CHRISTINA
and the
WHITEFISH

Stephen Vittoria

a novel

ALTERNATIVE
BOOK PRESS

Cover Design by Cassidy Hart
Interior Design by Robert Guillory & Cassidy Hart

Cover photograph "Asbury Park, New Year's Day"
© David Rucker. Used by permission.

Poem "Wild West"
© Kathleen Kremins. Used by permission.

LIBRARY OF CONGRESS CATALOGING-IN-PUBLICATION DATA

Vittoria, Stephen / Christina and the Whitefish / First Edition
Fiction, General.
Fiction, Psychological.

ISBN: 979-8-9924613-0-5 (hardcover)
ISBN: 979-8-9908531-9-5 (softcover)

Printed in the USA

To Ellen & Shannon...
and all those fantabulous summers on the Jersey Shore

CHRISTINA and the
WHITEFISH

CONTENTS

Part One
FRAUD

Part Two
ME

Part Three
ANGELS

CHRISTINA and the WHITEFISH

WILD WEST

As if a Jersey girl in Utah wasn't wild enough
said girl kissing her first girlfriend, first love

on the edge of Inspiration Point, crimson
hoodoos rising spire-like across

Bryce Canyon at sunset, days later
balanced at sunrise at Sunrise Point

stretched into space looking for the best angle
leaning over the jagged crags to catch a photo

shot after red-rising shot, rapid-fire as I totter
slip, trip – now in my slow-motion memory –

reach back with my left hand toward earth
the Nikon from my right hand, tumbles

into the abyss of the gorge. I still feel your fingers
dig into my shoulder, pulling me back from uncertain death,

the blast of the crashing camera echoing like my bones—
certainly not the last time you saved me from me.

— KATHY KREMINS
THE CURVE OF THINGS

Part One

"I come from a boardwalk town
where almost everything is tinged with a bit of fraud."

Bruce Springsteen

FRAUD

CHRISTINA and the WHITEFISH

1
Babalu.

I'VE ENJOYED THIS SONG a thousand times.

Okay, that's probably an exaggeration. But I'd wager it's at least three hundred times. The record is scratchy as hell, but the historic jet black label is damn near pristine: "RCA Victor, The Master's Voice," with that dog staring right into what they called a gramophone. In fact, my grandmother had a real beauty at her place down in Ocean Grove – that stick-up-its-rump town that hails itself as (get this) "God's Square Mile at the Jersey Shore."

Now, the gramophone didn't work, which is no surprise, but she did have her "newfangled record player" that spun her treasured Mario Lanza records. Man, did she adore the powerful tenor, his sweet timbre floating on an ocean breeze – but "not too loud," she'd whisper, since the local holy rollers wouldn't approve of a swarthy Italian from South Philly. I'm not kidding. Until maybe ten years ago, they actually had a law on the books forbidding cars to roam their streets on Sundays. Ocean Grove. Talk about childlike behavior.

In point of fact, I've memorized the "Babalu" label: "RCA VICTOR... THE MASTER'S VOICE... FOR BEST RESULTS USE RCA VICTOR NEEDLES... BABALU... MARGARITA LECUONO (that's who wrote the song – then, of course) DESI ARNAZ AND HIS ORCHESTRA... VOCAL REFRAIN BY DESI ARNAZ... (and then curved along the bottom in circular fashion) RCA VICTOR, DIVISION OF RADIO CORPORATION OF AMERICA, CAMDEN, N.J., MADE IN U.S.A.

Steel trap, huh? I mean, I could be reading it right now and who would know? But I'm not. If I learned anything from my Nonni down in "God's Square Mile," it was not to perjure yourself. I live by that. You know, most of the time.

And when I say I've enjoyed "Babalu" a thousand times – here's what I mean – because I'm not kicking back on the sofa digging some Latin Jazz. What I do might be considered insane or at least hovering on the outskirts. You'll understand soon enough, but here's my gig – and keep in mind: nobody knows I do this, except now, of course, you. Because it's probably time I share my secret. (If not now, when?)

Dig it. I have a basement that's neatly divided into two sections. Consider it bing and bang. So when you walk down these rickety stairs (that I need to replace at some point) and you hit rock-bottom, you'll immediately veer to your right into this subterranean grotto that resembles an art studio, mostly because it is. You see, I consider my painting what they call "performance art." Although there's no audience. Except for the performer. I know, that sounds masturbatory, but it's not. I like to think of it as a never-ending rehearsal period. And also a pretty good workout for my constantly deteriorating forty-six-year-old body, an organism that's been to hell and back and fortunately lived to tell about it.

So, the first thing I do is strip down buck naked. Just like when I arrived: October of Anno Domini nineteen hundred and forty-seven, disembarking at what the hoity-toity proudly called the "Raleigh Fitkin-Paul Morgan Memorial Hospital" over there in Neptune.

Now, at this point, my six paint cans are cracked open, ready to go. There's a brush in each: sky blue, navy blue, king's red, another kind of orangy-red, amber, and then bright white. The colors never change. My art, if anything, is redundant. So I move to the center of the room and neatly position my newly acquired trash can. Standard issue. Gunmetal gray. No deep ridges or depressions. I want it as flat as possible. New or used, it doesn't matter. As long as it's a regular put-out-by-the-curb trash can.

So there it is – in the middle of the room, this lonesome dove, ready to be assailed-attacked-maybe-even-ambushed by yours truly. Nice alliteration, right? This canister, this naked galvanized steel trash can, if it had feelings, would sit there persecuted, waiting for the assault to begin – anticipating an onslaught of paint, getting waxed up if you catch my drift. Just like its many siblings born in this sacred basement, all of them formerly known as "just a trash can."

I drop the needle (or "stylus" for you audiophiles) onto my trusty Technics turntable that immediately reads each little wiggle and bump in the pressed vinyl as a distinct sound vibration, which then gets translated into electrical signals or soundwaves that roll through the pre-amp in my Pioneer receiver. And this baby, with its one hundred and twenty watts per channel, feeds gigantic Cerwin-Vega loudspeakers, two beauties that'll blow your fucking doors off.

And then it's "heaven in a basement" as Desi's conga drum belts and beats for precisely twenty-four seconds – and for all twenty-four seconds I'm facing the can, my right leg pulsing with Arnaz's fiery drum. Then right at twenty-five seconds the orchestra kicks in, which is my cue to commence hostilities. But in actuality, it's not very hostile at all. The can never fights back. It's a willing partner in our pas de deux.

I start with sky blue as Desi roars, "Babalu... Ba-ba-lu! Babalu, aye!" Now, you gotta visualize that the sky blue takes up a good portion of the entire circumference of the can – so I hit it with a generous coat. And by the way, I use house paint. Oil-based and preferably Dutch Boy, so it covers really well. Next, as the rumba starts to really cook, and I'm zigzagging around the can like a whirling dervish, I transition to the navy blue, which forms this kind of "shield shape" right on the front – very foundational. Next comes the orangy-red. It's the backdrop for what I like to call "the marquee." I want it to come off super theatrical – and I'm sure the original designer did, too, just like "The Roxy," corner of 50th and 7th Ave. NYC.

And so my goal is this, because you oughta know: sky blue, navy blue, and the orangy-red are all applied before Desi and the boys wrap it up – all told about three and a half minutes. Usually it's not a problem.

Then I change records, replacing Desi with the aforementioned Mario Lanza, as I embark on the detailed portion of my work: the tomatoes and the subsequent words. I consider these two elements the very guts of the piece, so everything slows down. Think snail's pace. I throw on my paint-stained robe, which is ancient and resembles something Sonny Liston might have worn into the ring. Furthermore, I grab my bifocals because, like I said, I'm not the man I used to be. I park my ass on a mushroom-like cushioned toadstool for a more focused, albeit relaxed, approach.

Why? Well, as I often tell folks, greatness exists in the minutiae.

#

CHRISTINA and the WHITEFISH

2

Tadasana.

It was dawn, and Christina felt like she was hovering on the edge of the world. From a purely geographic standpoint, she was standing on the rocky western coast of North America. The edge cartographers considered a slice of the Pacific Rim. And if these same cartographers were forced to pinpoint the exact place where Christina's bare feet now rooted themselves into the moist ground, they'd most likely label it Santa Monica. Palisades Park to be GPS exact. That thin strip of manicured grass that loitered just above Pacific Coast Highway and its adjoining stretch of sandy coastline, one that usually framed a surfer named Dusty or Corky, and then of course that giant deep sea that bubbled between her bare feet and the Orient.

The Mountain Pose—or Tadasana (tah-DAHS-anna) in Sanskrit—looked like a simple pose, especially to the sweet elderly couple who strolled by with their gray Miniature Schnauzer hooked on a hot pink leash. But the pose was anything but simple. Internally, Christina's muscles were strong and working hard. In fact, over the last few months, she discovered two truisms associated with Tadasana—be mindful of your muscles that must be engaged but be equally mindful, maybe more so, of your muscles that need to remain soft and tender; a beautiful contradiction. It's why she loved her rather nascent yoga practice, a real godsend on her self-imposed journey toward peace. Or at least a negotiated cease-fire. Anything, please, that resembled a much-needed armistice.

But, for Christina, this bumpy journey wasn't about geography, although by now—in the summer of 1994, more than two years after she'd arrived—this Jersey Girl was very familiar with the safe confines of Santa Monica, California, a pretty city named after Saint Monica, the mother of famed theologian Saint Augustine. It was also the final stop on America's self-styled "Mother Road," aka Route 66.

She liked her new home. There was a bohemian café on Wilshire that wasn't half bad. There was the Ye Olde King's Head Pub that served sumptuous Irish cider straight from the old country. And without a doubt, sipping God's nectar at their long, ornate bar reminded Christina of Mom & Dad—and that was a good thing. There was also the ancient and battered pier with its hokey amusement park that charmed her nonetheless, especially when the Sun dipped over the usually calm Pacific. And, of course, the People's Republic of Santa Monica offered a decent contingent of leftover hippies and barbarian surfers, cats who occasionally offered those fragile doses of peace, that harmony and stillness Christina desperately craved but found so damn elusive inside her trembling darkness—a shadowy storm that began building exponentially six years before, back in the white-hot summer of nineteen hundred and eighty-eight.

But as of late, and after a good deal of hard work, she'd been able to hold this tempest at bay. Or was the damn thing simply gathering steam as it hovered out there just beyond the horizon? Growing more ferocious as it prepared for a renewed frontal assault?

There was another possibility: Was Christina actually winning the battle? Good questions. Unfortunately, at this time, all without answers.

She landed in Southern California via spaceship courtesy of the people who actually own and operate this third boulder from the Sun. And once she was back living with regular, run-of-the-mill Earthlings, her leaders up the chain of command supplied her with the currency necessary to start and sustain life—at least for a short while. After that, she was expected to support herself and assimilate with the nice folks who populated this laid-back colony, those who received their mail at 90405.

Along with her most cherished comrade (who had since blown town), she rented a bungalow on Ocean Park Boulevard—one of those concrete boxes built during the 1940s when the Douglas Aircraft Company turned bucolic Sunset Park and most of Santa Monica into a company town.

For months, the small house was stark and colorless. Her most cherished comrade once called it "drab and pallid." But recently, Christina tried to make her living space warm and cozy, picking up used eclectic furnishings from nearby garage sales. And for the most part, she'd succeeded. She hung lace curtains in the tiny kitchen, curtains that softened the early morning light. Usually at daybreak, a small yellow tea pot whistled on a blue flame. Christina would sit at a small red Formica table, sipping Chamomile and picking on some whole wheat toast with jam. Breakfast (and all meals for that matter) was now part of her newly adhered-to First Commandment: KEEP EATING.

The dancing squirrels in the courtyard provided friendly entertainment.

She found a large Buddha for the main room (chipped and scarred but only ten bucks!) along with some beanbag chairs and a small 1950s sofa: burnt orange and marshmallow soft. A framed poster of the seven chakras hung in solitude, forcing one's gaze to the heart of a silhouetted woman seated in lotus pose, a mystery lady that embodied all the appropriate chakra colors. The bedroom was sparse and rarely used. There was a mattress on the floor with some rumpled sheets, a couple of pillows, and a large gray footlocker that supported a healthy Philodendron. But mostly she slept in the orange marshmallow next to her small clock radio that played low throughout the night. K-Jazz out of Long Beach. She needed the soft music for fear that the silence would drive her stark raving mad. Stillness was one thing. Silence was torture.

Christina took a job at a neoteric coffee shop called Starbucks on the corner of Hill and Main. It was only a fifteen minute walk, which meant she didn't have to drive, something she hated doing in Los Angeles anyway. She was first lured to this coffee spectacle by the green and white mermaid on their logo—but also their name—a character in Melville's *Moby Dick,* one of her Dad's favorite novels. She worked five or six days a week, and her shifts were anywhere from six to eight hours. Usually eight. "Why? Because she's good under pressure, that's why," Ricky, her manager, would tell his disgruntled employees who wanted more hours. "If I had to pick someone here to be in a foxhole with, it'd be this firecracker."

Ricky also had a thing for Christina, even though he was probably twenty-five years older than his Frappuccino whiz. She knew Ricky was into her, but Christina was also well-practiced at dodging the male species: first the boys in high school, who were always on the prowl, and now men (for some reason usually older) who were constantly interested in the conquest, a reminder of what they could never achieve in their youth.

But Ricky was harmless, she figured, just a window shopper. And the bottom line for Christina was simple: she wanted the job and actually enjoyed the work. Time passed quickly and she was surrounded by the hustle and bustle of human company without having to truly engage.

Best of all, when she left for the day, the job and her green barista apron stayed behind, protected under the watchful eye of that beguiling siren hanging over the front door.

❖ ❖ ❖

Although at dawn on this early summer morning, standing out there on the edge of the world, with her bare feet rooted in the moist earth, the now rapidly moving Sun was no longer simply hinting at a new and warmer day. Nope, it was surging fiercely over the distant Mojave, set to plough right through the Inland Empire, and then accelerate across Hollywood—taking direct aim on Christina, who had transitioned from Tadasana to Adho Mukha Shvanasana and then into Virabhadrasana: the Warrior Pose. This winsome, tanned-skinned woman of Black Irish descent was rock-solid, steady as she goes, maybe a few beads of sweat modeling on her forehead, just beneath her wavy, thick, and cascading black hair that somehow looked amazing no matter what tornado was passing by. And for a moment, just a nanosecond, this twenty-three-year-old was confused.

Again.

Because that ol' playful Sun was up to new tricks—rising harsh over scorched desert and jagged cliffs instead of sweeping majestically atop a massive ocean, one that stretched across her childhood gaze, like it did so many dawns ago.

In New Jersey.

Up and down the windswept coast in places like Red Bank, Brigantine, Manasquan, and her favorite—the mysterious, ghostlike, and many would say "infamous" Asbury Park.

Because from Christina's point of view, the goddamn Sun was supposed to rise over water.

&

3
Progresso.

I WAS PARTICULARLY HAPPY with this latest rendition. As per usual, the colors popped. But that's never been an issue. For me, it's always about the quality execution of the words, especially since I'm freewheeling on the letters, no stencil bullshit like Warhol. Of course, it's also very much about the tomatoes. You have to get the shadowing just right to create the illusion of depth and texture. It took me a while to learn that shit.

Okay, picture this: Emblazoned across the top of the blue shield, we have "PROGRESSO." Large white capital letters with the two Rs dipping just below the baseline. I think I nailed it on this third day of July, nineteen hundred and ninety-four. Point of fact: I always put the date on the ass end of my cans. Down low. Out of the way. In quotes for some odd reason: "3 July 1994." Like the Brits, right? Classy bunch of savages.

Below the large PROGRESSO letters, I pulled off a real workmanlike rendering of "Recipe Ready" along with its corresponding design lines. And then below that, I nailed the bright amber letters "Crushed TOMATOES" set against that orangy-red oval backdrop – the aforementioned marquee. I finished off the blue shield with Progresso's all-important after-sell: "With Added Puree." This detail, along with the "Recipe Ready," can be demanding since the letters are italicized. That stroke, or penmanship as we used to call it, took some time to refine. I think I'm close.

Now, for the piece de resistance – the tomatoes. Five plump beauties, one cross-section slice, and a few leaves for the trim. And I must tell you – I nailed the tomatoes. In my opinion, maybe the best ever. Indeed, if this replica trash can depicting Progresso crushed tomatoes was Cassius Marcellus Clay, it would shout to the fucking world, "I am the Greatest!" Like I said, I nailed it as if some great painter like Georgia O'Keeffe crawled inside my britches; actually shocked myself. The fruit looks as if it just tumbled off the vine – of course in a manner that a New York City art critic might suggest was "effected in an abstract expressionist kind of way." Truth be told, I find the leaves (which are nothing more than trim) to be pedestrian at best, but who's looking at the leaves, right?

All in all, I'm ecstatic with this new interpretation. I might actually take a couple of months off before I engage with a new can. Plus, I have to keep up on the writing. This chronicle of sorts is kicking my ass. Moreover, why the hell did I talk myself into doing this? Posterity? Maybe. "Tell your story," they say, "People will find you noteworthy." I don't know; it sounds like smoke getting blown up my ass, since I know of no time capsule waiting anxiously to include my words.

Hell, I could type on this old Underwood for years and end up hammering out three hundred pages of chaotic gibberish.

And in case you're wondering, I've taken two creative writing courses up at Brookdale Community, so that's a help, no doubt. I've also been told it's probably in my blood. That claim I'm not so sure about.

But what I am sure about is reading. I'm what they call a voracious reader. So was my Ma. She influenced me greatly. Over the last twenty-five years or so, I've read a lot of words from numerous big-time brains. All the usual suspects: Joyce. Orwell. Hemingway. Steinbeck. Clemens. James Baldwin. Salinger. Virginia Woolf. Faulkner. Both Jacks – London & Kerouac. Pasternak. Gabriel Garcia Marquez (Gabito!). Harper Lee. Margaret Atwood. Mailer, of course. Most everything Hunter Thompson wrote. Also, a lot of lesser-known authors like Frantz Fanon and this hip cat from the Pacific Northwest, Richard Brautigan. Great first-person narratives. And if you start to find my writings derivative or, like I said above, chaotic gibberish, well, there's always lighter fluid and a match. That usually does the trick.

On the other hand, painting offers me structure. It has edges. Identifiable dimension. The focus is right there, right in front of you. Concept: reconstruct an everyday and mundane can of Progresso crushed tomatoes. Bingo. The canvas, or in my case, an actual trash can, becomes your entire world. Boundaries.

But writing, Christ, writing is willy-nilly, very unruly... and I fear that I might easily go wayward, like a small boat on a big ocean. Too much freedom freaks me out. I need a constitution. Hard form. I need to be wedged between a rock and a hard place. In fact, given the chance, I'd make a shitty God. He or she (or it) started out with nothing, right? Blank slate. And then you gotta figure out all the bullshit. "Corn gets harvested in the early fall. The penis goes in the vagina. Cats eat mice. The Earth revolves around the Sun. The Sun revolves around the center of the

Milky Way. Water starts freezing at forty degrees; nope, that doesn't work; how about thirty-two degrees? And how the hell do you pull off a virgin birth?"

Seriously, sit back for a second and think about being God. Just the planning will fuck you up. Think about how much shit could go wrong. Off the fucking rails wrong. I mean, even if I was given one job in this ever-expanding universe: "Hey you, yeah you, with the receding hairline – you're in charge of getting the buses to run on time. Make it happen." Dollars to doughnuts, my rapid transit system would be a goddamn catastrophe – or kind of like it is right now.

At this juncture, I think it's important to tell you a little bit about the Underwood that's banging this crap out.

It was my father's, or the "old man," as my mother liked to call him. He really wasn't that old when I was growing up, younger than I am right now. He was a reporter for the old "Newark Evening News" – founded in 1883, but the great daily folded in '72. In fact, I had a Newark Evening News paper route every day after school. Pop was proud to call his employer "New Jersey's paper of record" and not "that fucking rag, the 'Star-Ledger.'" The old man bounced around from one bureau to another: Morristown, Montclair, a few months in D.C., then Trenton for a good spell, until his longest and final stint "down the shore" – Belmar. Mostly he covered local politics, but always added what he thought was a necessary disclaimer: "All politics is local, folks." I've come to find out truer words have never been spoken.

He died in 1965. Actually, he was murdered in 1965. Shot in the chest three times during a grocery store hold-up in Toms River. My mother asked him to pick up a few things on his way home. He was forty-two. And she was never the same. Ma passed in '89, five years back. I was their only child. They were good parents, for sure. One of Pop's fellow reporters, a sportswriter named Joe Flynn, gave me the old man's typewriter – this Underwood. Flynn said he was positive that Frank wanted me to carry on his legacy. Flynn also thought the Underwood might come in handy for college.

Which never happened.

Unless, of course, you count the University of Vietnam.

#

CHRISTINA and the WHITEFISH

4

Trauma.

Following the Gulf War in 1991, a number of U.S. military battalions received "Valorous Unit Awards" for "extraordinary heroism against an armed enemy." Units with names like *1st Squadron—4th Armored Cavalry Regiment* and *Co C—1st Battalion, 41st Infantry*. Also cited for valor was Christina's unit, known as the *522nd Military Intelligence Battalion* and she loved every man, woman, and asshole in that battalion. Most were known only by their last names: Washington, Phillips, Vásquez, et cetera. A few had nicknames—Spanky, Pizza, Boomer, and Munchkin.

They would die for her, and she for them.

❖❖❖

Two Years Earlier
Christina packed her bags in the spring of 1989. When she left and locked the front door, she suddenly realized that this old colonial gem was the only home she had ever known—perched on a hill just south of the Delaware Water Gap.

She was now the official owner of a two-door Jeep Cherokee, the rugged four-wheel drive her Dad kept in mint condition. It was raining on the day she left, escaping really with her best friend Jaime—these two American kids heading south along the old river, past Easton, PA, and then west on U.S. Route 22—the dark red Cherokee chugging straight toward their final destination: Las Vegas, Nevada.

A new start.

They were lovers since sophomore year at Belvidere High School in bucolic Warren County, a place advertised as "New Jersey's Best Kept Secret." Their relationship shared the same tagline.

In many ways, Belvidere could have been constructed by "the Rembrandt of Punkin Crick," Mr. Norman Rockwell. Situated on the banks of the Delaware, this quintessential Victorian hamlet offered what you might expect: gingerbread dollhouses boasting elaborate Queen Anne trim; most of the homes exceedingly colorful.

One late October afternoon represented Christina's vanguard memory: walking home from school with Jaime, their hands touching and grasping, sunlight slicing through painted leaves, some floating as if animated by gravity. There were no words, just the serene whisper of nearby cascades belonging to the Pequest River, a tributary to the Delaware. Poets might call her snapshot "a moment carved in time."

Growing up in Belvidere, there was only one uncomfortable reality for Christina: Her mother and father both taught at the high school; Darlene weaved her way through U.S. and world history, and Jack extolled the virtues of American literature. But they were both cool, rarely crossing the Rubicon into her sacred teenage world.

Throughout high school, Christina always figured she'd follow in the family business—not because Jack or Darlene pressured her regarding pedagogy; they did not. Her lifelong exposure to the intrinsic value of teaching had simply seeped into her DNA. Plus she was really good at math and science, loved numbers, and fancied how astronomy was, in essence, ruled by those same numbers. And when she read Carl Sagan's seminal book, *Cosmos,* she was officially hooked—with one of Sagan's lines becoming her lightning strike:

> *If you wish to make an apple pie from scratch,*
> *you must first invent the universe.*

Christina spent time with her Dad in the Warren County Library researching colleges, schools that offered programs in astronomy and astrophysics. They were leaning toward UC Berkeley or possibly UC Santa Cruz. She wanted nothing to do with ivy-covered walls. The left coast seemed right, especially after they visited both schools between junior and senior year. Christina was accepted at both, and the decision process became a comical and daily ping-pong match of alleged absolute decisions: Berkeley-Santa Cruz, Santa Cruz-Berkeley, until one day the senior at Belvidere High said, "Santa Cruz, that's final."

Graduation was exciting and Christina's cross-country moving plans were all in motion, except for the elephant in the room—Jaime, who was "sorta-kinda" thinking about maybe attending Trenton State or nearby Warren Community. Or maybe taking a year off.

For Jaime, a sturdy free spirit, college and a career were mere afterthoughts, much to her parent's chagrin. She was brilliant, no doubt, and political, loved wearing her grungy "Che" t-shirt, but her cynicism regarding convention kicked institutional education to the curb.

So Christina and Jaime made grandiose plans and big promises for rousing visits with both eighteen-year-olds smiling through the obvious tribulations, both hiding behind façades that masked their doubt and pain. And then without warning, life—as it's apt to do—dropped a hand grenade.

Death arrived at Christina's front door... and not for a game of chess.

Jack & Darlene perished in a helicopter crash somewhere over an Alaskan glacier—a goddamned shore excursion from their cruise ship docked in Juneau. That was in the summer of 1988, just months before her frantic escape to Nevada, a dire attempt to free herself from the agonizing grief.

She wanted out. Of her body. Of everything. And of course Jaime was there for her. Every day. Every hour. Every minute. For Christina, college—like heaven—could wait. She wanted to run. So she ran. And Jaime, being the quintessential free spirit, galloped out of Belvidere right by her side, even though Vegas seemed weird and arbitrary. But Jaime figured why the hell not; heading to the desert with Ti might offer her soulmate a chance to heal. At least somewhat, even though Jaime knew that Ti needed a mountain of healing.

❖ ❖ ❖

The dark red Cherokee exited Interstate 15 at Russell and then hung a hard right on Las Vegas Boulevard. A few seconds later, these two Jersey girls came face-to-face with legendary signage:

WELCOME TO FABULOUS
LAS VEGAS NEVADA

They rented a one-bedroom apartment on Silver Dollar Ave, and both landed peasant-level jobs at the venerable Sands Hotel and Casino—Jaime as a pool and recreation attendant and Christina working for the Boutiques Manager.

They made decent money, drove to work together, and for Christina, the noise-clamor-and-crazy-racket of a Vegas casino helped to numb the agony, the heartache.

Cue the matador music: "Ladies and gentlemen, give a big Sands Hotel and Casino welcome to the one and only, Mr. Warmth—Don Rickles!"

&

5
Boardwalk.

THE PLANKS RUN NORTH AND SOUTH between 6th Avenue to the north and just past Cookman and Lake Avenues down south. It's a stretch of about seven-tenths of one mile. That's it. This short run constitutes the legendary expanse of the Asbury Park Boardwalk.

There are multiple iconic structures that embolden each end of the seesaw. In the north you have Convention Hall with its famed Paramount Theatre and Grand Arcade, a cavernous complex that's an eclectic melange of Italian and French designs, very Neo-Classical – at least that's what they tell me. At one time, this now crumbling edifice was stunningly beautiful, with spectacular brick workmanship surrounding numerous and inviting archways. Colorful terracotta – as well as what they call "verdigris" ornamentation – adds a certain European elegance to the joint.

Side note: "Verdigris" for the uninitiated is a bluish-green pigment that forms on copper or brass by way of atmospheric oxidation, which consists of basic copper carbonate. It's a beautiful embellishment.

It should also be noted that this imposing Convention Hall structure was designed by the same esteemed architects that built Grand Central Terminal in a city called New York. No doubt the powers that be had grandiose plans for this place.

When you wander down to the south end of the Boardwalk, things get funky and curious, a vibe that defines all of Asbury Park to this very day. You have the massive Casino – again, very Beaux-Arts. This multi-use complex, a rock pile of brick and limestone, was also designed by the Grand Central guys. The popular Casino housed a wide variety of amusements and games. You had Skee-Ball and pinball, fortune tellers, those warped carnival mirrors, funnel cake, saltwater taffy, and even a damn ice skating rink, not to mention scary rides in the dark. It was your typical "big top" shenanigans.

And then connected right next door, you'll find the stunning Carousel House – an ornate copper and glass rotunda that (as the name suggests) harbored wooden ponies galloping on a "Lucy in the Sky with Diamonds" merry-go-round – hand-carved and flamboyantly painted by the Philadelphia Toboggan Company a way back in 1928. Think early psychedelic.

Side note #2: Remembering those wooden ponies and their crazed art work, I gotta believe that the good folks at the Philadelphia Toboggan Company were smoking some truly fierce Roaring Twenties ganja.

Adding injury to insult, this celebrated merry-go-round was sold just last year and then hijacked down south to the goddamn Confederacy (Myrtle Beach).

Like vultures picking at a carcass.

One last structure of note (albeit a dump): Palace Amusements. This 19th century albatross, which was open for exactly one hundred years, still sits right next to the iconic Carousel House on Kingsley. If you've ever been to Asbury Park, it's that greenish-teal barn-like rattrap with the maniacal visage of "Tillie" painted on the side – this giant freak staring out into oblivion.

Tillie resembles a ghoulish Dick Nixon. (I know, redundant.)

A real shitshow of a fun house, the Palace was usually jam-packed and always drenched in mescaline. The grounds also boasted a conspicuous Ferris wheel that completed our skyline (my first kiss was up there with Mary Beth Walsh). This is the same Palace Amusements made famous by one B. Springsteen; his name may ring a bell, or possibly you've heard his anthem, "Born to Run"? "Beyond the Palace, hemi-powered drones, scream down the boulevard." Yeah, same Palace, same shithole.

Now, this being the east coast, when you walk southerly down the planks from Convention Hall, the ocean is on your left – and if you have to think about that, well, I can't help you. To your right are the actual boardwalk establishments. Or at least what's left of them in nineteen hundred and ninety-four. I'll get back to that.

But let's digress to 1871. That's when the town of Asbury Park was founded by a New Yorker named James Bradley, a so-called "captain of industry" and a proud Jim Crow segregationist. Bradley christens our quaint hamlet (his resort schema) after an 18th century preacher man, a Brit, who roamed the colonies selling medieval fairytales. Town historians have written that Mr. James Bradley, their founding father, had a dream: to build a thriving seaside resort town (for whites).

Side note #3: "Captains of Industry" don't have dreams. That's bullshit. They have what Ralph Kramden banked on: get-rich-quick schemes.

Side note #4: Town historians forgot to mention in Mr. Bradley's bio that he was labeled by many as the "Jim Crow of the North."

Side note #5: Many of the city's grand hotels and stately Victorian homes were built by the Sand Hill Indians (a local tribe descended from the Cherokee clan) as well as Blacks escaping from the Jim Crow South. Ironically and all too typically, the same working families that built this city's cash cows were systematically barred from living and enjoying the fruits of their labor. Old story.

Lo and behold, Bradley's "dream" materialized smack-dab in the middle of prime New Jersey beachfront. And the centerpiece? A magnificent money-producing boardwalk. The original construction included an orchestra pavilion, public changing rooms, bathhouses, as well as an impressive pier that extended well out into the thrashing Atlantic.

Word spread like wildfire, attracting throngs of tourists from Pennsylvania and New York City, as well as the great state of New Jersey. Of course, this throng of cash-carrying tourists seduced voracious entrepreneurs who delivered top-notch amusement to this growing enterprise.

By the late twenties, with the Great Depression getting ready to throw some devastating haymakers, vacation wonderlands like Asbury Park prepared for the gravest of outcomes. And sure enough, by the time the market crashed, American amusement parks and their associated businesses were crumbling fast. My personal research into the limited intel of the day indicated that by or around 1930 some 1,800 amusement operations and/or locales were up and running throughout the country. When the dust settled, all but 303 entities were gone with the wind. So forget worldwide economic calamity; the Great Depression wreaked hell and havoc on the American amusement park!

Side note #6: But even the Depression had a silver lining, albeit grisly. As the great Will Rogers once suggested: "When Wall Street took that tailspin, you had to stand in line to get a window to jump out of, and spectators were selling space for bodies in the East River."

Not sure if the jumping actually happened, but we can dream, can't we?

Somehow, Asbury Park survived. My theory? The town and its tourism magnets were built with "old money," not scraps from the nouveau riche – and old money doesn't like to lose. The blue hairs and stuffed shirts jammed their collective finger in the dyke until the obedient serfs returned. And return they did. The city and its boardwalk surroundings climbed back on their feet – rapidly. In fact, by the mid-thirties, Asbury Park boasted more than two hundred hotels and motels ready to accommodate the throngs who finally rotated back to their vacation wonderland.

But then some weird out-of-nowhere shit started happening that curiously boosted business even more, like the "Morro Castle Disaster" in 1934. In hindsight, this tragic event should have been tagged as a warning shot, an omen if you will, sent from the gods of history with a message that, when decoded, simply read: get the fuck out.

Anyway, the "S.S. Morro Castle" was an American ocean liner sailing from Havana to New York that suddenly burst into flames just off the Jersey coast. Hours later, and with all passengers and crew having abandoned ship, either to their death or dismay, the still-burning hull of this giant ghost ship grounded itself right into the goddamn boardwalk.

Side note #7: Exactly eighty years before, in 1854, IN THE EXACT SAME SPOT, a ship named "New Era," carrying German emigrants, helplessly grounded in dense Jersey coastal fog, killing 150 people. Talk about your Bermuda Triangles!

For months, the S.S. Morro Castle became a sightseeing attraction – an out-and-out circus sideshow, which, as you know, is always great for business.

Another big-time money shot in the arm took place in 1943 when the New York Yankees held spring training in Asbury Park – that's right, the "Bronx Bombers." You see, all rail transport to Florida was being conserved during the war. My old man told stories about seeing the likes of Bill Dickey, Charlie "King Kong" Keller, and his favorite: the slick fielding shortstop Snuffy Stirnweiss.

In fact, World War II, the so-called "good war," just kept on giving. Asbury Park became a major receiving station for the Royal Navy. Something like five thousand British officers and enlisted men were stationed in our little homestead, including – get this – legendary actor Sir Alec Guinness, who you may know from "Star Wars." I tend to associate him with real movies like "The Bridge on the River Kwai" or when he played Fagin, the old Jew in "Oliver Twist"–

"What's become of the boy? SPEAK OR I'LL THROTTLE YOU!"

Unfortunately for Asbury Park, the war ended... and the postwar years were anything but kind.

The suburbs grew fast and furious; their shopping centers (and later their malls) lured businesses every which way out of places like Asbury Park. And it was easy because in '55 we saw the emergence of America's "Appian Way," otherwise known as the Garden State Parkway (with those goddamn toll baskets). Hell, for the preceding fifty years, the two hot spots on this coast were Asbury Park and Atlantic City. But the Parkway was a game changer – the entire Jersey seaboard was up for grabs.

Some of you may have also noticed jet travel. Well, so did the residents of New Jersey.

As the 1950s and 60s began spreading their wings, those archaic husbands and wives (the ones who once strolled the Boardwalk in Gatsby straw hats and petticoat dresses) disappeared en masse, the ladies' flamboyant parasols floating away like swallows to Capistrano.

So did all those families who used to vacation here every summer – with names like Ward, June, Wally, and "the Beave." "Ward, let's go to Florida. Miami Beach. Collins Avenue is all the rage!" Sure, people still went "down the shore," but suddenly the shore was a helluva lot bigger, one hundred and forty miles bigger. The new Parkway dumped all these travelers on pristine beaches from Perth Amboy to Cape May.

By the mid-1960s, most of the $$$ had exited Asbury Park stage left.

You know what else took place in our fair city?

Oh, c'mon, you know what it is – the ugly reality that has permeated the Amerikkkan states since the beginning of time.

Hatred.

Which triggers the exact opposite of life, liberty, and the pursuit of bullshit. Which causes division. Which causes trauma and terror. Which, in turn, causes uprisings. Like Watts in '65. Newark and Detroit in '67. DC in '68. And lest we forget, there was also Asbury Park in 1970: 4 July through 10 July, when the seeds of racial hatred gave birth to revolution.

Although, when lily-white Amerikkka hears "revolution" – and then is forced to face the ugliness borne by their collective actions – they run for the hills. And baby, did they ever white flight run.

But you already know how the rest of this story goes. Because if you're an Amerikkkan with at least half a brain and your eyes open, maybe thirty percent of the time, you don't need an explanation of white supremacy and its all-too-expected vicious cycle. Hell, we've all lived it since at least August 1619. You don't need a soapbox screed from me (although that sounded like one).

But a simple tale might underscore the reality of why people in straw hats and petticoats REALLY did turn their back on Beirut by the Sea.

When I first rotated back to the States and drove down that shiny new Parkway, I met a man on the Boardwalk early one morning. He had a name: Chester Cook... and Chester filled me in about growing up in Asbury Park.

He explained how the authorities and local business owners wouldn't allow him and his friends to swim on the city's world-class sandy beaches – except, of course, way off the beaten path, down where the main sewer pipe emptied into the sea. I know exactly where that is. So fuck them.

While gazing out at the Earth's ocean, Chester painfully recalled that he and his buddies had to walk miles to use a decent integrated beach down in Belmar. Land of the free? So fuck them.

Before Chester took off for work that morning, he told me how the hotels and various establishments used to ship in white help from out of town rather than hire from the local Black population, which accounted for a large percentage of Asbury Park's citizenry (mostly segregated on the West Side). So once again, fuck 'em. Ship in the white help.

You see? Shit doesn't just happen.

Okay, my left brain, pain in the ass that it is, just yelled, "Wrap it up, Mr. Man on the Underwood." Yessir.

So on days like today, when I stand on the Boardwalk in front of my joint, I often wonder if I should put up one of those Sister City signs like you might see around the country:

GREETINGS FROM ASBURY PARK
SISTER CITY WITH
EPHESUS
SELCUK, IZMIR PROVINCE, TURKEY
SINCE 1965

Why Ephesus? It's the damn ruins, stupid. Take heed.

Both cities look alike, with the excavated city in Turkey offering its stark remains that reflect centuries (actually millennia) of history – from Ancient Greece to the Roman Empire. And it's a strange thing. The Ephesus ruins look beautiful AND beat to shit all at the same time. Not unlike Asbury Park. Hollow shells of what used to be. Last week I saw some graffiti scrawled on a nearby wall suggesting "This Too Shall Pass." Kind of poetic, right? But underneath the poetry, someone offered the prosaic answer: "Fuck You." I get 'em both.

Right now, in 1994, this place – once a posh retreat for Philly and New York society – is crumbling beyond recognition. I read a lot. Making up for an education that never happened. "Great scribes," the old man used to say, "can place their readers anywhere with very few words, as long as they're the right words." Well, I'm not a great writer, barely even a writer, but if I had to pick some phrases to describe home sweet home, I might submit:

"Post-Apocalyptic America" or "Dystopian America" or "Marooned on Monster Island" or maybe "After Doomsday." We could also go in another direction, like that film "Night of the Living Dead." They all work.

Trust me. We're at rock bottom. Abandoned by civilization. Even the parking meters are rusted shut. When you stroll along the Boardwalk, you suddenly realize that all the sounds of life have disappeared. Oh, you can still hear the Atlantic crashing to the east, still hear seagulls whining about not having enough food, but that's about it. Maybe an occasional passing car – probably Springsteen fans on a pilgrimage to some imagined promised land, wondering as they drive, "What the hell was Bruce talking about?" (More on "The Boss" later.)

Now, if people are being "nice" as they pass through our fair city, they might scoff and tag us "Newark by the Sea." But if they're in a nastier, bombed-out frame of mind, it's probably more like the aforementioned "Beirut by the Sea."

I used to actually try preaching to the dilettantes that came through, offering pithy and intriguing tidbits like a paid mouthpiece for the Chamber of Commerce:

You know, at one time, some of the most lavish buildings in the country lined these boulevards. Saltwater pools dotted this boardwalk. Did you know that famous people like the Marx Brothers played the Paramount? What about Glenn Miller and Artie Shaw blasting out the dance halls? And dig this: Great Black music thrived on the West Side. Artists like Count Basie, Duke Ellington, and let's not forget the beautiful ladies like Josephine Baker and Billie Holiday - they played those clubs on a regular basis. Bud Abbott and Danny DeVito were born here, for crissakes.

Here's another historical nugget: Asbury Park was once a hub for homosexuals - a kind of protected haven for those seeking shelter from the storm.

But alas, I was wasting my breath.

Although, truth be told, if it wasn't for the hippies and the bikers, and your hardcore rock 'n rollers, your gays and freethinkers – those folks the establishment likes to call "the counterculture" – this place would have died a lot sooner. Who knows, maybe that might have been better.

Anyway, I could go on forever, but I won't.

Side note #8: In the summer of 1987, there was a slight comeback afoot. Only slight, but a comeback nonetheless. I know for a fact because I was making more money and so were all the other guys & gals. And then a fifty-mile slick of garbage - including discarded medical and hospital waste - hit the Jersey shore like a tsunami, courtesy of our friends up north. Bye-bye, comeback, and bye-bye birdie.

The S.S. Morro Castle. Giant ghost ship. Its still-burning hull slamming something fierce into Asbury Park.

Like I said, a prophetic forecast of things to come.

#

CHRISTINA and the WHITEFISH

6

Damage.

After the initial mushroom cloud of her parent's death obliterated Christina's true north, the lethal dust settled on the edges of her fragile consciousness. Like a gang of apex predators, say Komodo Dragons or Saltwater Crocs, her despair would hover just out of sight—then without notice nor invitation, and from every perceptible direction, they'd creep up in formation. And they'd form a noose. She could feel it. These psychotic interlopers gnawing away at her nervous system, which at this point was nothing more than a trellis of live wires.

First they came daily. Then hourly. Sometimes by the minute. Until Christina was existing inside a living, breathing dichotomy. She could sense, in real time, the definable split. A dismantling of psyches, like an unseen alchemist was frenetically fucking with her brain chemistry, instigating a variety of internal battles. It wasn't good versus evil, but rather gut-wrenching loneliness and sweeping panic versus normality— or whatever "normal" used to be.

In plain English, the loss of her beloved parents hit her like a ton of bricks.

Sadly, as the weeks went by, Christina sensed that this evolutionary freefall was still looking for a bottom. The chasm between these two warring sides grew larger with normalcy withering on the vine, damn near gone.

Vegas was an odd place to be fighting this personal battle. Working at the Sands, inside the belly of the beast, was like being nauseously sick and then trying frantically not to puke on a twisting roller coaster. It was how Hunter Thompson described the Vegas rhapsody:

> *This is not a good town for psychedelic drugs.*
> *Reality itself is too twisted.*

When she was at work, somehow-someway, who the hell knows, Christina kept the internal mêlée under wraps. She offered frozen plastic smiles for the weeble-wobble customers that frequented the schmancy hotel boutique. Her supervisor, Dorothy, was a 1950s creature from the Black Lagoon, preserved by equal doses of gin, nicotine, and formaldehyde.

All that really mattered to good ol' Dot was that you showed up on time and that your cash drawer balanced out at the end of your shift.

It was at home, with Jaime, when things got rough. That's when Christina powered down the force field, revealing a shell drained of any vitality whatsoever, like unplugging a robot. Jaime realized that Ti's performance in public must have been a Herculean task, robbing every last ounce of energy from her once vivacious nineteen-year-old partner. Languid and lethargic didn't begin to describe the off-hours at the apartment on Silver Dollar Ave. Shades pulled down, Christina would nibble at what seemed like a perpetual bowl of soggy Cheerios, the grainy television playing old reruns—at best it was life on hiatus; at its worst, life swirling down a comatose drain.

Jaime showed amazing patience for just another nineteen-year-old on the road to Kingdom Come. She offered unconditional support. And, of course, love. There were nights in bed or on the floor in a blanket when Jaime would simply hold Christina as she wept, sometimes trembling. Jaime offered few words, just her touch, a subtle kiss. When they had a day off, Jaime would drive them out to the desert or up to Mount Charleston along an incredible scenic drive, some 11,000 feet above the deadly low desert roasting pan. It was here that Ti was more like herself, hiking breezy, cool trails in search of beauty and peace. Jaime was thrilled to recognize her best friend again. And, for the first time in a long time, they ditched the trail and made love in their own Garden of Eden.

There was no doubt: These rare days on the mountain offered Ti a brief respite from fighting the darkness.

One late afternoon in 1989, almost dusk and almost Thanksgiving, Christina left the Sands on her lunch break. For some reason, and for the first time, she thought the clutter of gyrating neon lights looked pretty against the sky's purple backdrop.

She was hungry, which was unusual, and wanted tacos from this joint just off the Strip. It was Jaime's favorite—"Taqueria de Hector." Christina ordered two carnitas and a Coke. No ice. While waiting, she had a good laugh with the sweet man who owned the tiny establishment. He helped her with the pronunciation of "Michoacán"—the state in Mexico where Hector said the carnitas taco originated. They volleyed back and forth until she got it right: "Mee – choh – ah – kahn." "Mee – choh – ah – kahn." Hector said he could have her fluent in no time. She blushed and waved him off, "I'm horrible with languages."

When Hector slid her taco plate across the yellow picnic table, she realized it felt good to laugh. They volleyed once again:

Mee – choh – ah – kahn

As she was leaving, Hector showed up with a creamy horchata, on the house. "Gracias, Hector, that's so sweet." As she walked back to the Sands, with the neon dancing bright, she glanced at the horchata and thought, "Holy shit, where have you been my entire—"

A baritone voice interrupted, "Good evening, ma'am, do you have a minute?"

Caught off guard and for the first time in eons feeling footloose and fancy-free, she sipped the horchata and casually said, "Sure, what's up?" A friendly conversation ensued, which quickly evolved into a major life-altering decision.

It was a decision Christina would later believe to be—*actually know to be*—the worst decision of her short life.

&

CHRISTINA and the WHITEFISH

7
Club Southside.

I MOVED AROUND A LOT AS A KID. Not by my own volition, since you don't have much choice when your old man is an intrepid newshound for the Newark Evening News. But I really didn't care, it didn't matter, as long as the three of us were together. I spent a good deal of time inside my head, buried in books that me and Ma would check out from the library, usually the local bookmobile when it came rolling around. "Huck Finn," "The Hobbit," "The Catcher in the Rye," you name it. Also sports bios, love that claptrap – Lou Gehrig, Jim Brown, Joe Louis. And then the comic books. "Superman" for sure. "Tales from the Crypt." "Wonder Woman." "Iron Man." "Captain America." Boatloads of entertainment for ten cents a pop. Like I mentioned earlier, I've always been a voracious reader.

We finally settled down in Belmar, which is roughly ten minutes south of Asbury Park. Besides the Atlantic, the town is situated on a body of water called the Shark River. Although, I never encountered any sharks.

Side note: There's been some heated disagreement as to whether Shark River is actually, in fact, a river. I witnessed a fairly brutal fistfight one night between Lil Abner and Goots regarding this very issue. Abner staunchly believed that Shark River was actually "a saltwater tidal basin fed by the Atlantic," simply separated from the mighty ocean by a thin strip of dirt. But Goots doubted Abner's "ludicrous findings," suggesting that this was a common misnomer among the "woefully uneducated." Goots declared that it wasn't "the motherfucking ocean that fed the Shark" but actually several freshwater tributaries ten miles upstream. "You know nothing," Goots declared, "about what supplies this river's watershed. You're out of your element."

We finally broke up the Friday night slug fest with both combatants rather bloody, although the crowd ultimately gave the bout to Lil Abner since one of Goots' teeth was buried in Abner's knuckle.

As a kid in Belmar, my favorite place to hang out was up in Asbury Park at the Monte Carlo Pool. It sat just beyond Convention Hall at the very northern end of the Boardwalk. The pool was quite famous and hailed as "THE WORLD'S LARGEST SALTWATER POOL." And to my knowledge, there was no disagreement concerning this fact. The pool's water supply was piped in directly from the ocean and then treated through filters (at least that's what they claimed). With the buoyancy, you could float forever in a saltwater pool. There was also an underground tunnel where you could walk from the pool straight to the beach, which was fairly unique.

I spent many a summer day in that pool. Ma would pack sandwiches in the morning and we'd take the bus. She rarely came in the water, preferring her magazines to the bedlam that uncorked itself in the Monte Carlo. Little did I know as I was floating in the flapping waters, gazing up at Jersey cloud formations, that I would someday be the owner/operator of my own boardwalk establishment – the Club Southside.

And, at the time of this writing, it's going on twenty goddamn years.

During my formative days, say '55 through maybe Jack Kennedy getting whacked, those summer afternoons ushered in playful summer nights. We'd make it home in time for dinner with the old man, jump in our Buick Wildcat and head back to the Boardwalk, of course with the Yankees on the radio. Ma always laughing when Rizzuto shouted,

"HOLY COW!"

Hell, in those days, the Boardwalk was a happening place for kids. Seemed like endless rides: Tilt-a-Whirls, bumper cars, and then the big boys: "The Galaxy" coaster and a weird oblong-shaped Ferris wheel that went stupid-fast, something called "The Zipper." Strangely enough, the old man loved taking me on these rides. But he never wanted to play those intoxicating (and yes, infuriating) gallery games – target shooting, throwing hard balls at stacked metal bottles, all that shit. "Listen, kiddo," he'd pull me close, "These SOBs have the whole thing rigged. It's a racket. You want that stuffed Popeye? We'll buy it at Woolworths." He'd whisper in my ear so Ma wouldn't hear him, "Fuuuuuck them."

Then we'd grab a slice over at Patsy's, and Ma would pick up one of her toffee apples, and while she was busy dealing with that thing, the old man would deftly procure a Breidt's and down that baby in two or three swigs. And then zap, the bottle was buried in some trash can. Slick as a motherhumper. I can still picture that massive "Breidt's Beer & Ales" sign hovering above the Boardwalk. Damn thing belonged in a ballpark with one of Mickey's 500-foot blasts clanging off the letters, lights exploding.

Side note #2: All those rides, along with a host of other attractions, vanished in the early seventies, just as I was ramping up the club. Son of a bitch.

After two tours of killing Asians in Indochina (and desperately trying not to catch a blast myself), I returned home thinking about my next move. I was discharged honorably, listed as "rendered physically incapable of performing assigned duties." That's a fancy clinical way of saying I walked funny after combat. I had some meager VA benefits that were so fucking inadequate as to render them useless... and the urge was profound to tell Uncle Sam to eat shit and die with his garbage handouts. Bastards nailed me right out of high school – any thought of college was put on hold once the Pentagon sent me my invitation via the Selective Service System. To put it mildly, Ma was angry as hell and said something along the lines of –

"I'm sick and tired of old men sending young men to die." (Or maybe George McGovern said that.)

Her brother (my Uncle Ralph) died in the South Pacific back in '44. There wasn't even a body to send home. And the day I was drafted, she showed me his papers: "Killed in Action, Body Not Recovered." The pain still haunted her soul. That very same night, she was ready to make plans for us to drive to Winnipeg, where she had cousins who would offer safe harbor. "Besides being socialists," Ma explained, "Danny and Gracie are dyed in the wool pacifists. Your father told me they have a whole network up there. They'll never find you."

I was able to talk her down off the ledge. Hell, I didn't want to bolt to Canada like some scrawny hippie. Plus, I knew guys who were already on their way to Southeast Asia. Who the hell was I not to go?

Side note #3: But from where I stand today, and how crazy it sounded back then, she was most definitely correct in her thinking. Long live the scrawny hippie.

So, when Johnny came marching home again (Hurrah! Hurrah!), I returned to Belmar with Ma.

```
The men will cheer and the boys will shout
The ladies they will all turn out
And we'll all feel gay when Johnny comes marching home
```

Needless to say, it was joy and sorrow. I was home, I was breathing, and I was standing upright. That was her joy. But one glance at me walking... and that vision became her sorrow. Tessie's only child was damaged. For good. And Lord, she didn't even know the half of it.

I got a job at Pier 51 – a restaurant slash tavern at the very south end of the Boardwalk. The last structure. A standalone. Lou Fontaine was the owner and immediately took a shine to me. I was waiting tables, bussing tables, doing food prep, running errands – basically working my ass off while moving around like Quasimodo. And then Lou, bless his heart, gave me two bucks more an hour to start handling the booze inventory. I liked that job because it came with some trust and responsibility. Plus, Lou knew I didn't drink (back then). Between my hourly and the tips, I was doing pretty well. And then, living with Ma and paying no rent, I was able to sock away some cash.

This was 1971. Asbury Park's heyday was receding in the rearview mirror... but the town still had some piss and vinegar... and it still had rock 'n roll. That year the Allman Brothers and Alice Cooper played the Sunshine Inn on Kingsley, along with Yes and Pink Floyd selling out the Convention Center.

In fact, I was front row for that epic Alice Cooper Fourth of July show. He played "I'm Eighteen" and brought down the goddamn house.

```
                 I'm eighteen
          And I don't know what I want
                   Eighteen
         I just don't know what I want
                   Eighteen
             I gotta get away
         I gotta get out of this place
       I'll go runnin' in outer space
                  Oh yeah
```

Well, it's 1994, I'm almost forty-seven, and I'm still here. "Oh yeah."

But Pier 51 has been mine since late '74. Lou and his wife Lorraine had no kids, and with all the Boardwalk businesses nosediving by the minute, the aging couple had their sights set on Florida – Sun City, just south of Tampa. He was teaching me... and I was learning the business by osmosis. Then one day Lou sat me down, "Kid, if you could somehow scrape together the dough, this place could be yours. Whatever the real estate guy says, for you, fifty cents on the dollar." And Lou didn't bullshit me, saying it was going to be a bitch to keep any business in this town alive over the next few years. "But," and then he paused, "And this is a big but, just like Lorraine's... BUT, people still need to drink. They don't necessarily need to eat, but it's the booze, my friend." Lou likened the business to funeral parlors as he grabbed two shot glasses and poured some Wild Turkey, proffering the bottom line: "People die and people drink, and in this shithole of a town, they tend to drink heavy."

I had some money saved up, but not nearly enough to do what Lou suggested.

Enter Ma.

No doubt, she had some available cash from working full-time ever since Pop died (Code Enforcement Office, Borough of Belmar) – but hell, I would've felt like shit tapping into her savings, not to mention the old man's insurance payout. Now, at the time, I wasn't aware of these things, but she suggested "taking out a second," which sounded like Klingon to me, but once she explained how mortgages worked, it seemed like a no-brainer.

So before the deal was official, I remember walking down the Boardwalk early one Sunday morning as the HOLY SUN was just about to mount its daily insurrection on the Jersey Shore. Not a soul alive. It was me, the planks, and those fucking birds. I was contemplating the whole shebang: "Was I up to this? Could I fill Lou's shoes? Run a bar? Handle a restaurant? Deal with straggler-only business in the dead of winter? Especially in this godforsaken place?"

As I passed under the Howard Johnson's sign touting its "Panorama Room" and "Cocktails," I started to get cold feet. Shit, these bastards are the corporate competition, suits funneling in $$$ whenever necessary.

But then a saving grace light bulb went off in my head: "Who the hell wants to imbibe in a goddamn Howard Johnson's? Frumpy housewives and lonely insurance salesmen, that's who – and shit, I don't want them in my place anyway. Still, I was worried. I didn't want to squander Ma's dough. There had to be a safety net. Something to augment the booze and the food. And that's when it hit me –

What am I, dense? I know exactly how Lou supplemented his business. And the supplement was year-round. I never thought of just asking. Probably because it seemed off-limits. But what the hell, it's worth a try. Could be my ace in the hole.

The Sun was now blazing on a low trajectory, and I had a bit more giddy-up in my strange Good Morning Vietnam gait. I must have been smiling with the new idea because when I passed Madam Marie's so-called "Temple of Knowledge," the famed Madam – Marie Castello – waved me down, "Hey Chief, what are you so happy about?"

I stopped by a second and queried the Queen of these planks, "Why you here so early?" She grumbled, "Ah, Walter left some shit in the hut."

I always wanted to ask her, so I did, "Hey Marie, my mother says you actually read Judy Garland's fortune. Is that true?"

She poked me, "Listen to your mother, kid."

I queried again about her unique Asbury Park history, "Who else, Marie?"

She was smiling, "Whattayou, a cop? Christ, I dunno, a bunch of huckleberries. Perry Como, Ray Charles... by the way, a prince of a guy. That little squirrel, Woody Allen. Gorilla Monsoon. Mick Jagger, loved him. Don't you have somewhere to be?"

I laughed, kissed her on the cheek, and Quasimodo'd my way down the chevroned planks.

Maybe Marie planted the thought in my head with her vast psychic powers or some such bullshit, but as I approached Pier 51, like I said, situated at the south end of the Boardwalk, I suddenly decided to change the name. As soon as the joint was really mine.

"Club Southside"

Along with Lou and Lorraine, we finished out the summer of '74. It was a better summer than we anticipated. We completed the paperwork on the building and the business, and whaddaya know: I was suddenly a scared shitless business owner (not to mention real estate "mogul") on the Boardwalk in Asbury Park.

But I was also hopeful. Because Lou and Lorraine were actually thinking about that possible and aforementioned "ace in the hole."

#

CHRISTINA and the WHITEFISH

8

Hey grunt, 'war is hell.'

"WHAT? You have got to be kidding! That's, I dunno, *INSANE?*"

The bedroom was dark except for the transient dance of passing headlights. For the five or so minutes since the return of their almost forgotten but still tender lovemaking, Christina and Jaime held each other in the peaceful perfection of their private calm. Until Christina opened her B-52 bomber bay doors and dropped a titanic payload on Jaime's unsuspecting world. At first, Christina's whispered revelation sounded like gibberish to Jaime. It began normal enough: *I've been thinking the last few days*—okay, that made sense, intelligible for maybe a minor observation about looking on the bright side of things regarding her current emotional state.

> *I've been thinking the last few days... about joining the Army,*
> *maybe focusing on something more than myself.*
> *It could be a good thing, right? Maybe a really good thing.*
> *You know, before going to college. Two or three years.*
> *Force myself to get serious. Get my head right.*
> *And they'll pay for it, the college. I mean, who does that?*
> *They have an entire program.*

Slowly, throughout Christina's discourse, Jaime untangled from their cozy knot and hoisted herself up on an elbow. "WHAT? You have got to be kidding! That's, I dunno, *INSANE?*"

She flicked on the small bedside lamp. Jaime needed to read Christina's face. She wasn't interested in the words, as Ti continued:

> *I need to do something other than this. And James,*
> *this isn't about us. Really. You see how fucked up I am.*
> *Maybe if I just go to the moon, I might come back*
> *like it was before, like we were before.*

Rarely did Jaime run her hands through her long, satiny black hair, but she did when offering her confused and dubious comeback, "If you go to the moon? What the hell does that mean?"

Christina tried stroking Jaime's arm, hoping to diffuse what she knew was about to transpire. "You know, get rid of all this baggage, see the world." That was Jaime's cue as she bounced out of bed and flitted naked through the room.

"See the world?! Jesus, Christina—buy a fucking plane ticket! I'll go with you. Anywhere. Paris-Rome-South America. How 'bout Tokyo? Right? You love cherry blossoms. You know you do!"

❖ ❖ ❖

For years, her hair was an unofficial trademark, but the U.S. Army couldn't give a rat's ass about style and/or "what great hair you have." That's how Corporal Anne Banks put it just before she significantly cut away the newbie's black wavy locks. "Sorry" was the last thing Christina heard before she underwent a proper military grooming, a butcher cut to just above the collar, nice and tight. Christina didn't care. She perceived the haircut as part of her transition.

The first time she fired her standard military-issued M-16A2 rifle, Christina was scared shitless. She'd never experienced that kind of violence. She almost wanted to drop the damn thing at her feet and run off into the woods. But she didn't. She hung in there, and rather quickly the intense muscle and furious power of the weapon started to feel good, started to feel right. She also knew she had to buckle down to keep up with the other grunts, many having years of civilian experience firing weapons for sport and killing Bambi's mother. Plain and simple, an Army recruit cannot graduate without proving they can handle their weapon without shooting themselves, their fellow classmates, or one of their instructors.

Ever the good student, Christina absorbed every nugget the instructors tossed her way. She liked when they pushed her, thinking it was the only way she'd cross the finish line.

At night, she'd memorize the M-16's details: "It's a fifty-six millimeter rifle, it's lightweight, air-cooled and gas-operated. You can fire from your shoulder or your hip. The M-16 is designed for three-round automatic fire or single shot semiautomatic fire." There was more. In fact, one afternoon an instructor called on her to verbally describe her weapon. Christina did so without a hiccup. She religiously practiced the disassembly and reassembly of her weapon. She also enjoyed cleaning her M-16. The gun became a natural extension. One instructor, toward the end of training, told her she was "a decent shot." Coming from this particular SOB, that was reaching the mountaintop.

After ten weeks of boot camp and then her subsequent basic training at Fort Jackson, South Carolina, Christina shipped out, first stationed at Camp Zama, Kanagawa Prefecture, Japan. About fifty minutes southwest of Tokyo.

The move proved to be an odd throwback to Jaime because when Christina arrived in the spring of 1990, the storm of cherry blossoms was bursting everywhere. Way more than those happy-go-lucky days with Jaime when they'd escape to Branch Brook Park in Newark and disappear into a cloud of pink heaven.

But here in Japan, my Lord—such an odd juxtaposition between the mechanized ways and means of the United States Army as compared to her free hours taking the train down the coast to Miurakaigan Station, followed by blissful walks to Komatsugaike Park; an endless maze of pink blossoms, some deciding to flurry, whispering to her as she passed. More than anything, Christina wanted Jaime to hear those whispers too.

At Camp Zama, Pvt. Christina MacKenzie was assigned to the 311th Military Intelligence Battalion. Based on her basic training as well as further evaluations, the Army believed she was a good fit for "MI," and they were correct. She excelled. And as rumblings of war escalated in the Middle East, Christina was transferred to the 522nd Military Intelligence Battalion in Wiesbaden, Germany, just days after the Iraqi Army invaded Kuwait in August 1990. The cherry blossoms now a fairytale.

Iraq's invasion brought immediate economic sanctions by both Washington and London. Was Saudi Arabia next? Possibly, since Saddam Hussein denounced the U.S.-backed Saudi state as an illegitimate guardian of the Islamic holy cities, Mecca and Medina. America and its coalition partners were on heightened alert. The geopolitical chess game and related theatrics ignited the U.S. military's unrivaled wherewithal, especially when it came to military intelligence. Christina regrettably remembered laughing way too hard when her superior quipped the old adage that "military intelligence" was the perfect oxymoron.

She not only embraced her new duties and the intrigue associated with the knowledge-gathering business but also buried herself in military life. Pvt. MacKenzie's escape into the gears of martial righteousness and American exceptionalism proved a remarkable whitewash over her pain and suffering. It was never an antidote for her particular poison but rather suitable camouflage. Pun intended.

In Wiesbaden, Christina worked in air-conditioned offices jam-packed with supercomputers and workstations linked to every conceivable electronic portal, including reconnaissance satellites blinking high above the planet. She was grounded enough to clearly recognize that at this stage of her nascent career she was a grunt, not in a muddy foxhole but sitting behind a steel desk. A glorified secretary who could also handle an M-16 or M4 assault rifle. But you had to start somewhere. The Army told her a thousand times: *We're all important cogs in this mechanism.* "Freedom is hard work, soldier."

American GIs around the world, including reservists at home, could sense that an all-out air and ground combat effort was inevitable, especially when the U.S. Commander in Chief began comparing Saddam Hussein to Adolf Hitler. Christina and her fellow warriors in the Five-Twenty-Two understood that the gig was getting close. They were all well aware of major U.S. troop mobilizations domestically, as well as key deployments from foreign bases. In the local Wiesbaden biergartens, over Dunkeles and Radlers, Christina would hear the long-timers banging the drums of war. She could tell they were getting salty—"itchy for the shit," as one Sergeant from Kentucky put it.

And then once the Pentagon dispatched their heavyweight naval battle groups into the region—assault capabilities built around locked and loaded aircraft carriers—everyone, including the dorks at CNN, could smell the dogs of war. Operation Desert Shield was burrowing deep into the Persian Gulf.

Christina communicated with fellow service members by email, but the American public was not yet hooked up with the likes of AOL—still a short jog away—so it was yellow pads and ink for Christina and Jaime, who were faithful letter writers. Both Jersey girls remained committed to their relationship, but it sure as hell wasn't easy. Nevertheless, Jaime was encouraged by the upbeat tenor of Ti's letters, as well as the occasional phone call. Jaime's support endured, albeit under silent protest. She was still in the apartment on Silver Dollar Ave, but was starting to seriously wonder why. Without Ti, Vegas felt like a supermax prison with neon lights.

For Christina, still within the safe confines of American-occupied Germany, the prep for war felt more like one of those Atari video games. But that would change quickly. Orders came through for a large segment of her battalion to head to the desert along Iraq's southern border. It wasn't until Pvt. Christina MacKenzie was strapped inside a C-130 Hercules transport at 22,000 feet over the Mediterranean that she said to herself: "What the fuck did I do?" And then two days later, on a prodigious caravan through the Arabian Desert, Christina decided she'd much rather be traveling through the Mojave with Jaime, maybe on their way to Joshua Tree.

Chatter amongst the soldiers focused on the immense build-up of U.S. troops now in the region, some suggesting almost half a million. "What the hell are they expecting?" became the prevailing asked and unanswered question. Both official and scuttlebutt predictions varied about how many dead and wounded the U.S. would ultimately suffer. Christina's comrades knew the American and coalition forces were superior fighters—also better equipped than the Iraqi forces—but what about Saddam's elite Republican Guard?

There was also tense concern about Iraq's chemical agents, both sarin and mustard gasses, which they recently used freely in their war with Iran, killing thousands. But that didn't intimidate a certain Kentucky sergeant, who pounded his chest, "Fuck them and their gas. Stormin' Norman's gonna wipe these faggots out!" Cheers. Another grunt yelled, "DEATH FROM ABOVE." More cheers. A tough chick from Maine made it clear, "We'll send these sand crabs crawlin' back to Mesopotamia." The pep rally continued.

That same night in camp, in her all-female barracks, Christina was amazed by two realities: how impressive their temporary housing was in this desolate hellscape; and that she was part of the largest single deployment of women into an American (or any?) combat zone. "Maybe," she thought, "I'm part of history"—another vital instrument in what was now being called "Operation Desert Storm." Just like World War II, the job needed to be done. Hundreds of thousands of soldiers embracing their humanitarian mission.

Lying on her bunk, reading *Stars and Stripes,* she learned that forty-one thousand women, both officers and enlisted, were deployed—pilots, medical personnel, truck drivers, intelligence analysts, communication teams, security experts, you name it. Ironically, they were infiltrating a society built on ancient tribalism where women were, if lucky, fourth-class citizens. In fact, Jaime once wrote in a letter to Ti, a letter of support, words Jaime couldn't believe she was scribbling, "Think of it, Ti, you're now at the vanguard of history!"

Jaime hated bullshit, most of all her own. Then why did she write it? Oh yeah, that's why, it all came roaring back as she felt the barrel of that emotional gun pressed up against her temple.

By Thanksgiving 1990, Christina's team was knee-deep in the ramp up to hostilities. Even though she was a peon, the day-to-day machinations and stratagems of military intelligence were strangely invigorating to all involved, including the young grunt from Belvidere, New Jersey. But she was still a stranger in a strange land. Especially during Christmas, which felt bizarrely out of sync until a large group of soldiers, Christina included, went out caroling throughout the camp. It was a big hit. So was the Polaroid Jaime sent of herself in a skimpy elf outfit. Christina was incredibly turned on but made sure to bury the photo deep in her footlocker.

Christina also thought, "Who the hell took that photo?"

Since fighting was imminent, the first two weeks of January were crazy as hell. MI felt like Penn Station at rush hour. Instead of trains crisscrossing, it was intel flowing every which way. Recon and surveillance poured in 24/7; everything was checked, double and triple checked, and then checked again.

16 January 1991. Game time.

U.S. CENTCOM, on orders from the Pentagon and the White House, began a colossal forty-day aerial bombardment over Iraq. Coalition forces flew more than 100,000 sorties that decimated Iraqi civilian and military infrastructure. Christina found herself conflicted: On the one hand, she applauded with gusto the utter destruction of Iraqi society—and why not? This was war. And war, like a famous general once said, was expected to be hell. And, no doubt, this obliteration would ensure her safety as well as the safety of her fellow comrades ("Better them than us"). Plus, they all knew a major ground campaign was right on the heels of this blitzkrieg, so let's clear the runway for the real flesh and blood.

But wait, she thought, what about the flesh and blood and grisly entrails already flowing on the ground in Iraq and Kuwait? Gobs and barrels of civilian blood. Every day, Christina would read the Pentagon's Iraqi death toll estimates, courtesy of the nonstop carpet bombing launched from bases in Saudi Arabia as well as the six carrier groups positioned in the Red Sea and Persian Gulf. It was a damn turkey shoot. Clearly, she had no other choice but to start wondering what it was like living and dying under this barrage of death—in Baghdad neighborhoods, in villages throughout the countryside. The so-called dogs of war.

Pvt. Christina MacKenzie was about to find out.

A team of five grunts from MI were ordered to pick up new computer equipment at the U.S. Army's Quartermaster Corps in the Saudi Arabian city of Dhahran. They sent a small five-ton truck for the cargo, along with a locked and loaded Humvee on escort. It was 25 February 1991—a day after the U.S. ground assault began in earnest, an onslaught brimming with Abrams tanks and Bradley Fighting Vehicles, as well as howitzers thundering across the desert, all of it covered from above by Apache and Cobra attack choppers.

The MI team left HQ after dark at around 1900 hours. Without incident, they cruised through the desert until just a few minutes outside of Dhahran when they heard a warning siren, which usually meant a possible Iraqi SCUD missile attack. They could see the temporary U.S. base as they pulled off the highway and then suddenly witnessed a screaming missile slam into a large barracks as they pulled inside the compound—the detonation producing an ornery firestorm. There was immediate bedlam as the orange inferno lit up the night. And then, along with all the others on base, the grunts from MI raced in to help, followed shortly thereafter by ambulances and fire trucks.

What Christina witnessed was absolute bloody chaos: Every U.S. soldier in camp was either putting out fires, digging through rubble, or tending to the shrieking and gravely wounded, or the charred bodies and severed limbs, the shrapnel spiked into the howling near dead. Medics looked haunted as they tried desperately to save lives. Blackhawk choppers suddenly appeared to airlift out the wounded. The agony and suffering were horrific.

A day later, the 522 retrieved their computer equipment and started back. Driving through the desert, no one spoke. Christina and her mates were still covered with soot and dried blood.

The Jersey Girl stared blankly at the passing, dead-brown landscape. It was one of those million-mile stares. Martha sat next to her. She was from Sitka, Alaska—the soldier they called Munchkin; and up to this point, the twenty-year-old was gnarly and tough as nails. But here, in the middle of nowhere, after absorbing a human meat grinder, Martha was quivering and weeping as Christina held her close, tears welling in both of their eyes.

Christina knew history. Jack & Darlene made sure of that.

Their summer road trips were geared to filling in the blanks inherent in all of those boring textbooks. So it wasn't surprising that Pvt. MacKenzie could see well beyond the passing Arabian sand dunes toward the lush green hills of Tennessee, the seemingly undisturbed countryside Christina once visited. She remembered walking through large whispering oaks that stood high above the Shiloh Battlefield—or it could have been Vicksburg or Antietam. Hell, it really didn't matter. Because this was all about her Dad's lesson that day, a lesson centered around one man, Commanding General of the United States Army, William Tecumseh Sherman, who famously cautioned the world with three simple words.

And sure enough, on this bleak day some seven thousand miles away, Tecumseh Sherman loomed large over the Arabian Desert, reminding Christina and anyone else who would listen, "See? I told you so."

&

9
Purple Haze.

SINCE THIS ISN'T A MOVING PICTURE SHOW, visual descriptions are probably in order.

Let's start with my club – about to commemorate its twentieth anniversary. Not too shabby, right? Especially when considering I've been navigating through an economic wasteland. One of my regulars, Bagel, an ex-New Yorker, refers to me as "The Toots Shor of Asbury Park." Love the fact that Bagel sees certain qualities of the renowned saloonkeeper in yours truly.

Our city's oceanfront esplanade hosts two very disparate looks. Most of the structures on the planks or around the Boardwalk are humdrum, jerry-built constructions, usually painted in a boring whitish-gray. But then, like a classic red Rolls-Royce amidst a sea of white Ramblers, a classic historic edifice emerges with its elegant brick handiwork highlighted by that bluish-green patina trim, which is the verdigris detailed earlier. But other than Convention Hall, there's very little color, especially on a dreary bleak day – and in Jersey those are plentiful. Granted, HoJo's has their trademark orange and there are a few signs along the way that offer a hint of colorant, mostly red, with obligatory messages like "Fudge" or "Peanut World."

But it's only when folks amble by my place that color kicks 'em right in the nuts. And they're either drawn in or they want absolutely nothing to do with the Club Southside. Why?

Well, first off, it's set back about fifty feet from the Boardwalk proper, so people have to make a commitment to wander over. Most folks are not explorers, but there are some with a Vespucci gene – and I prefer the curious anyway. Secondly, the club is a long, rectangular freestanding structure, painted in a motif that can only be called "Purple Haze." Looming over the entrance we have giant signage:

C L U B   S O U T H S I D E

Each individual letter is painted on faded driftwood planks in a hue I've dubbed "Jimi Gold." When you get a chance, take a look at the album cover for "Are You Experienced?" and then simply invert the colors. That's the example I showed the sales guy at Sherwin-Williams. "See this album cover? I want that purple and I want that gold. Exactly. Mix your magic."

All four exterior walls adhere to this palette. There are two front windows, both blacked out except for a neon beer sign humming in each: "Pabst Blue Ribbon" and "Ballantine Ale." They're both original and both still work.

Side note: I also hired a noted sign artist from Brooklyn to paint the club's main signature as well as various words and adages, like the main draw: "TAVERN / FOOD: NOON TO MIDNIGHT... or some poetry: 'Scuse me while I kiss the sky. (Catch that? Most folks think it's "Excuse me")

She did a remarkable job with all my signage. Elegant and edgy but not hokey. Museum-quality. Dora still comes down once a year for touch-ups but she won't take any money, so I make us a steak dinner (T-bones and mashed), and I break out one of my very decent California cabs – a bottle that the winos and boors down here are way too pedestrian to appreciate.

Let's go inside.

Now, when the club changed hands back in '74, I set aside three months for a complete refurb on the interior. Ma was actually a big help. She had a great eye. God bless that woman.

We'll get to the upstairs (where I live) and to the basement (which you've already glimpsed) later, so let's focus on the club itself.

My vision was stark simplicity in low amber light.

The belly-up bar is a beauty. Didn't want to touch that baby at all – a Pier 51 cornerstone. Stunning mahogany (and not that fake shit from the Philippines but the real McCoy from South America). Lou and Lorraine told me his name, which I can't remember, but the guy that built my stretch bar was a skilled artisan. Dig it: dovetail joinery with hand-carved particulars. He crafted raised panels on the front and added ornate corbels that buttress the bar's surface. Of course, down under, he installed brass foot rails and, believe you me, you have to polish those suckers but good. The stools are also the originals from Pier 51. Leather half-backs with a nice thick cushy seat. They don't make shit like this anymore, unless, of course, you go for your lungs.

The concrete floors needed to be ground down and polished with a dull luster. I did most of that myself. Backbreaking work but well worth it. The exposed brick walls were original – beat to hell reddish and white; I just left them as is (Ma's idea). Great character. You have to know when to just walk away. Although, there can be drawbacks to exposed brick: the hard-clay material is porous and can absorb moisture, which leads to mold. So I hit the walls with a heavy-duty sealant. Works like a charm.

And I wanted no clutter, I hate clutter, so I just hung a few strategically placed black and white photographs. No overall theme, just large images that grabbed my attention at flea markets or in those shops out in New Hope and Lambertville. But here's the key: It's all about the framing. The photographs cost me next to nothing. Instead, I decided to sink a few bucks into the frames and the matting. Gave the job to a real pro – Eddie's Framery out in Freehold – because I wanted each frame to be the exact same style. Sizes could change but not the look. I went with thick black wood because you need a serious portal leading into each image.

I have three favorites: a deadly serious Babe Ruth staring right into the camera, probably late in his career; then there's a rough and tumble Ulysses S. Grant in his rumpled uniform, looking off in the distance like he's deciding which southern sonovabitch was next; and then finally there's Jane Fonda on a bombed-out street in Hanoi. She has a camera hanging around her neck and there's a young North Vietnamese regular peering in over her shoulder. Three iconoclastic Americans.

I also left the ceiling alone. Hell, we're talking about original copper tin tiles with a simple box pattern. Classic. Nothing's better than that. Just wipe 'em down. Done and dusted. But I did get rid of Lou and Lorraine's table situation. Suffice it to say, their inventory was beat to shit with no oomph. Excuse my French, but it was fucking firewood.

Then I hit the jackpot: A fish joint down on Long Beach Island went bankrupt and I scored five nail-trimmed dining tables that needed nothing more than a few gallons of Shellac. I also walked out with three big semicircle booths – upholstered with those dark red cushions. For me, it was like Christmas morning.

And then just recently, I added a leather Chesterfield sofa in case one of the regulars can't make it to the door.

Add all this shit together and my club evokes the perfect vibe for the perfect watering hole: a classy dive. The kind of place Charles Bukowski might like to bury himself in a booth, slug bourbon and write something like –

"But now and then, a woman walks up, full blossom, a woman just bursting out of her dress a sex creature, a curse, the end of it all."

Or Jimmy Breslin, like my old man, a rough and tumble muckraker who found angles, human angles. For instance, back in '63 when the press – in its entirety – focused solely on "the spectacle" of JFK's funeral, Breslin (writing for the "New York Herald Tribune") instead focuses solely on Clifton Pollard, the man who dug the 35th president's grave at Arlington National. I can absolutely envision a cloistered Breslin drinking in my bar, ferociously writing this remarkable story, capturing a day of national grief as he chronicled the gravedigger making $3.01 an hour.

"Clifton Pollard was pretty sure he was going to be working on Sunday, so when he woke up at 9 a.m., in his three-room apartment on Corcoran Street, he put on khaki overalls before going into the kitchen for breakfast. His wife, Hettie, made bacon and eggs for him. Pollard was in the middle of eating them when he received the phone call he had been expecting."

You might be wondering, what about the guy banging on this Underwood?

Well, I'm hard to miss. I've been bleaching my hair "ash blonde white" ever since that shit-heel Reagan got elected. Talk about a pig fucker. Ronnie Raygun. But that's for another day. I figured if the country was going in that direction, I should immediately detour in another.

In point of fact, bleaching is pretty easy. One of the supplies I need is bleach powder – and you actually need a cosmetology license to buy this shit, so Sally over at Surfside Beauty hooks me up.

Four components are necessary: coconut oil, developer, toner, and ammonia-free bleach powder. The process begins when I go to bed, and it's complete by the time I show up for work. So, yeah, if you see a guy walking the planks with a pronounced limp sporting long bleached white hair, chances are it's probably me.

For the most part, I wear two basic outfits. The main look is simple and consists of faded rag-tag jeans with Hawaiian shirts. The more colorful and outrageous the better. The secondary look consists of the same jeans, but Hawaiian shirts are replaced by authentic hockey jerseys. I have twelve, home and away, for each of the original six NHL teams. Frankly, I consider any team organized after the original six to be imposters.

Over a bottle of Napa cab one night, Dora, my amazing sign artist from Brooklyn, suggested that I was "coarsely handsome." I guess that's a compliment. I also think she was somewhat surprised that night, as well as all the other nights she stopped by to say hello, that I never made a move. And from where I stand, there's no doubt that Dora from Brooklyn is a looker. In fact, just my type.

I just figured it was better to keep our relationship strictly business.

# #

CHRISTINA and the WHITEFISH

10

Cinders.

The trudge to Dhahran and the subsequent bloodbath were unfortunately only Act One in Christina's Middle East horror show. A few days later, orders came through for an advance team that included Military Intelligence to head out to Highway 80 in Iraq, the road that connected Basra with Kuwait City. It was a fact-finding mission on what would soon be called the "Highway of Death." On 28 February 1991, one hundred hours after America's thunderous ground assault commenced, the U.S. president declared a ceasefire. Kuwait had been liberated with Iraq down for the count. But in the wake of mass destruction and death, there was still much in question.

Since the middle of January, the retreating Iraqi Army had been setting countless oil wells on fire, creating an asphyxiating canvas that turned day into night. Coinciding with this land-based firestorm was the strategic dumping by Iraqi forces of untold millions of barrels of crude oil into the Persian Gulf—the ecological nightmare aimed at foiling any amphibious landings by American Marines.

So, as chaos reigned, Pvt. Christina MacKenzie was assigned to one of the various MI teams covering the region for intel—and the 522 headed straight to the Highway of Death. What she saw there and what she experienced there was another hell on earth, only a thousand times more gruesome than the barracks in Dhahran. These were realities no individual can unsee. As the team moved through what seemed like a never-ending killing field, the reality of seared human beings roasted alive in their charred vehicles was beyond surreal—images that drilled deep into human psyches. It was like willfully drinking poison.

Wandering off by herself, Christina stopped by one particular truck. The enemy soldier must have been trying to climb out of his shattered windshield but didn't make it. The flames incinerated him whole, his body nothing more than blackened bone and silver ash. His eyes were cinders, his skeletal skull somehow still upright. The contortion of his mouth was not human.

Indeed, Christina's Kentucky sergeant was spot-on: Death from Above.

En bloc, convoys of Iraqi forces had been fleeing Kuwait when U.S. aircraft loaded for bear trapped their snaking retreat: F-117 Nighthawks with their laser-guided missiles, A-10 Warthogs unleashing armor-piercing shells loaded with depleted uranium, and then nimble Apache choppers launching cluster bombs as well as a nonstop machine-gun pounding.

Boomer, one of Christina's 522 comrades, moseyed up like he was back home in a Boston bowling alley, "Man-O-Man, those boys barbecued these motherfuckers." He looked at Christina with a devilish grin and then pounded the incinerated Iraqi with the butt of his rifle. The scorched body collapsed into itself. "Yowza Hajji!" Then walking away like a warrior philosopher, Boomer shouted to the world, "Dust to dust, sand nigger!"

Standing there in this cadaverous graveyard, Christina's innocence, or whatever the fuck was left of it, joined the charred Iraqi with those cinder eyes.

For the remainder of this brutal operation, which lasted about a week, Christina was sleepwalking through a personal Hades, an unrelenting abyss, and her fellow soldiers knew it. Munchkin was the only compassionate GI and fought the others to "back off, give her a break! Jesus." A screaming crew cut got in Munchkin's face, "Shut the fuck up, you cunt. She's dead fucking weight!" Munchkin didn't back up an inch, "Fuck you, ass wipe, she might be the only sane motherfucker out here. We're all acting like this shit is normal!"

Under protest, they covered for her until they got back to base. On the mission, Christina spent an inordinate amount of time in the Humvee. Or dry heaving. Or riding the waves of severe panic attacks. Sweating. Shuddering. Bouts of hyperventilating. More than once, she lost control of her bowels. Munchkin had to ride her hard when it came to eating and drinking, especially under the suffocating toxic cloud driven by the reek of burning oil. At night, in transient tents, Christina would lie awake, mostly wanting to die as she constantly wiped black mucus dripping from her nose.

Her life on the idyllic banks of the Delaware felt like far-flung days, existence in another solar system.

Shortly thereafter, on orders from her superiors, Pvt. MacKenzie spent a few days of R&R at the King Abdul Aziz Air Base in Dhahran, the provisional home of the Air Force's 1st Tactical Fighter Wing out of Langley, Virginia. Two in-country physicians, an Army doc, and a consulting civilian psychiatrist, spent time with Christina, mostly the shrink—an expert from Stanford on mental disorders consequent to warfare. The shrink went deep with the young unraveling soldier. When she learned about the recent and tragic death of Christina's mother and father—and that it wasn't even listed on her recruitment records—the doc realized how dangerous the situation had become for this friable young woman.

Before she knew it, and along with other personnel, Christina was on a military-contracted commercial aircraft bound for Los Angeles International Airport. In her bag, she carried her Administrative Discharge papers. The medical staff in Dhahran told her it was an "ODPMC"—a termination defined as "Other Designated Physical and Mental Conditions." This classification covered various issues that deemed a soldier unfit for service. The Stanford doc also prescribed a few magic pills. The only name Christina could remember was Klonopin since the shrink made a big deal about the drug, telling her patient, "Whatever you do, even if you start feeling okay, DO NOT go cold turkey off Klonopin. Very dangerous."

From LAX, an unmarked van took her as directed to the Wadsworth VA Hospital near UCLA, ominously neighboring the VA's vast National Cemetery. Based on her doc's recommendation, Christina was scheduled to spend at least two weeks under the care and observation of VA docs before returning to civilian life. After only a day, the thought of leaving this tranquil place, surrounded by breezy palm trees and warm blue skies, felt scary as hell. Like a womb, her mother's womb, Christina contemplated staying here forever.

She fell in love with a small derelict white chapel on the VA compound, a church that belonged on good ol' Greenwich Street in Belvidere. One of her more erudite counselors told her that this small "Queen Anne jewel box of a church" was the oldest building on Wilshire Boulevard. Christina was bummed that she couldn't go inside—closed since an earthquake in 1971.

Still, she loved sitting outside on the front steps.

She thought about her Mom, who loved churches—not the religious aspect but the architectural. She was always teaching her daughter the various terms and concepts, like "apse" and "nave," and how they figured into the schematic; also how the "transept" created the symbolic shape of the cross. And don't even start on stained glass. There wasn't an old church in New Jersey, big or small, that Darlene MacKenzie couldn't rattle on about—especially the artistry of the stained glass.

If her Mom were here, Christina thought, she'd catalogue and store every element of this "Queen Anne jewel box of a church."

It was weird but a song started playing in Christina's head as if it were coming from inside the chapel—a tune she remembered Darlene singing as the record played on their stereo. The album cover was strange with the Mamas and the Papas stuffed in a bathtub. Why this memory? Why now? Why a bathtub? And only some of the lyrics lined up with the tune playing in her head:

> *Stopped into a church...*
> *On my knees I pretend to pray...*
> *The preacher... he knows I'm gonna stay...*
> *California dreamin'... on such a winter's daayyyyy...*

She didn't expect tears, but there they were. Along with the breezy palm trees and warm blue skies.

Sitting on the steps of this boarded-up white chapel, Christina figured she had two things in common with the old place: they both fell into a state of disrepair and both probably had bats in the belfry.

&

11
Vigorish.

BACK IN LATE '74, when Pier 51 changed hands and was officially mine, Lou and Lorraine finally opened up about the elusive "ace in the hole." They were willing to talk. I think the reality of retirement finally settled in and they wanted out of everything. Watch sunsets, delight in the grandkids, and at long last enjoy each other without the constant grind of booze, food, screwball patrons, and the pile of sludge that is the Jersey Shore. And the beauty part? These two kids really did love each other, even after decades of marriage. It was refreshing to see. I should be so lucky.

I was always aware that their parallel "bizness" broke numerous New Jersey statutes, but this was Asbury Park. The gendarmes from Trenton were a million miles away and couldn't care less, and their local blue brethren usually looked the other way, especially since these cops were either utilizing Pier 51's services or they were knee-deep in their own corruption.

Lest I give you the wrong impression, Lou and Lorraine weren't exactly Bonnie & Clyde, but they were significant bookmakers in and around Monmouth County. I knew what was going on but never indulged since the "house" – like Vegas or AC – has everything stacked in their favor. I've always viewed gambling as a fool's errand, a reckless folly for sad sack degenerates. Even professional gamblers, sophisticated sharks in the sports biz, only win at about a fifty-five percent rate. Tops. But now I had a chance to be on the other side. Funny how your perspective changes when the fence moves.

However, this is what I didn't know: Lou and Lorraine were merely front of house on this operation, ordinary ticket-takers. Bureaucrats. The real brains behind this sports book, the true bookie, the actual turf accountant, was Lorraine's identical twin sister, Lorelei. This demure and straitlaced granny was mostly wheelchair-bound and lived a quiet life right next door in Ocean Grove. Remember? "God's Square Mile at the Jersey Shore."

I hate that fucking place.

Lorelei was a staple at the old Methodist church, even sang in the choir. But her husband, Gaetano "Nicky" Antuofermo, was a legendary sports book employed by none other than Newark's first family, the Boiardos.

Starting out, Nicky worked closely with the infamous family's patriarch, Ruggiero Boiardo, lovingly known as "Richie the Boot."

Side note: Why was Boiardo nicknamed "The Boot"? Simple, really. Early in his career, during Prohibition, Richie picked up the catchy moniker based on his brutal technique of dealing with his enemies: crushing their skull with his boot. I bet you can't unsee that shit.

In the '70s, after Richie retires behind the walls of his suburban Essex County fortress, Nicky answered to Richie's son, a character named "Tony Boy." Over the decades, Nicky proved to be one of their best earners, funneling piles of cash to his North Jersey bosses. When Nicky was dying of cancer, he spent the year teaching Lorelei all he knew – you know, as a possible retirement plan, if she so desired.

Truth be told, Lorelei loved the idea and wanted in. She was a virtual sponge. A true disciple. Nicky quickly realized that his choice of heir apparent was spot on: Lorelei was shrewd and sharp like a fucking tack. You see, Nicky worked out of their old brownstone on Garside Street in Newark, and apparently over the years, his wife had been paying more attention to the New York Football Giants than she was to the Braciole.

A year after Nicky passed, Lorelei retired and moved down the shore to be with her twin sister. That's when Lou realized he was sitting on a possible goldmine, which of course was Nicky Antuofermo's widowed wife and former acolyte. Lou figured if Lorelei could step into the breach, they could cement one sweet partnership far from the Newark cabal. When asked, Lorelei told Lou and her sister that the old man had been slipping for some time and that she was the one holding things together. "With a wry shit-eating grin," Lou explained, "Lorelei posed the following rhetorical question: 'Who do ya think made that killing on Joe Willie back in '69?'" Lou said she broke out laughing hysterically as she rolled herself toward the toilet, "All me, Lou. Those last two years poor Nicky didn't know where his fuckin' dick was. Excuse me, I gotta drop a deuce." Now Lou was laughing hysterically.

On my behalf, Lou called a sit-down over at Lorelei's. At first, to be respectful, I called her Mrs. Antuofermo, to which she laughed and kindly suggested that I call her Lorelei, that she hated "the fucking name" and it only reminded her of those "bubblegum gangsters" up in Newark, "especially Richie the Boot and his fuckin' backyard incinerator. These thugs give Italians a bad name."

Side note #2: I remember my old man telling me about an expose that his paper was doing on the Boiardo crime family. He said it would make a great TV show. He's probably right. My father had terrific instincts.

It was easy. Lorelei and I struck a deal – the same deal she had with Lou. My club would be the clearinghouse and she'd run the numbers along with the business. I got a cut of the vig or vigorish as well as a taste of the action. Lou and Lorraine would get me up to speed before their Sunshine State escape, and Lorelei would educate me on the fly, "Baptism by fire, Mister Boniface. My sweet kid sister, by eight minutes, says you're pretty sharp."

When I got home, I looked up "boniface." You learn something new every day.

We consummated our illicit marriage over blueberry scones and some delightful Earl Grey. Lorelei regaled me with some upcoming action: college and pro hoops, NHL hockey, and there was, of course, the imminent Ali-Foreman fight about to happen in Africa, but when the discourse turned to the weekend's NFL action, there was a glint in her eye. She waved her fancy teacup like a magic wand, her mouthwatering as she ran off the games jotted down on scraps of paper: "Lions minus three-and-a-half, yeah, I'll buy that. Hasn't moved all week. We got the Rams giving a touchdown for crissakes, let's shave that a bit. And then on Monday night, the Cowboys giving eight is a fucking ball-buster, especially with Staubach out. And trust me, that line ain't coming down. I'll go the eight but get these losers to parlay that shit with the over-under. That oughta nullify things." After a long pause and a dainty sip of tea, she dubiously sighed, "sons of bitches," as her look drifted far past the window.

Then, matter-of-factly, "Vegas makes our job a living hell."

Lorelei could sure work the spread. She'd be adjusting right up to game time. It was like watching a mad scientist. And then balancing the books, minimizing losses – nobody was better. She operated with fucking precision. It was a thing of beauty. The woman could've waltzed into any Vegas sports book and those cretins would've rolled out the red carpet.

Over the years, we made some very nice coin together. Took a lot of pressure off my bottom line. Most of the time, a trusted associate by the name of Joe Fats worked the phones. We had a runner, a Puerto Rican kid named Albert. Good guy. He also doubled as my number one waiter. Unfortunately, he went back to the island. Then, of course, we had some muscle just in case one of our clients decided to go on an unscheduled vacation. Luckily, we kept the violence to a bare minimum. Threats laced with creative hyperbole goes a long way.

Poor Lorelei died in her sleep three years ago. She was still working at ninety. One morning she didn't answer the phone. Half-hour later, I found her in bed, stiff as a board. As always, her desk was neatly cluttered. Star-Ledger sports section folded just so. Red, green, and blue Sharpies ready for action. Multiple stacks of square notepaper that she trimmed herself to save money. Up on the window sill there were two small framed photos: one of Nicky outside his beloved First Ward hangout – the "After Work Political Club," and the other was Nicky and Lorelei in front of a Newark landmark, the window sign read: M. Giordano Sanitary Bakery. The photo was a study in juxtaposition: Nicky was smiling ear-to-ear... Lorelei was not.

I once told her that I thought she was "idiosyncratic." She looked up from her paper, smiled the warmest smile I'd ever seen – and then told me to go fuck myself.

I miss her so much.

#

12

Shell Shock.

The phone number at the apartment on Silver Dollar Ave was no longer working. And it was almost two months since Christina wrote Jaime a letter—even longer since she received anything back. The Dhahran missile attack followed by the Highway of Death atrocity turned their normal means of communication sideways. One of Christina's counselors at the VA Hospital allowed her to use an office phone to reach out and find Jaime. Somehow, she actually remembered Jaime's home number and called a few times with no answer, not even a machine. Christina desperately wanted to reach her.

Therapy at the Wadsworth VA began one-on-one. Dr. Morea, a young empathetic psychiatrist, began to unpack Christina's background—most importantly, the loss of her parents, of course, forever married to her recent battlefield trauma.

From simple observation, the doctor surmised that her patient wasn't sleeping. And as the days clicked by, Christina confirmed her sleepless nights, also revealing muscle pain, shortness of breath that she hated, as well as debilitating fatigue—and by the end of week number one, she revealed to Morea a large raspberry rash on her thigh. She said the panic attacks weren't as severe or as frequent as they were back in Iraq or the Kingdom, but they were still happening. Morea knew these symptoms painted a classic example of what was now being called post-traumatic stress disorder. From Los Angeles to East Orange, VA hospitals were flooded with cases—Vietnam leftovers and now a new supply of fresh meat from the Persian Gulf.

As Christina stared out the window, watching cars sail by on Wilshire, Morea remembered one of her professors saying that PTSD used to be called "soldier's heart or irritable heart." Or the one everyone remembered: "shell shock." But what worried Morea the most was when Christina tried to describe certain episodes—"attacks" is what she called them—scary bouts that really freaked her out; what Christina referred to as "visits from Iraq."

"I'll feel... sudden pain, like in my stomach," Christina tried to explain, "not nauseous but like a stinging slicing ache." She struggled to continue, as if it might start throbbing at any moment. "Or maybe I'll hear something that reminds me of Dhahran or—" Christina suddenly stopped cold, trying hard to find the words. Morea was always patient, always serene.

"Sometimes I can even kind of smell something or maybe it's a smell that reminds me of something, I don't know." She stopped again. Morea knew there was more. Christina was staring at her fingers, then nervously gnawed on a cuticle. It was as if suddenly the doctor wasn't there and Christina was by herself, alone on an island. Morea recognized it as a dissociative state, also to be expected. Christina snapped back, "They're sort of like these moments, I dunno, maybe more like electric snapshots? That's weird, right? I know, but they're, they're fast. They just come and then... It's like you can hear a snap or a sizzle, but they don't stay, and that can change, like there might be another, but it's not connected somehow. Does that make sense? Or they don't stay, they just leave. These visits."

Morea needed more definition, more insight; she wanted to be sure. "Christina, what do you see in these electric snapshots?"

The once vibrant kid in high school, the girl in love with life, the woman who had everything stretched out before her, life as she knew it, stood up nervously, as if to make a speech in front of a thousand people. She stared intently at Dr. Morea for a very long moment and then turned to the window that faced Wilshire, turning like she was following a slow-moving sound—but there were no sounds.

When she finally spoke, Christina started to cry; yet she was unexpectedly calm, "I see exactly what I saw. For like a split second, I'm actually there again, back there again. I mean it's hyperreal, like I'm even closer to whatever it was the first time. I mean physically closer."

Christina walked over to the Wilshire window, "Maybe it's more like visits *to Iraq*, not from. Yeah, it's more like I go there."

In her file labeled "Pvt. Christina MacKenzie," Dr. Morea noted that the patient "shows early signs of triggering trauma-related episodic memory fragments – seemingly caused by perceptual cues that are tied to strong perceptual priming in her implicit memory system." Morea also wanted to play alchemist with Christina's drug regimen, most notably recommending: "Christina, let's get you off the Klonopin to another benzo. Let's try Lorazepam. It's more commonly called Ativan. Some new studies are very promising. The team here is very impressed. Three to four weeks."

Later that same morning, Christina was sitting on the steps of the white chapel, her makeshift sanctuary, when a young woman, they were probably equal in age, approached with a smile and a basket. She was dressed like a nurse from the Royal London Hospital circa 1880. But here in the City of Angels, she was known as a candy striper. She smiled and reached into her tisket, a tasket, a brown and yellow basket and offered Christina a small double-flag tied together on sticks. Somehow, the candy striper's smile grew magically large:

"A grateful nation says thank you."

Christina awkwardly smiled back and took the gift. The candy striper moved on down the path, seemingly back toward the 19th century. Christina's eyes followed her until the girl disappeared into an adjacent building. Then she glanced at the flags. One was Old Glory and the other was white with blue and red letters:

"A grateful nation says THANK YOU."

As Christina stared at the flags, she felt it again—that scary shortness of breath. She'd feel this sensation sporadically, no pattern whatsoever. And it seemed like it was followed by a hacking cough, one that was getting more pronounced.

Back in her room, there was a small spider plant. Christina stuck the flagsticks in the dirt. She thought the flags looked silly, but where else could she put them? The trash can was a fleeting thought.

Then, an hour later, she finally got through to Jaime.

Actually, Mrs. Nguyen answered the telephone and was so happy to hear Christina's voice. Jaime must have been upstairs because her mother excitedly yelled for her to pick up. Christina sat alone in a small sterile office: green metal mid-century desk, filing cabinet, and a very uncomfortable chair. A Physician's Desk Reference acted as a doorstopper to the toilet.

"I got it, Ma. Hang up!" were Jaime's first words, orders really.

Christina couldn't help but crack a smile, that was so Jaime. Mrs. Nguyen sweetly took forever to wrap it up. Christina could imagine Jaime getting irritated waiting for her mother to finish. She also visualized the Nguyen house on 4th Street—a Victorian they called "Italianate." She knew almost every inch of the interior. The white kitchen with rose-colored shutters. The lavender parlor. Red sofa. Jaime's bedroom, where they first kissed. The dank, unfinished basement where they first made love. "I love you, too, Mrs. Nguyen."

Christina and Jaime both waited for the click.

&

13
The King.

BEFORE I DESCEND INTO THE LINEAGE that is the "King of Asbury Park," let me round out a few items in the Club Southside that usually pique the attention of the diverse demographic that frequents my establishment.

JUKEBOX.

I really looked into this nostalgic bit of Americana because, as we all know, "music is the moonlight in the gloomy night of life." Some ancient cat wrote that, but I appropriate it here for effect. I also dig this contraption's backstory, its name derived from the Gullah or Creole people's word "juke" or "juke joint" – those bawdy musical haunts that popped up in the American south after emancipation. Workers and sharecroppers needed a place of their own to unwind, dance, drink, maybe gamble, especially with ol' Jim Crow rearing his ugly face, barring these good folks from whitey's various establishments.

After researching the possibilities, there was only one jukebox I wanted for the club: the 1956 Seeburg Select-o-Matic. Not the Rock-Ola or the famous Wurlitzer but rather this box of musical perfection. I tracked one down at a bar in New Castle, Delaware. Made an offer on a machine that wasn't officially for sale, but the owner couldn't unplug it fast enough. Cherry mint condition. This baby houses eighty 7-inch vinyl records, and I meticulously handpicked every recording, tenderly tossing out most of the music already living inside.

Side note: My bookie partner, Lorelei, helped me type up all the new card labels, like-

"CRAZY"
Patsy Cline
"I FALL TO PIECES"

"OYE COMO VA"
Santana
"ABRAXAS"

First thing I did was disable the mechanism for depositing coins and then rigged it so it's free selection for all Club Southside clientele. And, of course, I included anthems for everyone—from Coltrane and Etta James to Elvis Costello and Warren Zevon. Also some newer cool shit like Nirvana's "Smells Like Teen Spirit." Love that fucking song. And even Pavarotti makes an appearance, "Nessun Dorma!"

POOL TABLE.

Now, I'm no Minnesota Fats, but I like a nice table: slate bed, decent pocket liners, and of course perfect felt. The surface is a gorgeous burgundy red. The choice of pool balls is also very important. I went with the Brunswick Centennial. Top of the line. And the best thing about a pool table? That unmistakable-unambiguous-and-undeniable sound when someone launches a thunderous break.

STAGE.

Don't get too excited. It's nothing more than a cheeseball platform jammed over in the northwest corner. I built it one Saturday afternoon, painted it black, and hung a red drape over the back brick wall. Ma donated her old beat-to-hell upright Baldwin that we anchored to the side. There's also a decent mic and a small Peavey amp. As well, I recently installed a dancer's pole.

It's funny about that stage. Like the club, it's very multipurpose. I've had a few comedians (none of them funny), a barber shop quartet (not bad), a few run-of-the-mill wannabe Dylans (all of them boring as hell), some leftover Beat poets (stop trying, boys and girls, it's dead), a jazz trio known as "Two Jacks and a Jill" (as close to a house band as I care to get), and then there's our on-again off-again afternoon delight – Donna the Stripper. (Truth be told: If she applied for work in a classy strip club, she'd be lucky to land Monday morning before lunch.)

Side note #2: Regarding the Beat poets - or more accurately, the current crop of losers... Sure, I'd extend an invitation if one of them could actually write something like:

"I saw the best minds of my generation destroyed by madness,
starving hysterical naked,
dragging themselves through the negro streets at dawn
looking for an angry fix"

Yeah, that guy or gal would get an invitation.

###

There's one other act that's become legendary in these parts. It's known as –

"The King of Asbury Park"

Somewhere along the line, I became a big fan of George Carlin. I often promote the notion that Mr. Carlin is our Mark Twain. And when you watch Carlin perform, like one of his Home Box Office specials (that I steal off the local cable distribution box), it appears like he's riffing, right off the top of his head. Well, that's ridiculous considering the perfection of his delivery and the power of his words (words that cut through the dung of American society like a machete). And that shit doesn't just happen. He writes it, rewrites it, and then works it until he has a finely tuned Stradivarius.

That's how I work – but by no stretch of the imagination do I put myself in the same universe as Mr. Carlin. That would be preposterous. But I follow his lead, his work ethic, not to mention his manic passion, his innate ability to make folks feel just a bit uncomfortable.

For years, I've worked a routine I authored entitled "The King of Asbury Park." I offer it here as a gander inside my heart of darkness, one epitomized by dark comedy, as we find times when comedy and tragedy walk hand in hand. Just ask that old English wordsmith who penned the great "tragicomedy" – The Merchant of Venice. It was my old man's favorite play. There's a main character named Shylock who I sort of relate to in various ways. Unfortunately, Shylock is destroyed not only by his own blunders but also by the persecution levied at him by the play's various lovers, all of whom marry and walk off into happy endings. Hence, the tragicomedy.

My partner in crime for this absurdist and vaudevillian performance is none other than the aforementioned Lil Abner, who is one strange looking dude, perfect for the Asbury Park freak show. He was constructed by the Lord Himself for a routine such as this. Abner's probably in his late thirties, can't be more than four-foot-ten, downright emaciated, and it appears like the SOB withers right in front of you – and he ALWAYS wears an old red fedora that's at least one size too small. He's asthmatic, so he wheezes like an old radiator. When Abner left his Elysian Park brownstone in Hoboken, his prominent hawk nose led the way. Simply put: a Looney Tunes character that belongs in an animation cell (I actually have one framed on the wall – Elmer Fudd).

From the handwritten draft, delivered from my small stage to a packed house, one Saturday night – 26 January 1991 – at the very height of the Persian Gulf War when folks needed a little breather from the Empire's theatrics...

LIL ABNER already on stage.

House dark, solo spotlight on stage. Two stools: one empty, one with a tumbler of scotch neat, and its bottle nearby – Ballantine's Finest.

On a table the props include a Boombox, small American flag, piano wire, and a putter.

Conspicuous on a black stool sits a large gold crown atop a marble pedestal.

LIL ABNER:

(hit PLAY on Boombox – "Hail to the Chief")

  Ladies and gentlemen, please welcome to the stage, New Jersey's preeminent saloon keeper, not to mention the reigning King of Asbury Park–

(turn up the VOLUME)

  "The Whitefish."

ME:

(enter acknowledging your loyal subjects, during applause light a cigarette with the Ronson flip-lighter)

(admire the crown, pick it up, play with audience, music fades away)

  "The King of Asbury Park..." Is this an honest-to-God monarch with royal authority? Historic figures like Alexander the Great, Henry the Eighth, Tutankhamen, William the Conqueror... or maybe a legendary king, say King Arthur... or hell, what about the Burger King?

(wink & point to someone, crown down, new direction)

The tradition started back in '55 with a guy named "Jack the Golfer." This cat drove a gorgeous cornflower yellow Buick Riviera, of course a convertible... damn thing got maybe eight miles a gallon. And when Jack pulled into town, holy shit, it was like an asteroid blasting through the stratosphere. A real piece of work.

(beat)

Now remember... this is a world with Elvis on the TV and every American male walking around like they're dipped in grease. And the girls? They're fussing about in poodle skirts and cardigans. C'mon, postwar America: Happy Days and sock hops. We had "Grandpa Ike" making every man-woman-and-child feel safe, especially with those Russkys hiding behind every dumpster... and Sputnik flying around the globe.

("oops," forgot to intro Abner)

Sorry, folks... my esteemed partner hailing from the great city of Hoboken, deep in the heart of Hudson County, a man who is never without his classy red fedora - ladies and gents, Lil Abner!

(applause, Abner tips his hat, back to storytelling)

Alright, back to Jack... and you're probably wondering: What's this guy do for a living? Well, you're not gonna find this on a resume: Ol' Jack was a hustler - big time money on all these manicured links up and down the Jersey Shore. A fucking legend. Nerves of steel.

LIL ABNER:

And for a small guy...

(swings an imaginary club)

WHACK!

(watches it fly toward the horizon)

Lemme tell ya, Jack hit a real big ball.

ME:

And make no mistake about it, Jack the Golfer was "King" of this town for quite some time.

LIL ABNER:

Absolute warrior... Something like twenty years.

ME:

Until one fateful afternoon out at Spring Meadow when Jack sinks a 7-iron for about ten large.

LIL ABNER:

Unfortunately that gorgeous shot led to Jack's grisly demise.

ME:

Indeed it did. Some local Don Cheech wasn't exactly enthusiastic about Jack's shot-making abilities... this one from about a hundred and fifty yards out. Unheard of.

LIL ABNER:

Witnesses said the shot had wicked back spin, like Providence itself controlled that unholy Titleist.

ME:

Shortly thereafter, Don Cheech orders one of his lieutenants to strangle Jack right in the parking lot.

LIL ABNER:

(holds up piano wire, indicates the gruesome action)

Piano wire. Almost took Jack's head clean off.

ME:

Then for good measure, Bobby HaHa buries a pitching wedge in his skull.

LIL ABNER:

Poor Jack lying there resembling a dead Kennedy.

ME:

And then like vultures on a carcass, Cheech's crew starts grabbing anything they can get. His watch, wedding band - which actually took some doing... I think Beans got like three-four hundred dollars cash, even took his shoes. Damn scene was like Christmas morning.

(grab the putter)

Me? I got his putter. Vintage Tommy Armour.

(line up a putt, whisper voice of a TV golf announcer)

This folks for the U.S. Open...

LIL ABNER:

Who got the convertible Riv?

ME:

Who do you think?

LIL ABNER:

Yeah that's pretty obvious. But I still have one thing to say: Long live the King!

(rallies audience)

LONG LIVE THE KING! LONG LIVE THE KING!

ME:

(wait for them to calm down)

There's no doubt in my mind that Jesus Christ was SO proud of his disciples on that warm New Jersey afternoon.

(lose the putter)

So, the Golfer is replaced by a sleazy bastard named Chick Venus, somewhat of a folk hero from here down to A-C. Some moniker, huh? Chick Venus.

LIL ABNER:

That's a bullshit name as far as I'm concerned. Sounds made up.

ME:

Chickie owned two nightclubs, three fish restaurants, a cheesy strip joint, and the bastard's also running a very profitable numbers racket out in the Black neighborhoods.

LIL ABNER:

Predatory fucking capitalist.

ME:

No doubt. Greed was good. But Chickie Boy doesn't last too long.

LIL ABNER:

No he doesn't... a simple twist of fate.

ME:

One night at Captain Kidd's-

LIL ABNER:

That's Chickie's crown jewel eatery down in Egg Harbor-

ME:

Dude eats some real bad tuna, turns a whiter shade of pale, and dies in a toilet. Just like that.

LIL ABNER:

Here today, and then boom, you die in a restaurant toilet. Life is full of fuckin' surprises.

ME:

Chickie the King suffered from something called "scombroid poisoning." Apparently his tuna contained extremely high levels of histamines. Off the chart kind of stuff. Doctors were baffled. It was like a gunshot through the heart.

(aside to audience member)

Sonovabitch owed me a grand.

LIL ABNER:

(rallies audience)

LONG LIVE THE KING! LONG LIVE THE KING!

ME:

Next in line, Ralph Giancarlo.

LIL ABNER:

(makes subtle sign of the cross, stage whisper)

Father, son, Holy Ghost.

ME:

Most folks called him "Sarge," because more than anything else, Ralphie wanted in on that little dinner party we threw over in Southeast Asia.

(take a long pause)

I'm sure you're all familiar with that minor debacle. I know I am.

LIL ABNER:

(waves the small flag)

What-ya-call an addendum to the Monroe Doctrine.

ME:

I mean this fucker was gone. Dude bought his entire wardrobe at the Army-Navy Surplus... Hell, Ralphie would sit there and cheer the Vietcong death count like he was watching the goddamn Mets.

LIL ABNER:

But Sarge had one problem.

ME:

Yes, indeed. He was five-foot-one and weighed about three thousand pounds. There wasn't an army on God's green earth that would march into battle with this tub of shit.

LIL ABNER:

So what does he do? He starts pullin' stunts.

ME:

Because Ralphie needs to prove to the entire world that he's as tough as any six-foot-five farm boy from Nebraska.

LIL ABNER:

Speaking of Nebraska, that album remains Springsteen's unrivaled answer to Reagan's "Morning in America" bullshit.

ME:

Some of his best work: stark, haunting... hell, if you listen closely, you can hear the ghost of Woody Guthrie. And dig it, Bruce records the damn thing on cassette. I mean that takes balls. Sorry, I digress... So, Ralph starts picking ridiculous fights - battles he has zero chance of winning. He also starts doing wacky shit like running old cars into brick walls.

LIL ABNER:

We're talkin' thirty-forty miles an hour.

ME:

(laugh at a memory)

In fact, right out back, the maniac dares our friend, Lil Abner here, to hit him flush on with his fucking pick-up truck.

LIL ABNER:

At first I said no... "Jesus, Ralph, I'm gonna kill ya."

ME:

But then Ralph gives Abner a C-note for his trouble - even signs a goddamn waiver, which of course ain't worth the paper it's printed on.

LIL ABNER:

I hit him good, like twenty miles an hour. Flush on. BAM.

(warmly remembers the moment of impact)

And you know what? It actually feels strangely rewarding to whack someone with your car. I mean who knew?

ME:

Did Ralph get back up?

LIL ABNER:

Three months later.

ME:

Fuckin' whack job... but that's just prologue... because the piece de resistance for King Ralph was his famous final scene.

LIL ABNER:

The ol' swan song... Sarge's gasoline shower. FILL 'ER UP!

ME:

What a trip. Here's how it breaks down... Ralphie's old lady owned and operated the now defunct Point Pleasant Sunoco station out there on 88... and Ralph's doing this act where he douses himself with what Europeans call "petrol."

LIL ABNER:

Sunoco 94 octane shit. Fuckin' rocket fuel.

ME:

He's doing tricks with lighters, matches, M-80s, anything that ignites. I mean this is crazy, rubber room kind of shit. And by now, Ralphie the King is drawin' big crowds.

LIL ABNER:

The guy's mimeographin' off flyers, people are coming in from all over.

ME:

And that's when some sick and twisted sonovabitch-

LIL ABNER:

And to this day, we still don't know who-

ME:

Tosses a lit cigarette at ol' Ralphie. It was hideous. He went up like the fucking Hindenburg.

LIL ABNER:

  (expect an awkward silence)

    LONG LIVE THE KING! LONG LIVE THE KING!

ME:

  (wait for crowd to calm down)

    And with Sarge gone, the throne was - as they say -
    vacated.

There's a big finish landing later in this work. Hang in there.

#

14

Booby Hatch.

Three days after their phone call, Jaime was on a Continental flight from Newark to LAX, worried as hell—scared shitless really—now that she knew the ugly truth: why she didn't hear from Christina for so long. But she melted when she heard her voice. Jaime could tell instantly that Ti was seriously messed up. When you know another soul as well as she knew Christina MacKenzie, as much as she loved Christina MacKenzie, you become über perceptive. Over the phone, Ti's voice was low, almost a mumble throughout. But that was only part of it, the minor part. For Jaime, her initial worries quickly became her fear, and then mutated into outright panic. It was obvious to Jaime: Christina was scared. For her life. And she needed help. And they needed each other.

Jaime knew she could wrench her out of the quicksand. Or so she believed. Or hoped.

The day before her flight, Jaime finally picked up the book that had been sitting on her dresser for well over a year, last year's Christmas present from Ti—Carl Sagan's *Cosmos*. She was embarrassed that she never even cracked it open, especially a book that was so important to Christina. With a plane flight coming up, better late than never. Actually, better *now* than ever, she thought, as she re-read the inscription:

> *J*
> *My South China Sea*
> *You've heard me go on endlessly about these words*
> *Yes, if I had a religion this would be it*
> *I share. I hope. I love you.*
> *Merry Xmas!*
> *C-Mac xoxo*

Jaime forgot that nickname. C-Mac. She was there when Mr. Brennan started calling her that in physics class junior year. Matter, space & time; motion & forces; optics & light. C-Mac loved that stuff, and luckily for Jaime, C-Mac helped her study. She also helped her cheat. If Ti was the brains of the operation, then Jaime was the spirit, the rebel—the Lennon to her McCartney.

During the cab ride up the 405, which was more like a crawl, Jaime was weirdly nervous about seeing Ti. What the hell was she walking into? How much had she changed? Maybe a lot. Christina was in a hospital for mental reasons?! Worse yet—A VA HOSPITAL?! Not for a broken leg or a bullet wound. That would've been easy. But she's here, in the government's motherfucking loony bin. Their nuthouse. Funny farm. Once, in a cartoon, they called it a "booby hatch." Did they have padded cells? Rubber rooms? A psyche ward fronting for a snake pit? Screams and howls echoing down squalid hallways. Jaime was worked up, "I have to get her out." The cabbie answered, "What?" Jaime thought that was her inside voice. He tried again, "Did you say something?" Jaime just stared at a passing Pico Blvd sign, "Sorry, no, I'm talking to myself."

When the cabbie finally swung off the 405 at Westwood, Jaime caught a glimpse of the massive Veterans National Cemetery—headstones covering the expansive and sloping landscape for what seemed like miles. "At least she's not in there." Fortunately, this time, she used her inside voice. In the turnaround at the VA, Jaime dug out some cash as the cabbie pulled her suitcase from the trunk. He seemed happy, so she figured the tip must have been decent. As the car pulled away, Jaime stood frozen in the driveway. Her second thought was completely absurd, "I've never seen a green cab before. I DO NOT LIKE green eggs and ham."

But her first thought was actually a question, "Which way to the booby hatch?"

As Christina walked into the waiting area, she felt painted head to toe with equal coats of guilt & shame. But when her eyes met Jaime's, she realized that those smiling dark eyes, eyes she missed so much, were already moving fast across the large sterile room, toward Ti like a runaway freight train—and the patient wasn't sure what was about to happen. An elderly couple sat nearby. Just for an instant, Christina glanced their way—the couple's inquisitive eyes were now involved in this about-to-be collision, this pile-up, this wreck on the highway.

But the elderly woman was the first to smile as Jaime hugged her best friend like a stuffed bear. Christina finally realized what was happening as her guilt & shame surged out of the infirmary and splashed into the gutters out on Wilshire, joining the urban drainage designed to stream rainwater toward the not-too-distant Pacific, which would carry it all west, toward Hawaii, where the Sun and lava would cleanse and erase this corrupt and government-inflicted man-made horror.

After a few seconds, Christina (aka Ti, aka C-Mac) threw her arms around Jaime, their eyes closed and shielded in each other's bodies. Could they fly away like this? Whoosh! Or maybe leap into a time machine? Destination: who cares. Anywhere but here. The elderly man smiled and reached for his wife's hand; this waiting room couple now a part of the love radiating off these two lost souls.

The hug shifted as they parted slightly, their hands falling naturally together, between them, like their soft hands fell so many times before. Unfortunately, Jaime and Ti did not soar away, nor did that time machine ever show up.

But they were together, and for now that was at least something.

❖ ❖ ❖

As they strolled around the well-maintained grounds, the guilt & shame slowly returned to Christina's psyche—not with a dramatic crash, thank god, but with a slow, familiar cozy up and whisper: "I'm back." Seems like guilt & shame never made it to Hawaii, but C-Mac tried her best to fight through it. And Jaime was one smart cookie. She kept it all mellow, small talk, and oh so humdrum—brought her partner up to speed on hightailing it out of Vegas, the idiot landlord, the hassle getting her last paycheck from the Sands, some dull shit back in Belvidere, it was still cold in Jersey, "Look, it's starting to grow back," Jaime stroked Christina's short hair. She held Ti's hand. "I did our walk along the river like six times." They both smiled, remembering in perfect unison, "Cold like a witch's tit." A well-oiled inside joke that still worked.

When they reached the white chapel, Christina felt relieved, like in some bizarre way she finally made it home, wherever home was in the spring of 1991. Jaime immediately noticed the shift.

"You like it here? At this old church?" They sat on the grungy steps.

"Yeah, it's nice here…" Christina closed her eyes. The Sun felt good—a sweet embrace, welcoming as it's apt to feel in Southern California. Finally, her eyes popped open, smiling, "When I'm here, I have conversations with you. Just boring junk. You're a good listener."

Jaime laughed as she cuddled close, "I aim to please." A truck downshifted in the always hectic West LA traffic. "Sweetie," Jaime was careful and easy, "Are they helping you here? What's going on? *Only if you wanna talk.* I'm cool just sitting here."

Christina was ready; she wanted so much to share the truth with Jaime. Although, the first few words were tough. "Yes, here, it's been better. Better, yeah. I like my doc. She's young and seems to care, I guess." Sirens made a racket out on Sepulveda, disappearing into the din of the nearby freeway, then a lawn mower, followed by distant hammering and construction in Brentwood.

Jaime held Ti's hand, which seemed to trigger more thoughts as her body relaxed and her head gently landed on Jaime's shoulder.

"Over there, I was so freaked out. I mean you have no idea, James. It's like a nightmare times ten fucking million. You can't even imagine and it's all crazy sick because it's real. Not some make-believe war movie or a really bad dream. The shrink there started me on medications. Without them I'd probably be dead by now." Like a feather, Jaime touched her hair, terrified to even contemplate what Ti saw "over there."

Christina MacKenzie and Jaime Nguyen sat in the warm sun a little while longer. Jaime was pretty sure Christina fell asleep cuddled next to her. When she nodded awake, Christina kind of blurted out, "They call it PTSD. I have group therapy today. I hope I'm not late." She held Jaime's hand. "James, are you coming tomorrow?"

"Of course. What time?"

Tomorrow came. As did the next day. Also a few more. And then the VA finally discharged Christina with a bag full of pharmaceuticals, some books and pamphlets, as well as a proposed schedule for group therapy and a few one-on-ones with Dr. Morea. Christina joined Jaime at the Royal Motel on Santa Monica Boulevard. A real shithole. Made the apartment on Silver Dollar Ave feel like The Ritz.

Of course these two Jersey Girls would talk, but not like the old days when their connection was skintight, their words like playful librettos, emotions wondrously freewheelin'. It was a friendship that classmates would openly mock, their envy obvious. Imagine if they knew the whole truth!

Although now, as the dust settled from a life gone haywire, they were trying—each in their own way—to regain their rare and effortless bond, their union under siege since that goddamn plane went down in the wilds of Alaska. And back then this siege was just getting started as it morphed into outright slaughter in the blood-drenched sands of Iraq. Courtesy of a United States Army recruiter on the Vegas Strip. A costumed robot working for a psychopathic cult leader named Uncle Sam. In fact, that was exactly how Jaime regarded the way their lives went sideways, especially Christina's. Jaime wasn't a violent person, a pacifist really, but she'd love to get her hands around the neck of that goddamn recruiter.

Together they were dealing, kind of sort of handling Alaska—but then enter stage left: Tin soldiers. Cannon fodder. Carnage and butchery. "Christina, what the hell did you do?"

Jaime never said it. She never wrote it. But she believed every word of it. Nothing but brainwashing and Christina was ripe for the harvest. Although Jaime knew that someday, hopefully soon, they'd cross over this bridge of sighs and deal with the truth.

But for now, they would talk about other things. Not the elephant in the room. And boy did they need that damn time machine—and it didn't have to be one of those top-of-the-line models that can transport you back to Ancient Egypt or the French Renaissance or just before the Big Bang. Nope. Just a cut-rate machine capable of carrying them back to a Tuesday night in 1987. The U2 *Joshua Tree* show at The Garden. Great seats. A birthday present from Jack & Darlene. Little Steven and the Disciples of Soul was the opening band. *What a show. What a blast!* Jaime remembered they made a pact that night to move to Manhattan as soon as they were free from their suburban shackles. But now, three and a half years later, with buckets of blood having passed under some clichéd bridge, they had to make some decisions about who-what-where-and-when.

And none of those decisions involved the Royal Motel on Santa Monica Boulevard.

Jaime sat at their small kitchen table. She thought Ti looked cute in her oversized gray Princeton t-shirt, her hair perfectly disheveled from sleep—or whatever it was that Ti did during the night. Christina started making them oatmeal for breakfast. Their "efficiency room" had a pathetic kitchenette with a hotplate, two crusty pots, and a shitty dorm room fridge. There was an equally shitty clock radio that Jaime was trying to dial in the necessary tunes—ahhh, there we go, Tom Petty and the Heartbreakers. 95.5 KLOS. As she went back to her book, *Cosmos*, Jaime noticed that Christina had stopped stirring and was staring blankly into the simmering oats. It began to unnerve Jaime because it wasn't one of those absent-minded moments. It looked eerie. "What's that word?!?" Jaime couldn't remember, then she did, "Catatonic."

"C-Mac?" Nothing. "Christina?" Still nothing. Jaime moved up easy to Christina. "Hey Ti." Jaime held the pot and then the spoon, trying to make eye contact. "Hey, Ti, you alright?" Christina finally broke her thousand-yard stare and looked into Jaime's face. It was a look Jaime didn't recognize. And when she spoke, Ti's voice sounded like it was coming from some other place. "Wha-I-did-do." It sounded weird, jumbled. But then suddenly Christina was sharper, more coherent. "James, it's the worst thing I've done. What-did-I-do?" And just as Jaime was going to offer something in return, or maybe just a hug, a jolt of adrenaline surged through Christina's body as she bolted away looking for something.

"Where is that fucking thing?"

"What thing, sweetie?"

"That thing with those fucking sticks."

Jaime was lost. She moved the oatmeal off the hot plate and followed Christina. "What thing with sticks?"

"You fucking know. There's two of them."

Christina then went zero to sixty unhinged, "WHERE THE FUCK IS THAT THING?! I'LL FUCKING KILL SOMEBODY!" Now Jaime was scared. "I'll help you find it. We'll find it together." "WHAT THE FUCK DO YOU KNOW?! FUCKING CUNT!" And then just as fast as she went rogue, Christina downshifted back to serene, when she finally spotted her elusive prey—the two small flags on sticks.

Christina passed by Jaime, smiling and holding the flags like she finally tracked down the Holy Grail. Jaime tried some normalcy, "Let's eat our oatmeal, right?" "Absolutely, James. I'm starving. Let me first dispose of this thing." Christina stopped on a dime in the kitchenette proper and turned back to Jaime, "It's really not a thing, it's a creature."

She whipped open the small fridge and, in one motion, tossed the flags inside the box and slammed the door shut. Like the Gates of Hell.

"There, gone forever."

Turning on a dime, Christina was excited about breakfast, "Okay, right, oatmeal. Two bowls. Brown sugar and cinnamon, right? We love cinnamon."

Jaime watched closely, fixated on one very clear thought: her anticipated vision of a booby hatch, the scene she had feared when she first arrived at the VA, the "psyche ward fronting for a snake pit," was now, sadly, making oatmeal on a grimy hotplate. The eagle had landed.

Carrying two bowls, Christina walked over grinning, "Behold, breakfast... Yay!"

And a grateful nation says THANK YOU.

◊

CHRISTINA and the WHITEFISH

15
The Vikings.

IT'S VERY DIFFICULT (truth be told: impossible) to cremate a body properly when conducting a Viking funeral. An official crematoria will burn a body at about 2012 degrees Fahrenheit (or about 1100 degrees Celsius for you Canadian fuckers out there). And even at 2012 degrees for two full hours, you still have to grind down the leftover bone fragments. How do I know this macabre shit?

Because there's a postscript on Mrs. Lorelei Antuofermo.

You see, Lorelei's "Last Will & Testament" contained very specific wishes. There were all the normal directives: The money was split between her siblings plus a pet rescue fund in Matawan; her baseball card collection, which was massive and in mint condition (with enough Mickeys and Willies to fund two years of college), went to her longtime mailman Oscar Washington; and then the big prize – the house in Ocean Grove – went to her son, Carl, who Nicky ex-communicated from the family when the old man found out that his only-begotten son was "a fuckin' homo." To her credit, Lorelei waited a few months for Nicky to substantially decompose and then hired a non-mob lawyer to draft a new will, reinstating Carl as her son and primary beneficiary. She also added Oscar Washington to the document. The first lawyer, a "family consigliere," not only refused to reinstate Carl, but also said Nicky "would never allow a shine in his will." Lorelei told him to die of cancer and then hired her new attorney.

But her most unique wish was a Viking funeral. (You heard that right.) She told me about this provision roughly a year before she died. Apparently, Lorelei remembered some Kirk Douglas movie where he played a Viking and his fellow marauders ended up burying Kirk at sea. In the film, the Norse clan prepared the body on a giant canoe-like boat and launched him out to Valhalla. Then, on cue, an assemblage of marksmen fired flaming arrows into the boat, setting Kirk on fire, all in the hope of elevating his chances into the afterlife. Hollywood bullshit, but very dramatic. Memorable to say the least.

But really, why a Viking funeral?

Lorelei said she grew to hate all that "deranged Italian crap," especially when it came to funerals: you weren't allowed to cremate the body, and at the wake, you had to deal with histrionic rituals like wailing Italian scrubwomen throwing themselves on caskets. Lorelei was emphatic, "Get the fuck out of here." Then, of course, she wanted nothing to do with all that church shit. Again, she was emphatic, "Too goddamn medieval." And, as you might imagine, Lorelei wasn't done: "Then you got some drunken Monsignor, who doesn't even know me, spewing bullshit to a bunch of gavones with one thing on their mind: going home and shoveling lasagna in their piehole. I ain't goin' out like that."

As usual, Lorraine's twin sister was right.

At the reading of her will, the invited beneficiaries included: Me, her son Carl, Oscar the mailman, a chap named Cosmo Mintz from the animal shelter, and one sister, Ruthie, who represented all the siblings. The even split of Lorelei's currency was well received. Ruthie, along with Cosmo, both cried. Oscar was blown away. He said they used to talk baseball all the time, noting, "Lorelei knew more about the game than anyone I knew." Her collection was later valued at nineteen grand. Oscar even gave me a few choice cards for framing (Yankees, of course): Roger Maris, Tom Tresh, Yogi, Whitey, The Mick, and the always entertaining Joe Pepitone. In a nice montage, they all hang behind my bar.

The son, Carl Antuofermo, was dumbfounded, flummoxed, and bemused all at once. The Manhattan pastry chef was completely unaware that his mother had him reinstated in the will. He wasn't even planning on driving down from the City, but in the eleventh hour decided what the hell.

He's a very sweet man. And now he has a vacation home on the Jersey Shore. Good for him.

Side note: Let me pull out the soapbox and say something here about "fuckin' homos" - in the parlance of one Nicky Antuofermo.

Shut the fuck up, you thug piece of shit.

You treat your son... your own flesh and blood... like worthless garbage? (Or anyone for that matter who dares to live outside your ignorant Neanderthal boundaries.)

Who the hell are you to deem any human being's way of life unacceptable? Christ, you're an uneducated goon... a maggot who worked for deranged killers... and, according to Lorelei, you were banging hookers like they were going out of style. Ever hear of glass houses, you "pencil dick motherfucker?" (Lorelei's words, not mine.)

Me personally? I could give a shit if someone's gay, lesbian, a transvestite, or whatever makes you whole. How does that reality affect me one iota? It doesn't. It's none of my business and it's none of yours. Outside of applauding someone's courage and their righteousness, I have no say about anything.

I'll never forget this one night in my club: Some asshole from Philly accuses Ronnie Esposito of being "a dandy," – which he is not, but that's of no consequence. Ol' Ronnie throws a straight right and the guy drops like a sack of shit. Cheesesteak climbs back to his feet but he's summarily "escorted" out the back door by Lil Abner, Joe Fats, and of course myself (just to make sure things didn't spiral completely out of control). I told Ronnie to relax, finish your drink, we'll show cheesesteak home.

Now, I regarded this little episode as a teachable moment for the unstable huckleberries that patronize my club, some of them not as enlightened as yours truly. Here's a paraphrased transcript as I remember the conversation, just after we left Mr. Philadelphia lying prostrate in the alley, my guess bleeding:

ME
"Alright, ladies, tell me why we just tossed that asshole out?"

JOE FATS
"What's that? A trick question? 'Cause he called Ronnie a fag."

ME
"First of all, Fats, he called Ronnie 'a dandy' – same thing, but get your facts straight. And secondly, that's not why we beat him senseless with a perfectly good trash can."

LIL ABNER
"Then I'm confused. Why did we beat him senseless?"

ME
"Because he disparaged and denigrated someone's sexual choices, that's why. No one has that right."

JOE FATS
"But Ronnie's not even whaddayacall gay."

ME
"Fats, it's not a personal thing. It's communal. Universal. And it's not going to happen in my club. Who the hell are we to decide what's right and what's not? I may be King, but I'm not God. See what I'm talking about? And also keep this in mind: We live in Asbury Park – once a safe haven, an oasis for those that society mocked and scorned. You don't know the history like I do – an oasis. So mark my words... at some point in the very near future, people will accept different lifestyles without even blinking an eye. It's called the march of history. Evolution. Now please get me a club soda. I got agita."

###

As you might surmise, I'm a bit of an anomaly down here. In another life, I would have roamed the Americas, an insurgent for sure. Instead, I was a lackey for Uncle Sam, shootin' up the leech-infested rice paddies of Vietnam. There I was, Mr. Gung Ho, chanting, "HO CHI MINH IS A SON OF A BITCH!" – when I should have been absorbing important principles, for example:

"Let me say, at the risk of seeming ridiculous, that the true revolutionary is guided by great feelings of love."

Excuse my Underwood detour to visit an absolute hero of mine – Ernesto Guevara, a physician and true revolutionary. Che wrote the above dictum in his amazing document entitled "Socialism and Man in Cuba," a book that sits by my side as I type. This Argentine Marxist left his native country to facilitate fighting oppression elsewhere – his life and fight greatly influencing my own spirit, embracing the idea that we should be driven by moral incentives rather than material wealth. His revolutionary courage scared the bejesus out of the United States, probably why CIA-fueled forces executed Che in the mountains of Bolivia back in 1967.

True giants like Guevara (and Tom Paine, Fred Hampton, Rosa Luxemburg, et cetera) need to studied by the sheeple; they need to be revered for their intellect as well as their courage. They function like mirrors in the face of corrupt societies.

That's why those in power always vilify truth-tellers, the true revolutionaries.

But alas, I dream. For I am nothing more than a Court Jester attempting to civilize the denizens of this quaint hamlet with small doses of empathy. There are those who would accuse me of "tilting at windmills." So be it.

###

Lorelei's "Last Will & Testament" listed me as the beneficiary of her 1985 Cadillac Eldorado – as long as I carried out her funeral wishes. The will specified that "Mr. Whitefish is the only individual I have faith in to actually pull this off." Man, did I want that car. Convertible. Original alabaster paint job with fire engine red leather seats. Gorgeous wheels. And only 7,000 miles on the ticker. A cherry of a car.

I immediately looked into Norse funerals.

As you might imagine, once I researched the details, I had some real obstacles to conquer. In fact, most of Lorelei's Viking funeral would have to be theatrics via sleight of hand. Understand this: not all Norse funerals were carried out on burning boats, but some were – and that's what Lorelei wanted.

I read about a typical ceremony out on the Volga River. The "festivities" began with some serious binge drinking, followed by the expected plunder and ransacking of the host village, then, of course, some prearranged ritualistic sex – all of it climaxing with the customary human and animal sacrifices. Once all the fun was over, it was time to launch their chieftain adrift, setting his burial ship ablaze.

Frankly, it seemed like state and local authorities might take issue with this unusual scenario, so I needed to create an alternative, a B-side.

I kept the actual details close to the vest. Only Abner knew the plan, and that bugger is like a goddamn bank vault. But for the Lorelei faithful and their immediate circle, we advertised and invited them to her requested and much-anticipated Viking funeral.

All the info was very generic: sunrise on a Tuesday morning, ground zero was the beachhead just south of Convention Hall. I knew the Boardwalk would be desolate. The cops, as always, nowhere to be found. I secured an old boat, and Lil Abner pinched a mannequin that we outfitted in one of Lorelei's familiar dresses. Then we covered "Lorelei" under much flora and pomp. To the initiated, this heap of combustible material is known as the "pyre." We figured most folks wouldn't be hip to the 2012-degree Fahrenheit reality, so it was all about theatrics... and then they'd go home with a story to tell.

Luckily, Abner is an accomplished jet skier, so he towed our wooden boat out past the ebb and flow where, upon my signal, he dramatically ignited the kindling and flora with a blowtorch. (C'mon, how the hell was I going to come up with twenty Norse marksmen on such short notice?) Abner unhooked his towline and rode off, letting the show unfold.

And there it was: a roaring blaze that sent old Lorelei hurdling toward Valhalla.

One other thing went hurdling toward Valhalla: my "ace in the hole" bizness with Lorelei Antuofermo, for a number of reasons. First and foremost, doing it without her made no sense at all. I'd have to replace her with an unknown entity, and that's a dangerous proposition. Bookmaking is already an enterprise that might land you in Rahway for a few years – and that's true even when trust is sacrosanct. I also figured that I skated past the authorities long enough, maybe getting out scot-free was the smart move.

Bottom line: Doing it without Lorelei just wouldn't be any fun.

I arranged Lorelei's actual cremation at a local funeral home. No service. Straight to the broiler. Her ashes live in a very tasteful urn that sits prominently in my art studio.

I figured her chirpy spirit would live on in every one of my brush strokes.

# #

16

Danger Will Robinson.

The bouts continued for Christina. Wild mood swings. Constant fatigue. Anxiety. Ongoing respiratory issues. The recurring flashbacks were followed by terrifying panic attacks. Enduring depression. And, of course, the pills—constantly adding and switching, with the shrinks at the VA resembling clowns juggling bowling pins, "Let's try this, what about that? A new Stanford study argues... Harvard believes otherwise...."

Christina simply went along. "They're doctors, they know what they're doing." But Jaime surmised that this ongoing witch's brew was little more than the military and their civilian cohorts playing alchemist, trying to find a magic PTSD potion. Or even worse: Vets as guinea pigs. Jaime read the critiques: Ever since Vietnam, when legions of broken men rotated back home, these snake charmers had been searching for that magic pill, mother's little helper, anything to help erase the crippling repercussions of their failed wars.

As 1991 unfolded, stories were circulating that other soldiers were returning with sudden and perplexing disorders. Mental and physical. Depression seemed to be number one on the hit parade, but other alarming ailments, similar or identical to Christina's, were also rocking these Vets. But the Pentagon brass made sure to trumpet the "fact" that the vast majority of America's fighting force were not reporting "strange illnesses" or "abnormal conditions."

Even if that were true, Jaime argued one night, it's not surprising since the vast majority of American soldiers, unlike Christina, didn't see action—the slaughter of Iraqis came from overhead strafing and bombing, not to mention missile strikes from distant naval launching pads. For many, it was just a very cool video game. Wax your joystick and it's Miller Time.

Jaime read about the possible side effects associated with the heavy toxins released from the massive oil fires. In fact, Jaime read a lot of stuff. She needed breaks from Christina and would spend hours in the

Santa Monica Library looking for clues—but there wasn't much to go on, mostly outdated studies based on the Vietnam War. Current reports and investigative exposés were few and far between. She even researched the drugs, wondering if Ti's daily cocktail could actually be making things worse.

Jaime approached every question and every hurdle with the same trilogy, the same mantra: *diligence, science, and empathy.* She never lost sight of the big picture—that Christina's psychological condition was the result of two major successive shocks. The sudden loss of her parents, her very foundation rocked to its core, followed by the utter madness and brutality of war. And not the bullshit TV version. Christina, a raw and innocent neophyte, experienced a brutal bloodbath followed by a ghoulish nightmare in broad daylight. All of it exasperated by shoving powerful benzodiazepines down her throat like Skittles—and voilà: *head on a post.*

Jaime figured you didn't need to be Sigmund Freud to piece this horror show together.

Money was tight. They'd have to find jobs and move into an apartment if they were going to stay in Southern California. Jaime didn't mind being the breadwinner until Christina was better, or at least well enough to work. Jaime also knew there was an uncle handling Christina's newly acquired house back in Belvidere as well as her financial inheritance. But this much was clear: Christina wasn't ready to touch what was now rightfully hers. And Jaime understood her feelings, but only up to a point. Obviously, there would come a time when Ti's life had to move on. The question was when; and judging by Christina's downward spiral, Jaime started to wonder if that time would ever—

She didn't want to finish her thought. Too soon.

On most days, Jaime would walk with Christina to her therapy sessions at the VA. In fact, Jaime thought the group sessions were the most beneficial. She definitely noticed that after group, their walks back to the motel were a short-lived reprieve. They'd stop at Winchell's for coffee and then split their favorite treat: a chocolate cake donut with chocolate glaze. Jaime would relish their thirty minutes of normalcy.

One afternoon, as they playfully fought over the last giant donut crumb (that unfortunately ended up on the floor), Jaime proudly announced she had finished reading *Cosmos* while sitting on the steps by the white chapel. She said she couldn't wait "to discuss this amazing book, especially this one mind-blowing quote. You're so right. Sagan's incredible. Such a smart dude." Listening to Jaime, C-Mac smiled sweetly, her eyes sparkling just like the old days, "Cool beans."

Jaime went to grab refills. As the lady poured coffee, Jaime watched Christina watch the traffic zipping by outside. Every moment was an adventure, "Is she still smiling? Is she still together?" She seemed fine, so Jaime ordered, "One more chocolate with the glaze." Hell, live it up. More coffee, more donuts. "Right now," she thought, "Winchell's is our sanctuary." Jaime knew the sparkle would be fleeting. A momentary refuge from those lurking shadows. She giggled to herself, "Even the demons needed a coffee break." Delivering the goodies, she kissed Christina on the cheek.

Christina broke off a bite and returned her gaze to the traffic. "You're spoiling me, Nguyen."

Sipping her coffee, Jaime rubbed her back, knowing full well there was no one else in Ti's corner. Sure, there were VA docs, but that was nine to five. Christina didn't ask, no one asked, but Jaime Nguyen was elected caretaker, to help her escape from this fucking spider web.

Jaime also knew Christina was lost in a hall of mirrors, a dark labyrinth, so to keep her own sanity, she constantly tried to pare things down to the practical facts—don't somersault down rabbit holes. Never lose sight of the big picture: Ti had been sprinting away from one massive earthquake and then inadvertently crashed into another. What you're dealing with now are the aftershocks. Jaime's mind was clear: be her filter, her clearinghouse. Keep chanting your trilogy: diligence, science, and empathy. She was also very aware of the dance associated with recovery: *one step forward, two steps back.*

There was another landmine always lurking nearby—the blame game, and Jaime was smart enough to also have a mantra for that: *Don't. Blame. Christina.*

She even wrote about it in a cheap notebook. It was a ramble—a stream of consciousness aimed, once again, at her own sanity:

Invasion of the body snatchers. The girl I know embraces LIFE not death. Her heart's in the heavens not hell. Fool some people, can't fool me!

REMEMBER she just made a bad decision. People make bad decisions all the time. So? Ti made the same mistake that millions made before her! Go to work for a killing machine. I read the history books. (The right history books!) They can't burn everything! THESE KIDS have no idea. They get brainwashed, it's like an injection that lasts forever.

Maybe these kids are just gullible (or maybe too dumb to realize!) "Sure, I'll trade my soul for college. Does the University of Mercenary have cheerleaders?"

These thoughts kicked around in Jaime's head all day long, ricocheting around like rogue bullets. Zing-zang.

One night in bed, Jaime watched Ti sleep. In these rare moments of deep slumber, the pain seemed to vanish from her beautiful face until consciousness rudely returned with the rising light. But in the midnight hour, Jaime knew that her best friend was still in there—the really smart girl, the gentle soul, the kindhearted woman who never (ever) would have picked up a gun or marched off into some unholy alliance.

Jaime understood the mission. She read about people that deprogramed victims trapped inside cults. Christina had been hoodwinked and filched by a cult: the United States military—how else could you convince kids to kill and die for Raytheon or Lockheed Martin or democracy? (Snicker-Snicker.) And for sure the fix wasn't going to come from these VA charlatans, "Shit, they're the damn problem, the guilty party." When the hell did solutions come from inside the problem?

Christina turned back from the traffic excited, wiping a smidge of chocolate glaze off her lip, "C'mon, tell me, what line blew you away?"

Jaime dug inside her big black bag and pulled out the dog-eared paperback. A page corner was folded back. "Okay, okay, this quote reminded me so much of you. It's what you used to tell me about, that 'astral' stuff,' right? I think it really shows who *we* are." Jaime touched Ti's arm, but there was a disturbance at the cash register. A homeless guy was trying to finagle something from the young cashier and the situation was escalating. "Not here," Jaime ditched the book in her bag. "Let's boogie."

They walked to a small city park just a few blocks away. Two moms were watching their kids sway on the swings. Jaime and Christina found a bench near some weeping willows. Jaime opened the book and read slowly, appreciating each phrase.

> *Every one of us is, in the cosmic perspective, precious.*
> *If a human disagrees with you, let him live.*
> *In a hundred billion galaxies, you will not find another.*

As she read, Christina quickly recognized the iconic Sagan quote. Her smile wasn't forced or manufactured, it was the magnetic smile that Jaime hadn't seen for what seemed like forever and a day. Ti held her hand and they kissed gently. These last few minutes felt like the old days.

Then it happened. Christina's smile slowly dissipated, as if she was now uncomfortable. Her eyes diverted to the children on the swings. Her hand wandered away from Jaime's as the city's racket moved into their peace. The sweet and perfect connection was lost in just under ten seconds. Did the mothership call Christina back? Even the children's laughter seemed to grow in volume, in angst, sounding more like a scathing laugh track mocking Jaime's decision to read Sagan. *Danger Will Robinson*—and Jaime knew it.

She tried to salvage the moment. "He's saying we're out here alone, right? It's important to cherish how unique this is." Jaime motioned to their connection, their love, "How unique we are." She barely got it all out before Christina was squirming and then walking away.

For sure, that's what Sagan meant. But Jaime knew he was also talking about other things, epic things, things that Earthlings have perfected with great success: hatred, torture, carnage. Jaime was hoping that Sagan's truth, a truth that once fueled Christina, shaped Christina, would be a truth that might guide her back.

Jaime trusted that Christina could handle the truth.

CHRISTINA and the
WHITEFISH

17
Rangoon Creeper.

I **NEVER KNOW** when the freaky episodes might play out in my head since my zoetrope machine only cranks up at night. When I'm asleep. But it wasn't always like this, relegated to theatrical nightmares. It used to be a helluva lot worse.

Side note: The "zoetrope" was developed in the 1830s when photography was still in its infancy. This rather simple device featured a twirling disc or drum mounted to a center spindle. The walls of the revolving drum were covered with segmented or phased drawings; depictions of various things in motion: horses or maybe people walking on a city street. The drum (which some folks called "the wheel of life") would rotate while early audiences peeked in at these herky-jerky short animations. And they loved it. It was very exciting, especially in a prehistoric pre-film world.

At first, when I returned home from the ancient kingdom of Nam Viet, these episodes (really more like "mind-bends") would happen whenever they damn well pleased, many times during my waking hours. Popular culture drolly labeled these waking nightmares as "flashbacks," or more precisely, in my case, "Vietnam Flashbacks." Writers and movie types would portray us as cartoon zombies reliving some jungle hellscape that was flickering just behind our corneas. It was always the same: the eyes would glaze over and then wildly bug out as audiences could then be treated to some horrific incident.

They got that last part right.

Usually these Vets were seen as mentally deficient, fevered whack-jobs. So be it. The war was unpopular, to say the least; nothing less than a wanton genocide perpetrated on the people of Southeast Asia. You know the old saying:

Kill one person call it murder.
Kill millions call it foreign policy.

No doubt, the whole lot of us (pilots, grunts, et cetera) were culpable assassins working for the real guilty bastards, those bloodless monsters perched way up the chain of command, which included the Pentagon brass as well as their boss politicians – war criminals one and all. If they were judged at Nuremberg, they'd be hanging on a wall.

As for us grunts in country, we were also guilty, but one thing we were not: whack-jobs. So, hey, Mr. and Mrs. Yuppie, put down your slightly chilled Chardonnay and walk a mile in my sandals before you debase and defile our so-called flashbacks.

Imagine you're taking out the garbage, minding your own business, just strolling down the driveway, and suddenly, without warning, you "sizzle out" and enter what the headshrinkers call "a dissociative state." That's when taking out the garbage is replaced by another reality, this one probably gruesome and from some other point on the space-time continuum. My "normal" reality of taking out the garbage would quickly shift to a new and "exciting" (read: horrific) reality, one that unfolded in a place with a name I'll never forget: Plei Trap – a fertile valley nestled in the Central Highlands of Vietnam, very close to the Cambodian border. It was late October 1966. Just weeks before, I was in Saigon drinking beer and listening to Armed Forces Radio as the Orioles swept the Dodgers in the Fall Classic. Frank Robinson was the MVP.

But here we were, 3rd Brigade-25th Infantry Division, deployed first to Plei Djereng, and then we began sweeping northwest toward the southern end of Plei Trap. Other divisions were also moving into position. Our objective was simple: clear out and destroy enemy base camps throughout the valley.

Side note #2: Keep in mind, these were "enemy base camps" that existed inside the "enemy's" own country.

As we slogged along, we had a number of skirmishes and were forced to engage platoon-sized units from the People's Army of Vietnam (PAVN) – founded way back in World War II by Ho Chi Minh. Unlike my brethren, I understood their actions: they were defending their country against foreign aggression. But hell, it was either me or Charlie, so I was trigger-happy with my trusty M16 Jammomatic!

Once situated in Plei Trap, it started to get hairy. We came under increasing mortar fire, and then PAVN launched a major human attack wave, battalion after battalion. Yessiree Bob, we were officially in the shit. Our wounded were piling up – but then the skies rumbled and opened like the Book of Revelation! Unleashing one epic John Ford western, and baby, HERE COMES THE CAVALRY – two orbiting U.S. Air Force Skyraiders engaged our firefight with maximum gusto, and these boys don't play around: first the napalm (some nasty shit) and then the cluster bombs (designed by Satan himself). And then, what seemed like only minutes later, three helicopter gunships began spraying machine-gun fire over enemy positions. A true workmanlike performance. Impressive.

The Empire struck back.

By midnight, the remaining PAVN forces withdrew from the area. In the morning, helicopter recon reported at least one hundred PAVN dead on our perimeter and another four hundred dead on their base. There's no doubt in my mind – without the Air Force's boys and toys, we were mincemeat. Some other squirrel would be playing chopsticks on this Underwood.

We were lucky. But not Company C, 1st Battalion, 5th Cavalry Regiment. They were patrolling right on the Cambodian border when one of their platoons was completely overrun by PAVN before U.S. air and artillery support could arrive. Many of those poor bastards were either killed or captured. On any day, it could be you. Russian roulette.

About forty-eight hours after this major engagement, PAVN started poking our defensive positions at night – and good ol' Texas boy Sarge was grumbling about the "rules of engagement." It's a fucking war for crissakes. We were cool, we were ready, and we were holding them at bay. They weren't close or getting closer. Let it be, Sarge. Just let it fucking be. But on the third night, Lone Star had enough, "Fuck this!" And Sarge decides to go rogue, taking the escalation of the Vietnam War into his own hands.

Kind of like John and Yoko (WAR IS OVER!) – only in reverse (WAR IS ON!).

Sarge grabs me, Ralphie, Ricky Dick, and Whale. He wants to flush these fuckers out here and now, figuring they were making more noise than danger. "LET'S MOVE!" he barked. So we start bending around to the right, and Sarge sends another team circling the left flank. I thought it was a mistake from the get-go. PAVN's actions didn't warrant an offensive posture. Pro football has the prevent defense. Ali had the "Rope-a-Dope."

You just wait the fuckers out.

But this was the Army, and thinking wasn't allowed.

It was a beautiful night, actually. Clear as a bell. I remember a crescent moon. And I also remember thinking, "What the fuck am I doing here? What the fuck are we all doing here? And please, tell me again: Why are we here? Because I keep forgetting. I'm wasting dinks and gooks in their own country... and for what reason exactly? Please, President Johnson. Please, Secretary McNamara. Why are we here? Tell us our bedtime story one more time."

Obviously it was dark, but you could still make shit out. When they have to, your senses get very nocturnal. I even recognized certain plants and trees because Ma loved that shit. I would talk to the locals and then write home about the flora, figuring that some peaceful correspondence would help her not to worry. Ma seemed to like my descriptions, especially one spectacular blooming vine that a village woman, in her very broken English, called "Bangoon Reaper" – at least that's what I thought she said. Later I found out it was called "Rangoon Creeper," which makes sense because it's a beautiful climbing plant where the flowers grow in hefty bunches of bright white... and then they turn a vivid pink and finally deep red.

`They're beautiful.`

As we passed around a bend, Sarge was leading but then slowed down, raising his hand for us to stop. Obviously he heard or felt something. Instinctually, we took a soft knee, our 16s ready to rock and roll. Sarge was still standing. Two shots rang out. His body lurched backward and down, like he was yanked on a chain. We immediately started firing back. Into the black. And then silence. Except for the gurgling. Sarge was hit twice: in the chest and in the face. He was a bloody fucking mess. More shots rang out – you could hear and feel the rounds as they whizzed by. Again, we're firing into the darkness. Whale was on the radio, giving base camp our position, begging for medics. We could also hear more firing from our distant left flank. Those guys were also engaged.

Ricky Dick crouched low, ran out, and grabbed Sarge under the arms, "Move back, get the fuck outta here!" Ralphie followed, grabbed Sarge's feet while Whale and I kept firing cover, to help us get on the move. Suddenly there was a torrent of shots ripping through the trees.

Ralphie was hit first and dropped hard. Whale was hit twice. I could see his body go left and then right. It was a goddamn shooting gallery. I can still hear Ricky Dick yelling out, "Cover! We gotta find cover!" He kept dragging Sarge, and I kept firing at god knows what. We slid down a slight embankment that offered scant cover. Almost nothing. My heart was pounding out of my chest. Fucking adrenaline. I'm sure it was the same with Ricky Dick. At this point, Sarge was still alive, even though half his face was gone. Through the darkness and shadows, I could see that Ralphie was pulling himself along, but Whale wasn't moving. I had to get out there and pull Ralphie in. Ricky Dick covered me, first with a grenade and then automatic fire. I moved out low and fast, grabbed Ralphie, who threw his arm around my neck and we struggled like motherfuckers back behind the embankment. Ricky Dick was reloading.

Ralphie wailed, "IT'S IN MY SIDE!"

I had to go out for Whale. I made it once, why not again? He could still be breathing. Plus, he had the radio. Ricky Dick nodded and started firing more cover as I darted back out. Whale wasn't moving, but his radio kept crackling. I grabbed him under his arm, but he was lifeless like a rag doll. I could feel blood everywhere. I was yelling his name over and over, but there was nothing, no response.

When I snatched the radio, ready to bolt back without him, something hit me in the stomach, my lower stomach, like a sledgehammer. I thumped backwards and landed like a snow angel. I was losing control, convulsing, and I remember hearing a voice on the radio, but the words didn't register. It felt like I was coming apart.

That's the last thing I remember. The voice on the radio... and the bizarre reality that I was pouring out, like a gusher of blood.

And damn, I think it's the first time I've written this shit down. I talked about it in group, two or three times, but never saw it typed out in black and white.

Mick & Keith had it right: "Let It Bleed."

Back in the day, when these images would take over and play out as reality, it was never, of course, in its entirety. But rather in sporadic bits, fragments jumping frenetically in a surprisingly linear and coherent fashion, as if my old man wrote the teleplay.

Now, in 1994, those "daydreams" are gone. Thank motherfucking god. The visits only come at night, in dreamlike reveries – authentic and surreal at the same time. Facts mixed with fiction. Like hallucinations. And then I shudder awake, my heart pumping in that fight or flight mode.

Try that a few hundred times.

Side note #3: One night recently I experienced an abnormally vicious visit back to Plei Trap, jolted awake, wanting to leap out a side window in a single bound. My TV was still on, tuned to C-SPAN (good white noise), and there was this U.S. Senator (I'm not sure which asshole) and he was presenting a big shiny medal to some Vet in a wheelchair, and the senator says with all the affected gravity he could muster, "Lieutenant So & So, a grateful nation says thank you."

To wit, I say, "Fuck you, Senator."

# #

18

Jekyll & Hyde.

Jaime was feeling guilty. Really guilty. She was also experiencing a Doctor Jekyll and Mister Hyde existence. In public, Jaime was the Rock of Gibraltar; despite the many grueling and grim waking hours with Christina. Jaime was there, plugged in: kind-loyal-supportive-understanding-indulgent-mindful-and-almost-always-constructive. You could add additional adjectives. She wasn't a pushover, but she wasn't a Drill Sergeant either.

Ti, on the other hand, was a disengaged car on a roller coaster, rogue and possessed as it veered on and off the tracks. Although, thankfully, there were still random glimmers of the old C-Mac, her goodness sporadically peeking through the mist. But those moments were increasingly few and far between.

Unfortunately, most days were filled with personality swings, unhinged transformations that "manic" doesn't even begin to define. Yet Jaime, like a grizzled boxer, withstood the pounding. She took everything thrown her way, believing that together they'd reach the end of this fun house tunnel.

That was Jaime's "public" posture. Equal parts of faith, hope, wish, pipe dream, and castle-in-the-sky. This was her Dr. Jekyll.

But Jaime's private posture, her Mr. Hyde, felt almost evil to her, disloyal-heartless-selfish-and-cruel. In these moments, her internal banter would hammer home what became a familiar theme: survival and self-preservation.

Her internal voice would ask and answer stinging rhetorical questions:

Are you willing to sacrifice your entire life?
THIS ISN'T WHAT YOU SIGNED UP FOR, JAIME.

Are you willing to give away your entire youth?
PTSD DOESN'T JUST GO AWAY WITH REST AND TYLENOL.

What happens if this gets worse?
EVERY DAY SEEMS LIKE A NEW ROCK BOTTOM.

What happens if you babysit the situation for ten years and she ends up institutionalized? Or she kills herself? Or you?
YOU ONLY HAVE ONE LIFE. IT'S NOT SELFISH TO PROTECT YOURSELF OR YOUR FUTURE.

Would she do this for you? Would she?
YOU'RE NOT BEING COLD-HEARTED. YOU NEED TO ASK YOURSELF THESE QUESTIONS.

❖ ❖ ❖

At least a year had passed since they escaped from the Royal Rattrap Motel in West L.A.

Through an acquaintance, Jaime found a great place: a bungalow on Ocean Park Boulevard—one of those concrete boxes built during the 1940s when the Douglas Aircraft Company turned bucolic Sunset Park and most of Santa Monica into a company town. The small casita was stark but very clean. Freshly painted cream-colored walls. Decent gray hardwood floors. The kitchen, which had pretty light in the morning, was workable with a fairly new fridge and gas stove.

They spoke about furnishing the place once they had some extra money. Jaime landed a job working the front desk at a busy yoga studio on Main Street. It was great since the owner honored Jaime's commitment to Christina. The flexibility allowed her to schedule work around Ti's shrink and group sessions, as Jaime continued trekking back and forth to the VA with her partner. Jaime struggled with Ti's total dependency but still felt the need to accompany her in transit during the dying hours of 19-hundred and 92.

Jaime took advantage of free yoga classes, hoping one day to entice Ti to join her, which at this point, when asked, Christina would instantly shake her head NO—and then for an hour, a day, or maybe just five minutes, she'd sit there in a place Jaime internally named "wacko lunch break," like a time-out for a toddler. And for Jaime, it was maddening because it was akin to driving your head into a brick wall. She knew she needed to ask, but the answer was always a done deal. "Hello, brick wall."

It was also infuriating because Jaime knew in her heart of hearts that the yoga (as well as some meditation) would undoubtedly help Christina—more than those magic pills, courtesy of the ongoing chemistry experiment being conducted by the VA apothecary. Jaime suggested smoking some weed as a way to help relieve Ti's stress and trauma, especially the depression. But Jaime wasn't expecting the shitstorm that came ricocheting back, with Christina accusing her of interfering with the doctors and their plan.

"Jaime, these are real experts! Don't be stupid! It's the U.S. military. *We take care of our own.* These are serious doctors with a plan. You're just someone doing yoga!"

Uncharacteristically, Jaime shot back with unbridled anger, *"What fucking plan?* Drugs and Army gibberish? It's all garbage, Ti! I've been reading a lot of stuff. These bastards have been using the same bullshit since Vietnam, when those guys came back all fucked up. *And they're still fucked up!"* Christina suggested that Jaime was "a real asshole."

Unflappable at this point, Jaime took the gloves off. "You know it's all a charade, right? With shell shock or battle fatigue or PTSD or whatever the fuck they'll call it next… Just apply drugs—and when that doesn't work, apply more drugs, and when that shit doesn't work, then fuck it, apply new and improved drugs! *It's fucking insane!* And you're only getting worse. *YOU WALK AROUND LIKE A GODDAMN ZOMBIE!"*

Christina bolted, crying, "GO TO HELL," as the front door slammed.

⅋

CHRISTINA and the WHITEFISH

19
Gravy.

I EAT THREE SQUARES a day.

Now, there's nothing unique about that whatsoever. But what is unique is that each meal, every day, has been exactly the same since I moved my living quarters into the Club Southside back in March of 1974. For those keeping score, that's twenty-plus years.

For me, it's about consistency. Reliability. Some of you may find this unbroken streak wackadoodle. I understand your assessment. I can also feel your side-eyes. But hey, as Sylvester Stewart, aka Sly Stone, once suggested, "Different strokes for different folks." Everyday People.

I wake up without hesitation at 6:11am. Fifteen minutes later I'm on the Boardwalk: fifty-five jumping jacks, forty-four sit-ups, twenty-two push-ups... and then I hike, walking briskly north to the borough of Allenhurst. Roundtrip is about an hour, a little over three miles. The terra firma I navigate across includes planks, pavement, and beaches.

I have a well-appointed but small kitchen in the upstairs residence. Breakfast consists of Quaker oatmeal. That's it – a large bowl of horse food sprinkled with raisins and a few walnuts. (Cardiologist says oats are good for the ticker.) One cup of A&P's Eight O'Clock dark roast at 7:47am. And then another at 9am. I use a French press that I bought from a traveling salesman.* One sugar and a splash of cream, and this perfect cup of coffee accompanies my jaunt through the paper – or as my old man used to call it, "that fucking rag, the Star-Ledger."

*(ode to my Uncle Pete, an old Fuller Brush salesman)

After breakfast, my morning consists of inventory and then ordering from our various food & booze purveyors. And even though my club is spic and span, I also dedicate some time every morning for cleaning this or polishing that. (How do you think it stays so spic and span? Elves?)

Lunch unfolds at 1:11pm. While trying to stay out of Lou's way (he's my cook and usually busy at that hour), I make the midday meal in the Club's galley and eat at the bar. Chat up the regulars, who enjoy the repartee. Sliced char-grilled chicken breast over a green salad (arugula when we can get it), some brown rice, and plump Jersey tomatoes. Salt, pepper, and a spoonful of Roquefort dressing. Arnold Palmer, easy ice.

And then, in the midst of every sundown that I'm still privileged to anticipate and lucky to enjoy, I prepare my dinner. For me, it's equal to art, tantamount to DaVinci creating "The Last Supper." So instead of Leonardo in the Italian High Renaissance, it's me in the upstairs apartment of the Club Southside... Asbury Park 07712. Even as I type this, the comparison is not only stupid but nonsensical. And yet I write the words anyway in the hope of a smile.

It's my belief that the concept of "cuisine" (or "gastronomy") can only be possible at the third and final meal of the day. What I prepare has remained simple yet elegant, not unlike most great Italian recipes. A few fresh ingredients go a long way. Delicate preparation is required. Philistines need not apply.

It starts with music. Either Mario Lanza's 1958 album, the "Seven Hills of Rome," or the Decca recording of Puccini's opera "La boheme" – circa mid-fifties. Two of Ma's favorites. For years, I played the vinyl (her vinyl). Of course now it's cassettes on my boombox. And if I live much longer, it looks as if I might be forced to transition to compact discs. Chalk that up to what they call "functional obsolescence."

The recipe for my red gravy, which you may refer to as "tomato sauce," was gifted to me from Angelina – the Ma of a Boonie Rat buddy I visited down in South Philly years ago. Her gravy was sweet nectar of the gods. I had to have the exact formula. So this terrific lady wrote it down on scrap paper and then made it for me once more before I left the next evening. I absorbed every detail as we sipped some wine and chewed the fat about the ghosts of Philadelphia. Now, as you might already know, making gravy is actually quite simple – but what makes Angelina's gravy so perfect occurs in the nuances.

In fact, I framed her handwritten recipe and it hangs over my kitchen table.

I start with seven cloves of garlic (like the seven hills of Rome). You peel them clean and then slice into perfect slivers. Her recipe calls for one-half of a white onion, but over time I've dropped the onion. Ultimately, for me, the additional essence is somewhat of a distraction. I place my large skillet (she said no deep pots) on a medium flame and then heat one-quarter cup of olive oil. You then add the garlic but you don't let it brown. As soon as the garlic starts sizzling, you add your 28 ounces of Progresso crushed tomatoes. Then you add a pinch of red pepper and a teaspoon of kosher salt. Stir gently. By now, the music and the prep have all fused into one dance. That's when I take a large sprig of basil (with the stem still on) and toss it on the tomatoes until it wilts. You submerge it and stir again. I then let it simmer for about fifteen minutes until the gravy thickens and the oil on the surface becomes a deep orange. Remove the basil and then hit it with a quarter cup of Chianti. Lower the heat, simmer and stir.

As I boil my salted water, I make a green salad with cherry tomatoes and red onion. I'll add balsamic and EVO at the table. Once my water hits that magical 212 degrees F, I toss in my go-to brand of pasta: De Cecco – either Penne Rigate no. 41 or Thin Spaghetti no. 11 – and then cook until al dente. If the pasta gets soft or limp, I'll boil a new batch. Al dente is non-negotiable. Of course, an Italian rosso wine is a must. My distributor has a nice selection and I'll cycle through the various offerings, usually opting for a Sicilian Nero d'Avola or a Tuscan Montepulciano.

Plate the pasta, spoon over the gravy, and grate a significant amount of Pecorino Romano that falls to the dish in slow-motion, like snowflakes on Christmas Eve. You go to the table and mangia bene.

Side note: On Sundays, I add three meatballs, gotta have my meatballs. I mix ground beef, veal, and pork with some garlic, raisins, and a little Romano cheese. "Jesus, Mary, and Joseph" because each meatball has its own name.

One hour from now, when I leave my trusty Underwood, I will punch up Mr. Lanza and begin tonight's prep. But first I promised to include the big finish to my one and only performance of "The King of Asbury Park." When we left off, I was on my cheeseball stage with Lil Abner under a solitary light. The Club Southside was packed to the gills, and the booze was flowing. In the previous narrative, we had just wrapped up with a former "King" – one Ralphie "Sarge" Giancarlo. Wannabe soldier of fortune.

Let's rewind a few seconds so we can dig the vibe... or as they say on TV:

"Previously on L.A. Law"

ME:

And that's when some sick and twisted sonovabitch-

LIL ABNER:

And to this day, we still don't know who-

ME:

Tosses a lit cigarette at ol' Ralphie. It was hideous. He went up like the fucking Hindenburg.

LIL ABNER:

(revs up audience)

LONG LIVE THE KING! LONG LIVE THE KING!

ME:

(wait for crowd to calm down)

And with Sarge gone, the throne was - as they say - vacated.

(relax on a stool, fire up a joint with the flip-lighter)

Which brings the lineage to me...

(highlight the joint & lighter)

A nice fresh Bob Marley... and this Ronson flip-lighter was my old man's.

LIL ABNER:

A gift from the now-defunct Newark Evening News.

ME:

Now, as some of you may know, my old man was a hardboiled newspaper guy. Wrote the living shit out of stories. His heroes were ball-busting SOBs like Izzy Stone, Pete Hamill, and one James Breslin.

LIL ABNER:

If you never heard of these guys, hit the library. The last two are still breathing fire. Tough guys don't dance.

(tips his hat to me)

Just like the King.

ME:

And believe it or not, folks, I'm trying like hell to turn this little seaside town around.

LIL ABNER:

Even though today, 26 January 1991, it resembles Pompeii right after Vesuvius shot its load.

ME:

You're all probably wondering about the obvious demise of Asbury Park. Well, folks, just another victory for what they call "the cross, the sword, and the almighty dollar." Yessiree, boys and girls. Even on the Jersey Shore.

(take a healthy swig of scotch, swagger into audience)

Now, there's no doubt that I run this place with fairness, maybe even a little compassion... and make no mistake about it: I'm in charge. I run Asbury Park. And not the "brutality," otherwise known as the po... lice...

LIL ABNER:

(uses the putter as a Tommy Gun)

"Come and get me ya lazy coppers, ya dirty screws!"

ME:

Not the City Council...

LIL ABNER:

To hell with City Hall. THIS CLUB is the Temple of Justice.

ME:

Not even the mayor.

(drain the scotch)

LIL ABNER:

And definitely not Springsteen.

ME:

You are correct, my fine feathered friend. I run this sewer, this Augean stable...

LIL ABNER:

What the hell does that mean, Augean stable?

ME:

Gather round children...

(enjoy the joint as Abner drops to the floor, story time)

In Greek legend, Augeas was the King of Elis and the son of the God Helios. Of course, Mr. Augeas was wealthy as shit and owned hectares and hectares of livestock, including a giant herd of at least 3,000 oxen jammed into his stables - no doubt a veritable shithole that probably wasn't mopped up in thirty years. And, of course, not known for their labor equity, the Gods gave their clean-up duty to one sorry sonovabitch.

LIL ABNER:

I know this story... Heracles the Strong Man!

ME:

Bingo... Now we all know him by his Roman name, HERCULES... but here's the beauty part: With no help whatsoever, this mountain of a man cleans out these manure-packed stables in one, get this - one motherfucking day.

LIL ABNER:

How'd he do it, Boss?

ME:

Well, as you might guess, he was rather ingenious. Check this out: Young Mr. Hercules digs four huge trenches that originate from these filthy stables... and then runs them right into two mighty rivers. I mean, this guy wasn't fucking around. Then with a little mythical magic, wham-bam-thank-ya-mam, he reverses the course of both rivers, and then directs the raging waters right back into the stables...

(be dramatic with this)

So dig it. He's got two massive pumps flushing all this shit to the other side of town.

LIL ABNER:

Ingenious indeed. But what's the point?

ME:

I thought you might ask.

(back at stage, help Abner to his feet)

You see as King, I revere this fable... so much so, that it's become my mission statement for Asbury Park.

LIL ABNER:

(incredulously)

Flushing dung to the other side of town?!

ME:

Christ, when you say it like that... but damn, for a little man in a red fedora, you're one smart cookie.

LIL ABNER:

May I query you, King?

ME:

Shoot.

LIL ABNER:

Okay, let's review. You've identified and articulated your ruling platform, albeit with a too-long and convoluted story.

ME:

I have. Flush the stables. Drain the swamp. Actually, folks...

(arm around Abner)

It's impressive that Greek mythology, as analogy...

(take his red fedora, wear it)

Was not lost on this young man from Hoboken.

LIL ABNER:

Don't forget, by way of Bensonhurst, the Republic of Brooklyn.

ME:

So Abner, what's your question?

LIL ABNER:

(walks into the audience, now one of them)

Okay, King, let's cut through the embroidery. As ruler of this crumbling fiefdom: What means more to you than anything else?

ME:

Ah, you're unlocking one helluva Pandora's Box.

(another sip of scotch, enjoy with gusto)

Ballantine's Finest. Ask your waitress. Hand me that Boombox.

LIL ABNER:

This one?

ME:

How many fucking Boomboxes do you see?

LIL ABNER:

Take it easy, King Lear... here you go.

ME:

Brand new Sony, right? Top of the line. Cost me like three bills. It's got the CD, auto reverse tape decks, woofers-tweeters, whole shebang.

(HEAVE & DESTROY THE SONY INTO CONCRETE FLOOR)

See? Material shit means nothing to me. Houses, cars, jewelry - nothing but distractions.

LIL ABNER:

(surveying the destruction, runs hand thru hair)

Jesus. What the hell? That was a great fuckin' stereo!

ME:

I guess Doubting Thomas needs more proof.

AUDIENCE MEMBER YELLS OUT:

Are you a communist?!

ME:

Smart man. Hell...

(savor this slowly)

"Civilizations will gleefully release the rope given to them by God... for nothing more than a handful of gold."

LIL ABNER:

According to you, it's "the root of all evil."

ME:

(take out a wad of $20 bills, keep waving it around)

Now you're talking, little man. Money's the biggest distraction of all. Some folks will kill their mothers for a big payday. Am I right? We all know what money does. Hell, there might even be an honest-to-god mother killer in our audience tonight. You? You? Maybe you?

(smile... laugh, relieve the tension, then turn)

C'mon, you read the papers - kings and presidents will wipe out entire populations for it. I know. I used to serve at the pleasure of the Empire.

(flip fedora back to Abner)

Tell us why Abner?

LIL ABNER:

Because it represents power. Ultimate power.

ME:

Bingo! Republic of Brooklyn is in the house...

(beat)

You know, folks, there's an old adage - "Steal a little, they throw you in jail... steal a lot, they make you king." For me, it's the exact opposite.

(grab flip-lighter, hand bills to Abner)

Here, hold these out one at a time. Let's burn Andrew Jackson at the stake. Hell, the SOB has it coming. Anyone know why?

(anticipate silence in the house)

Nobody? C'mon, folks, gotta look this shit up. Okay, let's go...

(Abner holds out each $20, then drops it to the floor as I light & burn the rest)

Here we go: TWENTY...

(to audience)

C'mon, count with me...

(they will)

FORTY... SIXTY... EIGHTY... I'll burn 'em all night. C'mon, ONE HUNDRED AMERICAN DOLLARS. Abner, hold out the entire wad...

(he does, light the wad)

MONEY - MEANS - NOTHING.

LIL ABNER:

So then, what exactly DO YOU care about?

ME:

Well, that's a much different question, Mr. Abner. What do I CARE about? As opposed to what MEANS something to me... I care about the poor, the disenfranchised, the New York Football Giants...

LIL ABNER:

Alright wise guy, I get it. Let's bottom-line this thing, you semantic fool: WHAT THE HELL ACTUALLY DOES MEAN SOMETHING TO YOU?

ME:

Why didn't you ask me that to begin with?

LIL ABNER:

I did, you stark raving lunatic.

ME:

"Who's on first, What's on second..." What's the question again?

LIL ABNER:

Once more or I'm fucking leaving - pay attention: What means more to you than anything else IN THE ENTIRE FUCKING UNIVERSE?

ME:

Well, sir, now that you've put it that way, my answer's easy...

(Abner sighs relief and plops down, I walk through the audience as a "sage pioneer")

Our collective history in the Garden State began a way back in the last century... we were nothing more than a small seed planted on a countrified homestead, an entity that fast became a prosperous settlement... ultimately, a thriving community that miraculously transformed itself into a shimmering seaside hamlet. A refuge.

(pick people & tables to get intimate with)

> I believe you all know the place, or knew the place, this celebrated escape on the world famous Jersey Shore... People came from far and wide to stroll our Boardwalk, our hallowed planks... to swim in our ocean... to enjoy real food, and no doubt, refreshing drink... Families – you remember those – they flocked here en masse to ride our amusements and play our games... games that made them smile, joyful.

(stop for dramatic effect)

> History witnessed what one writer called: "an effervescent vacation haven." Indeed, you all know the place, hanging on by the proverbial thread...

(long pause)

> My friends, until the candles go out... let us embrace.......... Asbury Park.

(stage light out)

LIL ABNER:

> Ladies and gentlemen, your host and the undefeated King of Asbury Park – the Whitefish.

(applause & take bow, music)

###

With apologies to the "The Ancient One" (Honest Abe) –

The world will little note, nor long remember, what Lil Abner and I said here, but it can never forget what they – the founders of Asbury Park – did here. It is for us the living, rather, to be dedicated to the unfinished work which they who fought here have thus far so nobly advanced.

# #

20

Just the facts, ma'am.

It was going to be the hardest thing Jaime ever had to do. At least up to this point in her twenty-plus trips around the Sun. Their fights continued. As did the unpredictable spells of respiratory symptoms, which included an on-again, off-again hacking cough, shortness of breath, and a nagging tightness in her chest. The pulmonologist told Christina that the symptoms were temporary and should disappear soon.

But the dark cloud of depression remained, seemingly unfazed by the expanding bag of pharma cure-alls. Dr. Morea had relocated to some other VA hellhole and was replaced by a new guy, who was replaced by another new guy, until a third shrink, a woman from NYU arrived, who Christina seemed to trust. Jaime was cautiously optimistic about this new connection, but the chemistry experiment continued unabated.

Jaime wasn't sure why she didn't think of this sooner: forget the library and its limited intel on these brawny drugs, including her worst fear: the possible mutilation of the human brain. Yeah, forget the library. And yes, she did have an attitude. She told herself, "Put on your shoes and walk over to the corner drugstore. Talk to the pharmacist. These dudes oughta know about this shit." And that's exactly what Jaime did—hoofed it down to the local Thrifty Drugs with a list of Christina's notions and potions, and then chatted up the dispensing chemist behind the counter.

Charlie was a nice guy and more than willing to share his wealth of pharmacology. Jaime told him, "She's been taking Lorazepam for, I don't know, at least a year and a half." There was a long and disturbing pause as Charlie just stared—and then blurted out in disbelief, "She's been taking Lorazepam for eighteen months?" The alarm in his voice scared the shit out of Jaime. "Yeah, she has. Why?" There must have been a bit of a detective or psychiatrist in Charlie, "Is this really about a friend? And not you?" Jaime instinctually raised her hand like she was on the stand, "I swear to God. She's my partner. A Gulf War Vet."

A customer was getting antsy by the register. Charlie excused himself, said he'd be right back. Jaime was incredibly worried as she fixated on the shelves behind the counter—shelves filled with umpteen bottles of pills, a damn pill for everything. Bags of pills waiting patiently for their rightful owner: "Gimme-gimme-gimme." Jaime Nguyen from Belvidere, New Jersey, was so troubled thinking about Christina's dependency on these military cocktails that when she spotted some candy bars on a rack, she just helped herself to a Hershey bar, tore it open and took a bite.

Charlie returned as Jaime found herself wiping chocolate from her mouth. She awkwardly fessed up, "Sorry, of course I'm paying for this." Charlie couldn't care less and was right back at it, "Eighteen months. Lorazepam. The package insert from the manufacturer is crystal clear. It's only for short-term use. I mean really short term." Afraid of the answer, Jaime asked, "What's considered short term?" As he adjusted his glasses, Charlie knew his reply would send shock waves, "Weeks, maybe three or four."

Walking home, Jaime was close to tears as Charlie's blunt description of side effects kept zigzagging through her own central nervous system: "Tremors causing severe night sweats." There was also something Charlie called *"brain zap."* Jaime almost walked into a mother and stroller as she pondered brain zap. She was mumbling to herself, "What the fuck is that?"

Clearly, she didn't want to go home. She wanted to think about how to present Charlie's new reality because this devolving version of Christina was a master at constructing barricades to almost anything that refuted the almighty gospel of the Veterans Administration. Like a junkie, their word was her ticket to keep poppin'.

Jaime ducked into the Yum Yum Donut Shop on Pico—their neighborhood's version of Winchell's. She needed a change. A vanilla-iced cake donut. She felt weird, like she was cheating on Christina. She also realized she was doing more things without Ti, and if she was honest with herself, and she was, this was by design. Sitting at the counter and looking out a streaky window at the Westside's nonstop traffic, Jaime was heartbroken by this sad truth. She also decided she wasn't going to sugarcoat the drug intel she just discovered, like she was starting to sugarcoat most everything else with Christina. "Give her the facts straight up," she thought. "No ploys or schemes. Don't soft-pedal this shit. Drop the hard truth and then leave for work."

When she arrived home, Christina was relaxing in a lawn chair on their little patch of grass out front. She was hiding behind dark shades and wearing cut-off jean shorts with a bikini top. In fact, this California girl image reminded Jaime of an old sunbathing photo. Maybe Cindy Sherman? Maybe not. Jaime only wished she had a camera because this image—especially with Christina perfectly framed between two stubby palm trees—might win her awards as a fashion photog or maybe land her a career as a war correspondent in Bosnia or some other far-off land. Regardless, this late afternoon image was remarkable in that Ti, on the outside, was as beautiful and carnal as ever. "A cinematic show-stopper," she thought.

Of course, that was only half the story. The unimportant half. For there was a dreadful undercurrent that essentially nullified all else.

Jaime finally sat on the patch of grass at Christina's feet. Without looking or moving, Ti softly acknowledged her partner, "Hey." Jaime returned serve, "Hey, you." A peaceful, quiet moment, filled only by an unintelligible TV and a brief car alarm. Finally, Jaime told Christina about her chat with Charlie, the pharmacist, a caring guy who really knew the score. Jaime offered the baseline without editorial or hyperbole. Somewhere in this giant city, Sergeant Joe Friday was intoning, "Just the facts, ma'am. Just the facts."

When Jaime finished her short précis, Christina never budged and never said a word—as if she became the photograph Jaime never snapped, dreamily melting into the soft emulsion.

For a few minutes, Jaime sat quietly, expecting a response. A grunt. A cough. An invective-laced diatribe followed by pounding fists. Anything. But then the car alarm went off again, this time Jaime's cue to escape. Her shift didn't start for two hours, but it was still time to leave.

When she arrived at the yoga studio, her sanctuary really, she was glad to see her friend, Julian, who ran the business for a mystery guru who never left Topanga Canyon. Julian was a sweet man, a neighborhood fixture. Jaime was scheduled to take over the front desk for evening classes.

In his late thirties, Julian was Jaime's confidant regarding the ongoing Christina situation—for two basic reasons: she knew she could trust him, completely; she also knew he had his own dark personal experience with depression and the associated drug dependence.

When she walked in, Julian immediately knew Jaime was having another tough Christina day. She told him about her pharmacy trip and the disturbing news regarding Lorazepam. She said she also asked about something called Zoloft, some brand-new antidepressant they just started her on. "This pharmacist guy blew my mind when he said Lorazepam was only for short-term use, like three or four weeks." Again, the nervous dread climbed back up her spine, "For fuck's sake, she's been on it forever."

Julian warned, "You really have to tell her."

Jaime insisted, "I did. She didn't even react." But then she caught herself, "This pharmacist guy says when she stops, *if she stops,* it has to be slow— he used a word, I can't even remember."

Julian guessed, "Weaning?"

Jaime nodded, "They created a damn addict." Julian framed the reality, "With Lorazepam, they also created a time bomb."

Jaime knew he was right, "Yeah, this guy said suicidal tendencies were like a thing, especially when you go cold turkey off this shit." Jaime closed her eyes, hoping to find some relief. Julian could sense her internal battle, sense how scared she was for Christina. No doubt, stuck between a rock and a hard place.

Jaime remembered something else the pharmacist said, "At the end, he told me another fucked-up thing. He says these shrinks want to 'disease-i-fy' every bad experience their patients have. Says he sees it all the time. And that's the word he used, 'disease-i-fy.'"

Julian got it, "The guy's right. If someone's on edge just dealing with some heavy shit, they robotically see an illness." Jaime nodded, "He said normal's being confused with comfortable. 'Here, take these magic pills. You'll feel better. Have a nice life.'" Jaime remembered, "My Dad said this all the time, 'If your only tool is a hammer, every problem looks like a nail.'"

Julian agreed, "That's exactly what this is."

Weeks before, Julian had opened up to Jaime about his own history with dependency and addiction and about almost losing his life. "Weed was all day," he told her, "Everything I did revolved around getting high. Waking up, eating, going to work, to the movies, you gotta sleep, you gotta smoke. Luckily, the coke was short-lived, but then there was meth, and that shit's great, but you build up a tolerance superfast, so it becomes all the time. Cravings beyond belief. You're so fucked. And then you crash. Heavy depression, really severe. There were a couple of times... what professionals call 'suicidal ideations.'"

Julian explained how his behavior, "If you could call it that," ripped his family apart and then destroyed his relationship with Bree, his fiancé, someone he called, "his girl next door." Counseling helped, "But it was like a Band-Aid, and then I was right back at it." His stories were god-awful. But Jaime needed to know, "How did you get so healthy? Like you are right now?"

"Two words," he started, "Tough love." A memory gave him pause, "You know, people talk about 'tough love' like it's an absolute, but it's a really loaded concept... and trust me, it's not always successful. With my friend Grace, really sweet and smart, everyone said the only hope was 'tough love, tough love,' and then they... we, we all walked away. And it backfired. Right into an early grave. So I get the danger."

Jaime wondered, "But for you, it worked?"

He shifted in his chair, turning the page from Grace, "I was lucky, yeah, for me it worked." After a long pause, he added, "So far."

Julian sensed she needed more. "My brother knocked the shit out of me, physically and mentally, mostly mental." Jaime saw the hurt in his eyes, "I'm sorry." Julian added the punchline, "With my head banging against the front door, Billy made it abundantly clear: 'You will not destroy this family. We're fucking done unless you get help. Try life on your own for a while.'" After another long pause, "Then he threw me off the porch. The house I grew up in. Neighbors had a front row seat. I was bleeding pretty bad and just walked away. It was...." She gently rubbed his back. He forced a smile. It was important to Julian that Jaime understood the bottom line, "But listen, your situation with Christina is different from mine, everyone's situation is different, so I mean, who knows. Be careful."

Jaime tried to find common ground, "But there has to be parallels, right?"

He shrugged, "I dunno, I am no expert. Sometimes the experts aren't experts. I mean, a hard line may not work with Christina. Her situation with the war, her parents. It's really tough."

It was clear that Jaime was desperate. Because on this day, in the quiet anteroom of a yoga studio, Julian sensed that she'd already made up her mind. She just needed a foundation to stand on, more than just "I can't take this anymore." And if Ti stood a chance, Jaime needed to try something life-altering.

Julian explained, "When I was screwed up, needless to say, I didn't respond very well to 'enabling behavior.' I took advantage of everybody and just kept on rolling. But when I suffered real consequences, at least for me, you start thinking about change. Here's the key." Then he really emphasized, *"You have to first be able to envision change...* you have to be able to see it." His words were making sense. Julian continued, "There needs to be hard and fast boundaries. Addicts need to know exactly what they stand to lose. And Jaime, *I mean really lose.* In my case, the price I paid was... I mean, the loss would have been devastating. For others, who knows, they might not even hear it."

Julian held her hand, "This shit's vicious... the drugs, the trauma, it screws with people's heads, their actual brain chemistry. Remember, she's almost not the same person. She's not thinking clearly like you are... it's fucking scrambled eggs." For some reason the "scrambled eggs" triggered some gallows humor, helping her to keep it together. Julian offered, "You're hoping for the right connection at the right time, some click, some brief moment of clarity that allows her to absorb what you're threatening, allows her to see the line in the sand. Does that make sense?"

Jaime nodded and then shared with Julian how she sought help from this non-VA clinic she found over on Fairfax—a group for Vets dealing with and suffering from depression, drug addiction, "and fucking shell shock, let's call it what it is." Then she stressed, "The doctor there said that drugs should be the last resort. My plan, somehow, is getting Christina involved over there. Funny, they also talked about tough love."

Jaime quietly broke down. Julian held her. As the class ended and people started to leave through the small lobby, Julian helped her wipe away the tears.

❖❖❖

That evening, when Jaime returned home, all the lights in their bungalow were off. She knew something was up. Right from the squeaky gate that ushered her inside the courtyard, she knew. Their place was dark. A light was always on.

Jaime unlocked the front door and moved in slowly, "Christina?"

From inside their bedroom, a loud whisper, "Lock the door. I finally got them outside." Jaime locked the door and moved to the bedroom, where Christina was sitting on the floor, against the wall, holding her pillow tight. The streetlamp offered enough light for Jaime to see that Christina was naked. "Did you lock the door?"

Jaime knelt next to her, "I did. We're safe, sweetie. What happened?"

Christina closed her eyes, "They were in here."

Jaime took a moment, "Who was in here?"

Christina was shaking, "These three people dressed in red uniforms. They wanted me to go with them, outside, in the alleyway. They said it was time to cut myself. Get rid of the poison. It would be good for me."

Jaime remained calm, fighting off the freaky vibes, "What did you do?"

Christina held the pillow tighter, "They grabbed me, so I fought them off. I can take care of myself. They teach you that, you know."

Jaime pried gently, "They touched you?"

Christina pulled the pillow away, "More than touched me, ripped my clothes off. Look."

Jaime was quietly dying, "I'm sorry, sweetie. I'm here now. Nobody's gonna hurt you." And when Jaime touched her shoulder, Christina turned on her like a caged tiger, shoving her away with one violent jolt— and before Jaime knew it, she skidded and bounced off the closet doors. Jaime's heart was thumping, "How strong is she?"

Christina lashed out, "HOW DO I KNOW YOU'RE NOT ONE OF THEM?!"

Jaime struggled to her feet, "It's me, Christina. It's Jaime. I love you." Speaking softly as Christina panted, Jaime slowly backed away, thinking she might lash out again, "I need some water. You want some water? I'll be right out here. I'm just gonna turn on this little lamp, okay? Some light'll be good. See, it's me. We'll just rest, we'll sleep. I'm tired, you must be tired, too."

Jaime moved into the kitchen. She was breathing heavily as she poured whatever was left of their cheap white wine and drank it fast. Jaime thought maybe Ti forgot her meds; maybe that explained the monster huddled in the bedroom. She checked the pill sorter. Nope, she was on schedule. Jaime opened the fridge door and simply gazed inside, as if some secret answer would materialize from the magic box. There was nothing except the cold mac and cheese she was mindlessly consuming. When the bowl was empty, she gingerly moved to the bedroom door; maybe if she offered the monster some food—but Christina was on the mattress, stone-cold asleep under the blanket.

That night, as Christina slept, Jaime slipped a tape into her Walkman and buried her head in Neil Young's *American Stars 'N Bars*. Stretched out on their shitty used sofa, she began writing a long letter to Christina. In a spiral notebook. *Where the hell do you start? I know what I want to say. I know what I have to do. WHERE THE HELL DO YOU START? I can't do this.* But she did.

> I know things about you that no one else will EVER know. Like why you cry when it snows. Like why you were always more comfortable with your Dad than your mother. Why you love butterflies. Why your favorite star is "Rasalhague" – 56th brightest in the night sky, it's a blue star, and we used to watch it with your telescope. Nobody loves you like I love you (& vice versa!!!) But that's not what any of this is about.
>
> This is not about being selfish. It's about saving your life AND saving mine. People say that desperate times call for desperate measures.
>
> No room for moderation, right?
>
> Something happened on our way to Nirvana (or was it Shangri La???) Something horrific. I can't even pretend to know how you feel about losing Jack & Darlene. They were your world. As they should be and they were taken way too soon. It was so fucked up, Ti, my god, but I was so proud of you, how you were fighting through all the pain & all the shit. The way you were "handling" it. I knew you were going to make it. WE WERE GOING TO MAKE IT. I know we were. Vegas sucked but you were going to make it.
>
> But then the monsters from hell arrived and somehow, some way,

behind my back, they stole your soul. Wrapped in flags and fucking experts at brainwashing, the lies we're all forced to swallow – and they preyed on you, these bastards know exactly what they're doing. So in that regard you're really not special. This is what they do. They steal brains *DAILY!* and then the bodies & souls follow. And there's no doubt in my mind that if Jack & Darlene were around none of this would've ever happened! It's grotesquely unfair.

You weren't born to be abandoned. And that's who these bastards target for their fucking killing machine. People who've been abandoned. Or poor people. Or people that have no choice (or they think they have no choice). Brainwashed into their cult. I know that sounds super dramatic but many smart people think it's true. I do.

I've actually thought about this: If we ever have a child, I would lay down on train tracks to stop that kid from ever being taken like you were taken. You weren't born to be used and abused and then discarded. You were only born for one reason: *TO BE LOVED. TO LOVE OTHERS.* The rest is bullshit.

So I can't watch this anymore. I have to shift my geography. I hate what we've become because of them. They're a disgrace. It's degrading. It's dehumanizing. A crime against humanity. So it's up to you – you have to reach back and find who you were – or really find *WHO YOU STILL ARE!* You're the only one who can do it! You need to reclaim what's rightfully yours & *OURS.*

Fuck them.

At one time, not that long ago, the C-Mac I know would have spit in their faces and then laughed. I'll say it again: there's only one person who can get you out of this. One person. *YOU!*

And it's not me (because for real: you don't even hear me anymore).

AND TRUST ME, it's not those goddamn army shrinks! with their bullshit pill-popping! It's you. You're the ticket out.

I know I've told you a lot of this but it always gets lost in the yelling and the fights. But here's the deal: You need time to grieve, you must grieve – for Jack & Darlene, once and for all. *AND NOT RUN FROM IT.* Face the pain, face the grief (and maybe face it without the drugs).

And I can't make this any clearer: The shit that went down in Iraq is not your fault. You are not responsible. Yes it was fucked up. I can't even imagine. BUT THIS IS YOUR LIFE, not that. They put you there against your will – you just haven't faced that yet. It's like being kidnapped and brainwashed. And yes, PTSD (shell shock!) is real. We know that.

Every day, it's obvious what you're going thru. They give you uppers and downers and fucking mind blast cocktails that devastate your brain, your nervous system. Drugs are killing you. They say okay you have PTSD so here take this and you'll fly out of here, right back to whatever NORMAL was – but it never happens.

Think of it this way: These bastards put you in this horrible situation – HOW & WHY would they have the answer to get you out? They could give a shit. They got what they wanted.

Okay, like I always do, I did a ton of research and I found this amazing doctor and his group, they're really something. I TOTALLY LIKE THESE PEOPLE, you have to go meet them. The place is on Fairfax. Take the bus. It's easy. It's called "PEACE HOUSE" and they get their $$$ from Veterans groups as well as antiwar & peace collectives. Private donations.

Call them: Dr. Genovese (213-555-4328).

Give them my name and your name. I already met with them for you (TWICE) and they told me point blank: Soldiers come home from war and they're really messed up, suffering tremendously – but none of that is what they call "pathology" – it's grief, IT'S BAD BUT IT'S NORMAL. You have to face this shit with people who can help. Doc Genovese can help. It's what he does. Making people whole without their magic pills that only fuck with you.

AND LISTEN CLOSELY TO THIS!
LISTEN CLOSELY TO THIS!! LISTEN CLOSELY TO THIS!!!

He says BE SURE to keep taking your pills until they can ease you off. They told me about this one chick who went cold turkey off that Klonopin shit you used to take, and she couldn't deal with it, she walked right in front of a bus. On purpose. You weren't born to suffer like this.

Now here's the hard part (also the fucked-up part). You will most likely hate me - but I can't do this anymore. I'm enabling your behavior and that's not good (you may not even know what behavior I'm talking about). You need to fight this without me, you need to grieve without me. You need to kick the pills without me. You need to say "fuck you" to Uncle Sam once and for all. Look at what they've put you through. For what? They trapped you in hell AND YOU DIDN'T DO ANYTHING!

They sold you a LIE! A big one about liberty & democracy. They need human cannon fodder, that's what I heard them call it. It's evil shit, Ti. Stealing souls, stealing people's kids.

I've given Dr. Genovese all your information. EVERYTHING. He's been dealing with Vietnam Vets and now Persian Gulf Vets and he's helping them a lot. I MEAN TRULY HELPING THEM. His whole staff. They're really compassionate. They have one on one sessions, group, whatever you want. And they have a shitload of experience.

Also, Julian at the yoga studio said he'll help with anything. Free yoga. Meditation. Even help you find a job. Or just hang out if you need someone to talk to.

And you can have all the money in the checking account. I've left all the info. I'll get the rents to pay my way back home.

How can I make you believe this??? IM NOT RUNNING AWAY. IM FORCING YOU TO BE CHRISTINA. This might not work, sweetie, but you've got to understand what's at stake. A guy there called it being "scared straight." Some people turn around, others fuck up even worse. But you have to try. If you don't want to lose ME & YOU, go to Genovese.

Fight like hell.

I'm always loving you, you know that. And if you need me, I'll be there to talk. Over the phone. But you have to do this without me. They've put shackles on you. You have to bust this shit up. You'll always be my first and my last. (I know, fuck me, that sounds like Hallmark crap.)

Get away from the VA (as far as you can run) and head straight to Genovese (213-555-4328). I want your darkness gone. I want your sweet face without all the pain.

And because I know things about you, YOU KNOW I DO, I know this for sure: You always talked about visiting those old places down the shore where Jack & Darlene used to take you. You wrote that short story in English Lit about the red bucket and how you lost it there, in the ocean. Was it Atlantic City? I can't remember. But please Christina, GO FIND YOURSELF. Go find that goddamn red bucket. It's who you are.

And when you do I'll meet you anywhere.

Oh Christ, I'm writing WAY TOO MUCH. No sappy ending. Tough love. DON'T HATE ME! Call Genovese immediately IF NOT SOONER.

(213-555-4328) and go see Julian. He's cool.

You were born to be loved. We were born to love each other. But look at us now. I blame the bastards. So should you.

James xxxooo

(I left lots of food. KEEP EATING. KEEP EATING. KEEP EATING.)

(TAKE YOUR PILLS! TAKE YOUR PILLS!! TAKE YOUR PILLS!!! Until the doc gets you off – remember, it's only your goddamn life in the balance.)

(213-555-4328)

No matter how many times Jaime said it. Or wrote it. Or thought about it. Or even those times when she believed leaving was the absolute right thing to do—it just felt like she was abandoning Christina. And in many ways she was, in fact, walking out, but told herself it was for all the right reasons.

Truth or lie, it was gut-wrenching.

The great escape was set in motion: Jaime told Christina she had to work a morning shift, so Christina would take the bus alone to and from the VA. She'd done it a few times before. No big deal. And once Ti left, Jaime would lay out the letter and all the associated paperwork for life without her: bank stuff, rent stuff, extra cash, the medication scorecard, et cetera. All the important but mundane shit that Jaime handled. Genovese's info and paperwork were in another specially marked envelope.

Three times Jaime tried to leave their apartment, and three times she failed. Crying, shaking, and once hyperventilating. On the fourth try, she managed to get to the bus stop with her two bags. An hour later she was at LAX checking in—United 525 nonstop to Newark. Two hours after that, she was climbing to 37,000 feet somewhere over the California desert.

Seven hours from LAX, Jaime was curled up in the backseat of Mr. and Mrs. Nguyen's Honda Civic, heading home on Interstate 78, through the damp darkness that was presumably western New Jersey.

⸎

CHRISTINA and the WHITEFISH

21
Jack Palance.

THIS IS THE KIND OF DAY I LIVE FOR... long for... the kind of late summer day that you just don't want to end. It's when a sultry afternoon bends into golden hour. Orange western skies. God's daily perfection drifts lazily into a warm, muggy night. But alas, this Jersey Shore magnificence must end – for me usually after midnight – when it's time to plunk down at my trusty Underwood and start banging away, documenting why I revel in the alchemy and bewitchery that is the Club Southside.

obsessive (adjective)
ob ses sive
    a: tending to cause obsession
    b: excessive often to an unreasonable degree

Yep.

###

Every so often, I offer the good folks of Asbury Park (and nearby shore communities) a special evening of food, drink, and dance. Special menu, special cocktail, and live music.

Tonight, the magic started when Mother Nature dropped dinner on my doorstep. My crabbing guy hails out of Great Egg Harbor and delivered three bushels of giant blue crab at a stupid price. This crusty SOB is named Raimo and looks twenty years older than his trips around the Sun. He prefaces every financial pitch on seafood with his hackneyed rendition of "I'm gonna make you an offer you can't refuse." I think if Brando ever saw this rank butchery, he'd string the guy up like Mussolini – Il Duce! But Raimo had a big haul, so I grabbed three bushels for three bills and immediately set one of our crab night extravaganzas into hyper speed.

Lou, my cook, is always up for special nights. He gets anxious when faced with too many monotonous days in a row. I reclaimed Lou off the proverbial scrap heap. He was one of the head kitchen guys at this posh blue blood eatery called The Breakers in Spring Lake – that is, until he was drinking his weight on a daily basis (and Lou ain't small). But I gave him a shot, and then three more shots in between stints at Beach House Rehab up in Red Bank, where me and a Checker Cab delivered him like Chicken Delight. They should have installed a drive-thru just for Lou, "Tuck and roll, big guy!"

But ever since Father Time clicked 1990, Lou's been rock-solid, a trusted warrior who proffers workmanlike performances day in and day out – and on Club Southside crab nights, he's a rock star. He brings in his nephew Stef, and together they work it like any top-notch Chesapeake shindig. Point of fact: Lou's garlic butter recipe for blue crab has been celebrated by every beautiful cash-paying customer this side of the Parkway.

I placed my massive sandwich board out front, significantly encroaching the planks; it read:

CLUB SOUTHSIDE TONITE

BLUE CRAB EXTRAVAGANZA
MINT MOJITOS (half price)
SPECIAL MUSICAL GUEST!

With a giant finger pointing thataway.

Then I started making phone calls – Abner, Bagel, Donna, Mickey Finn, Joe Fats, Texas-T, even Madam Marie – and then these good people start calling a host of others, spreading the word amongst their closest allies. And my math is usually pretty good: If I get a twenty percent turnout from this degenerate phone bank plus whatever stragglers my sandwich board rustles up, we'll have a packed house from about six till maybe ten-thirty. Then the booze and peanuts carry us through to midnight. Tonight, my math was spot on.

Also, on nights like this, I usually dress up a bit – and tonight called for one of my original six puck jerseys. And for some reason, it felt like the Montreal Canadiens. Base red with navy blue and white trim. For those interested, the large "C" stands for Canadiens; the smaller inner "H" is for hockey and not "Habitants," as some amateur historians have surmised. Officially, it's le Club de Hockey Canadien. And I'll tell you, with my hair flapping around, working the club like a madman, I felt like Guy Lefleur (Le Demon Blond) flying down right wing. If only.

Now, for blowouts like "Blue Crab Extravaganza," I need to up the entertainment ante from David Bowie on the jukebox to some blood-pumping live act. And guess who owed me a favor? (Actually three favors!) Give up? None other than Johnny Maestro and his Friggin' Brooklyn Bridge, who just happened to be available (which comes as no surprise). Now, I'm not sure whether we landed the entire Brooklyn Bridge, but I know it was Johnny and three of his sidekicks. We scheduled the headliner for forty-five minutes at 8:30pm and another forty-five at 10:15pm. The group was jam-packed on my small stage but still sounded great. Johnny's a helluva talent and shined sweetly tonight with his signature serenade:

`"But it's the worst that could happen... to me."`

My usual jazz trio, Two Jacks and a Jill, played through dinner and also closing. I brought Donna in to waitress along with her strip club confrere Roxanne (Va-va-va voom!). They made some decent scratch, at least this time with their clothes on. Abner's twin sons, two real knuckleheads, shared duties as busboy and dishwasher, and only once did I have to wing something at 'em, which I consider a victory. My regular bartender had the night off, so yours truly worked beverages with my part-time alewife, Doris – who has probably quit at least a hundred times since the late seventies. A few times twice in one day. It's like a routine now; people don't even pay attention, although when she quits and tosses in the apron, she really believes it. On this night, she did not quit. Probably too busy.

Things simmered down around 11:30pm. Johnny and his boys were packing up with Two Jacks and a Jill playing standards (ending on a very seductive "Someone to Watch Over Me"), and the kitchen staff was busy swabbing the deck. Doris hit the bricks, and my regular crew gathered around the bar – a real ragtag bunch.

LIL ABNER, you're well acquainted with... And, as you know, JOE FATS dates back to my sports book. These days he's selling used cars over in Wall Township, trying desperately to gain enough weight so that one day he'll just spontaneously combust.

BAGEL – aka Lenny Katz – made his small fortune in one of those Lower Manhattan casinos. His plush Gordon Gekko office overlooked the East River, right on the corner of Wall and South streets. Bagel cashed out on a high note and immigrated to a ritzy section of Monmouth County, a community he calls "Jewish Newport." Bagel is what you call a real mensch.

Then we have our three Texaco stars: VINNIE, DANNY, and JOEY. They own Angie's Texaco out on Route 35 – inherited the business from their old man, who established the venerable old filing station back in the fifties. You will almost never see this hat trick of grease monkeys out of uniform: Texaco greens with a prominent red star perched over their breast pocket.

Truth be told, we were due for a lively conversation and we nailed it between midnight and about one – a real humdinger in the Absurdist Hall of Fame. Dig it: up for discussion, a proposed knock-down drag-out fight, a real pitched battle between unexpected celebrity foes. Here's how I remember the jousting.

`Casually clipping his nails, Joe Fats set the scene.`

"Alright, here we go," he belched under his breath, "Eastwood and Bronson against Stallone and Jack Palance." Baffled, Vinnie quickly inquired, "Who the fuck is Jack Palance?" Fats scoffed, "Jack Palance. Tough guy. Jesus, he played Bronk." Bagel swatted a fingernail off the bar, "Hey Joe, keep your filthy clippings out of my scotch." Still baffled, Vinnie pushed his query, "Who the fuck is Bronk?" With utter contempt, Fats rolled his droopy hound dog eyes and said, "Don't you ever leave that fuckin' gas station? Jack Palance as Detective Alex Bronkov???" Joey stuttered, "I-I-I-I'm lost, t-t-too." Abner wryly suggested, "Must be from inhaling too many Texaco fumes, these fuckin' pump jockeys." Laughter.

Fats quickly filled in the Texaco troika on the old CBS series in question, "Bronk" – created back in the 70s by none other than Carroll O'Connor. And that set Vinnie off again, "WHO THE FUCK IS CARROLL O'CONNOR?" Abner laughed, "Archie Bunker, ya moron."

At this point, I felt the need to interject some historical context. "Gentlemen, stick to the facts: Bronk was one tough bastard, soft-spoken but tough. And let's not forget that Palance also played one of the most ruthless SOBs in Hollywood lore." Sipping his scotch, Bagel knew exactly, "Indeed, barkeep, the classic western, 'Shane,' starring Alan Ladd. Palance played a cold-blooded killer. Chilling." Abner advanced the narrative, "So, Mr. Fats, what about weapons?" The used car salesman drained his beer, "I'm thinking bats and chains."

Bagel slapped the bar, "Down and dirty, ladies. Bats and chains." "Wait a second," Vinnie protested, "I gotta tell ya, not knowing this fucking Palance guy puts some of us at a real disadvantage." Abner lovingly punched Vinnie in the arm, but hard, "Live with it, Numskull." Vinnie fired back, "Fuck you, ya fuckin' midget." Teflon Abner rolled on, "Well, if it's bats and chains, I gotta go with Eastwood and Bronson." I immediately asked Abner to explain his thinking. "Experience," he confidently offered as if he earned a PhD on the subject. "Eastwood and Bronson have been through way more than Stallone and this here other guy. And ladies, there's no substitute for experience."

Bagel offered the opposition, "Actually, Abner, it's really no contest. You're sucking wind banking on experience alone. I'm actually surprised by your naivety." Abner was in his face, "I don't know what that means, but I ain't sucking wind." Unfazed, Bagel admired his scotch swishing on the ice, and then laid it out, "Yeah, sucking wind. Palance can handle a bat, that's a known fact... and if it gets down to bare knuckles, and it just might, Stallone can punch like a mamaluke jackhammer. And for my money, Eastwood's nothing more than a figment of his own imagination, and Bronson's slow like an ape." Abner was waiting for an opening, "You know, I love when the Jew uses words like mamaluke." Bagel tipped Abner's fedora, "It's from hanging out with ginnies my whole life."

Laughter ensued.

Later that night, outside, Vinnie was curious, "Hey Fish, tell me more about this here 'Shane' movie." I gladly obliged (sort of), "Vin, it's a great flick. What a cast: the legendary Clark Gable, the always ravishing Marilyn Monroe, and, as you heard before, fuckin' Jack Palance. Talk about a gritty, tense western. I think Huntz Hall even made an appearance in this picture. Check your TV Guide, probably Channel 9, the Million Dollar Movie."

Vinnie left, still noodling my Hollywood gibberish. I crossed the Boardwalk to the railing that faced the inexhaustible Atlantic – beautiful with lunar light streaking the whitecaps. What a day, huh? All ending with friends and laughter. You can't beat that.

I thought again about Shane and that iconic ending with the kid yelling out to Alan Ladd as he rode away, "Shane! Come back!" And for a moment it was kind of surreal because I actually thought I could hear the kid yelling over the booming ocean. But then I realized the voice, or actually two voices, male and female, were emanating from down below, right under the Boardwalk.

Early morning rapture. Young love. As the world turns.

#

22

Dorothy (Part One).

A funny thing happened on the way to hell. Christina successfully traversed her trip from Santa Monica to the VA and back again. She walked home from the bus stop along Cloverfield. When she opened the squeaky gate to the courtyard, she had a weird feeling that something was different.

Sure enough, when she walked inside, Jaime's notebook letter was positioned prominently on their small kitchen table, along with other paperwork and a few hand-labeled envelopes. Christina picked up the notebook as if it were burning hot.

The first time she read the letter, she remained standing at the table, not moving a muscle except to turn the pages, her tears alternating as they fell, some hitting the paper, some reaching the floor.

The second time Christina read the letter, just minutes later, she was slouched on the shitty sofa, reading with the very real hope that Jaime's words might morph into different words, better words.

The third time she read it, again minutes later, she sat on the bedroom floor, her back up against the wall like she was nailed to the structure—a few times looking to her left and right as if she too might see and bear witness to Dismas and Gestas, the other two famous thieves crucified on Golgotha two thousand years ago, one good the other unrepentant.

Christina sat there for a very long time as the late afternoon shadows stretched to dusk.

The initial shock of it didn't seem real. She kept waiting for something to happen. What that something was, she wasn't quite sure—but Jaime would never do this. Just leave? Jaime wasn't someone who just left, like one of those crafty escape artists. She was someone who was always there. Never say die.

Sitting there on the bedroom floor, Christina would read random sentences, thoughts and words, and then that damn phone number. She actually smiled and snorted at Jaime's tenacity, listing the phone number four times. Well, at least that was evidence of the real Jaime.

⟩ *(I left lots of food. KEEP EATING. KEEP EATING. KEEP EATING.)*

She was actually getting hungry—and hell, if Dismas and Gestas could take a dinner break, so could she; Christina wasn't sure she could follow any of Jaime's other demands in this goddamn letter, "that bitch," but she could "KEEP EATING"—that seemed doable. And indeed, it was as she sat at the kitchen table, gazing outside, the courtyard lit up with colorful hanging lights that adorned various bungalows. Her neighbors' cabins never looked so pretty, she thought, as she polished off some cold lasagna from La Vecchia. Then a leftover turkey burger that she dipped in Heinz 57, tickled by the giant size of the bottle because Jaime "that bitch" loved ketchup. She put it on almost everything. Christina figured that her partner would be pleased she was paying attention. Christina was trying. KEEP EATING. "Listen to Jaime, 'that bitch'—she wants to make everything better."

To Christina, the letter resembled orders from CENTCOM. She was good at this. Following orders. *Sir. Yes, sir.* Only this time it was Jaime's orders. And she liked "that bitch" Jaime a whole lot better than *Sir. Yes, sir.* Cool thing about the letter? It was laid out perfectly, just like the Yellow Brick Road. She finished the burger and scooped up some rogue ketchup, licking her finger clean. Spotting her reflection in the window, haloed by the colorful lights, she spoke to herself, out loud, "Follow the Yellow Brick Road, you have to work your way back. Hell, 'that bitch' left. And now you have to get her back. Because now that you're alone, that has to be the plan."

To Christina, the colorful lights in the courtyard seemed to slowly dim. Any semblance of hope dissolved. Was reality setting in? Of course it was, as her last thought kept replaying in her mind:

Because now that you're alone, that has to be the plan.
Now that you're alone...
Has to be the plan.

Now that you're alone. The foreboding reality was now, suddenly, devastating.

She felt the table as if for the first time. Then she pounded the table—the third time viciously. JAIME WOULD NEVER LEAVE LIKE THIS! Christina ran to the bedroom and whipped open Jaime's closet. Empty hangers. She ran to the bathroom and flung open the medicine cabinet. Jaime's things were gone. Christina looked at their little table. Hairbrush gone. It was always there.

Christina sat on the toilet and suddenly kicked at the table. James loved when Christina brushed her long and silky black hair. It was so beautiful. She kicked the table again. And again. And then again, only harder, only this time screaming:

"HOW COULD YOU JUST FUCKING LEAVE?!"

She flopped forward, pounding the small table, which was now nothing more than firewood, still screaming, "HOW COULD YOU JUST FUCKING LEAVE?!" She was throwing the broken pieces and anything else she could grab all over the tiny bathroom, including glass. She was on her knees crying and hyperventilating. And then she vomited violently on the floor. A few scary seconds later, she exploded again, this time against the wall.

And then she recoiled, like a fetus, into a quiet place. So quiet, you could hear freeway traffic from nearby I-10.

Christina whispered to herself, "How could you just leave?" Eyes wide open, Christina's curled-up body remained frozen in the damage. But then her vision shifted, as if she were watching herself from a bird's-eye view. She didn't like this weirdness but had no control to stop it, as if she were paralyzed. She thought she looked pathetic, alone on a toilet floor, in a pool of her own vomit—the smell repulsive or whatever was worse than repulsive. From outside, she heard a car engine turn over, followed by unintelligible music.

She thought she heard her father's voice because the timbre (is that what they called it? Timbre?) was very distinguishable, kind of a Tom Waits voice, but softer, easier. And for eighteen years, whenever he spoke to Christina, it was always tender, always caring, as if he were speaking and listening at the same time. She always assumed that's why he was such a good teacher.

And now, in a city that lied about housing angels, she gaped down at herself trapped in this fucking bathroom. She could hear Jack's voice and that meant he was listening—and she needed him now more than ever.

Please Daddy. I'm dying.

And then she cowered, trembling more than before, now under attack as an earsplitting motorcycle growled hot out in the alley. Was her father just about to say something? "Goddammit," she threw a table leg. "GODDAMMIT!" She whacked her hands over her ears, now whispering at Easy Rider, "Shut the fuck up. Shut the fuck up." The Harley roared off into the night; she could hear this cocksucker for blocks. Would he ever fade away? Ever? And then she heard her father, not his actual voice, but the simple things he said over the years—his thoughts, his ideas—his philosophy about love, the only truth he actually believed in.

He was never super heavy or grandiose, just generous.

But here, on the bathroom floor, surrounded by shards of glass, cracked wood, vomit and blood, Christina could hear her father, Jack MacKenzie, as if everything he ever shared had been distilled down to one stream of consciousness:

Trust, Christina. Trust yourself.
Trust those you love and those who love you.
The ones who really love you, unconditionally love you.
You'll know who they are...
because you'll be able to count them on one hand.
We're out here alone, kiddo, we have nothing else
but our love and trust... with each other.
And without love, we're no better than the rocks and trees.

His canon ran through Christina like a main circuit cable. It was part of her DNA. She had great allegiance to his humble words. And it wasn't like he pontificated. In fact, Jack MacKenzie rarely offered a sermon. But when he did, when his words did come around, it was like Halley's Comet; it mattered.

Like this one time when the newly minted teenager sought emergency guidance. They were in the den, father and daughter, and he was grading papers but stopped everything because she needed him. Christina was thirteen, and it was mother versus daughter, round fifteen for the heavyweight crown. They had been at each other's throats for days. In her whispered but agitated tone, Jack listened intently to the teenager's plea. And then, in his soft yet gravelly voice, he began calming her down, offering simple and straightforward advice. It was pretty much the same canon Christina evoked as she trembled on the cold bathroom floor. Of course that night in the den, in New Jersey, he didn't take sides, but he made sure his daughter recognized Darlene as one of the two people on the planet that loved her the most—and it was time for Christina to trust that love, trust her mother's judgment. "She'll never do anything to hurt you, sweetheart. Ever." Jack underlined "ever."

Were her father's words now endorsing Jaime?

Alone, on the revolting floor, amidst the vomit and destruction, Christina began to recognize what rock bottom might actually look like. Jack & Darlene, dead. College and the cosmos, dead. G.I. Jane, atten-hut, also as good as dead. And Jaime, gone with the wind.

But the beautiful love of her life, the girl from Vietnam, that shy kid she met on the swings in 1975, who could barely speak English, had now (in 1994) dropped her a lifeline. Was this a rope to salvation? "Fuck, just get me off this bathroom floor."

Her next move was probably the most important move of her entire life, a move that felt like an endless crawl from the toilet to the kitchen table. Christina pulled herself up to a kitchen chair and grabbed the letter, scanning the words, trying desperately to stay one step ahead of those demon voices, the familiar ones in her head, voices that might gain control of the situation at any moment.

She was breathing heavily, panting. Was it nerves or the respiratory damage? Probably both; who the hell knows? Who the hell cares? She was laser-focused on a new revelation: the cause and effect of Jaime's fast exit: "I must be a fucking monster." Her next thought was not out loud: "What am I supposed to do? She's gone."

The idea of being alone must have drilled in, absorbed as reality, defined as tragic loss, because Christina was already trying to grasp what the hell to do next: "What am I supposed to do? She's gone."

The thought kept repeating itself. "What am I supposed to do?" Her panic prompted the question, "We're supposed to be together. Can I fix this?" She scanned the letter.

> But you have to do this without me. They've put shackles on you. You have to bust this shit up. You'll always be my first and my last.

There was something else.

> GO FIND YOURSELF. Go find that goddamn red bucket. It's who you are. And when you do I'll meet you anywhere.

"What am I supposed to do?" was no longer an empty thought. It became a real and tangible question. "What am I supposed to do?" A question that demanded an answer, an answer that required action. "What-Am-I-Supposed-To-Do?"

Let's say professional gamblers had been studying Christina for the past eighteen months. To a person, they would have wagered piles of cash on her soon-to-be demise. That would be the smart bet. And no doubt there were numerous shitty outcomes to embrace. Take roulette, for example—if you want the best chance of winning, a savvy gambler will probably plunk their chips down on a red/black or an odd/even bet. The bet doesn't pay as much, but you'd be right about fifty percent of the time. And in Christina's case, the smart gambler would be cheering for suicide because that's the smart bet. And why not? All the earmarks were there: a massive personal trauma followed by a harrowing and bloody shell shock, then a deep depression laced with high-octane pharmaceuticals—and now, topping off the banana split—a tremendous emotional loss.

Plus, and this is a big plus, Vets suffering from PTSD commit suicide at alarming rates. Almost four times higher than the general public. Gamblers would factor that in.

So the roulette wheel was spinning and the ivory pill was bounding about as Christina stared into her wall of faded kitchen tile. And that's when she had the most bizarre of memories, one that offered a fleeting moment of clarity, possibly even one that saved her life—at least for the nonce.

She suddenly remembered her favorite flick as a child—she saw it once in a dark New York theatre and then numerous times with Darlene sitting on that sunken couch in their comfy den, the VHS tape playing over and over. Christina was mesmerized by the phantastic world of little people speaking with strange voices, enthralled with a beautiful GOOD witch doing battle against an ornery BAD witch. And then there was Dorothy from Kansas, the girl Christina fancied as herself, a girl who just had to get home, had to get back to Kansas.

But now, in this tiny kitchen, in the People's Republic of Santa Monica, flashes of that movie came roaring back; Christina's very smart brain (along with any residual help Big Pharma might offer) was working overtime.

                    GLINDA
    Remember, never let those ruby slippers off...

                    DOROTHY
    But how do I start for Emerald City?

                    GLINDA
    ... all you do is follow the Yellow Brick Road.

                    DOROTHY
    ... what happens if I--

                    GLINDA
    Just follow the Yellow Brick Road.

Christina closed her eyes; she could hear all the little people urging Dorothy on.

                    MUNCHKINS
    Follow the Yellow Brick Road.
    Follow the Yellow Brick Road.

Then she remembered the Munchkins gathering around Dorothy and her little dog Toto; they were all singing—one big send-off: Dorothy, Toto, and their three new friends skipping toward a promising new land.

                 ALL THE MUNCHKINS
    You're off to see the Wizard
    The Wonderful Wizard of Oz

In a weird way, this movie gibberish started to make sense: Jaime's letter became Christina's immediate call to arms. Her personal Yellow Brick Road. But there's always a flip side, day turns to night, light becomes dark. Christina's demon voices were also rising up, taking their rightful place—the voices demanding that Christina recognize this Jaime letter

(THAT BITCH) as the cowardly pack of lies that it was, all bullshit, a confidence game.

Like a fighter climbing to their feet in the fifteenth round, Christina still had some punches left, even after the last few desperate hours. She managed to block out the cacophony of fiendish voices and concentrate on Jaime's all-time favorite saying that was currently echoing in her head: "You have to have a plan. You have to have a plan." With newfound clarity, she scanned the familiar handwriting.

It's about saving your life AND saving mine.

WHO YOU STILL ARE!

not those goddamn army shrinks! with their bullshit pill-popping!

I did a ton of research
I found this amazing doctor

Take the bus. It's easy. It's called "PEACE HOUSE"
Call them – Dr. Genovese (213-555-4328)

but none of that is what they call "pathology" – it's grief

it's grief

You have to face this shit with people who can help.

I'm enabling your behavior and that's not good

He's been dealing with Vietnam Vets
and now Persian Gulf Vets

Julian at the yoga studio said he'll help with anything.

If you don't want to lose ME & YOU, go to Genovese.
Fight like hell.

Get away from the VA (as far as you can run) and head straight to Genovese (213-555-4328).

I blame the bastards. So should you.

(I left lots of food. KEEP EATING. KEEP EATING. KEEP EATING.)

TAKE YOUR PILLS! TAKE YOUR PILLS!! TAKE YOUR PILLS!!!

> *it's only your goddamn life*
> *(213-555-4328)*
> *James xxxooo*

As those first days passed, the voices continued their chorus on Christina, like constant body blows: *The Army takes care of its own... of course the VA cares... of course these pills work... we're the experts, we're the United States of America... this other guy is a radical quack... they're all a bunch of renegades—plus, Jaime ran out on you, left you high and dry, fuck her... and fuck this quack.*

Throughout all her head clamor, two very different thoughts kept ping-ponging: "I must be a fucking monster," and the flip side, "Follow the Yellow Brick Road."

Monsters and Dorothy. Juvenile? Maybe.

But C-Mac was learning how to fight back. Jaime's letter told the truth. And her father would never steer her wrong. She was alone and broken and started drawing direct lines to the guilty party. "To hell with the fucking government. They're the reason I'm in this shit."

❖ ❖ ❖

Dorothy (Part Two).

Christina kept swallowing her pills (Yin) and kept eating (Yang). But one day she stopped taking the bus to Westwood. The VA noticed that their patient was AWOL, and the office called a few times, Christina telling them the flu hit her hard. They said, "Feel better."

She said thanks, goodbye.

A few days later she gathered enough courage to climb on another bus, this one stopping on Fairfax, just down the street from Peace House. At first, she wasn't so sure. About Peace House or about the people inside. Christina thought they were weird. Even kind of cult-like. But strangely, at the same time, she also liked them. After two more visits, she liked them a little more and signed up for the program: group counseling and one-on-one sessions. These included a comprehensive health and drug rehab plan. Cricket, the receptionist, smiled when she looked up from her clipboard, "Check, check, and check. You're in, Mac and Cheese." Christina laughed at the clever twist on her name. Cricket ran around and gave her a big hug.

No doubt, Dr. Genovese was tough as nails. So was his staff. But clearly they cared. She could tell. She also met a bunch of other Vets, many of these guys from Vietnam, except they seemed different. They were fighters. They didn't take any shit. Especially government shit. It was the same with the few Persian Gulf Vets at Peace House. They were all very different from the Vets she met at the VA. They weren't passive. They questioned everything. And they sure as hell weren't gung ho.

Slowly, Genovese started moving Christina off the VA's cocktail. One morning, another female Vet that the Long Beach VA doctors had on a similar cocktail, shared her story with Christina's group. Megan was nervous:

> When I finally came home, I stayed with my brother and his wife.
> I used to drive their daughter to school in the morning.
> Katie would get out of the car and wave goodbye and I'd just sit there
> with these gruesome thoughts about how the school's gonna blow up
> and shrapnel's gonna shred all these goddamn kids.
> Then I started thinking: Was I gonna be the one to do it?
> Was that my fucking job? Because if it was, I could surely do it.
> No problem. Just gimme the word. Luckily, I snapped out of it,
> "Why am I even thinking this? I don't wanna blow up these kids."
> But then again, I thought maybe I did.
> Especially when you can actually see the aftermath. Oh, fuck.

When she told the story, you could see the terror in Megan's face. Genovese called it "chemical mental torture." And the terrifying part for Christina was that she had similar thoughts. Many times. Thoughts about inciting violence that she never shared with Dr. Morea or the other VA shrinks, or in group, or even with Jaime. It was too fucked up. When Megan mentioned the school, Christina knew she had similar thoughts. She figured if she ever said them out loud, they might come true. Or they'd lock her up for her thought dreams.

Genovese and his staff—a few were also Vets—weren't afraid to fight back. Nor were the ex-GIs who came here for help. Like Jaime said, the enemies weren't in the Iraqi desert. They were here, at home. Behind desks in the Pentagon. In recruitment offices. Roaming the halls of VA hospitals. And most assuredly in those drug industry boardrooms—junkies who sold their pill-popping propaganda to anyone who'd listen; and of course the military aggressively trumpeted these magic beans. Why? Because they were guilty as sin and desperate for the PR optics: "Look how much we're doing, how much we care." When, in reality, Christina was learning at Peace House, the drugs were nothing more than a gag order on the ugly truth—not only was the Empire murdering Iraqis, they were knowingly killing their own. And worst of all, they didn't give a shit.

Christina decided Jaime should be working here.

Wheelchair-bound Eugene was a Vietnam Vet missing both legs. He always wore his tattered green Army jacket. Eugene said he lost "both pins" in '68, right outside the U.S. Embassy in Saigon. "Like my country," the grizzled Vet made clear, "I was in the wrong place at the wrong time, infamous Tet Offensive." Christina remembered reading about the Tet Offensive in school. Eugene continued:

> *It's been twenty-five years, boys and girls. And to this day,*
> *if I hear a door slam, I think it's a gunshot. Nerves are deep-fried.*
> *But you gotta face reality... just like my legs ain't gonna grow back.*
> *This shit's with me for good.*

The third week Christina showed up at Peace House, another Vietnam Vet came to speak to the entire population, another wheelchair-bound ex-soldier named Ron Kovic. He lived in nearby Redondo Beach and was "kind of famous," according to Cricket, "He wrote that book, 'Born on the Fourth of July,' you know, Tom Cruise played him in the movie." Christina never met anyone like Ron before. She thought he was so brave and courageous for speaking out. Just like Eugene said to Kovic, their wheelchairs parked side-by-side, "Thank you, brother, for not taking any shit. Call the bastards out. Fuck 'em where they live." Kovic had copies of his book. He signed each one. Christina devoured it over the weekend. She wrote passages from Kovic's book in a journal she started, a journal Genovese had suggested.

I wanna be free again. I wanna walk in the backyard on the grass.
I wanna put my bare feet in the ocean. I wanna run along the sand
and feel it on my feet. I wanna stand up in the shower
with the hot water streaming down my legs...

Once a day, like clockwork, Christina would read Jaime's letter. In its entirety. It became her bible. She started spending time with Julian. They'd meet for coffee and sometimes went hiking in the mountains above Malibu. She thought he was amazing. He finally wrangled her into some yoga classes. Also, meditation. He left a message for Jaime, wanting to tell her about the progress Christina was making, or so it seemed. He didn't hear back from her.

In a number of one-on-one sessions with Dr. Genovese, whom everyone called Frank, they dove into some deep waters about the death of Christina's parents, followed by the hell she walked through in Iraq and the Kingdom. "Suffering is the only response, Christina—for Jack, Darlene, and yourself. It's what we call 'the imperative grief process.' It'll hurt, and it will be painful. You'll hate it. But if you don't go through it and only rely on medicating your pain, then it's zombie-land forever. We have to deal with the grief, we have to deal with the depression. If not, it's a vicious cycle. No more Band-Aids."

The weaning off process from the heavy pharmaceuticals had begun. Genovese and his staff embraced a slow and calculated process. And along with the gradual cutback on chemicals, they implemented a natural diet and flush program for Christina. She enjoyed going to a place called Rainbow Acres, an honest-to-God hippie market for the natural foods and juices Genovese recommended. It was kismet how this daily direction and purpose integrated seamlessly with Jaime's Yellow Brick Road.

A month later, Christina told a female counselor that she was feeling "crazy horny for the first time in like forever." The counselor smiled and laughed. Christina was put off at first, "What's so funny?" The counselor made it clear, "I'm not laughing at you. I'm happy for you. You're feeling your body again. The drugs and the trauma kept you from feeling real things. Celebrate. Go get laid."

On the bus ride home, Christina decided "that the damn letter was kind of working." Jaime's harsh reminder. Of loss. Of consequences. To some degree, life felt "lighter" for Christina but far from peachy keen. She still had weird spells. Bouts of depression. Flashes of vicious imagery. Fatigue rolled in waves. Genovese and the counselors told her to expect these things, what they called "residual symptoms." Peace House's message was steadfast: "This is hard work. Some of it may last for years, and some things may never go away—like the anger, detachment, anxiety." Doc was always reminding anyone within earshot, "No magic wands, folks." And then his well-known mantra: "Magic wands are for wizards and fairytales."

About two months after showing up, Dr. Frank Genovese guided Christina in for a soft landing: she was off all medications. She was face-to-face with her grief and subsequent trauma. And it was scary as shit. Especially the panic attacks. But life was real. No more head on a post. And Peace House was there for her, as were the other Vets—and she for them. They all leaned into each other. In many ways, she had a family again. A brick-and-mortar sanctuary with a side order of saving grace.

❖ ❖ ❖

Life was returning in drips and drabs. Some days were good—and some were just fucking awful. Julian's friendship became so important, and together they thought it might be a good idea for Christina to look for a job. She was ready and found gainful employment at a neoteric coffee shop called Starbucks on the corner of Hill and Main, just two blocks from the ocean. She worked hard and made decent money. She was a barista with first-rate skills, making those overpriced coffee concoctions at $3.00 bucks a pop. She told Genovese, "I may have been a really crappy soldier, but I'm a natural with the espresso!"

It was the first time the good doctor hugged her.

As the calendar flipped, Christina was able to spruce up the bungalow, cobbling together a look together from various garage sales. She really loved her oversized Buddha that wore an old Dodgers hat. Thanks to Peace House and sweet Julian, as well as her budding yoga practice, there were moments when she felt glimmers of hope, flickers of once again loving herself and her life. Fleeting, yes, but traces nonetheless.

It happened one morning when she was hovering on the edge of the world, that rocky cliff high above Pacific Coast Highway—her bare feet rooted into the cool, moist ground. It was during her fluid transitions from Tadasana to Adho Mukha Shvanasana and then into Virabhadrasana (the Warrior Pose) that she made a monumental decision. And when she arrived home, she actually thought about calling Jaime to boast about her progress but decided against it. Absolutely decided against it. She might be, as the Indigo Girls suggested, "closer to fine," but she was nowhere near done, nowhere near Emerald City, the Land of Oz that Jaime's letter commanded her to visit, literally & figuratively.

Yes, journey to and visit. That seemingly mythical place where the Sun didn't rise over scorched desert and jagged cliffs, but rather over a massive ocean, like it's supposed to.

And if she was ever going to reclaim her soul, her joy, that's where she needed to be. At least for a while. Hell, if Jack & Darlene built this bird's nest for a reason, then it was time to fly back, seek solace, sidestep the tempest. Jaime knew that and said as much—and that was good enough.

And then, for some bizarre reason, Christina envisioned the letters of this seaside village miraculously appearing in the sky, letters emblazoned with sparkling fireworks, spinning on a colossal Ferris wheel, one moving way too fast for human consumption.

ASBURY PARK

&

23
Twenty minutes.

IT WAS SLOW, EVEN FOR A MONDAY. Lou wrapped up and was already cleaning by 7:30pm. The place was empty except for an elderly couple drinking coffee and sharing their apple pie (a la mode Breyers Vanilla on the house). At lunch, we pulled in a few bucks, and then I poured a bit during happy hour, but it was the kind of day that underscored my deliberations on whether we stay open or not on manic Mondays. I usually lose money, but for me it's always been a communal thing to stay open. Especially in the summer. I don't know, we'll see.

By 10:00pm, I was in the residence watching the ballgame. Yanks and O's were in extra innings at the Stadium. Rizzuto and Mercer were talking about the looming MLB strike, and I was sipping a White Russian. My third. And sonovabitch if I didn't get whacked with one of those jungle relapses. It was just a few goddamn seconds, but real as shit. Like I've said, it's been years since one of these visited during waking hours. Nonetheless, it was a brutal few seconds, replaying exactly when I got hit. Shocked me. A lightning bolt. You feel like you're losing control of both mind and body, as if you're getting sucked into some alternate reality, powerless to escape, scared shitless you won't be able to return.

Terrifying. Even for the King. Luckily, I returned from Plei Trap, still breathing, able to write about it.

When things settled down, what was left of my drink was on the floor with Randy Velarde ripping a single to right-center, knocking in Luis Polonia. Bombers walked off winners six-five, bottom of the eleventh. Always a silver lining, right?

I was shaky and just sat there as the tube droned on. It felt as if I might need Donna for one of our private sessions. It's never a sure thing for the Whitefish in this regard... but you cannot win if you do not play. And what's a few more shekels? I'm already down for the day. Maybe I'll close with a smile on my face.

I called her. She was still up. She wasn't happy, nor was she into it (if ever), nor did she like me very much when I asked... but Donna was never emotionally involved anyway... a C-note's a C-note. And there's no doubt in my mind that Donna Stefanelli is a dyed-in-the-wool laissez-faire capitalist.

She knows the drill. I leave the galley door unlocked, and the club is dark except for a lone spotlight on my empty stage. I'm sitting in the dark about thirty feet away. Buck naked, although she can't see me (for two reasons): one, she doesn't want to see me; and two, the spotlight flares out the blackness, blinding her to me and my antics. Better she can't see me. The shadows are my friend.

She always wears my requested tight-knit cream-colored sweater, no bra, and a short black leather skirt. She's also barefoot. There's no music and we don't say a word. I leave the front door ajar, so the not-too-distant ocean remains our gentle white noise. I get twenty minutes for my hundred bucks. Not a second longer.

Turns out, when I scrambled back for my buddy Whale, the poor bastard was already dead. I grabbed the radio to head back, and my first step triggered one of those homespun Vietnamese landmines. Like a VHS tape, I can replay the wartime schtick any time I want: a bright flash and then wicked white heat as the fucking thing blasts straight up into me – bullseye: stomach and groin. Down I went (a la Cosell: "DOWN GOES FRAZIER!"); metal shrapnel slicing and dicing, driving rocks and assorted debris into my abdominal cavity (the docs tell you that afterward).

The booby-trapped postcard from my fearless adversaries completely destroyed the scrotum, the penis, and did some serious damage to the pelvis, stomach, et cetera. You get the picture. For the museum mount, title this photo "Bloody Carnage."

But thank God for trauma surgeons... these guys were miracle workers; plus, the Pentagon gives them plenty of practice.

So, besides missing my balls as well as my dick, and walking a little funny, everything else returned to so-called "normal."

That is if you don't count my brain.

I know you have questions. Here, I'll answer two of them.

First, the easy one: self-catheterization.

The second one is a bit more complicated: correct – there are no orgasms in the traditional sense. I left the Garden State for Southeast Asia as a strapping, horny nineteen-year-old – and then returned a short time later as a eunuch. God Bless Amerikkka. But I have since discovered, quite by accident, that I can muster up an occasional "phantom" orgasm. That's right, folks – step right up! If my mind gets excited enough, demonstrably aroused and thrilled, then I can experience a revenant ejaculation – it's really more like a gratifying spasm. Truth be told, it doesn't happen the way it used to: seventeen and ready to blow, open up a "Playboy" – "HOLY SHIT, she's so beautiful," and you're so damn hard, BAM, it's over. But today, in 1994, with Ms. Stefanelli, ofttimes there's nothing. Although on a number of occasions it's been somewhat enjoyable. Especially when you stack it up against having nothing at all.

Life becomes relative, eh?

I could hear Donna come in through the galley – the squeaking backdoor, her quick footsteps across the linoleum, then over the glazed concrete. Still spry for almost thirty. She stopped briefly to take off her shoes and gather her facade. After all, this is a performance.

As I explained, I'm seated in the dark, watching from the murky shadows. She crosses into the spotlight on my slightly raised stage. She has this rather unique stage persona – it's as if she's the only human alive in a fifty-mile radius, and there's no acknowledgment of my presence, the existence of my club, or, for that matter, Asbury Park.

She grabs the chair that I've left for her, faces the eunuch in the abyss, and sits gracefully. I appreciate her concentration. She wears a delicate gold watch that's actually quite nice, a Christmas gift I gave her back in '91. She glances at her Bulova and now it's official. My twenty minutes have begun... and they begin the same way every time Donna takes the stage: with her bare feet starting the dance, up and down one calf, followed by one pes over the other, as if the left massages the right and vice versa. With her nails painted black, the toes appear to operate as separate appendages as they rub her creamy calves and then dig hard into the floor. She has beautiful, soft feet. For a street legal girl, she has somehow kept her feet flawless.

Her eyes are closed, and god knows what she's thinking, if she's thinking at all. Maybe she's meditating – all thought erased, cruising down a blank highway. Could she be into it? She sells it well, really well, but somehow I doubt it.

She looked especially good tonight. I thought that might be a sign of things to come. Her elbows begin to gently squeeze her breasts closer together, braless in her tight, inviting sweater. Sometimes her nipples are hard and sometimes they're not. But tonight, on this hot August night, they're surprisingly hard. I'm rubbing my nether regions – not that it matters, but it seems like the right thing to do.

Was I feeling anything yet?

Not really... except, of course, the skilled boyish function of gawking at sensual women, maybe checking out some dude's girlfriend when he's not looking or flipping through your favorite "Penthouse" – one that reduces women to an object – yeah, I know, I get it, and I don't deny it, but for crissakes, it's the way the Universe programmed the species, at least me. Let me welter in my wretched state.

Slowly, very slowly, she begins to raise her sweater above her soft tummy but stops just below her rather amazing breasts that now bribe me headlong into this thing. Her hands let go of the sweater, tenderly passing across her nipples, now pressing-feeling-grabbing everything – an obvious suggestion that I do the same; and if words defined this moment and not body language, it would sound something like: "C'mon, fuckface, stumble up on your ridiculous stage and grope a piece of heaven. But you can't, ha-ha!"

Her sweater rolls higher, deliberately flicking her nipples on the way by, revealing what I've seen many times, but every time it's like the first. And damn, if Stefanelli doesn't add a new wrinkle: As her sweater exposes every young boy's American dream, she slowly rolls her tongue along her lips. Jesus... is she looking in my direction?

Is she acting? Or is she genuinely feeling this? Experiencing this. She'll never let me know. The hidden secret of a great performer.

As the sweater passes over Donna's head, it tousles her thick reddish curls... they settle with panache, a TV commercial teasing "U Can't Touch This."

Goddamn, this woman is erotic. Soft. Beautiful.

All of that in ten minutes. Had I been "normal," the horse would have left the barn eons ago. And then without any fanfare, she runs her hands down her thighs, starting at the knees, then subtly directing her legs wider, lavender fingernail polish soaring off her milk-white skin. I plead with myself, "Please feel something, you useless absurd little man." The pep talk doesn't work, but I still have nine minutes.

Donna's fingers must be magic because now she's bent backward on the chair with one hand on her breasts and the other on what she calls the "pudendum" – never heard that word until this self-same Italian ingenue laughed her ass off educating me and the boys when it came to vagina-vulva-and-labia. Seven meatheads staring into the great divide.

Now, I must say, Donna is either taking personal acting classes with Konstantin Stanislavski or she was truly into tonight's episode, because Christ Almighty, she was arched way up off the chair, writhing in ecstasy-bliss-joy-AND-pain. All at once.

Was it pain from having to do this? Or ecstasy from actually getting off?

Her fingers were truly working the... pudendum. Or was Stanislavski simply worth his weight in gold?

Unfortunately, it's of no matter because we're in the homestretch, my twenty minutes ticking toward zero... please Apollo 11, kindly have liftoff... but it ain't gonna happen on this now very stone-cold August night.

And like that it's over.

Donna Stefanelli grabbed her sweater, then her C-note – Ben Franklin waiting, as always, on top of the Peavey amp – and like a thief in the night, she exits stage right, floating off from whence she came.

#

CHRISTINA and the WHITEFISH

24

Here-here, MacKenzie!

Working through the grief without chemistry was easier and harder all at the same time. It depended on the wind. When it was bad, it was in your face El Niño bad. Christina was already accustomed to dealing with death and mortality—not to mention entrails and viscera; but now—suddenly, her personal hell played out in the vibrant Technicolor of reality. Harsh, severe, and brutally violent. The kind of reckoning that exacted a price. There were even times when she thought, "Hell, suicide might be easier. Much quicker and we're all gonna die anyway, so what's the difference?" That's when she was being flippant. But when suicidal thoughts crept into her more serious and depressive moments, that's when walking the ledge between life and death became a perilous high-wire act.

However, when the sorrow manifested itself in dreadful ways, Christina started to understand the value of being pharmaceutical-free. Embracing a personal veracity felt like emancipation. She felt physically and mentally stronger, capable of putting the last three-plus years behind her. She came to realize that with a pushcart of pills, so-called reality was a muddled haze—a grayscale of life viewed in soft focus, every day a newborn dossier that the drugs were helping to rewrite on the fly.

As the days and weeks passed, Christina's heightened realism began to diminish. Her work at Peace House was brutal but genuine—going down like grain alcohol, but that's the price she paid.

J.P. was a recent Persian Gulf Vet. They became friends. In group one night, he talked about dealing with his trauma minus the camouflage of powerful meds. "For me, it's like walking down an alley, knowing you're gonna get sucker punched, just not knowing when or where. You're flying blind, but at least it's real."

For Christina, the clarity began to offer the same solid recognition: "You either deal with reality or reality deals with you"—a boilerplate adage that Doc Genovese drove home with every suffering Vet he counseled. In fact, the good doctor was like a pacifist drill sergeant offering a stream of tried and true personal aphorisms: "Your nightmares need to be exposed, processed, *and then accepted.*" He was steadfast and resolute. His tough love rang true with staff and patients alike—and that was all that mattered.

Christina also began to recognize how right Jaime was in her letter about the foundational difference between the VA and Peace House—Peace House wasn't working for the enemy.

Plain and simple, Christina inherited a new and altered POV from her newfangled brothers and sisters, one that was frequently counterintuitive: *bad is good.* She was now able to concede that the VA and their government stooges were simply medicating normal—for them, every day was Trick or Treat.

In group, Christina was inspired by an ex-VA counselor who said she "thankfully saw the light" after working both sides of the fence. Christina liked her a lot. Geena was super smart, even wrote books on the subject, always offering clarity: "Years ago, these guys rarely saw a doctor. They didn't get medicated. They dealt with grief by talking to other soldiers, their friends, parents, maybe a priest or a rabbi." A Vet named Bags, who was shy like a church mouse, blurted out, "But now it's a system, right?" Geena nodded, "That's the deal. If you're fucked up, go see the doc. Get your pills. Numb this shit before it spins out of control." Bags wasn't through, "Talk about the money. You gotta follow the money."

"Bags is right," Geena stood up and strolled the room. "Along with Big Pharma, these psychiatrists got together and started to define *YOUR* pain and *YOUR* reactions as 'deviant,' always something beyond their bullshit definition of 'normal.'" Now she was cooking, "Most of it based on nothing... there was no pathology, no MRIs, no blood tests. These jokers sat around in a room and codified a bunch of arbitrary standards, all of it beholden to financials and various billing cycles—abracadabra, voilà... there's your clinical criteria."

You could cut the anger in the room with a knife. Another counselor, a burly Korean War Vet named Hank, chimed in, "Bottom line, they're masking the anguish because it's good for business."

Another Vet, a big dude, a vestige from the U.S. invasion of Panama back in '89, hammered his prosthetic arm into a table, "These cocksuckers sweep their shit under a fucking rug... and for what? More blood money."

Monty was missing both feet and echoed the same anger, "It's like fucking Merlin. Sleight of hand. Don't look here, look over there!" An older Vet named Danny, who left both legs back in An Lộc, went deeper, "Sure, put you in a meat grinder for some made-up fucking lie, all the while pitching their patriotic bullshit. It's fucking shameless." Molly, the only other female Vet in group with Christina, suggested, "Just once I wanna hear one of these assholes, these shills, talk about the abject failure of war itself." Geena concurred, "Just like the media, they all talk around the problem, on purpose."

Hanging on each word and every emotion, Christina really wanted to contribute. But her thoughts, some jumbled and some clear, usually remained unpublished—until this moment on this day when she sensed an opening: "Molly's right... Ron Kovic wrote that in his book. He said the same thing when he was here." All eyes were now on Christina. She knew she had to finish her thought, hoping not to fuck up from memory. "Mr. Kovic wrote, 'No one will ever again be my enemy... No government will ever teach me to hate another human being.'" The Vet with the prosthetic arm banged the table again, only this time he was jubilant, "Here-here, MacKenzie!"

In fact, all these Vets in Genovese's growing clinic were learning that the government's overall rehab and treatment régime was nothing more than "a magic carpet ride with no end game." These exchanges were über cathartic for the wounded pawns, not unlike John & Yoko's primal scream therapy. It was liberating to speak candidly about the insanity they endured. Especially opportunities with outspoken critics like Kovic and Veterans for Peace, people who acknowledged the hard-boiled truth: The United States government had one desire—just move these rag dolls down the road. Out of sight, out of mind. Molly summed it up, "Sweep 'em under the rug... gives 'em clear sailing for their next imperial adventure." Hank from Korea iced the entire cake, "Never forget, these bastards always need new meat."

The next time Christina spoke at group was a week later. Greatly motivated by the Kovic visit and coupled with his autobiography, she followed Jaime's footsteps into the Santa Monica Public Library and fell upon the My Lai Massacre—when in 1968, during the height of the Vietnam War, the U.S. military brutally massacred some five hundred unarmed civilians in their tiny village of My Lai, code-named "Pinkville."

As Christina dug deeper, her anger grew, and it was maddening because her fury was now fueled by an inconvenient truth—one she never fully acknowledged before. Her Peace House comrades were always saying that once you see past all the myths and lies you've been force-fed your entire life, you'll never be the same.

She jotted down how Hank put it, "You can't unsee the truth."

One of her counselors asked three of the Vets, Christina included, to make short presentations to the group on any subject. So Christina went back to the library two more times to gather research. And just like Belvidere High, Christina handwrote a tight three-page paper. She only wished Jack & Darlene were there to proofread.

The auxiliary room at Peace House was packed for the presentations. Jersey (C-Mac had a new nickname) went last. She cleared her throat, reminding herself one last time that she was always a good public speaker—keep it slow and measured:

> On March 16th, 1968, in Quang Ngai Province, the wrath
> of American soldiers in Charlie Company came unhinged.
> Bloodthirsty doesn't begin to describe the My Lai Massacre.
> Vietnamese women and young girls were raped and their bodies
> mutilated before they were slaughtered. Vietnamese children
> were executed at gunpoint. The leader, Lieutenant William Calley,
> dragged dozens of villagers, children included, into a ditch and sprayed
> them with machine gun fire. Sergeant Michael Bernhardt later
> told reporters, and I quote, 'I saw them shoot an M79 grenade launcher
> into a group of people who were still alive.' End quote.

Two and a half pages later, when Christina finished, many of the Vets were crying, herself included. This was the second time that the good doctor, Frank Genovese, gave her a hug. This one lasted much longer.

❖ ❖ ❖

When Christina asked her manager, Ricky at Starbucks, for a month off, he quickly said, "No problem." He didn't want to lose her. "But please come back." Christina promised that she would.

That night, like most nights, she re-read Jaime's letter. For the newly minted "Jersey," it was like a boxer's workout. Each time, she'd absorb something new from James' prose (read: orders). At the very least, the letter helped to keep her on the straight and narrow, which she needed when those dark shadows came to visit. Then it hit her: "How do I get back to Jersey? James hightailed it out of Vegas with my Jeep." She laughed, "You stole my car!"

Christina also realized she had no credit cards, which made air travel difficult, although not impossible. Just pay cash for the ticket. Also, once back east, she needed a car. She had no intention of seeing Jaime first to reclaim the Jeep. She'd have to rent something at Newark—but don't you need a credit card for that? This intrusive reality would also nix renting a car to crisscross the country, which would cost beaucoup dollars anyway. She could buy a used car, but then she'd have to get insurance, and that would drain her bank account, especially when you factored in three thousand miles worth of gas, food, and motels.

"Hello Julian."

Nestled behind sunglasses made famous by Mr. Lennon, one of Santa Monica's best yoga instructors was sitting on a bench outside the studio when Christina ambled up. Julian shaded his vision as he eyed his visitor, suddenly smiling—he never saw her look so devilish.

"What's up, Miss Christina?"

She issued a friendly invite, "Can I buy you a coffee next door?"

They raised their mugs with a slight clink. Julian was curious, "So what's up?"

For a moment, Christina studied the perfect caramel color of her coffee, then quickly gazed up at her friend, "I think you know I've been doing better lately."

He clinked her mug again, "I can tell. That's beautiful." She continued, "And I'm thinking about... no... I'm positive... I'm going back east."

Julian was excited, "To see Jaime?"

She hesitated, "Well, not really... at least not yet because... I don't know, not yet." A bit baffled, Julian glanced over his sunglasses. Christina nodded, "I know, I know, it's complicated, but James wanted me to go back, back to Asbury Park. First. That's down the shore. In New Jersey."

Julian sipped his coffee. He knew there was an ask.

Christina sipped, too, then went in for the kill, "Here's the thing. James took my car back to Jersey when she left Vegas, which is cool. I mean, what else was she supposed to do, right? I was gone."

Julian agreed, "Makes sense."

Christina then wondered reluctantly, "Do you still have that other car? The Nissan?" Julian sensed she was uncomfortable, "I do, but officially it's a Datsun. '83 Pulsar. Why? You want to borrow it? Sure."

Christina felt like she could breathe again, "You'd be okay with that?" Julian sat back with his coffee, "It's got a lot of miles but it's a good car. I was going to sell it last year, but you know. No big deal. I'll just put it back on insurance."

Christina was excited, "I'll pay the extra."

Julian waved her off, "Don't worry about it, just make sure you bring it back!"

Christina raised her mug, "Deal. Oh my god, you're great."

He smiled, then added, "We should have it checked out before you leave."

They relaxed in the warmth of a late afternoon, finishing their coffee. But then Julian remembered something, "Oh, can you drive a stick?"

&

25
Big Bambu.

EARLIER ON, we explored the basement of my Club Southside. But that's only fifty-percent of my footprint. If you recall, we ventured down my rickety stairs and then veered to the right, where we visited my subterranean art studio. Although, at the bottom of those rickety stairs, if you instead turned left, you'd enter another large space that is home to my pristine 1985 convertible Cadillac Eldorado – museum-like condition boasting muscular mag wheels.

With the top down, this alabaster work of art reveals luxurious fire engine red leather seats that scream, "Come to Papa."

This vehicle is one of the great joys of my life. By far the greatest gift anyone has ever bestowed in my direction. It would be impossible for me to forget, even for a second, the plucky Lorelei Antuofermo. In fact, I touch the urn every time I pass it by, on a shelf in my art studio. Her impact on my life remains forever rooted. And when I'm in the basement, like I was today, buffing up one of GM's finest moments, it's her spirit that I feel. And when I fire up the Caddy's engine – a throttle-body fuel-injected 4100cc V8 – it's like Lorelei's sitting next to me on those plush front seats – red cushions that belong in a leather-padded den, not a car. But then again, this is a Cadillac.

Today, Lorelei and I popped in my new cassette – the song stylings of English guitar god, Mr. Robin Trower, wailing away on "Bridge of Sighs."

Lord have mercy... and thanks to Big Bambu, we did a tightly rolled J-bird and defiantly cruised the Jersey countryside.

That's right: We headed west along 33 through Freehold, across to Hightstown, weaved our way north past Princeton, and then traversed the sloping farms toward the Delaware. We crossed the river near Lambertville. And then, like General Washington, we headed south along the famous river until we stopped for a drink in Yardley, PA – a colonial treasure where George and his boys raped and pillaged the town folk. (Okay, I made that last part up, although it's not out of the realm, is it? Be honest.)

But, as you might have surmised by now, we never left the basement... "Playing those mind games for–ever."

Now, there are only a few folks who know about my strangely entombed Cadillac. For each and every one of them (five Asbury Park residents in total), it's a real head scratcher how this goddamn car landed in my basement. Lil Abner remains the most confounded. I let him spend an hour down there investigating. "Knock yourself out." The man came up with nothing. He simply accused me of being a warlock or possibly a wizard. I just stared at him. With dead shark eyes. I never witnessed a grown man break out into flop sweat that fast and that severe.

Tonight, we had a small birthday party for Donna. She turned thirty. I try to celebrate as much as I can with the gang – anniversaries, birthdays, and various milestones—like a couple of months ago when the Rangers won the Stanley Cup and then a few years ago when the Giants won two Super Bowls. Those were some major blowouts. But for Donna, I thought we'd do something classy (as you know, we have a unique relationship).

Ten of us gathered around a private candlelit table. Lou made prime rib. I broke out a few nice Italian reds. Dear Madam Marie conjured up dessert – a magnificent chocolate cake. Thirty candles. Jill from Two Jacks and a Jill knew a violinist that I hired to stroll discreetly on the perimeter. In fact, I told this fiddler to keep it classy, play tunes like "Edelweiss" or Debussy's "Clair de lune." None of that "Devil Went Down to Georgia" crap. Donna deserved a nice, elegant evening. She's endured a lot of pain with her family and some asshole boyfriend. Real abusive shit.

Despite our sometimes cantankerous banter and those debased late-night trysts, we've had numerous heart-to-hearts. She's a tough kid, a good kid, trying to find her way.

Later in the evening, I thought I really could have rubbed one out with Donna, a good one. I felt it looming just over the horizon. But then I watched her smiling face as she was blowing out a sea of candles – and then hugging Marie like the mom she never had.

It appeared to be a rare and magical moment for one Donna Stefanelli. She was beaming. In many ways, the entire dinner party felt magical. This young woman was starved for nourishment, craving love. The last thing she needed was my bullshit.

Dial it back, Whitefish. Put your imaginary cock back in its holster.

#

Part Two

"No one expected me. Everything awaited me."

Patti Smith

ME

CHRISTINA and the WHITEFISH

26

Road Trip (Part One).

As Christina made the turn from Pico onto Cloverfield, she smiled. And there was good reason. The '83 Pulsar shifted effortlessly from first to second and then miraculously to third gear as she headed toward the I-10 Freeway. Julian was an outstanding stick-shift coach, which made sense since he was such a loving yoga teacher. He exhibited great patience while Christina practiced with the Pulsar—the car resembling a bucking bronco.

She downshifted to a red light just before the busy entrance ramp, the launching pad to her next metaphoric hill to climb: the I-10 artery of the Los Angeles freeway snarl, a challenge that has beaten many a sentient being. Although she was still smiling, basking in the glow of a flawless downshift. 3-2-1. Waiting for the green light, she nodded, thinking, "All those hours in the Ralphs parking lot are really paying off."

❖❖❖

Day 1: Santa Monica to Barstow, CA to Flagstaff, AZ

Green light. The belly of the beast beckoned. "Be cool. You got this. Feel the car," Julian would say. "Anticipate, clutch, shift. Anticipate, clutch, shift." Suddenly she was going fifty and she was still alive. Still breathing. "Gotta get over. Got-to-move-over. Let me over. *C'mon, asshole, let me over.* See my blinker? I don't want the 405. C'mon, douchebag, have a heart. Fuck you with that horn. Now I'm in front of you. Eat my dust!"

That was Jaime's favorite line on their road trip to Vegas. *Eat my dust.*

Julian belonged to Triple-AAA and went with Christina to pick up "these very helpful Trip-Tiks for navigating your way across the USA." Then he smiled and started singing out his window, "See the USA in your Chevrolet!" Followed by an uncharacteristic belly laugh. Christina had no idea what he was singing or laughing about. *Was that a commercial? Was Julian showing his age?*

As she passed Downtown L.A., she thought the Sun looked cool dancing on the office building windows, a skyline that seemed to rise from nowhere. And Julian was right: These Trip-Tiks were great. She maneuvered through the intersecting craziness that led to the Inland Empire—zipping by West Covina, Covina, Pomona, and then Ontario, where a commercial jetliner was on final approach to the freeway-close airport, and for a few weird seconds it appeared like her freeway had become the plane's runway. "Jesus," she thought, "That was trippy."

Next up the I-15 interchange: Barstow & Las Vegas—and the Trip-Tik concurred, although Christina didn't expect the sudden swing in her emotions as LAS VEGAS emerged on a huge green directional sign. Hell, just the idea of that place made it hard to swallow. In many respects that neon Strip was ground zero for Private First Class Christina MacKenzie. Atten-hut! And she knew it. Out loud, she tried to reassure herself, "You're not going there. Not even close. You're heading east way before Vegas. You're going home."

It was indeed creepy. Because by the time she reached Barstow and realized she was about to connect with I-40 East, she couldn't remember driving, shifting, or even changing lanes for the last hour or so. "That can't be good," she thought. Thankfully, once on I-40 East, cruising through the Mojave (and away from Vegas), the more at ease Christina felt.

She flicked on the radio and listened to whatever gibberish shouted out as she clicked the scan button—a commercial for DiNapoli's, a new Italian restaurant in Barstow where you could get a free—click: Dolly Parton singing "9 to 5"—click: *You walk out from under the covering of God and you're on your own. Jesus told us, "I saw Satan fall like lightning from Heaven." Listen brothers and sisters, my precious flock, without Jesus—* double click: "Ahhhh," she smiled, mumbling, "Righteous redemption" as Lennon's "Imagine" took over, ditching the good pastor and propelling Christina past Daggett and Newberry Springs. Windows down, she was digging this dramatic and wraithlike desert with its quivering heat waves and flashes of hot air. Julian suggested keeping "that rinky-dink A-C off" when pushing through the desert. A few minutes later, parallel to the Interstate, two F-18 Super Hornets flew low across the desert floor. Christina caught a peek, casually thinking, "Probably out of Edwards." She changed the station—click: *When we come back, an update on the O.J. Simpson case. Stay tuned.*

It was late August, and the days were still long as she pulled into Flagstaff just before sundown. Of course, it wouldn't be Flagstaff without getting waylaid by a train crossing. And Christina had a front-row seat as the gates lowered, warning bells sounded, and those pulsating lights danced. No doubt the freight train looked unusually long, so she popped on the emergency brake and shut off the car. She was spellbound by the rumble of the passing cars. Her memory banks flipping through index cards of various road trips she made with Jack & Darlene, the many days of a well-spent youth—and she loved every one of them: Québec, Williamsburg, Miami Beach, Cherry Blossoms in D.C., and, of course, every inch of New England. There was even their ambitiously crazy cross-country trek through Chicago-Denver-San Francisco-Portland-and-Seattle—and then back east along the Trans-Canada Highway. What a summer, legendary in the MacKenzie family album.

The caboose finally thrashed by, once again revealing reality as the giant neon HOTEL MONTE VISTA roof sign flickered on. A few moments later, she was off.

❖❖❖

Day 2: Flagstaff, AZ to Tucumcari, NM to Amarillo, TX

Early the next morning, Christina left her Best Western and downtown Flagstaff and headed straight into the rising sun. I-40 cut straight through Navajo Nation and the magnificent Painted Desert. Jack & Darlene talked about a road trip through the southwest, spending time exploring New Mexico and Arizona. Christina made a dramatic motion as if she were going to whack the steering wheel with her fist, but then gently tapped it, "Well Dad, well Mom," she said out loud, "At least one of us made it."

Framed by rugged red mountains, the Pulsar dissected the arid desert. Christina was taken by the jagged ravines and the never-ending presentation of mesas and buttes—all of it trucked in by Central Casting for just such occasions. A massive yellow and red billboard touted the TOMAHAWK INDIAN STORE, only "120 miles to go!" The sign jarred a memory about her mother, the dedicated history teacher, going head-to-head with the Belvidere school board regarding her lesson plan, one they thought veered radically from the orthodoxy of the American gospel. Darlene did not yield. Armed with Howard Zinn's *A People's History of the United States,* she continued to tell the truth about physical and cultural genocide. About continental land theft. The terror of slavery.

Oh yeah, Darlene was a soft-spoken flamethrower.

Maybe it was the theatrics of the surrounding landscape or possibly local spirits honoring Mom's courage. It could also be the giant cup of accelerant java she just polished off. Regardless of why, Darlene's lesson plan was flowing into Christina's consciousness like the Colorado surged into Lake Mead. Clarity felt good. She was remembering U.S. Army massacres like her own name: Skeleton Cave, Sand Creek, and of course Wounded Knee. Her Mom was a helluva teacher.

Then she remembered Iraq and her employment with the same company. "Fuck me." Clarity had been going so well. Christina downshifted behind a slow-moving 18-wheeler. She flipped on the radio, just like her white noise at night, hoping to quell the onslaught. The twangy voice declared, "Next up on the platter, Messrs. Willie Nelson and Bob Dylan, a duet they call 'Heartland.'" This plaintive country tune carried her well past Winslow.

> ♫ *There's a big achin' hole in my chest now*
> *Where my heart was*
> *And a hole in the sky where God used to be*

For the next one hundred miles, there were TOMAHAWK INDIAN STORE signs up the wazoo. Christina became enamored with this bigger-than-life souvenir shop boasting "Jewelry, Kachinas, Pottery. Indian Arts, Lowest Prices." Finally, just before I-40 crossed into New Mexico, there were giant tepees surrounded by a throng of ugly signs littering the landscape. Christina pulled over for a pee. A short time later, as another massive sign welcomed her to "The Land of Enchantment," there was a beautifully-feathered dreamcatcher hanging from the rearview mirror.

Purchased in honor of Darlene for having the guts to say NO.

She stopped for gas just east of Albuquerque, and by Santa Rosa, she was sick of eating Cheetos and chomping on Dentyne. Fifty-two miles later, behold: Tucumcari. The Pulsar cruised down the exit ramp, its driver famished for a proper meal. There was a decent-looking diner smack-dab on Route 66. Of course she pounded more coffee, and the diner's laminated menu spoke glowingly about their "famous blue corn pancakes." And for an additional fifty cents, the waitress offered "real" maple syrup. Christina smiled and went the distance: "Make it real."

Outside a crystal-clean window, there was a deep blue sky with wispy cloud formations framing a distant mesa. She swore she could hear Jaime's voice instructing her to "KEEP EATING!" She smiled when she caught herself gesturing, "I am, I am," as if someone was sitting in the booth with her. Self-conscious and sure that the eyes of Tucumcari were upon her, she glanced up, relieved that the coast was clear. Luckily the coffee was pretty good at this East Bumfuck Diner, so she settled back, opened the Trip-Tik and studied the next leg of her trip.

As advertised, the blue corn pancakes were yummy, deserving of the fifty-cent upgrade.

She pulled into Amarillo late in the afternoon; might as well call it early evening. Texas was hot as hell. She found another Best Western that looked clean and safe, at least from the street. And they had two excellent selling points: a pool and HBO. She rolled in.

Cletus, the young man checking her in, was not shy about checking her out. Most likely, he attended the recent Charlie Manson seminar on "How to Abduct Young Women & Chain Them in Your Basement." As always, Christina was gifted at quickly identifying a male's visual grope and then stealthily dodging their oafish advances. But this Texas boy, Christina thought, was overt in a way rarely seen. When he handed her the key to Room 120, his pelvis gently swayed, her clothes already tossed in a pile over on the floor. "Note to self," she mused, trying desperately not to laugh as she left the office, "Slide furniture in front of door."

Christina also decided to scratch swimming off her list when he called out, "Hey, Christine, I'm off in ten minutes. You like Cajun? Jambalaya? I know a place. On me." His Texas drawl working like a gag and puke trigger. She simply waved goodbye and never looked back.

Fifteen minutes later, she was walking toward a nearby grocery store to pick up some fruit and snacks for the room—HBO was playing *What's Eating Gilbert Grape.* She loved Johnny Depp. As she crossed the parking lot, she watched Cletus climb into the passenger seat of an old Chevy. It looked to be his mother driving. The duo pulled out into the steamy Lone Star dusk—and suddenly swimming was back on the schedule. Of course, right after the Grape family burns down the house.

Unfortunately, the peaceful night swimming never happened in muggy Amarillo. There was a visit to Room 120 that interrupted her plans.

The latest panic attack (one Christina would later classify in her journal as "heavy") was considerate enough to wait until the film's credits were rolling before unleashing itself on the unsuspecting Depp fan. If there was a silver lining, it was that the attack didn't last very long. With breathing and meditation, two techniques pushed hard at Peace House, Christina gained more and more experience in dealing with the attacks and flashbacks in real time.

The Amarillo episode was scary as hell—the desperate feeling of losing control of your mind, your body, and if you can identify your soul, then yeah, losing your soul. She immediately recognized the attack and began counterattack measures—not with equivalent angst and fury but with a calming and serene technique, one centered around a mantra chanted softly, slowly, eyes closed—then gradually gaining control, banishing the imps, sensing their retreat back into the murkiness. For now.

By 10:30pm, she considered her room clear, as if TV cops rushed in, guns drawn, yelling, "Clear, clear, all clear!"

She still had one other concern: Would Cletus return, asking for her hand in marriage? Nah, he's probably already whacked off two or three times. She was safe and looking forward to another well-earned silver lining: whenever she fought off a vicious attack, she'd sleep like the dead.

❖ ❖ ❖

Day 3: Amarillo, TX to Tulsa, OK to Rolla, MO

As the Pulsar chugged out of Amarillo, past Shamrock, then across morning in the Panhandle, the driver was vigilant and steadfast, taking on her next sprint through America. Although it didn't take long for Christina to figure out why the usually interesting Trip-Tik write-ups about passing sights and history suddenly went mind-numbingly insipid in "the Panhandle." Shit read like an owner's manual. At least yesterday, before she reached Amarillo, there was the Cadillac Ranch—an art installation that was cool and worth the half-hour stop. But this stretch of north Texas was nothing more than a geological blunder. She passed a Smokey Bear sign that categorized the current fire danger as "EXTREME." One thought came to mind: burn, baby burn.

Oklahoma City was a milestone. Trip-Tik said it was the halfway marker for her journey, and it was OKC where Christina would transition to

I-44, which ran northeast straight through Tulsa and Cherokee Nation. Torrents of rain, a fundamental midwestern rite of passage, slowed the Pulsar down on its way to Tulsa. But skies cleared rapidly as Christina passed into Cherokee terrain—a magnificent swathe of land that covered the entire northeastern chunk of the state. Once again, she figured the spirits were welcoming her in honor of Darlene's fidelity to the truth.

The initial plan was to reach St. Louis by nightfall, but the rain altered things, so she grabbed a sandwich in the tiny town of Afton, right off the interstate, and then found a quiet spot on the Neosho River to eat, meditate, and spacewalk for a while outside the command module. The earth felt good. And at least for now, the demons and imps were locked up in that Amarillo motel room, planning their blitzkrieg on Cletus the moment he opened the door. "JAMBALAYA!"

As she cut a path through Missouri, there was a blazing sunset unfolding behind her (thank god for rearview mirrors). And for Christina, that elusive clarity was suddenly by her side; beautiful didn't begin to describe this sunset as thoughts and memories crystalized in bunches—her face stunningly soft, tranquil, so at ease, her perfectly disheveled wavy black hair cavorting on the window breeze, her eyes as deep a blue as the manufacturer offered. But it was her smile that belonged to clarity as the epic sundown conjured up distant words, a spotlight on Sagan's brilliance that unified science and art:

> *It does no harm to the romance of the sunset*
> *to know a little about it.*

An hour later, Christina downshifted into the parking lot of a Howard Johnson's Motor Lodge in the town of Rolla, dirt deep in the Show Me State. The orange neon inviting to any traveler with a heartbeat. Best of all, the HoJo's restaurant was still open. More clarity: Her Dad used to love these iconic orange mainstays, anchored along America's highways.

"Hey, Dad, let's grab supper!"

❖ ❖ ❖

Day 4: Rolla, MO to Dayton, OH to Wheeling, WV

Christina left a wake-up call for 6:00am. Her arm reached out from under the jumble of blankets and sheets, lifted the receiver, offered a muffled "thank you," tried to return the receiver to its cradle, but it bounced away. The room's AC continued its incessant hum as she grabbed more sheets to cuddle with, trying to dodge the bright slash of sunlight that cut across the bed. It was warmth she sought and it was Jaime she wanted. That satisfying tangle of limbs negotiating space and comfort, seeking achievable perfection.

It seemed so long ago because it *was* so long ago. Buckets of time had passed without even contemplating sex, lust, fucking. But today, Christina woke up aroused, instantly realizing the oddity of her desire. She wanted Jaime, and this goddamned clarity was having its way with her.

The feeling grew. Christina couldn't believe what was raging through her body. She felt some of it beneath her ass and then on her fingers, her other hand roaming her breasts. Then harder. Jaime was with her, that one moment during senior year, just before graduation, in the Nguyen's basement, when they knew they'd be alone for the weekend, no sex cops looking to nab the dynamic duo. Christina even remembered what they were wearing, the feel of the fabric, the looseness, the tightness—and now their wardrobe was somehow magically gone, their sheer bodies and impatient touch playing out behind Christina's eyelids like projected memories on some Nickelodeon of the mind. She could feel the streak of sunlight warming her face—Jaime's tongue inside, Christina's tongue the same. Could she taste her? If it's possible, then yes. Heaven.

Tooling along I-44, and sipping takeout coffee, Christina giggled to herself, "Thank god those weren't my sheets." And now, with eighteen hundred miles under her belt, the Datsun's stick shift had become a natural extension of Christina's right arm. If need be, she could hit the seven hills of San Francisco—Lieutenant Frank Bullitt, downshifting that badass Mustang like a jet engine. She always thought it was out of character, but Jack MacKenzie loved McQueen's iconic film. Now it was her hand on the shifter, "Fucking Bullitt," she yelled, passing the red-green-and-yellow Mayflower truck.

In St. Louis, as Christina gallivanted over Twain's Mississippi, I-44 seamlessly transitioned to I-70, ushering fellow trekkers toward Indianapolis, Dayton, and finally to her sleep-time destination of Wheeling, West Virginia—which is, according to the Trip-Tik—"the nail capital of the world."

On this night, Christina was a returning member to the Orange Roof Fan Club—and wouldn't you know it, Triple-AAA gave the Wheeling HoJo's three diamonds. Bingo. No need to look any further as Lt. Bullitt pulled into the parking lot, excited to get a room, and then hit the restaurant.

❖ ❖ ❖

Road Trip (Part Two).

The gentleman who checked her in was a sweet elderly man. No Cletus in sight. She spotted an *Outdoor* magazine on a coffee table with a catchy title and setup:

EXCLUSIVE REPORT

LOST IN THE WILD

On April 28, 24-year-old Chris McCandless
walked off into America's Last Frontier hoping to make sense of his life.
Four months later he was dead. This is his story.

Christina asked if she could borrow their copy for the room. Homespun courtesy with a smile, "No problem, Miss MacKenzie. Enjoy." Over supper, she cracked open the article written by journalist Jon Krakauer. From the very first sentence, the story grabbed her like a hurricane.

> James Gallien had driven five miles out of Fairbanks when he spotted the hitchhiker standing in the snow beside the road, thumb raised high, shivering in the gray Alaskan dawn. A rifle protruded from the young man's pack, but he looked friendly enough; a hitchhiker with a Remington semiautomatic isn't the sort of thing that gives motorists pause in the 49th state. Gallien steered his four-by-four onto the shoulder and told him to climb in.

Back in her room, Christina crashed in bed and keenly absorbed the second half of Krakauer's piece; when she couldn't sleep, she scanned and read the entire article again: "Death of an Innocent: How Christopher McCandless Lost His Way in the Wilds." Like the author, Christina debated the young man's actions: Was her contemporary and fellow space traveler suicidal? Did he have a death wish when he dove headfirst into the brutishness of the Alaskan wilds? Or was the young man courageously exploring the mystery of death? What the author himself called a "swirling black vortex," as well as "shadowy" and "forbidden." Was Chris McCandless trying to save himself by unlocking this "fascinating riddle?"

Before she turned off the light, Christina had two thoughts: In the morning, she'd "accidentally" forget to return the magazine; and then, like every night on this trip, not unlike at home, she flipped on the clock radio and searched for a good signal, one to accompany slumber—luckily she found the dulcet voice of a nocturnal DJ, some cat probably buried like dolomite in the surrounding hills of West Virginia: "You know him as Ricky Ricardo from the old 'I Love Lucy' show or maybe because of the song 'Babalú'—but tonight, I know him as Desi Arnaz and His Orchestra. Here they are with a beautiful rendition of the ballad 'Good Night' as I also bid you a good night." Christina turned off the light.

> ♫ Good night... and darlin' seal it with a kiss
> I'll always want to think of this
> As just goodnight and not goodbye
> Good night... and when I go to sleep I'll pray
> That very soon they'll come a day
> We'll be together you and I...

❖ ❖ ❖

Day 5: Wheeling, WV to Hershey, PA to the Delaware River

The reliability of the Trip-Tik was never wrong: Just south of Pittsburgh, I-70 transitioned to I-76, and this picturesque Interstate cut straight through to the Delaware River. The borrowed *Outdoor* magazine sat on the passenger seat, along with Ms. MacKenzie's trusty Trip-Tik. No doubt a venerated position in this Japanese car that offered terrific gas mileage.

About an hour out of Harrisburg, Christina started seeing billboards that were yelling and screaming about famous Hershey, Pennsylvania:

HERSHEY—The Sweetest Place on Earth; HERSHEY—New Motor Lodge, Amusement Park, Resort Hotel; NOW HIRING! Sweet Opportunities at our Hazleton Plant; HERSHEY BEARS HOCKEY at the Hershey Sports Arena.

Christina remembered visiting Hershey three times: with Mrs. Goldberg's third grade class; with Jack & Darlene when she was probably twelve—they stayed the night and ate way too much chocolate; and then senior year in high school for a "Future Business Leaders" field trip. The crux of the trip was bullshit, but sneaking away with Jaime to get high behind Hershey's faux factory called "Chocolate World" and then trying to dissolve Hershey Kisses while making out was fucking awesome.

BRAKE LIGHTS! BRAKE LIGHTS!
DOWN SHIFT! DOWN SHIFT!
BRAKE! BRAKE! BRAKE!

After a grinding, heart-thumping, and sideways stop, there were maybe ten inches to spare between the Pulsar and a Buick LeSabre. Christina was gasping for breath. "Jesus." Then she laughed. The PA license plate she almost piled into announced: "You've Got a Friend in Pennsylvania."

By the time she passed King of Prussia, a northwest suburb of Philly, Christina was hollering at herself and her open bag of Kisses: "STOP EATING THESE THINGS! GO AWAY!"

Factor in the jumbo Coke and she could probably sprint to the Delaware.

She crossed the river at the Ben Franklin Bridge and then stopped for gas at an Amoco station in Cherry Hill, right where I-276 transitioned to I-95 North. As the guy pumped gas and then actually washed the windshields front and back, Christina flipped through her Trip-Tik: Damn, by the time she gets to the Jersey shore, she will have driven two-thousand-seven-hundred-and-seventy-five miles from Cloverfield in Santa Monica. Wow.

"Eleven dollars," reported the young Italian guy suddenly in her window with that "How you doin'?" look on his face. As she dug out the bills, he wondered, "Hershey Bears fan, huh?" For a second, Christina was lost but quickly remembered the cute t-shirt she just bought, giving gas guy a redemptive reason for rubbernecking her chest. "Yeah," she handed him the bills, "Go Bears."

Gas guy was rubbing his hands together like he was about to carve a Thanksgiving turkey. "You don't see California plates around here. You visiting?" She fired up the engine. "Just passing through. I'm actually from Jersey." He started laughing before he took his lame joke public, "Hey, yo, what exit?" She couldn't help but laugh at Don Juan's delivery, saw an opening in traffic, and then pounded the Pulsar into second-third-and-finally-fourth gear as she smoothly merged onto the crowded highway.

Earlier in the day, probably around Shanksville, Christina decided not to roll into Asbury Park late. Spend the night somewhere in Jersey and then approach Emerald City bright and early.

Back in Hershey, she called the U.S. Coast Guard Station in Atlantic City. They said sunrise the following morning was at 6:17am. Perfect, that was her plan—to finally watch Earth's closest star grandly rise over a proper ocean.

Who knows? Maybe there was just enough magic left in that rusty old town to change the course of one more river, especially around the hour of a new day.

&

27

Confluence.

The Rhône and Arve rivers do it in Geneva. In Illinois, the Ohio and Mississippi hook up together at Cairo. The Jialing and Yangtze rivers in Chongqing, China. As do the Rio Negro and Rio Solimões rivers in the Brazilian city of Manaus. All of these examples represent "confluence"— the joining of two or more waterways. This merging of H_2O indicates the point where a tributary might join a larger river and then together continue on as the main stem, or it could denote where two smaller rivers or streams intersect and then upgrade to a big-time river with a brand-new name. Such is the case in Pittsburgh, where the Monongahela and Allegheny rivers join forces to create the now toxic and incredibly polluted Ohio River.

Some folks may see these geologic bumps as evolutionary chaos and/or haphazard collisions. But oftentimes in life, the confluence of human energy forms a uniquely emotional union—one that's possibly meant to be.

5:11am.

It was still dark when Christina pulled out from the Hampton Inn, just off the Interstate. She headed east on I-195, dissecting the Garden State like a blade slicing an eggplant in two. Her plan was to beat the Sun— and if Julian's car didn't break down, the race was in the bag. She drove through rural farmland that defined central Jersey, although she couldn't see much of anything in the passing darkness.

Somewhere along this early morning trek, Christina started to feel strange. About finally arriving. All across the country, she anticipated an exciting touchdown in Asbury Park. Her hope against hope was that this old boardwalk town might hold some elusive key to her recovery, familiar ghosts on the road to reclaiming what a French philosopher once termed her "élan vital." Or at least the visit might assist in these elusive endeavors.

Jaime had made this abundantly clear.

As an Exxon sign glinted in the distance, Christina (as she often does) summoned Jack & Darlene, contemplating those days and weeks wandering up and down the Jersey Shore, comfortable in their nomadic tendencies, Asbury Park, their home away from home. Why was Belvidere still even in their mix? Duh, she thought—long-standing tenured jobs? She laughed to herself, "Hello?" The shore memories swirled.

She passed a bright McDonald's sign that was fighting hard against the oncoming dawn just to remain relevant. As she blew past the 24-hour poison dispensary (Billions and Billions Served), Christina killed the last of her weak and now ice-cold coffee, still fixated on those frenetic memories, bits & pieces knocking together like bumper cars. "What was the allure? It was the seventies and eighties, the town way past its glory years." And it was weird, too, because she distinctly remembered her mother and father acting like it was still Asbury Park circa 1950. But even when Christina morphed into a know-it-all teenager, she still thought it was kind of sweet, Jack & Darlene's warm embrace of a dying history, a town waiting for a bed in hospice.

5:55am.

The morning light began to reveal the passing communities as I-195 gave way to local roads, ushering the California Datsun into the sleepy shoreside community of Wall Township. Christina would follow her Trip-Tik as far as the Asbury Park Boardwalk. That's where the nice lady at Triple-AAA ended the journey—where Christina would officially run out of land. Dawn continued to unfold, but she still had plenty of time.On Route 35, a few landmarks looked familiar; then she remembered a road that ran along the beach for a while. She recalled large and stately beachfront homes. "Head toward the water," she told herself, "You'll find it."

The streets were empty as she made a beeline east, the Datsun off the Trip-Tik, but no matter—she ran right into Ocean Ave, as anticipated, and then hung a left, knowing the Boardwalk was north. Her memory was intact: The stately homes still faced the ocean. She tooled along the deserted streets, the towns passing quickly. Belmar, Avon-by-the-Sea, Bradley Beach, and then she spotted a familiar landmark, thinking, "There's that damn sign, 'God's Square Mile at the Jersey Shore.' I hate that sign." Christina tapped the steering wheel, remembering how the MacKenzie threesome thought Ocean Grove was a foolish little town, her Dad preaching to the choir, "full of religious nutjobs, zealots."

Zealots.

She always hated that word. Just like bulbous, fester, and phlegm. "What were Mom's? Oh yeah: maggots, mucus, and jowls." For some reason, Dad always said, "Tinker to Evers to Chance." At first, Christina had no idea what he meant, but Darlene waved him off, explaining, "It's an old poem about baseball. He's nuts." Jack fired right back, "Nuts, my ass, it's a great poem!"

And then fifteen-year-old Christina was left dumbfounded when her Dad soared to new heights, reciting the limerick with gusto as he drove, his arm accentuating like a maestro:

> *These are the saddest of possible words:*
>   *"Tinker to Evers to Chance."*
> *Trio of bear cubs, and fleeter than birds,*
>   *"Tinker and Evers and Chance."*
> *Ruthlessly pricking our gonfalon bubble,*
>   *Making a Giant hit into a double—*
> *Words that are heavy with nothing but trouble:*
>   *"Tinker to Evers to Chance."*

From the backseat, the teenager wondered, "What the heck is a gonfalon???"

6:07am.

Christina beat the rising Sun to the south end of the Boardwalk. She circled around the narrow lake and then had no problem finding a parking spot—right on the corner of Asbury Ave and Kingsley Street. By the looks of this desolation row, it was probably tougher to find parking on the Moon.

There it was—the Boardwalk, right in front of her. "Am I really here?"

When she stepped out of the car, boom, she was face-to-face with that giant creepy clown, his mug painted twice on the decomposing green wall of Palace Amusements. She fumbled through her memory, "What's his name? Or is it a her? So fucking strange. Oh shit, TILLIE! Tillie. What is that fucking thing?" And it looked so much weirder than she remembered. Hell, add "Tillie" to bulbous, fester, and phlegm.

As she moved across Kingsley and up on the famed Boardwalk, she could see Convention Hall and the Paramount Theatre looming in the distance, the edifice brushed with a bluish morning light. She glanced toward the ocean, "It's right there." Another icon called her: the strikingly ornate Carousel House with the amazing merry-go-round she loved so much. She wandered up to the huge windows, now clouded with grime. Christina peeked inside. "Holy shit!" Stone-cold empty. Long gone were the flamboyant prancing horses. As were the guts of the adjacent Casino, famous for those crazy bumper cars, beguiling arcade games, and her favorite: creepy and spooky rides—Christina hanging on to Jack & Darlene for dear life. In disbelief, she mumbled, "Stone-cold empty. Jesus."

She wandered the empty Boardwalk and how weird the sense memory: the angled planks felt the same under her feet; her Dad explained they were "chevroned" or designed like a V. She strolled past the 1st Avenue Pavilion, wandering to the railing that faced Europe. She couldn't remember feeling so alone—not lonely, but like a shipwrecked Robinson Crusoe or the last astronaut stranded on America's first Mars expedition, the others devoured alive by slithering green creatures.

6:16am.

Christina was faced with a very strange truth: this place, this surrogate Emerald City, was beautiful and ugly in equal measures. Look there! Grandeur and brilliance. But look over here—defiled and pure dereliction. One moment glimmers of glory, hints of pageantry; a nanosecond later? Crumbling reality. Christina could feel ghosts dancing everywhere. Not in some mystic woo-woo kind of way, just a pragmatic salutation to those still existing between the ages, specters that weren't good or evil, angels or demons. Just spirits watching time disappear.

6:17am.

As per usual, the U.S. Coast Guard nailed it. Orange flames broke past the watery horizon right on cue.

Christina had witnessed many a sunrise in her twenty-plus years, but they simply didn't compare to the one exploding on this late August morning, nineteen hundred and ninety-four: stoic lakes of blue sky, streaks of pink and purple cut through shifting clouds, burnt orange billows and graphite swirls. And then the magnificence offered its crescendo—a sweeping surge of orange, a carpet of light unfurling over the Atlantic and then the empty massive beach; the painted sunlight coursing right up to Christina's feet and beyond.

Maybe it was the ghosts, and why not? What else would explain the freaky and motley assemblage of characters that flashed between the flaming orange ball and Christina's brain: Jack & Darlene & Jaime, Ricky from Starbucks, Julian, Munchkin, the guy with cinders for eyes, only now he was alive and smiling and whole, so was Ron Kovic sans his wheelchair, the gang from Peace House—Doc, Geena, Bags, Danny, Hank, Molly, and the big dude with the prosthetic arm, except now his arm was flesh and blood and waving high over his head.

For one bright shining moment, this was indeed Emerald City, in all its used-to-be luster, its ability to arouse spectacle. Or maybe it was just a strangely constructed flashback. No matter, Christina loved it, she was in awe.

6:26am.

The Boardwalk was getting brighter as this primo sunrise began to wash toward Allentown, Pittsburgh, and all points west. A friendly male voice from about ten yards away seemed directed at Christina:

"Close your eyes and tap your heels three times."

Christina didn't turn around immediately, thinking, "Was that real?" When she turned, it sure as hell was real—spoken by a middle-aged guy with long bleached-blond hair. He smiled and gave a little wave. He was sporting a bright yellow and green Hawaiian shirt.

He tried again, "Good morning."

She smiled, "Good morning," but was still curious, "What did you just say?"

He thought for a second, "Oh, 'Close your eyes, tap your heels three times.' You know, 'Wizard of Oz.'"

She was still smiling but confused, "Why?"

He pointed to her feet, "You're wearing those red shoes."

She looked down. Red Converse. "Oh, my sneakers."

He nodded, "Yeah, like ruby slippers. I know it's a stretch. Another failed attempt at being witty."

Christina waved gently, "I've heard worse. Did you see that sunrise?"

He looked past her for a moment, "Strange how the beauty sort of disappears when it comes ashore. At least in this neck of the woods." He moved a few steps away with that hitch in his giddy-up, "Excuse me, I have my exercises. Nice talking with you."

Christina shyly offered, "There's no place like home."

He started stretching, "How's that?"

She repeated louder, "There's no place like home."

He smiled and pointed at her, "Good one."

Christina began walking toward Convention Hall as this strange-looking but sweet man started his jumping jacks. The closer she walked toward the grandiose structure, this boardwalk monument, the more she began to focus on its gorgeous doorways with rustic green trim. Darlene called it something weird, but the word was long gone. Then she heard the exercising man yell out—

"Fifty-five!"

28

Check-in.

The place was exactly as Christina remembered—that is, if you don't count a century's worth of decay and decomposition that befell this town in only a few short years. Minute by minute, her heartwarming memories were being smashed by a dystopian sledgehammer. It was like ambling through the skeletal remains of some bombed-out Iraqi town. The irony wasn't lost on Christina. But then she would spot a landmark that looked exactly like it did back in the day, like Madam Marie's "Temple of Knowledge"—the old concrete shack with its eerie all-seeing eyeball nudged up against the hand-painted psychic menu on Marie's side wall:

"READINGS | TAROT CARD | CRYSTAL BALL"

But damn, that giant eyeball!

She was hungry as hell (KEEP EATING!) and looking forward to breakfast but meandered along the Boardwalk a bit longer, milking the epic sunrise for every last photon, figuring these were the minutes that Asbury Park looked its Sunday best. And if the town was haunted (as some folks whispered), then the ghosts were probably enjoying this moment of Zen, a well-earned breather from the full-time stench of entropy. Before she turned back, she soaked in one more look at Convention Hall and its historic Paramount Theatre (if walls could sing). But Christina's glance was ill-timed as the sunrise quickly withered, giving way to the day's harsh bright light, revealing not a grandiose monument, as she first mused, but a tombstone.

And then bang, like a dart of lightning from god knows where: "PATINA"—that's what her mother called the bronze-turned-green filigree on Convention Hall. *Patina.* The idiosyncratic element that intimates another world.

As she headed back to the car, she passed the exercising man now walking north with his rummy gait. She flashed a quick wave. He smiled easy, "See ya later, Dorothy. Be good." Christina thought the Dorothy reference was cute, but then after a few steps she glimpsed back, thinking, "See ya later? Sounded like he meant it."

❖ ❖ ❖

Christina ventured out for breakfast. Her Triple-AAA tour book suggested a few area eateries, including a diner out on Route 35—one of those main shore highways that dissect business hubs from Red Bank to Seaside. But first she had to navigate two of those infamous traffic circles that dot the Jersey landscape. Hell, it was a piece of cake for this former? current? Jersey Girl, holding second gear rock-solid. When she pulled up to the quaint "Johnny Be Goode Diner," her memory flashcards registered something but nothing concrete. The diner was one of those faux train-car-looking joints; this one covered in muted corrugated steel with dark gold trim and a bright red roof that stretched over an obvious expansion. There was a large neon-green treble clef that pointed down to the front door.

The interior of this classic Jersey diner was adorned with rock 'n roll paraphernalia that hung everywhere: old guitars, keyboards, and pieces from various drum kits. The fakakta décor was also dedicated to the various musicians that covered the diner's celebrated namesake: "Johnny B. Goode"—Elvis, The Beatles, Bill Haley and the Comets, The Beach Boys, The Grateful Dead, Judas Priest, Johnny Winter, Jimi, et cetera. The vinyl 45s and album covers adorned the walls. There was only one item missing: a St. Louis gentleman by the name of Charles Edward Anderson Berry, arguably the "Father of Rock 'n Roll." He was only the author of the damn song. Must have been an oversight.

Luckily, Christina didn't fly from Los Angeles because the culture shock of immediately walking into this Jersey diner may have short-circuited her already tenuous connection to reality. In fact, her cross-country trek was a perfect decompression chamber. They say "people are people" no matter where they're from. That might be nice for Hallmark cards and dime store novels, but as Christina gazed around from her comfy red booth, she quickly realized she had entered *The Twilight Zone* and Mr. Serling was nowhere in sight.

Wow, was she away from Jersey that long? Or maybe it had something to do with evolution? Or the lack thereof. She wasn't sure. Did the infamous boardwalk fun house move their freak show to the Johnny Be

Goode? Regardless, there was enough material here to feed comedians and anthropologists for years. The owner behind the ancient register looked and sounded like Buddy Hackett, wore multicolored suspenders and a tweed newsboy hat. The slew of waitresses were all costumed in 1950s car-hop outfits and were clearly bused in from the same decade. Layer cakes and pies were presented in a slowly rotating display case—monster creations the size of Buicks.

And then there were the customers. Holy cow.

Christina didn't want to be judgmental, but there was no other way to put it: They were all incredibly odd, or, as the Romans would say, "sui generis" (of its own kind). Like the Edsel: one-off prototypes, not designed for human interaction outside of Monmouth and Ocean counties. In fact, an alarm would sound if these villagers crossed the border, notifying all proper authorities.

The multitudes lured "down the Jersey Shore"—locals and visitors—were mostly refugees from the Newark/New York metro area, a few from Philly, as well as various outliers hailing from parts unknown. The older retired folks remained low profile—hit the bakery in the AM, post office before lunch, buy some halibut to grill, play a little gin rummy, and then thoroughly enjoy a sunset over Barnegat Bay. The doctors all accepted Medicare.

For the most part, the middle-aged population were seasonal visitors: families that rented for the summer—beach all day, barbecue anything that didn't move, and then it was miniature golf and ice cream under the stars. By Labor Day, they all headed back to their "little boxes on the hillside, little boxes made of ticky tacky"—those storage containers that all looked the same, in places with names like Livingston, Piscataway, Paramus, and Mahwah; all of them trying desperately not to screw the pooch.

The younger demographic stuck out like a giant infected boil perched on a baby's ass. The young ladies usually characterized as "pizza queens," the young men as "Nicky Newarkers." Of course these were stereotypes, and most folks like Christina knew they were stereotypes, but damn if those stereotypes weren't hanging out on every corner and burning to a crisp on every beach. The car of choice for most young ladies was the Chevy Camaro, although it was considered a minor miracle if they managed to wedge all of their hair inside the vehicle. The guys were either chiseled gym rats or blubber boys who thought they looked like chiseled gym rats. Christina figured this diner must be a vortex, some magnetized clubhouse for all of the above. She laughed to herself, thinking Hollywood ought to capture this zoo for a TV show.

For C-Mac, growing up in Belvidere, the cloistered northwest corner of the state, was as different (from these folks) as different can be. Couple her New England Yankee upbringing with her recent days in the yoga canyons of Topanga, and it became obvious that she had nothing in common with her fellow diners. Sprinkle in Iraq, prosthetic arms & legs, shrapnel bloodbaths, as well as heavy doses of K-Pin (Klonopin) and Tranks (Lorazepam), and it's no surprise that Christina was her own special kind of outlier.

Forget those Mom & Pop vacation days that embraced some bygone era; this part of Jersey was as familiar to her as the shrouded lava plains of Venus.

It wasn't by accident that her *Outside* magazine tagged along to the diner. It was like some weird crutch, reminding her that she too was an outsider, an interloper that just didn't fit in. Christina didn't want to be obsessed with the McCandless story, but that ship had sailed: She was totally gripped—and the more she pondered Chris' fate as well as his motives, the more fixated she became. She stared at the cover. Was it depression and suicide? Or was he trying to live out some Jack London-Last Frontier fantasy? Maybe he was just pathetically stupid and ill-prepared? Or maybe, maybe, this young man, who used two names, was actually schizophrenic? He left D.C. as Chris McCandless, then became Alex, and then finally morphed into Alexander Supertramp.

Or was the boy just a heroic seeker? A mutineer reckoning with the fact that freedom's just another word for yada yada yada? If so, were his actions a rallying cry? At this point, she didn't want to open the magazine. McCandless was hitting too close to home. Were the pages inside a scary reflection? Or maybe an invitation for her to join the club. "Dear Christina..."

She was momentarily saved by Doris: a beehive hairdo with a waitress standing below. "What's kickin' little chicken?" Doris plopped down in the booth opposite Christina, who was grinning from ear to ear.

"Good morning, Doris."

The waitress threw her head back and sighed, "Sunshine, I've been on my feet since five. Even if that fella Burt Reynolds walked in here right now and needed old Doris to throw him a shot, I'd have to pass him your way."

Christina tapped Doris' hand, "I might do you that favor."

Doris smiled, "Oh, he'd like you. What's for breakfast, sweetie?" Christina ordered orange juice, oatmeal, and coffee.

Her food was out in a flash. Doris dropped off the OJ and coffee, and then a minute later, a huge steaming bowl of oatmeal with all the fixings. "Enjoy, sweetie," Doris winked as the beehive receded into the loud and lively diner.

As Christina mixed her oatmeal, she watched two young guys in the parking lot argue over a fender bender. And now a third guy felt compelled to interject himself into the fray. Christina smiled, remembering when she and Jaime watched a similar tête-à-tête that actually led to fisticuffs outside Yum Yum Donuts on Pico. Jaime quipped, "Look, it's like dinner and a show. Hit 'em with the left!" Christina scooped up some oatmeal and offered Jaime a silent missive: "See, I'm still eating... and I got my ass to Asbury Park."

❖ ❖ ❖

According to her Triple-AAA lodging book, the Sea Breeze Hotel was still in business, although it only received one diamond, which meant it was barely "approved." Not exactly a glowing endorsement, but at least it wasn't the dreaded zero diamonds. She tossed the book aside, thinking, "Just go check it out."

Back in the day, the Sea Breeze was their inn of choice. Christina figured the MacKenzies stayed here at least four or five times.

She drove slowly down 1st Avenue, as if sneaking up on the place might make a difference. Sure enough, there was the familiar Catholic Church in all its solemn heaviness. In the church courtyard, a little girl rode her bike in loopy circles. Free as a bird, not a care in the world. And there it was—the Sea Breeze, a large Victorian structure, most likely a wealthy family's prominent home decades before. The main dark aqua color enhanced the architectural brawn, while the windows outlined in a cream white lent character to the old place. Christina remembered playing on the massive front porch with all those colorful rocking chairs.

The Datsun crawled to a stop right in front. "It doesn't look too bad," she thought, peering through her musty window. "Triple-AAA can't possibly know everything." She decided to go inside, see what's what. And similar to the Boardwalk experience earlier, walking up to the Sea Breeze, with its wood-carved sign on the front lawn, was as close to time travel as one might get.

The stairs creaked as she stepped up on the porch. She took a moment, took a deep breath, and then opened the large, heavy door with stained glass. Can you remember smells? She wasn't sure, but the small lobby offered a haunting scent. Not good or bad, more like if history had an aroma.

A short, pleasant woman, pushing eighty, sat at a semi-cluttered desk. Her greeting was probably said a million times, yet she still managed to keep it warm, "Welcome to the Sea Breeze." Christina told the innkeeper about staying here as a kid and then a teenager. Times past seemed to matter to the woman. Christina said she was in town for a few days and needed a place, "Could I see a room? One with a window on the street. I think that's what we had."

On their way to the second floor, which was somewhat laborious for the older woman, she asked Christina about her family, where they were from, what years they were here. Christina filled her in as best she could, but nothing seemed to land. "I don't remember much these days. My husband passed two years ago. I think he took most of the memories with him," she giggled.

At the landing, she took a deep breath and introduced herself, "I'm Millie, by the way."

"Hi Millie, I'm Christina."

Millie unlocked the door and they moved inside. As requested, Room 204 overlooked the street. As she glanced around, Christina was pleasantly surprised. It wasn't the Waldorf, but one Triple-AAA diamond was patently unfair. The room was clean and proper. Nicely furnished. Maybe a tad rundown, but no big deal. The hardwood floors were handsome, but more importantly, the bathroom was clean. Old but clean. Millie mentioned how difficult the upkeep was getting and maybe if business picked up she'd hire someone to scrub and paint, "maybe buy some newer furniture over at the swap meet."

Christina pooh-poohed Millie's contrition, telling her how much she liked the Sea Breeze.

"You're sweet," Millie said, "A good fibber to save an old lady's feelings. But sweet as pie. Probably just like your mom and dad. Is fifty dollars a night okay?"

"That's great," Christina said, gazing out the large picture window that overlooked the entirety of the church and its grounds. A group of older folks crossed through the courtyard while the same little girl (seen before) pedaled away from Christ the King, heading toward the not-too-distant boardwalk and beach.

The trees began rustling with gusto. The 1st Avenue corridor must shepherd the airstream west. Good name, Sea Breeze, makes sense.

Downstairs at the front desk, Millie asked Christina to sign in with her full name and address. As Christina obliged, Millie told her that tea was available all day, just ask, "And this isn't official Sea Breeze policy, but if you'd like to join me for breakfast, I'd be more than happy. Waffles tomorrow. Eight o'clock." Christina finished writing, "That's very nice, thank you."

Millie turned the book around, "California? I don't think we've ever hosted a guest from California." Millie adjusted her glasses, making sure she read it right, "Santa Monica." Millie handed her the room key, "Welcome, Christina MacKenzie, you're all checked in."

જી

CHRISTINA and the WHITEFISH

29
Ole Stumpy.

I DON'T BELIEVE in angels.

Heaven? Not in the manufactured or infantile way that religious con men have bamboozled the gullible.

A peaceful afterlife? If peace is not having to put up with this shit, sure, why not.

Hell? Definitely not.

Is there inherent goodness in human nature? Absolutely.

Is there inherent evil in human nature? Also, absolutely... probably times ten. Especially considering the abject horrors I've seen.

But early on this very morning, sunrise to be exact, I left the club for my morning calisthenics, followed by my vigorous hike up to Allenhurst and back. And rarely, if ever, have I been waylaid by anything: inclement weather, crazed lunatics wanting a piece of me, or even another cruise ship grounding itself ashore, which, as you know, happens here every so often. In fact, we're probably due for another.

I can only think of two incidents that canceled my morning cardiovascular.

During the first days of my tenure on the Boardwalk, I happened upon a skinhead spray-painting a swastika on the front of my club. At first, he didn't see me. But then this Nazi cocksucker got a really good look at the Whitefish as I brought a snow shovel down on his bald fucking head. Twice, as I recall. I swung that Sears Craftsman like Paul Bunyan. At first I thought I killed the bastard. But when I returned after calling the cops, Himmler was long gone, although he left his red Rust-Oleum behind.

The second incident involved a beautiful young naked woman prancing and pirouetting across the planks. Shit, I thought I died and went to heaven (now that's a heaven I can believe in). But then I spotted a camerawoman poised behind her 16mm movie camera locked on a tripod. Clearly she was creating art – the juxtaposition of human form against nature's magic. She yelled "cut" and then ran out with a blanket to cover her subject. She spotted me when I said, "Good morning." We started chatting by her camera, an Arriflex that I remember seeing in Southeast Asia. She was a filmmaker from Bucks County, PA, with a grant from some New York museum. Then she had a brainstorm – would I like to be in the next shot? I said, "Fuck yeah."

So the filmmaker (her name was Mercedes) gives me some direction, and she's swearing like a sailor. I loved it: "You enter from behind camera and then walk right here... you stop, you're mesmerized... Holy fucking shit, there's a naked nymph dancing right on your goddamn boardwalk. What the fuck, right? And then you take a really good look at those tits."

Mercedes runs to the railing, gesturing like crazy, "But then you see this fucking thing – this fucking sunrise – and whoa, no shit, that's an awesome fucking sunrise. And now you have to make a choice: either eyeball the nymph like you wanna grope the living shit out of her... or, OR... you get lost in the unadulterated balls-to-the-wall crazy-great sunrise." And then Mercedes says the choice was mine. "If you want the nymph, you gotta look at her like she's a goddamn steak sandwich... you're intoxicated and it's fucking carnal... and then after a few seconds, you just start dancing with her, go with the flow, she'll lead. But, BUT... if you pick the sunrise, forget the nymph, fuck her... just go straight to the fucking railing because you're awestruck by nature's epic beauty – and c'mon, tits are a dime a dozen." Then she pokes me: "And remember, stay in the moment until you hear me yell cut. That's important."

She pulls me back toward the camera, "C'mon, let's do this, we're fighting the goddamn Sun. Miriam, first position!"

I must be a natural, like Pacino or Lee Marvin, because I nailed it. One take... and then we quickly shot what she called "reactions and inserts." Mercedes seemed genuinely pleased and wanted to pay me. I said, "Fuck that, come on in for a breakfast beer. Guinness is rich in iron and good for the heart."

Two months later, she gives me a call, says her short film is "looping" in some exhibit at the Whitney or the Guggenheim – some fucking New York mausoleum. I never did see the thing. But the experience was good enough. So when you see him, tell Mr. DeMille that I'm still ready for my close-up.

Oh, you're probably wondering if I chose the naked nymph or the sunrise. I'll leave that up to you.

But today, on this morning, there was a vision that just bowled me over. And like I said, I don't believe in angels. But if an angel ever did show up, this particular young woman would be the archetype. Please call Betty in Central Casting, tell her "bravo" on sending over this celestial being. And at this point, I hadn't even seen her face yet. No matter because between the red sneakers, the cut-off jean shorts, the gossamer white hippie blouse, and then her magnificent thick black hair...

Well, George Harrison said it best:

My Sweet Lord.

But-but-but, but – I haven't even told you the good part: She was literally glowing in the sunrise. No, I mean seriously glowing. Much better than the nymph. And friends, let me tell you, I've seen a shitload of Asbury Park sunrises in my life, and I ain't never seen one like this.

Excuse my parlez-vous francais, but this was a motherfucking painting, very similar to that sunrise Monet painted in the Port of Le Havre.

And believe you me, this wasn't some sexual thing. Put it back in your pants, Slick Willie. This was exactly what Mercedes was trying to create, except in my version it was organic, not staged – and it was more powerful than hers because now the human form and nature were one, the handiwork of the same creative genius. Cohesive and coalesced. See the difference? It doesn't have to be a choice.

Then something remarkable happened:

I literally watched this angel push up on her toes and click her heels together. Like Dorothy in that fucking "Wizard of Oz." All the while staring into this exploding rebirth of a new day. Something formidable had to be spinning inside this young woman's head.

Now, you may be thinking that I'm overstating the drama of this brief vision – well, I'm not. And if you do, you're a bunch of heathens and infidels.

So let me put it to you this way:

If Mahalia Jackson stood by my side... and then Jesus himself jumped down off that cross and allowed his spirit to sing thunderously through her glorious pipes - and what the hell, add in Gabriel's trumpet signaling the Lord's return... that's how fucking A-1 perfect this moment was... Can you dig it?

Unfortunately, I broke the moment when I said something stupid like "Close your eyes and tap your heels three times." You know, the Dorothy trope. The young woman turned slowly, probably wondering, "Who's this jackass bothering me?" And then I saw her face.

In that instant... I wanted to be whole again.

I wanted to be who I was in '66. Before the war, before my gonads were launched all over the Central Highlands of Vietnam. Before I lost my innocence, a lot of my hair, as well as my looks.

And most definitely before I walked like Walter Brennan, "Ole Stumpy."

Me and the kid, we exchanged some pithy small talk, and then she tied a nice ribbon on my inane Dorothy from Oz bullshit, saying, "There's no place like home."

Smart kid.

#

30

Strawberries & Waffles.

For those first few hours of navigating life in Asbury Park, Room 204 at the Sea Breeze became a sanctuary, safe harbor caressed by the soft, dappled light shifting through the trees. There was a wonderful old high-back chair and a beautifully beat-to-hell ottoman that had tolerated a thousand feet. Christina positioned both pieces near the large picture window that faced the brooding church. For the next chunk of hours, this porthole framed her entire world. The church, not unlike the small white church back on the VA's property, was becoming a lodestone for this girl-daughter-woman—now an angel?—searching for her recently misplaced Holy Grail.

The church was built with massive and rugged reddish-brown stone and resembled a miniature cathedral. One large central spire with a bronze cross was surrounded by four smaller and obedient spires. Three ground floor archways offered sinners easy access to the Kingdom of God. Each portico supported by what looked to be stone-carved saints extending their arms in welcome and peace. And above the portals, on the front face of the structure, was a massive circular stained-glass window fronted by ornate and delicate lattice work—swirling geometric shapes that Christina found hypnotic. She could hear Darlene's description, saying that this matrix "suggested totality, timelessness, and of course God, the original circle whose center is everywhere and whose circumference is nowhere."

Oh, Mom. Your grasp of divine architecture is scary. Not to mention tax-free.

The church and adjacent courtyard were surrounded by what looked to be maple and oak trees that extended symmetrically along 1st Avenue. No doubt, Christina thought, Darlene would have loved this quaint papal outpost, probably identifying the painter best suited to capture its "New Englandy" essence. Her mother would think for a moment, as if flipping through her mind's Rolodex, and then announce with absolute certainty,

"Childe Hassam. American impressionist. Reminds me of his 'Church at Gloucester.' Look him up."

Christina watched life unfold outside her window. Two young nuns left the church grounds and were walking somewhere in lockstep—maybe on a mission? Hopefully escaping. The image reminded her of that book she read with Jaime, *The Handmaid's Tale.* Sinister as hell. Then a plumbing truck pulled up to the house flanking the church, probably the rectory. A greasy plumber emerged carrying his toolbox to the front door and rang the bell. A cop on a motorcycle headed east, followed by a garbage truck heading west. An old woman let the plumber inside. And then what was becoming a recurring image: the same little girl on her bike, only now she rode straight past the church, west, away from the Boardwalk and ocean—and she was definitely on a mission. Christina smiled; boy could that girl pedal!

A few minutes passed as if life outside was put on pause. Or maybe she dozed off. But then a young priest emerged from the church—handsome and All-American. He lit his cigarette like James Dean and strolled the courtyard, blowing smoke rings skyward, maybe sharing his fragility with the Lord. A fat man walked a small dog who started pissing on a tree. Christina also kept an eye on Julian's Datsun parked below, remembering her trek across thy fruited plain. The young, handsome priest finished his smoke, flicking his butt into the gutter before heading back inside. "A damn litterbug. C'mon, padre."

A cool breeze kicked up. The side windows in the room—both small, both open—invited the current to ebb and flow. The air was good-natured, especially for late August in New Jersey. Christina felt safe and protected.

When she woke an hour later, C-Mac felt like she'd been asleep for several hours. She decided to take Millie up on that cup of tea.

"I have chamomile and Earl Grey," Millie smiled. Christina browsed a bookshelf while Millie made the tea behind a curiously hanging tapestry that led to another room. She didn't recognize the first few novels. There were also dusty books on architecture, gardening, chess, classic cars, a world atlas, a baseball almanac, three Bibles, and two large books on the Hudson River School of Painting. Finally, a novel she did recognize, *Pride and Prejudice.* She pulled it from the stack. She'd read it in high school. Great characters, especially Elizabeth, or Lizzy, the protagonist; she couldn't remember her last name. Fearless and feisty. Smart, too— and Lizzy tamed that rich, pompous guy. "It's Bennet! That was her last name."

"Here you go. Earl Grey."

Christina slipped the book back on the shelf, "'Pride and Prejudice.' Jane Austen. I loved it." Christina wasn't expecting a delicate tray supporting a flowered china teapot with a matching cup and saucer. There was even a plate with three butter cookies. Millie handed her the tray, "I should get around to reading that book. I've been remiss to say the least."

Christina returned to her window view and enjoyed the afternoon tea and cookies. She perused the McCandless article once again, focusing on the sections she circled with a yellow marker that she "borrowed" in Amarillo. How civilized, she thought. Afternoon tea and stories of suicide, very British.

Alaska has long been a magnet for unbalanced souls, often outfitted with little more than innocence and desire…

McCandless tramped around the West for the next two months, spellbound by the scale and power of the landscape, thrilled by minor brushes with the law, savoring the intermittent company of other vagabonds he met along the way…

The butter cookies were amazing. Did Millie make these?

McCandless's last postcard to Westerberg fueled widespread speculation, after his adventure did prove fatal, that he'd intended suicide from the start, that when he walked into the bush alone he had no intention of ever walking out again…

Starvation is not a pleasant way to die. In advanced stages, as the body begins to consume itself… Some who have been brought back from the far edge of starvation, though, report that near the end their suffering was replaced by a sublime euphoria, a sense of calm accompanied by transcendent mental clarity. Perhaps, it would be nice to think, McCandless enjoyed a similar rapture…

Darlene's favorite tea was Earl Grey. Christina preferred coffee, the darker and bolder the better; her stint at Starbucks solidified that preference. And with coffee, she'd be dunking these butter cookies by now. Jaime also loved to dunk. Christina giggled, remembering when Jaime dunked a cheeseburger into her Coke. Christina called her a Philistine, so Jaime kept on dunking with a feisty defiance. (Ha! Like Lizzy Bennet.)

But here, in the delicate embrace of refined living, Earl Grey was quite nice. What's that flavor that enhances Earl Grey? Oh, yeah, "ber-ga-mot." Bergamot oil. Darlene also knew a lot about tea.

One of his last acts was to take a photograph of himself, standing near the bus under the high Alaskan sky, one hand holding his final note toward the camera lens, the other raised in a brave, beatific farewell. He is smiling in the photo, and there is no mistaking the look in his eyes: Chris McCandless was at peace, serene as a monk gone to God.

Such a confounding story. But one thing was for sure: the journalist was a superior writer.

Christina brought the tray downstairs and thanked Millie for the unexpected treat. The innkeeper was sweeping the floor, happy to see her young guest, "You can put that anywhere, sweetie." Christina asked, "Would you mind if I borrowed a book?"

The light in the room was changing. No doubt sundown. The day was long, productive, and she was in for the night. For an old bed, it was surprisingly comfortable. Christina huddled with her sheets up against the headboard. She was a few pages into *Pride and Prejudice*. (She loved feeling like it was 1813.) The bedside lamp offered just enough light, and the windows offered a necessary breeze as well as a distant hum.

As she turned the page, she noticed an odd piece of furniture up against the wall. Curious, she climbed out of bed, "What is this?" She flicked on the small lamp under a frilly lampshade that sat on top of this strange box with legs. Oh, it's a radio. Shit. How old is this thing? Tuning dial, small knobs. Then out loud, "RCA Victor." So weird—all this furniture for an AM radio? She turned what looked like the main knob, CLICK, and whaddayaknow, there was STATIC. She looked behind the cabinet. It was plugged in. This thing works? How's that possible? She turned the tuning dial: top numbers were "Broadcast," bottom numbers "Short Wave." 55. 60. 70. Just static. 80. 100. 120. More static.

But then a signal, and a fairly strong one—a news voice: "And finally, the Associated Press reports that the last battalions of the Russian Army have left both Estonia and Latvia, ending what was the last physical trace of Soviet occupation in Eastern Europe... Anthony Devlin, WJLK-AM, Asbury Park. Stay tuned for 'The 1940s in Music' with your host, Pinky Kravitz. Tomorrow continues to be sunny and mild, with a high of 78. The Phillies won and both the Yanks and Mets lost."

Christina turned the volume down. She crossed over to the big window and spotted the familiar priest leaning against a lamppost, taking a drag. She decided to wait and see if the litterbug would be flicking again. And then, as if he had special powers, he turned his gaze up toward Christina, followed by a large puff of smoke. What was next? An exorcism? Her head twisting around with Earl Grey splattering all over Millie's room? Fuck him. She didn't care. She'd outstare this soon-to-be defrocked holy man. Hell, he's just a guy defacing the gutter. Also, she couldn't be much more than a silhouette. Maybe she'd flash him. Give the guy a thrill. But he looked away, took a final drag, and of course flipped his tobacco roach, this time clear into the street. He glanced up once more as if to say, "Take that," just before he strolled back into prison. Maybe the encounter's negative vibes were all in her head, but regardless, this padre seemed like a dick.

She climbed back into bed as Pinky introduced Vaughn Monroe and the Norton Sisters (who???) singing "There, I've Said It Again." The two fresh pillows felt amazing, the dark room was cool and soothing. There were two lights that marbled the darkness: falloff from the nearby streetlamp as well as the amber glowing orb from the radio's ancient dial.

As the music played, Christina wondered if she'd have dreams of Pinky's playlist: Billie Holiday, Artie Shaw, The Ink Spots? Maybe Pinky himself, whatever he looked like. Or the smoking priest tied to a stake? Those nuns? Millie? Or what about the exercising man?

❖❖❖

It was still dark when Christina stirred awake, not really sure about the time. Could be midnight, could be anything. But it must be later since the local news replaced the old-time music. Her watch confirmed 5:31am. She figured if she left now, she could catch another sunrise. Digging through her bag, she grabbed jeans, a sweatshirt, and pulled a brush through her sleep-wild locks.

On this morning, her second in Asbury Park, she shifted her vision a bit and sat on the planks up against a "For Lease" storefront on the Boardwalk—same area as yesterday, just past the 1st Avenue Pavilion. She sipped some decent takeout coffee as that perpetual ball of flames turned a pearly and calm dawn downright fiery. And then, wouldn't you know it, the exercising man emerged out of thin air, same bat time, same bat channel. Clearly. He thought he was alone as he stretched and began his routine. Jumping jacks. Christina counted: fifty-five—and like the day before, he informed the ocean, "FIFTY-FIVE!" Now he dropped down for sit-ups. She counted again: forty-four, so did he, "FORTY-FOUR!" Then he rolled over for push-ups. Twenty-two, "TWENTY-TWO!"

But this time he was a bit out of breath as he climbed to his feet. Then he stretched to the heavens, did some jazz hands, and headed north on his hike. A solitary man.

"If I'm Dorothy, who are you?"

Christina's question stopped him dead in his tracks. She offered a cute little gotcha wave. He smiled, "Good morning."

She raised her coffee hello, "You know, I thought maybe you might be the Wizard, but that's too easy."

Whitefish agreed, "Typecasting. Way too obvious."

Christina smiled, "Maybe you need a brain or a heart? Or is it courage?"

Whitefish shrugged them off, "I got 'em all in spades."

Christina bottom-lined it, "Then who are you?"

He smiled on his exit, "Glinda... the Good Witch of the North."

Clever, she thought, this time raising her coffee goodbye. As he hoofed along with his odd way of walking, it seemed as if Exercising Man owned this boardwalk, like the leader of some invisible marching band.

After meditating on the eerily empty beach for a solid hour, Christina made it back to the Sea Breeze for Millie's waffles. The innkeeper was pleasantly surprised when her guest actually showed up. They ate behind the curious tapestry in a small but well-appointed kitchen. Belgian waffles from scratch. As Millie prepared the batter, Christina asked about the old radio, "I'm amazed it still works."

Millie wasn't. "Oh, my husband Charlie was a fanatic with the radios, always replacing tubes and things. There's one in every room... and they all work!"

Christina enjoyed a chunk of melon, "That's really cool."

Millie blended the ingredients, "I've had this recipe since the World's Fair in Queens, 1964." She held up a box, "Powdered sugar tops it all off." Millie drifted, lost in thought, "My Lord, that was thirty years ago." She snapped away from her memory and poured batter onto the waffle iron, closing the lid. Politely, Millie asked, "Would you mind slicing the strawberries for me?"

Millie left the kitchen as Christina began slicing the berries. Darlene always had kitchen duty for her daughter, tasks the daughter usually enjoyed. She remembered strawberry shortcake, her Dad's favorite—and Mom was making her pretty concoction for his birthday. Twelve-year-old Christina was the designated strawberry slicer and apparently did "a fine job." Her Mom, ever the teacher, encouraged her like a Thesaurus: "Christina, you're not only a safe and masterful chef, but adroit, skillful, and quite the prodigy, especially with that knife. A true workmanlike— or, shall we say, 'work-womanlike'—performance."

Geez, Ma, it's only strawberries.

Millie was back and right to the waffle iron, patiently waiting for the batter to get crispier and crispier, "You're going to love these, sweetie."

And she did.

&

31

Sometimes I give myself the creeps.

Betwixt and between crispy bites of heavenly waffles, they shared stories. Millie talked about her late husband Charlie, meeting him at the Fort Dix PX in 1940. He was a grunt in training and she was a salesgirl in what they called "The Exchange"—an on-base department store for GIs. They moved to Asbury Park shortly after the war, where Charlie started a small business as a commercial electrician, a trade he learned in the United States Army Air Corps. The business grew and then boomed when he was contracted by both the City of Asbury Park and the venerable Berkeley-Carteret Hotel. Millie was the bookkeeper and business manager. The duo did quite well. They sold the business back in '72 and then purchased the old Victorian manor on Asbury Ave.

Creating the Sea Breeze was a dream come true.

Christina kept her stories casual and close to the vest; she grew up in New Jersey, spent some time in California, and now she was back planning her next move.

She only wished it was that easy.

❖❖❖

Her eyes were closed as warm water swirled down her body, splashing to the tiles below; the shower spray gentle like a cozy blanket. Streams of water instigated streams of consciousness:

> *Can I stay in the shower an hour? Maybe two? Nowhere to go. Hot water heater's probably old, might break down. Can't do that to Millie. Although I wonder if Millie needs help around here? We could barter work for room and board. I'd do all the cleaning, the gardening, mow the lawn, maybe shop. Even start painting, top to bottom. Polish the floors with one of those machines you rent. Maybe even clean the rooms after guests*

leave. Help Millie keep the business going. Maybe I should think bigger? Settle down here. Become a partner. She might welcome that. Go get my money, invest in the hotel, make it the best—what do they call those? Breakfast... Bed and Breakfast. Make it the "Best Bed & Breakfast on the Jersey Shore." That's what the sign should say. And people would love those waffles. Triple-AAA would reconsider and give us four diamonds, call us "a real gem!" Travel magazines would write articles... "How the Sea Breeze turned this dying town around." A smart writer would call it "the Lexington and Concord of the Asbury Park renaissance." I'd be sought after and interviewed on TV—"a woman with great entrepreneurial spirit!" Maybe run for mayor... and my first act in office? Arrest that goddamn priest for littering, now a felony in our fair city... Of course, thanks to me.

After a few minutes, with her eyes still closed, her musings on being an innkeeper's apprentice-cum-mayor drifted away. Christina latched on to a more tangible brainstorm: photographs. She'd buy a few disposable cameras and capture as much of this place as possible. She came all the way here to find whatever—why not document the search? It might help, like her journal was supposed to help, but it didn't because she'd been woefully lazy and delinquent in that regard. She turned sideways under the spray, directing the shower's warmth through her hair, down her back. Yeah, photographs. She smiled. Maybe the red bucket might actually show up, like in those photos people snap, and when they come back from the drugstore, there's a mysterious ghost walking through the background.

She bought three Fuji disposables and a small notebook at the Wawa in Neptune. Driving back, Christina was excited. She hadn't been creative since high school. But the realization was unsettling, like when Millie remembered the World's Fair, "My Lord, that was thirty years ago." She felt her mojo rising, "This could be good. Really good." Cinematize her history and then write captions on the back. "Cinematize? Is that even a word?"

The Datsun needed gas before Christina explored the Boardwalk in detail. There was a Texaco station out on 35. She pulled in, heard the "bing-bong" as she rolled over the station's "doorbell," and then stepped out, looking grungy in her sleeves-cut-off flannel shirt that fell open over her Hershey Bear t-shirt. Her hair was still kind of wet and looked like she just stepped off a photo shoot. She waited, remembering that you're not allowed to pump your own gas in the Garden State. An attendant in gas station greens—with "Joey" stitched over his red Texaco star—walked up with a smile and then a grimace as he spoke, "Hi, m-m-m-ma-mam. G-ga-ga-gas?" Christina had fun, "Yes, please. Regular. *Fill 'er up.*"

As Joey jammed the pump into the Pulsar, a second attendant meandered over, this one named "Danny," and he was wiping his hands on a greasy rag, all cool and shit, "California, huh? And this thing made it the whole way?"

Christina lowered her sunglasses for effect, "Almost. I had to push it here from Philly."

Joey laughed and Danny pointed at her with respect. "Tough broad," he thought. As the gas pump juddered away, Joey squeegeed the windshield. Danny kicked a tire, "So, whereabouts in California?" Without missing a beat, Christina told him, "Death Valley." Suddenly there was a third green man who just appeared, "Did I hear you say Death Valley?" Danny confirmed, "Yep. She's from Death Valley." Vinnie could smell a rat, "I mean, c'mon, who the hell's from Death Valley?"

Christina pointed to his name and then to the others, "Vinnie... Danny... and that's Joey over there. Kind of like Manny, Moe, and Jack."

Vinnie laughed, "You may think that was a zinger, but we're big fans of The Three Stooges." Joey laughed, then grimaced again, "M-M-Man-Manny, M-M-Moe, an, and J-Jack!" Joey smiled as Danny offered more proof, "Nyuk, nyuk, nyuk. Termites!"

Christina was enjoying this impromptu get-together, what a bunch of knuckleheads. "Are you guys related? Brothers, I bet?"

Danny sounded like The Fonz, "You got that right, sister."

She laughed out loud, "Gotta love you guys."

Vinnie was quick, "How much do you love us?"

Christina was quicker, "Not that much."

Joey stepped up, "O-o-k-kay, ma'am. Thir-thir-thir-thirteen-fifty." She handed him a twenty. "Be ri-ri-right b-b-back."

As she pulled away, the station bell rang again, and when Christina glanced in the rearview, it was like a Texaco commercial circa 1957: all three brothers lined up waving goodbye, kind of sweet-schmaltzy-and-weird. Shifting gears and thumping down 35, the car radio offered a timely editorial on her life, one entitled "Basket Case," courtesy of Green Day; a little ditty about giving herself the creeps. Was she paranoid, stoned, or just plain cracking up? Christina swung around the 35 circle like a local yokel, singing full throttle with Billie Joe—

♫*Sometimes I give myself the creeps!*

From there, she headed for the Boardwalk, parking in the exact same spot she did the morning before, when she first arrived. She ripped open her first green Fuji package, thinking, "Is this how Annie Leibovitz got started? Disposable cameras? Probably not."

Her plan was to start here, on the south end of the Boardwalk—with the Carousel House and its adjacent Casino Arcade—and then investigate the grimdark, factory-looking building closest to the ocean. Crossing the street, she gazed to her left and slowed to a complete stop, "What the heck is that?" She didn't notice it yesterday. How is that possible? This rectangular two-story building, connected to nothing, sitting there all by itself. Last structure on this southern end of the Boardwalk. And it's painted purple and yellow. She gravitated closer, realizing it was more goldish than yellow.

'Scuse me while I kiss the sky
TAVERN | FOOD: NOON TO MIDNIGHT

Like a mannequin, she stood at the front entrance:

C-l-u-b S-o-u-t-h-s-i-d-e

The massive sign loomed above, each letter painted on slabs of driftwood. How fucking bizarre, she thought. Purple and gold? Then the artistic script, *'Scuse me while I kiss the sky?* Hendrix? Yeah, of course. Purple Haze. Jaime would be all over this.

Christina moved to the front windows to peek inside, but they were completely blacked out. But then, without warning, two neon signs sizzled on:

Pabst Blue Ribbon & Ballantine Ale

The front door creaked open, and Big Lou emerged carrying the massive sandwich board. He didn't see Christina as he walked the sign closer to the Boardwalk. On his way back, he spotted her and nonchalantly chatted on the move, "Joining us for lunch? I'm doing Reubens today. A real treat if you love kraut." And like that he was gone, the door creaking closed.

❖ ❖ ❖

SNAPSHOT, sound of clicking plastic, TIK-TIK-TIK, advancing film.

Christina took ten shots of the purple & gold C-l-u-b S-o-u-t-h-s-i-d-e, this 1960s objet d'art that looked airlifted out of Haight-Ashbury. Talk about a convoluted anomaly: In some ways it fit snug-as-a-glove on this derelict boardwalk, but in other ways, she thought, it was better suited for Jupiter, maybe Pluto. Reluctantly, she moved on, afraid she might miss something at this C-l-u-b S-o-u-t-h-s-i-d-e—like it might levitate off its foundation.

She continued on—next the famous Carousel House: It looked good through the viewfinder. SNAPSHOT-TIK-TIK-TIK-advance. She wrote observations in her notebook:

>*ornate rotunda, empty! where did all the horses go?*
>*beautiful green oxidized copper*
>*weird Greek medusa heads*

Next, she turned to the adjacent Casino Arcade. SNAPSHOT-TIK-TIK-TIK-advance:

>*gutted, broken windows, more green copper*
>*a real shithole*
>*like it was shelled from an off-shore destroyer!*

Christina walked inland a few hundred feet, following the narrow and somehow still pristine Wesley Lake, the damned-off estuary that also sat at the south end of the Boardwalk. SNAPSHOT-TIK-TIK-TIK-advance. Her notes and memories began to multiply with vigor, her thoughts faster than her hand could write:

>*tall mysterious building, DAD said it was a powerplant – steam for electricity*
>*I know there's a photo of ME+MOM right in front*

>*MOM said such an eyesore! Right on the beach*
>*DAD always pragmatic "easier to grab water, generate electricity"*
>*we took paddle boats on the lake, hours in the arcade – bumper cars!!!*
>*MOM loved crashing DAD*
>*I bashed a really mean fat bully kid who started to cry*

She stopped snapping and writing. Abruptly. This unscheduled regressive time travel came over her like a sudden thunderstorm. Up until now, she'd managed to keep Jack & Darlene at arm's length. They were there, but beyond her reality, still frozen in death. But suddenly, here at Wesley Lake, they strolled out like la-de-da, and it felt like they were standing right there. For Christina, this phenomena was chilling, as if she were hand-holding Jack & Darlene out of some dark graveyard, stone angels rising to life as lightning ignites nearby Ocean Grove, "God's (so-called) Square Mile at the Jersey Shore."

She sat on a concrete wall, wondering if there was another way to experience this moment. "Don't fight it," she told herself, "You gotta envision, I don't know, 1978? You gotta see the paddleboats, the blue sky, the three of you... maybe there's a warm breeze... try hearing the paddles thwacking the lake."

As she looked past the Boardwalk, and the beach, to the ever-present ocean, its thunder muted, Christina recognized that her yoga and meditation practice *was actually making a difference*. It had to be. She was facing all of this without doses of Big Pharma—and she was still standing. Yep, Jack & Darlene were standing right there, and it was painful, and it was harsh, but it was real. There was also a certain peace associated with truly grieving. She wrote one more thought in her notebook.

>*Hey Mr. Really Mean Fat Kid Bully*
>*I'm sorry*

Christina headed back toward the Boardwalk. She had one more shot in the Fuji. She turned the camera around and clicked an image of herself with the length of the Boardwalk (hopefully) behind her. It felt weird. Such an idiot. Who would take a photo of themselves?

It was 1:07pm. She was hungry as hell, and there was a giant sandwich board screaming right at her:

Grilled Reuben | Clams Oreganata | Meatball Parm

She figured, "What the hell, let's try this joint." She reached for the door, just as the neon *Ballantine Ale* sign sputtered off and back on, like it recognized her from before and was saying hello. Hmmm.

Christina opened the creaking door, and not to be outdone, the *Pabst Blue Ribbon* sign also sputtered hello.

She glanced at the weirdly impressive overhead sign:

C-l-u-b   S-o-u-t-h-s-i-d-e

Paused and then walked inside.

&

CHRISTINA and the
WHITEFISH

32

Lunch is on me, Miss Christina. Enjoy!

A few regulars were enjoying their midday meal. Lil Abner sat at the bar by himself, reading the paper and taking the last chomp on his meatball parm. Bagel and Madam Marie were laughing it up in a side booth, something about Bubba Clinton using state troopers to protect his traveling whorehouse. They both ordered the grilled Reuben and a Pabst lager. At a center table, four retirees were enjoying their clams oreganata—handsome married couples that represented "old" Asbury Park. Two city detectives were making their exit as they plopped down some cash and left with their visible hip badges and 9mm Glocks. Joe Fats emerged from the Men's Room with a *Sports Illustrated* tucked under his arm and joined Abner at the bar. Lou entered from the galley with a large tray on his shoulder, grabbed a folding stand, and delivered four lunches to the retirees. The Reuben was a sellout for the septuagenarians. A young busboy, maybe seventeen, cleared off the cops' table. The jukebox was picking random 45s.

"Eleanor Rigby" was in the house when Christina walked in.

Her first impression was "whoa"—the interior buzz certainly didn't match the exterior's odd vibe. In a flash, the place went from a hippie's crash pad to a classy Manhattan watering hole—a vibrant oasis surrounded by a dying town.

Christina felt all the curious eyes as she looked for a seat.

The busboy politely gestured, "Welcome, ma'am, sit anywhere you like." She had never been a "ma'am" before and parked herself at a deuce up against the brick wall, under a framed photograph of Clark Gable and Claudette Colbert.

As the kid moved toward the galley with his tray of empties, the Whitefish moved out to the bar with his lunch. "Hey Donnie, grab me an Arnold Palmer."

The busboy backed into the galley, "Sure thing, boss, and that lady just came in over there." Whitefish followed the kid's head-nod, recognizing Dorothy immediately. Abner looked at his watch, "Jesus, Fish, you're like a goddamn machine. One-eleven every day. Do you know how fucked up you are?"

Whitefish paid little attention, placing his lunch on the bar—as always, his blue plate special was picturesque: sliced chicken, brown rice, and arugula under Jersey tomatoes topped with a dollop of Roquefort. Abner was salivating, "Looks good."

Whitefish grabbed a small menu and headed toward Dorothy, "And don't fucking touch it."

As he ambled over, they shared knowing smiles. Whitefish handed Christina the menu, "So, Dorothy, we meet again."

She was glad to see him, "We do. Is this your place?"

He grabbed a chair, "Mind if I sit?" She motioned, of course not. "Except for the VA loan I took out last year to do a little refurbishing, it's all mine."

Christina scanned the room, "I love it... and you know, we can use our real names. I don't think Dorothy and Glinda are gonna cut it." She held out her hand, "Christina."

He returned the gesture, "Whitefish."

His name caught her off guard. "Whitefish or Mr. Whitefish?"

He made it easy, "Your choice, although friends and enemies call me Whitefish, amongst other more colorful things. Good friends just Fish."

She sat back, "I love it... Fish." He smiled, being a fan of witty banter.

The busboy delivered ice water and a basket of wrapped crackers. She thanked him.

Whitefish queried, "So, what brings you in today? Lunch, I hope."

She sipped some water, "The gentleman who walked your sandwich board outside mentioned grilled Reubens. Here I am."

Fish tapped the menu, "Everything's available. The Reuben's good and we also have two other specials, an eggplant parm sandwich and clams oreganata. Both are pretty good."

As she looked around, "You know, I really love this place, I do. Very cozy."

He picked up the crackers, "That was my goal exactly. Cracker?"

She quickly perused the selection and picked the Devonsheer Melba Toast. "Thanks." He snagged the Keebler Clubs.

Christina raised the stakes as she gently opened her crackers, "The exterior just blew me away. The Hendrix thing is remarkable. I mean, I couldn't turn away. I thought the building might just lift off the ground. You know, like levitate."

Impressed, Whitefish sat back, intrigued, "Yeah, like Abbie with the Pentagon." But then quickly realized he was referencing a dinosaur. "Sorry, I'm guessing you have no idea what I'm talking about?"

She took a bite of her cracker, "I don't."

He opened his Keeblers, "I do that sometimes... anyway, 21 October 1967—the March on the Pentagon, a massive demonstration against the war. All the usual suspects: Phil Ochs, Dave Dellinger, Ginsberg, and of course the star, Abbie Hoffman."

Christina perked up, "Sure, of course, Abbie Hoffman."

Whitefish knocked his knuckle on the table, twice, "So when this throng of protesters, I mean we're talking fifty thousand, reach the Pentagon, they're met by the boys from the 82nd Airborne... this is when that famous photo was taken where the protester sticks the flower inside the rifle barrel, right?"

Christina knew it, "Flower power."

Whitefish munched on a cracker, "Exactly... and then Abbie, along with Ginsberg chanting and doing his wacky shit, they both attempt to levitate the Pentagon. Norman Mailer swears he saw the goddamn thing (Whitefish dramatically raises his arms)... right off the foundation."

Christina was fascinated with the story, "Sounds like you were there."

Whitefish turned a bit melancholy, "Wish I was, but... you know," he stood up, "At the time, I was still playing for the other team, 'convalescing,' as they say... VA hospital, deep in the City of Angels. But that's another story for another time. What can I get you?" He enjoyed his cracker as she absorbed the VA twist of fate.

"Uh... I'd like to try the Reuben and, um... an Arnold Palmer if you have that."

Whitefish picked up the menu, "Arnie was a helluva golfer, hailed out of Latrobe, Pennsylvania"—and then as he walked away, with his back to Christina, he announced, "Lunch is on me, Miss Christina. Enjoy!"

His very strange gait now made sense. Vietnam. She watched him hobble back to the bar, thinking, "Kindred spirits, casualties of war... but with Mr. Fish, you can still see the insult."

At the bar, Whitefish tossed down the menu as Abner asked, "Do you know this chick?" The boss shot back, "What are you? A cop? Just read the paper." Whitefish leaned into the galley, "Lou, do a Reuben, table eight." And then to Donnie as he finally returned to his lunch, "Donnie B, one Arnie on eight."

She could hear the jukebox grind and grab a new 45—"Black Magic Woman." Whitefish announced, "Ladies and germs, Mr. Carlos Santana and his unmistakable Gibson Les Paul!" A few folks applauded. Abner whistled. What a weirdly great place, Christina thought, as she grabbed her notebook from her bag, wondering what gibberish she wrote down on her Boardwalk tour. But she couldn't focus. This twist of fate regarding the Los Angeles VA was still dancing the mambo on her brain. Donnie dropped off the Arnold Palmer, "Straw?"

Every once in a while, she'd gaze over at Whitefish quietly eating his lunch. He was watching a day game from the Stadium. The guy sitting near him, reading the paper and wearing a small red fedora, talked incessantly with Whitefish barely reacting. Christina sensed that the guy was driving her new friend crazy. Whitefish caught her gaze and raised his Arnold Palmer in salute. She did the same, clinking glasses across the great divide. He had a hard time looking away.

A minute or so later, Lou delivered her lunch—the corned beef, melted Swiss, and sauerkraut sat juicy on char-grilled rye, with Russian dressing oozing out the sides. It came with baked beans. Lou also plopped down a side arugula salad with tomatoes and Roquefort, "Enjoy your lunch, ma'am. Those Jersey tomatoes are unreal." And he said it just like Darlene used to say it, "ta-mah-toes."

The jukebox shifted gears to Elvis Presley crooning "Suspicious Minds."

Marie and Bagel were taking off, Bagel called out, "Yo Fish, thank you."

Whitefish didn't look up, "Bagel, be good." Now he did, "Hey Marie, what, no kiss?"

She never broke stride, "You're lookin' old today, King. Lookin' real old."

He smiled easy, carefully slicing his ta-mah-toes. Abner laughed as Whitefish's demeanor quickly turned, "Isn't it time for you to leave?"

Abner kept reading, "Very soon, pal, and then you're gonna miss me."

The proprietor inhaled a perfect forkful of salad, "I fuckin' doubt it."

Joe Fats downed the last of his beer and lumbered off his stool, "I'm heading back, Fish. Got a guy comin' in on a '90 Olds Eighty-Eight, a fucking cherry... and Joey Boy here needs a home run. I'm gonna put this schifoso to sleep."

On Joe's way by, Whitefish proclaimed, "Ladies and Gentlemen, Mr. Willy Loman."

Christina couldn't help but notice the easy flow of camaraderie in the Club Southside. She also couldn't believe how amazing the food was— she thought of Jaime, "See, James, I'm eating. I might even finish this thing!"

The ballgame droned on. The Yanks were getting spanked as the 45s kept spinning away. Christina was ready to hit the Boardwalk again. She moved up to the bar, wanting to pay for lunch, but Whitefish repeated his comp. She thanked him with another handshake as Diana Ross and The Supremes dropped, "Stop! In the Name of Love." Whitefish extended a reminder that they're open for dinner every evening and drinks till midnight. Christina assured him she'd be back, "I'm in town for at least a week."

As soon as she was safely out the front door, Lil Abner spouted out as if he'd been holding his breath, "Jesus Christ. She's like a fourteen on a scale of one to ten." Whitefish smirked at Abner, grabbed his now-empty lunch plate, and headed toward the galley. Abner scoffed, "Oh, all of a sudden. Sir Walter Fucking Raleigh."

That afternoon, Christina covered the Boardwalk right up to the corpse-like Convention Hall. She made notes and photo'd the entire stretch: 3rd,

4th, and 5th Avenue pavilions—

>*dead or dying storefronts*
>*saltwater taffy, custard, ice cream, pizza, white pizza*
>*games closed, graffiti, lemonade, t-shirts*
>*a rat eating red pizza*

She realized that the old Howard Johnson's in the round was one of the few places that gave this Boardwalk color: HoJo's with the orange, Club Southside with the purple haze, and then Convention Hall with the archaic hints of oxidizing green. HoJo's also summoned numerous memories—

>*HoJo on life support*
>*still orange, sat many a day w/ Jack & Darlene*

Christina had ten shots left on Fuji number three, so the once-famous (but now) gaping carcass of Convention Hall would be her final destination—a place that reminded her of a mighty terminus, like D.C.'s Union Station, a grand concourse that ferried humanity and echoed history.

Alone, inside the commodious structure, she began to sense that this standing wreckage still had a soul, one that was somber and stoic but a soul nonetheless. Did it want to be released from this dying planet? Saved like the wretched of the earth? She thought of herself, sitting on the steps of that derelict white chapel, where she too deliberated "release from this dying planet." Sometimes sweet death seemed easier. "Does it matter if I exit now or twenty years from now? Or even a hundred years from now?"

Standing there holding her pathetic disposable camera, she went even darker: Convention Hall still standing is one of life's little reminders about the ultimate joke—gotcha! The grand illusion is such a devious deception. We will never figure out how to cross the chasm, traverse the gorge. Go ahead, build as many monuments as you want! All of this shit will be gone, and get this—much sooner than later. Ask Rome, ask Greece, and Christina also knew, ask America. Before birth, nothing. After death, nothing.

A massive BOOM rocked Convention Hall.

She snapped out of it.

The Atlantic had mustered up a rock 'n roll wave, one that thundered and shook the bare bones of this ancient ruin, desperately shouting, "Look at me, look at me, I'm still here!" So be it: She took her first shot through this immense, dank cadaver toward the steely ocean beyond. SNAPSHOT-TIK-TIK-TIK-advance. C-Mac kept clicking away, thinking that all ruins share the same vibe—antiquities like Stonehenge, the Parthenon, the Colosseum, factories in Youngstown, Ohio, in Flint, Michigan, and now (SNAPSHOT-TIK-TIK-TIK-advance) this playful seaside palace.

When she moseyed back to the Boardwalk, she only had one shot left on her last Fuji. A bicycle bell chimed. She looked up and quickly smiled—this was the third time she spotted the same little girl riding her bike, a well-worn Schwinn. She passed by Christina and waved. Christina waved back, close enough to see that the girl was about ten. She called after her, "Can I take your picture?"

The girl yelled, "Sure!" and then circled back. Christina CLICKED and thought she captured a good shot with the little girl's arm waving freely over her head.

Then the kid circled slowly around Christina, "What's your name?"

"Christina. What's yours?"

"Shanice."

"That's pretty."

"My mom's name is Destiny."

"That's pretty, too."

"What are you doing?"

"Taking pictures."

Shanice waved, "Bye."

And off she rode. Down the Boardwalk. So independent. So beautiful.

❖ ❖ ❖

At the Sea Breeze, as late afternoon crawled slowly across the front porch, Christina had tea with Millie and filled her in on the day. Millie said she used to frequent the Club Southside with Charlie when he was alive but hasn't been back since. Millie said Whitefish sent flowers to the wake and then added, "He's kind of weird but a very sweet man. I've always liked him."

Across the street, the church offered music with a visual: the now recurring priest wandered out for a smoke, dramatically arriving with the gentle hymn, "I Need Thee Every Hour," playing on the pipe organ.

Millie was curious, "Why all the photographs? Everything is gone, at least almost everything."

Christina shrugged, "Yeah, I'm not really sure, beats doing nothing. I dropped them at the drugstore."

Millie understood, "Something always beats nothing."

Christina sipped her tea, "Maybe it'll bring back some memories."

Millie poured more tea, "Memories are good."

That night, Christina read more of *Pride and Prejudice,* visited Chris McCandless in Alaska, and then listened to the radio until she drifted off, the RCA Victor's faint light ushering in a series of dreams—outlandish images of the Club Southside shaking and growling, Whitefish chanting, arms raised, imploring the building to "Rise! Rise!" off its cracking foundation... the little man in the red fedora pushed a wheelbarrow down the Boardwalk, telling Christina he was on his way to fix up Convention Hall. "Wanna help?" She decided to follow this strange munchkin of a man as the Club Southside passed by overhead, pieces of flaming concrete falling to Earth, punching giant holes in the Boardwalk. They laughed, C-Mac and Munchkin Man, as they danced through the fiery debris.

When Christina opened her eyes, it wasn't from a nightmare but rather a comedy.

She was at ease and giggled at the cartoon dream, glad it wasn't Scud missiles pounding Dhahran. It was just monkey business in Asbury Park.

☙

33

Hear ye, Hear ye!

She was waiting for him at 6:26am. That perfect ball of hot plasma, heated to incandescence by nuclear fusion, was lurking just below the horizon. Christina wore yoga pants and her Hershey Bear t-shirt. He didn't see her when she asked, "Mind if I join you?" At first, Whitefish was clearly flummoxed—something that rarely happened.

He recovered quickly, "Top of the morning. Yes, indeed, your company will make the drudgery most worthwhile." Whitefish didn't realize he sounded like *Masterpiece Theatre.*

Seagulls squawking filled the short pause. Christina confirmed, "Fifty-five, forty-four, and twenty-two, correct?"

Once again, Whitefish was flummoxed, "You counted?" She smiled, "I'm really good at math."

He laughed as he stretched, "A regular Archimedes. Also quite observant. Where you staying?"

She stretched a bit but not nearly as grim as her senior, "Sea Breeze on Asbury."

Whitefish acknowledged its existence, "How's Millie doing? Haven't seen her in some time."

Christina stretched, her knee almost touching the planks, "She seems good. I don't know her that well."

Whitefish threw a few shadow punches, "She's very sweet."

Christina stretched back the other way, "She said the same thing about you." Whitefish felt loose, "What is that? Yoga?"

She stood up with ease, "Yeah, just stretching. Ready?" He was, "Let's do it."

55. 44. 22.

Whitefish yelled them out as they finished and then asked, "This is when I usually hike to Allenhurst. It's about an hour there and back. You in?"

She accepted, "Allenhurst or bust." Whitefish pointed thataway and off they went, the odd couple hoofing it north.

Two seagulls perched on the Carousel House watched as the humans walked—and if these birds could comprehend English, they would have appreciated the male's dogmatic spirit: "The journey of a thousand miles begins with a single step." The female asked, "Who said that?" The male replied, "Chinese philosopher Lao Tzu, probably five hundred years before Christ." After a few seconds, the male added, "It's pretty trite now, I saw it on a greeting card."

It was hazy and humid, but the Sun still cut through with some muscle. The Boardwalk was empty if you didn't count the seagulls and assorted birds. Christina was curious, "Why did someone call you the 'King' yesterday?"

Whitefish ran his hand through his long, thin hair, "Man, I wish you were here the other night."

Christina smiled, "Was there a coronation?"

Whitefish playfully knocked her on the shoulder, "Oh, a comedian, eh?"

She played back, fake yelling as they cruised along, "Hear ye, hear ye, fine citizens of the Jersey Shore, we crown him Whitefish, the King of Asbury Park!"

Whitefish threw a few air punches as they briskly walked, no matter his limp. "It's a thing here among the regulars, a tradition. It sort of documents this unofficial lineage from one whack job to the next... and yes, as you so eloquently put it with some surprisingly spot-on speculation, I am the current king."

Christina wondered, "Why do you wish I was here the other night?"

It may have been that slight anxiousness of exchanging thoughts with a new acquaintance, but Whitefish kept throwing the occasional air punch as they motored along, "I created a stage show dedicated to this ancestral bullshit. It was a real amateur hour, but people seemed to like it."

She was curious, "So, who were some of the other kings?"

Whitefish was surprised, "You really want to know?"

She did, "Yeah, gimme the TV Guide version."

Two other seagulls (who *did* comprehend English) picked up on the humans' conversation as the male offered colorful embroidery about Jack the Golfer, Chick Venus, and Ralph Giancarlo, mentioning something about "the fucking Hindenburg." The female was laughing so hard it seemed to hurt.

Christina spotted Madam Marie's psychic hut, "Is she still around?"

"I think you've already seen her. She was having lunch when you came in yesterday."

She thought back. "Yesterday?"

"Yeah, a fairly stout woman, somewhat hard to miss." He hand-painted a much larger woman than his words implied. "She's been spinning her psychic nonsense since the thirties. Nice lady, a real fixture. Now there's someone who really cares."

Christina remembered, "You know, I think she's the one who called you king."

Whitefish concurred, "Sounds like her. In fact, Springsteen mentions Marie in that Fourth of July song." He offered a quick singsong, *"The cops finally busted Madam Marie for tellin' fortunes blah-blah-blah.* He thinks he's Dylan."

She stretched as they walked, "I like them both."

He motioned to her t-shirt, "Does that bear come along all the time?"

She laughed, "Hey, I'm living out of a bag, gimme a break."

He threw another air punch, "Millie Carpenter's Sea Breeze... for a day or a lifetime."

&

CHRISTINA and the
WHITEFISH

34
Fred & Ginger.

SHE WAS WAITING FOR ME. Right at sunrise. Dorothy, aka Christina.

I don't know her last name. Actually, at this point, I don't know anything about her except that I like her. She's a good kid, smart as hell. Early twenties... seems confident and self-reliant, although there's a part of me that thinks she's struggling emotionally, looking for something. Lil Abner, our resident degenerate and all-too-common misogynist, says she's "a fourteen" on a scale of one to ten. He should know being "a three" on a scale of one to five hundred.

For some reason, his words have triggered this homily.

Notes on the Male Species... of which I am one:
(Sorry. Pullin' out the soapbox.)

Indeed she is – a "fourteen" in Abner's idiotic ratings game. Males think like that... and they also act like that. Especially with a woman like Christina. Strikingly beautiful – the kind of beauty that will unnerve the savage heterosexual male. Dead in their tracks kind of beauty. They can't think straight. They become totally consumed, like some poor bastard on his way to the electric chair. And I admit that I was a card-carrying member of this debauched club. At best, it's shallow as hell. At its worst, well, it can be horrifying.

You see, I've been trying to evolve over the last twenty-five years. Educate myself by paying attention to that minority of smart people who criticize the monolith that subjugates all the folks who supposedly don't count as much: women, Black people, the American Indian, Spanish and Asian people, homosexual people, children, old people... the list continues, but you get the picture.

Being a great reporter, my old man drummed these truisms into me from an early age. It was his religion: "Power concedes nothing!" Of course, at the time, I was too young and too stupid to hear it because, at seventeen, I already knew everything there was to know.

Shark River. Circa 1962.

Me and the old man were fishing for flounder and bluefish. I was fifteen and remember like it was yesterday. "Take notice," he said ("Take notice" was his clarion trumpet when he wanted to be heard), "Always listen to the victims. Their voices are the ones that matter. Remember, kiddo, history's always been written by the who?" My turn, "The winners." Followed by another Dad prompt, "And what do we know about power?" We'd say it together: "Power concedes nothing."

Then he'd make it personal, "When I work, I investigate and write my stories with that exact reality tattooed on my fingers. Screw the government, son, because all governments lie and they lie all the time. Never forget that. If their lips are moving, they're lying. I watch poor people get steamrolled and fucked over every day." Now, when he said "poor people," I'm thinking hobos and bums. And chances are he knew that, so he went out of his way to clarify, saying one of the most important things he ever said to me: "Kid, ninety-nine percent of us are poor. That's how these bastards at the top see it, that's how they want it – these thugs own the kingdom. Remember, they own you and they own me. They own the entire goddamn game... and the game is rigged, right? Voting's there to give us the illusion of freedom. That's why people with a conscience, people like us, we're never getting into their club. They will slaughter and pillage to protect what's theirs – their precious little treasure. Let this sink in: They're insatiable. Do you know what that means? (I nodded "yes," but I didn't.) Because there's not enough treasure that will ever be enough. Why?" Once more, we were in stereo, "Power concedes nothing."

When I swung back from Vietnam, his wisdom finally began to take hold. Unfortunately, it was about a year too late. Anyway...

I wanted to offer a little background on the seeds that define power for the Whitefish because Abner's all-too-common thoughts about this young lady indicates an ingrained and almost invisible power – what the academics call "systemic power" – and in this case it's about the rough and tumble world of male dominance. This hegemony cuts through civilization like a main circuit cable. It's been happening since the dawn of time. That's why yesterday, a weakling like Lil Abner (with that stupid fucking hat) feels comfortable enough to reduce someone to merely tits and ass. He felt it necessary to rank her like a piece of US Grade A meat.

Now, some may think Abner's remark was just a cute little innocuous aside. It's not. In essence, it implies unbridled power. This is how evolution works. It seeps in, like radium poison into groundwater.

I can hear some of you right now, "Calm down, Fish. You're overstating the case." You're entitled to your opinion. But you're still wrong.

I've read some very smart thinkers like Steinem-Friedan-Angela Davis... and they all talk about society reducing women to nothing more than "things" – or in the more abstract: objectifying women. Like I said, men have been doing this since they crawled out of the muck and mire. In many cases, it's outright terror, which includes violence and aggression, entitlement and privilege. Just look around. You don't need a presidential study or some report commissioned by Stanford to ascertain the truth. You only need your eyes to see and your brain to comprehend that the American male is a pathetic and violent creature. In fact, the mountain of evidence documenting this debased and unchecked behavior is massive, most of it ignored. The harm caused to women in particular – and society in general – is not just theoretical claptrap. It's very real. The harassment, the marginalization, and in many cases, the rape, are all erased, buried, or simply not taken seriously... by society itself and/or the proper government authorities.

Now, dig it... I don't suggest this line of thinking because I'm resentful and bitter, a male rendered incapable - the Whitefish professionally castrated in one of America's useless and pointless wars. Rather, I suggest it for three quantitative reasons:

ONE... I'm part of the male club and privy to the actions and thoughts of uninhibited males – so I can sing like a canary.

TWO... any objective and honest read of history over the last thirty or forty thousand years cannot ignore the amount of trauma that's been hoisted on half of the world's population (females) by the abject cruelty unleashed by males.

And THREE... I'm personally guilty as well. You might also say, "guilty as hell."

Take Donna for instance. She'd been stripping at a joint down in Atlantic City for about a year. And then the place suddenly goes out of business – the owner summarily dismembered by the Philadelphia chapter of the Knights of Columbus. So what happens next? I get the brilliant idea to bolster my business by installing a dance pole, a few spinning lights – all aimed at hiring Donna Stefanelli for three nights a week. It makes me some good money and also keeps Donna afloat (see the rationalization?) – and shazam: I became an active player in the game.

AND WOULD I DO THIS IF SHE WERE MY DAUGHTER? Then why should I do it to someone else's daughter? Or any woman? Ever been in one of those diners with the giant spinning cake displays? You tell me the difference.

Consequently, as I type this out now, I can see the crime in black & white. Therefore, under the heading of unintended consequences, it's high time for the Whitefish to take down the dance pole.

Sorry for the slight deviation.

So, Dorothy, aka Christina, showed up early this morning wanting to join my daily regimen. I was taken aback for a number of reasons; first and foremost, no one has ever joined me for calisthenics or my hike. I'm not sure anyone even knows about my routine. She even knew the countdown: 55-44-22. And then we started working out as if we'd been doing this for years. It felt like Fred & Ginger. I know it was only jumping jacks, et cetera, but there was a certain sync that felt natural. And my male vanity must have really been on guard since I was determined not to be winded – and somehow, thank you Jesus, I wasn't. Take that Father Time, you motherfucker.

Then we headed down the Boardwalk and along the beach to Allenhurst. It's an hour there and back. And it was Jersey humid, so I anticipated sweating like a rotisserie pig. But why should I care, right? I know for a fact that our connection has nothing to do with a mutual attraction (even though the unexpected sight of her takes my breath away – but that's just how God made me, so leave me alone).

And then right around Deal Lake, on Ocean Ave, it became all too clear why "The Fates" tossed the two of us together: Christina & the Whitefish.

# #

35

Girfer.

For Christina, the charming houses surrounding Deal Lake wiggled loose sweet memories. She recalled walking along this same slice of beach with Jack & Darlene. They always veered from the ocean path and strolled around the serene man-made lake—her Mom enchanted by the stunning architectural character and beautifully manicured lawns. Rarely did they use the "R" word, but here, down the shore, near Asbury Park, walking off their meal in the dying light of a July dusk, these two teachers from Belvidere said they might like to retire here. On this lake. In one of these homes. Preferably Victorian—"like this one, Jack... reminiscent of the style built in San Francisco between 1850 and maybe 1880. Ornate with symmetrical bay windows, small chimneys built in unexpected locations." And preferably painted in what her mother called "Dark Venetian Red." If nothing else, Darlene's vision was precise, etched in stone. Jack would always wink at Christina when her mom went on these flights of fancy.

Suddenly, Christina realized she hadn't heard much of what Whitefish said over the last few minutes as her mind floated above Retirement Lake. Last thing she remembered was rapping about the past year in Southern California and told Whitefish about growing up in idyllic Belvidere, which her hiking partner drolly referred to as the "Old West." Whitefish then fired off a condensed history about his father's career as a hard-boiled reporter for the historic *Newark Evening News,* declaring, "Frank Delgado spent a year in the Trenton Bureau, which is just south of your hometown. Classic muckraker... turned this state upside down."

A teenager strolled by carrying a shortboard—and then, out of thin air, Whitefish spun an arbitrary subplot regarding surfing on the Jersey shore:

> *Hey, it's not the North Shore of Oahu, but Jersey has some serious spots like Clam Alley down on Long Beach Island... and believe you me, the locals don't take kindly to some Barneys dropping in and*

grabbing their waves. There's a whole lot of tribalism. You know, watch all you want from the rocky shore, but these cats snag all the heavies for themselves.

And believe it or not, my dear old Ma used to love watching these barbarians surf. It was weird because if you knew her at all, surfing— even the idea of surfing—not in a million years, not even a thought. But luckily I had a buddy who let us park at his place right around ground zero. What a view! I made her a Thermos of coffee, packed a few donuts—she was in heaven.

Christina's attention wandered back to Whitefish, smiling and thinking to herself, "This dude can talk." But she liked the performance; what else could you call it? His stories, coupled with his exuberance, reminded her of Jack, who also preached a bit—not dogmatic or authoritarian, just noteworthy bits and pieces—like this memory somewhere in Oregon:

Did you ladies know that before Lewis and Clark left on their far west expedition, the President, Thomas Jefferson, was fully convinced they were going to have dangerous run-ins with herds of woolly mammoths and giant ground sloths? I kid you not. These were creatures long extinct. Thomas Jefferson.

Darlene would act like she was interested and then sneak her daughter a playful roll of the eyes. Whitefish's surf tale continued, his arms depicting the visual:

And if you know anything about surfing, dig this: the shore-breaks at Clam Alley come off a flat stone and sandy surface, which helps to create these sick, I mean sick, reef-like formations—and then these bombs break in almost the same spot every time. Boom, boom... It's fucking beautiful. I'm not sure about most things but I am absolutely positive that God's a surfer.

Christina jumped back into the conversation, "But if God's a woman, she's probably a *girfer*."

Whitefish slowed his pace; he really fancied her quip, "Ma woulda loved that." High-five.

As they passed the lake, Christina's memories scattered to the trees. She thought it might be time to reveal their funky fluky connection with regard to the VA Hospital at 11301 Wilshire Boulevard, Los Angeles, California 90073. "You know," she started slowly, "I think you and I share a weird sort of coincidence, freakish really." He was all ears, "Lay it on me, Dorothy." Christina reminded him about his Los Angeles convalescent story and then neatly weaved in the tale of her recent stint at the same VA dungeon hard by the 405 Freeway, albeit more than twenty-five years apart. Whitefish absorbed it all, seriously locked in.

Christina told her narrative in reverse—starting with Uncle Sam's half-baked excuse for a restorative hospital, followed by the outright hell of traversing the infamous Highway of Death between Kuwait and Iraq. And then she plunged headfirst into the carnage at Dhahran, working in her psychiatric stint at the King Abdul Aziz Air Base in Saudi Arabia.

She sighed, the exhale a final period. She realized this telling of her tale was probably the most frank and forthright ever—and that included sessions at Peace House. In fact, her drama and their connection slowed their hike to a complete stop in the ritzy town of Allenhurst—two damaged warriors standing under a rusty street sign marking the corner of Ocean and Spier. They were flanked by massive beachfront homes to the west and the pounding Atlantic to the east.

Whitefish was devastated. No words were exchanged. The ocean now had the floor. Clearly, the reveal of her war chronicle was still churning inside her gut. He unashamedly offered his arms, suggesting an embrace. She moved a step closer. He hugged her tight. She hugged him back. And for a very long moment, on this deserted corner, time stood still, the hike officially on hiatus.

No one really knows how long it took, but as a flock of seagulls squawked by, the two hikers had moved close to the water's edge, finding a seat on a large driftwood log. Christina continued, "All that shit was act two."

Whitefish said softly, "Christ, there's an act one?" She watched the waves break, trying not to break herself. He quietly stared at the horizon. He knew she needed space.

"A few months before I enlisted, my mother and father, my two best friends," she was having a tough time but held steady, "They were killed in a plane crash near Glacier Bay."

Whitefish mumbled, "Alaska."

She nodded, "One of those small shit planes, some cruise ship thing."

Whitefish ran his hands through his hair, overwhelmed by her pain. He stood up and stepped a few feet away. Fifteen minutes ago, he barely knew her. Now she was sharing her darkest pain, her foulest grief. Was it his turn? Could she absorb it? Could he?

Jesus, he thought, what started out as Fred & Ginger gracefully gliding stage left now felt more like Bonnie & Clyde exchanging submachine gun fire with the cops.

Whitefish decided it was his turn, "One-one-three-zero-one, Wilshire Boulevard, City of the Angels. I forgot the damn zip code." He sat back down.

Christina offered a slight smile, "nine-zero-zero-seven-three."

He welcomed her timing, her gallows wit, "You know it's also called 'The City of Flowers and Sunshine?'" She didn't know him well but knew he was trying to be gentle and soft. She didn't know the nickname. He shrugged, "Yeah, it's a shitty tag for a city anyway." He slid off the log, ran his hand through the sand. He looked up at the ocean as a large wave echoed by. Christina knew he was rummaging through some dark shit, looking for a stepping-off point. Finally.

"When I was there, late in '66, early '67, they called it the Wadsworth Hospital." He veered off and told her about a play he'd read concerning this guy they called "The Elephant Man, a Mr. John Merrick." Whitefish explained the poor guy's condition, his deformity, and the play, he said, was the sad tale of Merrick's existence, especially his days at the primordial London Hospital back in the 19th century. "From the old photos and drawings I saw, that was the Wadsworth in a nutshell. 'Welcome home, son, a grateful nation says fuck you.'" They shared a haunting but knowing moment. Whitefish reported, "I think they rebuilt it long before you rotated through."

Christina slid off the log and joined him on the sand.

Whitefish sat forward. His uninterrupted dialogue transported Christina to the Central Highlands of Vietnam, Plei Trap—that jungle paradise snuggled close to the Cambodian border. It was October of '66, and before he launched into the tragic tale, he realized that outside of his mother and a couple of fucking douchebags at the VA—those Army assholes with clipboards—this young woman would be the first "outside person" to know the full and ugly breadth of his story.

Life is so random.

Without editorial or embroidery, he walked her through his house of pain: Sarge, Ralphie, Ricky Dick, and the Whale. Then, as a consequence, his own destruction. Followed by his fevered and bloody removal from the meat fields.

It was at this juncture that he dropped the bombshell: his then, now, and forever malady—his status as Asbury Park's resident eunuch. And don't forget the catheter. Then he asked Christina, "What's your last name?" She told him. He continued on, telling her that outside of his mother and a couple of VA docs, "Christina MacKenzie was the only other person alive" that knew the crushing extent of his personal mutilation.

Whitefish's next statement turned out to be a strange period on his nightmarish hellscape: "One of my employees, Donna Stefanelli, probably knows a little something, but nowhere near the actual truth. So far she's kept it on the QT... but that's a whole other story."

He barely got the last line out when she reached over and held his hand. Tears spilled from their now swollen eyes, their collective gaze fixed on the waves. It felt like an eternity before Whitefish suggested, "Feel like swimming to Spain?"

She thought about it for a hot second, "I'd probably have to eat first." They nervously laughed in that awkward moment when people realized they were still holding hands.

Whitefish offered breakfast as their hands drifted apart, "You know I make a pretty good oatmeal... and I'm also in possession of some killer Guatemalan coffee... if you're up for it."

Christina stood, brushing off her hands and ass, "I can eat oatmeal and drink coffee."

They started back. Christina wondered, "Did you like Los Angeles?"

Whitefish was a bit stiff but kept moving, "I did, actually. Very much. Chili dogs at Pink's. Mustard, onions. Oh yeah."

She twinkled a devilish smile, bumping into him on purpose, "Sounds pretty mild for the Whitefish. Me? Mushroom Swiss cheese dog. Lots of mayo."

He yelled out, "DAMN, THAT SOUNDS GOOD!!!"

A dog barked. She had a recommendation: "Put it on your menu or that other thing, what's it called? A sandwich board? C'mon, you're the boss."

He yelled again, "YO LOU! MUSHROOM SWISS DOG. HEAVY MAYO. MAKE IT HAPPEN!!!"

Two hundred feet behind them, on that deserted corner of Ocean and Spier, another massive flock of seagulls passed over Allenhurst—this outpost where God and her angels were witness to an unlikely confluence of souls.

❖ ❖ ❖

As they retraced their steps back toward the Boardwalk, their far-off wars and alleged recoveries were put on hold. Whitefish regaled Christina with various moments in Asbury Park history—the great saltwater pool, those crazy amusement rides like "The Zipper," the giant "Breidt's Beer" sign that once hovered above mankind, the emergence of a skinny troubadour named Springsteen, and then, of course, the occasional shipwreck.

Walking south, they approached the yawning remains of Convention Hall—the ever-present architectural monster that consumed the Boardwalk whole; this anomaly stretched from the thrashing waves in the east to the empty streets heading west. And on this day, like most, its giant doors were flung wide open, inviting humanity to pass on through to the other side >>> toward Club Southside, maybe Havana, or possibly those massive ice sheets down in distant Antarctica.

Unbeknownst to either Christina or a pontificating Whitefish, the little girl, Shanice, was perched atop her trusty Schwinn, casually wandering through their boardwalk wake. She decided to swing right and then bounced down a ramp onto Ocean Ave, leaving the pretty girl and her limping companion as they morphed into silhouettes, swallowed by this Jersey relic, this dinosaur.

CHRISTINA and the
WHITEFISH

36
Gut-spillin' time.

I WAS WORKING FOR LYNDON BAINES JOHNSON and his Whiz Kid, Bob McNamara, when I took one for the team back in '66. It's been twenty-eight years since that fateful day in the wilds of Indochina. When I returned to this Monmouth County sandbar, I only confided and told my story to one human being – the woman who infused life into my lungs.

She deserved the truth.

As my pendulum clock strikes 1:00am, I've been sitting here trying to figure out why I spilled my guts this morning to one Christina MacKenzie – a young woman I've known for maybe forty-eight hours. We did my calisthenics together, and then she tagged along for the hike. In Allenhurst (of all places), we shared our collateral damage, our mutual nightmares. You already know mine, but Christina's, well, that's private – suffice it to say it's bad.

Now, there's no doubt we share a great deal of pain and suffering. No doubt we were both cannon fodder for capitalism – bamboozled by Uncle Sam and his hokum bill of goods: the alleged export of liberty and democracy. Good ol' Manifest Destiny. Bludgeon anything that's not Anglo-Saxon; good for bizness and empire building. And there's no doubt that Christina and the Whitefish were brother and sister in arms. That connection bonds you instantly – but I've known plenty of Boonie Rat buddies in my day and never had the urge to go full monty with my so-called secret. Not even close.

So why has today become gut-spillin' time with a virtual unknown?

I have a theory that may sound bonkers-barmy-and-a-little-bit-berserk. But it seems to make a shitload of sense. See if you agree.

Lying like a sack of rocks in the 24th Evacuation Hospital, Long Binh, and then again at the 6th Convalescent Center at Cam Ranh Bay, I had one overriding thought: I would probably never get married and most assuredly never have kids. Ma and I had just lost the old man, so it was common knowledge (at least in my head) that I'd find the girl of my dreams (or nightmares; it's always a crapshoot), get hitched (Ma would love that), and then start to repopulate the family with young'uns (Ma would really love that). Instead, I repopulated my end of the Boardwalk with a troupe of misfits – love 'em all... the way you love pets or fish in a tank. But not like your own children, not like the girl of your dreams.

Then years later, out of the clear blue, Christina explodes on my scene like a fallen angel, a rogue seraph who fled God's throne, escaped Isaiah's psychedelic vision, and landed here - in the land that time forgot.

I know, I know. I've probably romanticized Christina's arrival just a wee bit: "Dorothy in red slippers, standing in that magnificent sunburst, a fallen angel." Yeah, I hear it. Maybe over the top, but you have to admit: We were harmonious from the outset, long before our connection was even identified. And in that moment of clarity – that moment when we both became aware – that's when this young woman began to resemble the daughter (or woman) I never had, the daughter (or woman) I will never have. Hence, the basis of my theory:

Two space travelers sharing a rented rocket ship for a few ticks through time.

When we returned home, it was way past my scheduled breakfast, but I survived. I made oatmeal for two (a full cup of oats, double the water) and then pressed out two mugs of a new Guatemalan dark roast that is "scrumptious," as Ma used to say. Although, little did I know, Christina has a serious coffee background in Angel City, working at some joint called Star Bucks. She says they're going to be big everywhere. I wish them luck. We sat at my small kitchen table (no one ever has), and she filled me in on the art of being, what she called, "a barista." Sounds like she could make any coffee concoction in seconds flat. Suddenly, I was a bit nervous. Was my Guatemalan dark really as good as advertised? Lo and behold, she seemed to genuinely enjoy my brew.

We had our oatmeal and I shared another undeniable connection: I, too, lost a parent to a random tragedy. You already know the story: 1965. Shot three times during a grocery store hold-up. He was only forty-two. I was their only child.

Turns out Christina is also an only child.

Under the heading of misery loves company, I made more coffee, explaining to Private MacKenzie that the beans were from Guatemala's Antigua region—soil-rich farms situated between three volcanoes: Fuego, Acatenango, and Agua. Private MacKenzie carefully tasted the next batch and concluded after much deliberation, "Dark chocolate for sure and maybe toasted almond."

In this Corporal's opinion, the Private was spot-on.

\#

CHRISTINA and the
WHITEFISH

37

Emotional Rescue.

It was mid-morning when Christina left the Club Southside. Her private breakfast, an unexpected treat. But she felt dead tired. No wonder, she thought, the last three hours were a mental roller coaster. Oddly, that Stones' song, "Emotional Rescue," was playing in her head—but then she found herself smiling, remembering a night when that video came on MTV for like the millionth time as Jaime pranced around her room mimicking Jagger like a clucking chicken, pulling Christina into her crazy gambol. *"Ooh ah, ah, ah, ooh, ah, ah, ah."*

♫*I'll be your savior, steadfast and true*

They laughed so hard they collapsed on the bed. The universe must have saved some of Jaime's energy from that long-ago night in a cloud somewhere off the Jersey coast, enough to rain down a smile for Christina on this grueling morning. Good timing—she needed the emotional rescue on this humid scorcher. And then it dawned on her: You've been here for three days, go for a swim! Thoughts ping-ponged between her ears: *I have no bathing suit... but what's the difference? There's no one here except the occasional zombie... I've never gone in the water with my clothes on... Screw it. Take off your sneaks and get in the water, Christina.*

She gazed around, and outside of that giant freakish clown painted on the abandoned Palace Amusements, who the hell would know? First sauntering as if to sneak in unnoticed, but then running after the Boardwalk turned to sand, Christina tossed her red sneakers and keys near the water's edge and bolted straight into the tide. It felt cool, it felt amazing, and then she dove into a wave, swimming out the other side. Clothes or no clothes, the ocean offered a rush—and salt, she tasted salt, she forgot all about the goddamn salt! She bobbed and weaved as easy waves passed by, the horizon shifting, an oil tanker loitered in the distance.

Turning to face the beach and boardwalk façade, her view resembled the mise en scène of an old stodgy theatre, a gap in time where transient memories might emerge, like the one developing downstage, on the wet sand near the edge of ebb & flow, a discolored and faded Ektachrome snapshot—she was the little kid digging earnestly with her red pail and shovel.

She wondered, "Was this the area where that thievery happened?"

She figured it had to be since she clearly recalled that creepy clown, ugly Tillie cackling at her loss: her brand-new red pail and white shovel that Mom & Dad bought that very morning. At Woolworths. Her favorite store. And she was going to build a mighty sandcastle, one that lasted the test of time, but then she wandered away from the dig hole for what seemed like only a few seconds. She had the audacity to turn her back ON HER BELONGINGS while living an honorable life right here in the State of New Jersey, something she learned never to do again.

She was crying frantically as her Dad swooped in, trying to console his daughter back toward their beach encampment of umbrellas and coolers—she clung tightly to his neck as he cradled her along. She remembered Tillie snorting and snickering, blowing up its cheeks, wagging its slimy tongue. And even to this day, as the memory dissolved and the curtain dropped, Christina stared at that fucking clown, figuring Tillie had to be the mastermind of the great bucket heist.

> *You wrote that short story in English Lit about the red bucket and how you lost it there, in the ocean. Was it Atlantic City? I can't remember. But please Christina, GO FIND YOURSELF. Go find that goddamn red bucket.*

Does it mean something? Or does it mean nothing?

Or was she drifting too far from shore?

Is this how Chris McCandless felt when he walked into the wilds of Alaska? A chance to go out on your own terms? She could keep drifting toward Spain and Portugal. Go under. Swallow hard. And in the blink of God's eye, everything would evaporate, she'd say goodbye to the war, to the constant flashes of Jack & Darlene's mangled dead bodies—she read the report; she knew what the letters d-e-c-a-p-i-t-a-t-i-o-n meant. No more racing and pounding heart. Obsessive frantic thinking be gone! Along with the terrifying awareness that you're losing control— of everything. Go under. Swallowing hard means never having to wrestle your live-wire nervous system again! Or those furious attacks that someday, like an angry mob, will finally overwhelm your defenses. C'mon, it's fast, it'll be over before you know it. Leave on your terms. C'mon, all three MacKenzies gone, together, amen.

Still soaking wet and barefoot, carrying her sneakers back toward the car, she heard a commotion.

A throaty '69 Pontiac GTO was crawling alongside a young woman who seemed to know the driver but wanted nothing to do with man or machine. The GTO, painted a weird Earl Scheib blue, would occasionally backfire. If she slowed down or sped up, so would the car. In an attempt to escape the obvious harassment, the woman crossed toward Tillie and the forsaken old amusements, moving closer to Christina. The driver looked and sounded like a reincarnation of James Cagney, "Get in the fuckin' car, Donna, or I swear..." The woman slowed next to Christina and blasted back at the driver, "I'm going to work. GET OUT OF MY FACE!"

Cagney jammed on the brakes, and his sidekick jumped out from the passenger side, "Stop the bullshit, get in the car."

Donna's last chance was Christina, she asked softly, "Do you have a car? Can you get me out of here?" The Datsun was right there, facing in the opposite direction. Christina reached for her keys, "Get in, it's open."

Both women hopped into Julian's getaway car. Cagney yelled out, "Who the hell is this broad?!" Christina jammed it into first and peeled out along Kingsley, hanging a quick left down 1st Ave. Now the Cagney wannabe screamed at the sidekick, "Get in the fuckin' car!" As he floored it into a U-turn, the passenger door swung open wildly, his sidekick hanging on for dear life. The GTO jerked and kicked before stalling out, just as the sidekick fell out of the car. Then it backfired. Cagney screamed, "This stupid piece of shit!" The car wouldn't start as Cagney alternated twists of the ignition with punches on the dashboard: "Stupid piece of shit! Stupid piece of shit!"

Energized, Christina was impressed with her gear-shifting skills, especially under pressure.

"Fuck, you're a lifesaver."

"I'm Christina."

"Hi. I'm Donna."

"Stefanelli?"

Dumbfounded, Donna leaned forward, "What the fuck?"

"I know Whitefish. He just mentioned you. Said you were an employee."

"Oh shit. That's fucking weird."

A long moment passed as they cruised down 1st Ave, crossed the bumpy train tracks, and then headed north along Memorial.

Donna motioned with her Marlboro and lighter, "Mind?" Christina waved, "Sure, no problem." The Bic fired up, "That's where I was going before Quentin went batshit crazy. Blowfish put me on—sorry, 'Whitefish' put me on to waitress today." Donna exhaled out her window, "How do you know the Fish?"

Christina downshifted to a red light, "Met him a couple of days ago. We have some Army stuff in common."

Green light. "Sorry I got you involved. I'm trying to end this thing." Donna smirked, "As you can see, that's going well."

Christina asked, "Where can I take you? I have a room if you need some time."

Donna wasn't used to kindness, "Thanks, but I have to go to work. Your new buddy'll throw a shit-fit if I don't show up." Christina laughed as Donna gestured directions, "Just make a right up here around the park, on Sunset. We'll circle back at Ocean." Donna smiled, realizing, "You're all wet."

"I took a dip in the ocean."

"You know, they got this new invention out called a bathing suit."

Christina laughed, "Yeah, I've read something about that."

Donna took another long drag, "Where you from?"

Christina made the right on Sunset, "Used to be North Jersey but now Los Angeles."

"Wow. California. That must be nice."

The city park was a surprising oasis. “This is really pretty.”

Donna enjoyed her smoke, “I used to play in there.” The iridescent lake passed on the right as Donna stared out across the well-manicured park—unsullied greenery replete with small islands, walking bridges, and a lush canopy of elm and black gum trees.

And then, sounding very philosophical, Donna had a dream, “Someday, Christina, I’m getting out of this shithole.”

CHRISTINA and the WHITEFISH

38

Bronx Zoo, 1963.

Returning to the Sea Breeze felt like returning home. Christina wanted one thing: climb into bed and sleep. Turn on the radio and sleep. She teased herself, "Too much unsupervised reality." Her Dad had a saying when things got heavy: "Drop back twenty and punt." He was right. She needed to punt. The windows in the room were wide open, but the airflow was negligible on this humid day. She pulled the chain over the bed and the ceiling fan became an instant hero, generating a perfect zephyr that would make sleep possible. She also made sure to thank the Greek god Zephyrus for his unexpected help. (Christina knew her Greek gods.)

Curled up bare on rumpled sheets, she hugged her pillow tight. Outside, cars and a motorcycle zipped by. Children played, probably in the church courtyard. A train arrived at the nearby station—a minute later it continued on. The last thing she heard before dozing off was a radio newsman interviewing Governor Christine Todd Whitman. The MacKenzies would have voted for Jim Florio were they still alive.

When her eyes fluttered open, she knew she'd been asleep for a while. The light in the room shifted dramatically. The church bell rang five times as she rolled over to face the whirling fan, declaring out loud, "Jesus offers salvation *and* the time of day. Such a deal." Her energy was back. She felt like she could fly. Right now. Out the window and soar past the cross and steeple. The adjacent bay. Over verdant farmland. She'd find the Delaware River. Hang a hard right north toward Belvidere. Find the falls. Cut through town. Down the Nguyen's street. Around that giant oak tree. Float through Jaime's open window, wheels down for a soft landing. Slide into bed next to her. Where she belonged. Sleeping in each other's arms. Leonard Cohen singing for the poets.

Christina sat up. She thought about Donna having to deal with that asshole. She thought about how Whitefish made her breakfast, still amazed by their almost incomprehensible connection through time and space. She also thought about how much she loved this simple room. The view outside. The life-saving fan still performing its magic. Time to be practical: take a shower, get dressed, happy hour at the Club Southside. You need a drink. Or six.

She ran into Millie on her way out. The innkeeper was feather dusting the mantle above the old fireplace. Christina's newborn energy generated an impulsive invite, "Would you like to go out for breakfast tomorrow morning? My treat?" Millie was touched, and the invite seemed to raise her spirits on just another lackluster any old kind of day.

❖ ❖ ❖

Similar to the first time, Christina was pleasantly surprised when she walked into the Club—it felt so inviting, especially when stacked against the boneyard that existed outside. The jukebox was in a state of transition: Donovan's "Mellow Yellow" faded away as the mechanism grabbed the off-beat and unexpected "Frederick." Christina crossed toward the bar, thinking, "I love Patti Smith."

♫ *Hi, hello, awake from thy sleep*

Behind the bar, working over paperwork, Whitefish was chatting with Lou; Christina moved toward the empty seats at the far end of the bar. She carried her now tattered *Outdoor* magazine. "Alright, we'll shut down for two nights as long as it's not Friday or Saturday," Whitefish declared. "The kitchen's yours." He tapped the paper, "I'll take my cut on the nurses' gig plus ten percent because I don't want any of that cop money."

Lou liked the deal, grabbed the paperwork and was off to the galley, "Done. Thanks, boss."

Donna was busy. She moved up to the bar and put down her tray, "Two Guinness," then smiled toward Christina as she ducked inside the kitchen. Whitefish moved down near Christina and filled Donna's order, "Hey."

She gave him a subtle salute, "Hey."

As he pulled the Guinness pour, "I hear you and Donna had some excitement earlier."

Christina nodded, "She was in a jam. We had to Thelma and Louise it."

Whitefish smiled, "I never caught that flick but I get the reference." He leaned in close and lowered his voice, taking a serious tone, making it clear she was now privy to an upcoming reality, "At some point, Quentin will absorb a much-deserved ass-kicking." Back to normal, "What can I get you?"

Christina pointed to the Guinness, then changed the subject, "Sounds like you're gonna be closed for a couple nights." Whitefish placed the first two drafts up on Donna's tray, "Yeah, Lou gets catering jobs every now and then. He uses the kitchen. I get a cut and a night off." Donna pounced on her order, "Thank you," and headed back into the fray.

Christina wondered, "Why don't you want the cop money?"

He filled her Guinness, "I'm not a big fan of the gendarmes in general, especially the Gestapo in this town. They crack skulls for amusement. Here you go." Again, he lowered his voice, "And if you're gay or Black or god forbid both... these assholes have a long history, so I really don't want their fucking money. The Visiting Nurses Association? Absolutely. Those are useful people."

Whitefish spied something good coming his way, grabbed the soda gun like a microphone, and announced an arrival with his own sporadic reverb, like a prizefight at the Polo Grounds: "In this corner... *corner-corner,* hailing from the great city of Schenectady, New York... *York-York*—weighing whatever a middleweight weighs, the master of disaster, the mayor of Uppercut City, ladies and germs... *germs-germs:* Charles 'Tombstone' Lee! *Lee-Lee!*" A few scattered claps. "You're early, champ," as Whitefish shadowboxed his bartender. "Yeah, I know." Whitefish draped his arm around Charles, "Christina, say hello to Charles. Charles, Christina."

After the pleasantries, Christina asked, "Why do they call you Tombstone?"

Charles hemmed and hawed as he tied on his waist apron. Whitefish answered the bell, "Ah, he's too modest. *Ring* magazine once called Charles the next Sugar Ray Robinson. Dude had a sledgehammer right cross. Sent many a man to an early grave." She got it, pointing, "Tombstone." Charles leaned in toward Christina, "Yeah, until someone sent me to an early grave." She laughed.

Donna busted in, "Is there a bartender working tonight?" She winked at Christina, "I need two Rob Roys and a Dewar's neat." Charles swung into action as Donna headed to the galley.

Whitefish queried Christina, "You hungry? I'm making pasta if you want in." She nodded, sure. He wiped his hands, "Enjoy your beer. Gimme thirty to shower. Charles, the Guinness is on me."

It was sort of weird: On the ride over, a guy in a crosswalk reminded her of Prince, and now the jukebox was playing "Little Red Corvette." She sipped the Guinness and perused the room from her perfect vantage point; what a strange and curious—no, what a strange and deviant place, but also warm and comforting. Christina continued to find the juxtaposition shocking: dreary indolence outside, bouncing verve inside. It was like *whoosh*—down the White Rabbit's burrow.

More patrons kept arriving and assumed seats at available tables or at the gorgeously beefy wood-carved bar where she sat. Somehow, anarchy worked here. A heavyset man plopped down next to her, tossing his *Daily Racing Form* to the side, "Greetings and salutations, Young Tombstone." Charles already had a lowball glass in hand, dropped in two cubes, and poured a double Jameson, "Good to see you, Joe." Smooth as silk, the drink was delivered lickety-split. Joe Fats raised his glass, "Salute."

Charles asked Christina, "You still good?" She smiled, "Yes, thanks, Charles." Fats glanced her way and offered a nuanced salute, as did Christina, who detected an overbearing cologne wafting off her new bar mate.

The Club Southside also presented a collection of brutish faces, reminding Christina of those Fellini movies they watched in film appreciation class with Mr. Peterson. In some ways, the entire joint was a caricature of itself—and yet she felt oddly at home.

❖ ❖ ❖

The "living quarters" upstairs, as Whitefish called his apartment, was unique to say the least. Ever since breakfast, its overall milieu intrigued Christina—a small, cozy place, yet seemingly filled to the gills with life's ornaments; dimly lit, but no doubt strategically so. And for a single guy who always appeared somewhat disheveled, his "living quarters" were squeaky-clean—a major accomplishment, she thought, considering the density of his stuff. She wondered, "Maybe a maid?" Or maybe he's just OCD.

Christina relaxed on a stool in the kitchen as Whitefish cooked. She felt like she was in some out-of-the-way corner of a museum. She hadn't seen the bedroom, but three walls of the "parlor" were floor-to-ceiling bookshelves crammed with titles from *The Iliad* and *The Odyssey* to *The Bridges of Madison County*. The largest wall, the one without books, offered framed posters and photographs of varying sizes: Che Guevara reading a newspaper, Marilyn and Joe D in a happy moment, a portrait shot of a smirking George Carlin, Frida along with Diego's stomach, Thomas Edison holding a lightbulb, a 1920s woman named "Emma" wearing horn-rimmed glasses, a casual Albert Einstein smoking a pipe, Malcolm X holding an automatic rifle, one Lenin, and then the other Lennon. What a strange collection, she thought. But at the center of this hodgepodge, clearly on purpose, was the largest and boldest: a poster of a 1950s businessman looking at his reflection in a mirror with the overhanging signage that read: "THE MOST DANGEROUS ANIMAL IN THE WORLD." There was an inscription underneath, "Bronx Zoo, 1963." Wow, she thought.

In the middle of the parlor there was a writing station: a solid oak mid-century swivel desk chair in front of three smallish tables; one piled with books, another with two stacks of typing paper, and the center table supported an old typewriter along with a green glass banker's desk lamp.

"That smells amazing... and this wine is killer," Christina announced as *La bohème* played in the background. "Northern Italy," Whitefish specified as he chopped tomatoes and lettuce. "The winemaker employs what they call the 'ripasso' method, which uses partially dried grapes." He sipped for some immediacy, some context, "Great depth, no harsh tannins. Blackberries, blueberries. Dark fruit, right?"

Christina sipped a bit more, "I don't know, but it sure tastes good. Which opera is this?"

He pointed toward the unseen sound waves, "Decca recording of Puccini's 'La bohème,' circa mid-fifties. Ma's favorite."

Christina spotted a framed, handwritten piece of paper and moseyed over to get a closer look, "What's this? Oh, a recipe."

Whitefish tossed the salad, "That's what smells so great. My buddy's mother made killer gravy... that's tomato sauce to you Irish folk."

Christina enjoyed the banter, "Hey, I know about gravy. I've been around." Whitefish raised his glass. Touché.

Dinner was terrific. Christina couldn't remember the last time she felt so at ease, so safe. The meal was simple but perfect. She showed off three years of high school Italian, "Delicata. Deliziosa. Piacevole." They talked about growing up. They talked about their mamas and their papas. How Jack & Darlene loved teaching. How Whitefish mostly educated himself. He mentioned he was writing a chronicle of his life. She pointed to the parlor set-up. He acknowledged the connection, "Indeed. That's where I mangle the English language." He also talked about a special car he wanted to show Christina.

As they were cleaning up, Whitefish wondered, "What's up with the magazine?" Christina gave him a brief ten-thousand-foot view of the article about Chris McCandless. She asked him if he would read it and offer his thoughts. He said, "Of course, posthaste."

Whitefish suggested an after-dinner port down at the bar, "Let's see what the savages are up to." When they arrived, the bar was standing room only, and what a cast of characters: Bagel, Joe Fats, Lil Abner, the good ol' Texaco Three (always in uniform), a tall and lanky albino cowpoke they called Texas-T (vaquero wardrobe under a ten-gallon hat), not to mention a crusty old chap named Mickey Finn who stepped straight out of a Dickens novel. This mélange of human wreckage was topped off by the aforementioned musical group, "Two Jacks and a Jill"—the threesome enjoying a well-earned night off from their residency at the East Brunswick Holiday Inn.

As usual, a full-scale squabble was underway, a cacophony of blaring nonsense. Banging on the bar, Texas-T took control with his Lone Star drawl, "Alright, alright, listen up, you done beat that with a stick, let's start this thing over. Bless your heart, Vinnie, but shut the fuck up! You'd argue with a wooden Indian." Group laughter. "Listen closely, here's the shit," Texas-T laid it out, "Hoss from Bonanza along with The Rifleman, Lucas McCain... against Mr. Spock and Captain James T. Kirk."

Tombstone passed by Christina as he carried a bucket of fresh ice back behind the bar, "Some crew, huh?" She really liked the hard-working bartender.

Vinnie asked, "Hey jerkoff, any weapons?"

Texas-T confirmed, "Phasers and shotguns... unlimited ammunition." Doing his best Horshack impression, Joey anxiously raised his hand, "Whaaa whaa what kind of shh-shh-shotgun has un-un-unlimm-unlimited am-amm-amm-muuu—" Mickey Finn was busting, "Jesus Christ, spit it out!" Danny pushed Mickey, "Shut the fuck up. It's a good question!" Whitefish was pouring two ports, "Calm down, Danny... and Mickey, he's right, shut the fuck up." Texas-T was incredulous, "Oh, you can buy the idea of phasers and all that sci-fi cow-shit, but not shotguns with unlimited ammunition? Try thinkin' outside the box!"

Donna passed Christina and stage-whispered, so everyone could hear, "Get out while you can." Christina was really enjoying the insanity.

Joe Fats: "Are we in space or the Old West?"
Jill: "Does it really matter?"
Bagel: "Of course it matters. Environment makes a big difference."
Joe Fats: "Okay, North Dallas Forty, space or the Old West?"
Texas-T: "Put 'em in space, Jesus Christ."
Bagel: "See? Space is daunting. Right off the bat, you gotta think about gravity."
Whitefish: "Or the lack thereof."

Whitefish handed Christina her glass of port.

Vinnie: "Zero gravity favors Hoss. Turns that tub of shit into a killing machine."
Lil Abner: "Spock was never good with a phaser. You can tell. Only with that Vulcan Death Grip—and by the way, how's he getting that close to anybody? McCain'll cut him in half before you can say vivisection."
Danny: "Let's ask Miss California what she thinks."

Christina sipped her port and then didn't miss a beat—

Christina: "This is easy since I don't see Kirk as a factor whatsoever. The dude is an absolute ladies man interested in one thing and one thing only: getting laid—therefore Shatner's useless... and personally, I never bought the whole phaser thing... sometimes the target disappears, sometimes they don't, there's never any blood... and c'mon, Spock and Kirk both look slow as shit. And remember, Lucas McCain is a legendary gunslinger—greased lightning with that cannon. And Vinnie's right, 'vivisection' is the perfect word. I say this thing is over before it even starts. I'm going old school."

Lil Abner started clapping. So did Vinnie, adding, "Fucking eh!" Charles flashed a long-distance high-five, which Christina returned. Whitefish raised his port, "Miss California has spoken."

❖ ❖ ❖

When Christina finally left, the night air felt good. The humidity had lifted. Down on the beach, there was a gorgeous bonfire. She watched from the Boardwalk railing, rogue embers floating skyward. Forty or fifty young people had gathered around the crackling fire, drinking and partying. The ocean breeze whipped through, creating a rhythmic dance of flames. It was beautiful. She became fixated on the blaze. No doubt hypnotic, powerful. Since humans peered out from caves, she thought, fire has offered dominion.

Suddenly and without warning, Christina felt her consciousness waning, dissolving.

Terrified, she held the railing. Rigid. Shaking. As if something had shot through her body. She dropped her car keys. Her vision shifted. To some grisly reality that came roaring back. Sirens and horrific screams. Rotors and blades thrumming, shaking. *Please help! NO. NO. NO. NO!*

Now she could see it clearly: a de Havilland Beaver DHC-2 slamming into an icy glacier peak. General Sherman growling between her ears: "WAR IS HELL!"

In the blink of an eye, Christina's expanding safe haven and growing sense of normalcy went up in smoke.

֎

39
Shipwrecked.

WHEN CHUCK WROTE "It was the best of times, it was the worst of times," he must have been writing about today, in Asbury Park, this long day's journey into night. I'm writing this entry at three in the morning, acknowledging once again that the masters of war relish and revel in the act of dumping conscripts into the mix master, setting the motor on high, all the while chuckling and guffawing as they watch us spin and shred; and then once liquified, they turn us loose, back into the maze, no matter how severe the jumbled mess – minds rewired by madmen. "So we beat on," wrote Fitzgerald, "boats against the current, borne back ceaselessly into the past."

That's us. Human YO-YOs. And tonight it was C-Mac's turn. Tomorrow? Who knows, maybe me, maybe her again... but for sure any number of planetary members in the "Fucked to Hell Soldiers Club." SHELL SHOCK plays random selection. No rhyme nor reason. But there's one thing for certain, for both of us, and god knows how many others just like us:

There will always be another ride in the saddle.

I sit here wondering, damn near dreaming: Is she a mermaid who washed ashore in our golden hamlet, this low-rent Bermuda Triangle? Is Christina MacKenzie a ghostly relic from one of those forgotten Asbury Park shipwrecks? Or maybe a modern-day Lemuel Gulliver (Lemuella Gulliver?) touching down in our own unique land of Lilliputians.

Regardless of that nonsense, in a matter of forty-eight hours my recent esprit de corps with C-Mac (she told me friends sometimes called her C-Mac) has grown by leaps and bounds. Unfortunately, our connection was born in hell, yes, continents and oceans apart, but it's the same inferno. I can hear the sirens wailing now, creeping up on the stark poetry of Black Sabbath's "War Pigs"–

Generals gathered in their masses
Just like witches at black masses
Evil minds that plot destruction
Sorcerer of death's construction

That's where we found Christina tonight, shackled by witches leading black masses.

The trauma stays with you like a plague. Or more scientifically, like herpes or Hep B, or even AIDS. No doubt you can live a pseudo-normal life with the proper treatment and support – although it takes great endurance, and for some, medication... but usually that shit will render your head damn near useless. We used to call it "head on a post." And pray to God you weren't one of those untold millions, Vietnamese and Americans, exposed to Agent Orange, that pernicious and malignant defoliant dreamed up by Dow Chemical, Monsanto, and a host of other contract killers – this lethal venom used liberally and gleefully by the U.S. military.

There's a special place in hell for these war profiteers.

Now, I don't know for sure, but my guess is that Uncle Sam and those VA shrinks played Dr. Frankenstein with C-Mac. The bastards get more proficient over time at managing their damage – both mentally and physically. Especially after their most recent war of imperial vanity. They pitch the so-called antidote like a damn ad campaign:

"Don't worry, boys and girls, we'll build you back good as new. And check it out: revolutionary prosthetics with some space-age robotics. 'TAKE ME TO YOUR LEADER.' People will marvel! And if you just wanna forget everything, you've come to the right place! Just swallow these four times a day. 'What are they,' you ask? A dream come true - your personal magic carpet ride."

Joe Fats discovered Christina curled up on the Boardwalk. And as soon as I saw those eyes and lack of spirit, I instinctively knew what went down. I asked Tombstone to carry her back inside. Everyone already left the club except for me, Fats, Donna, and Tombstone. Soon it was just me and Stefanelli. We buoyed C-Mac up on the sofa. Donna was on water and damp towel duty (which I believe is tantamount to boiling water when a woman goes into labor). I was on coaching duty (not that I was qualified).

Christina was still reeling... and, frankly, petrified. She was staring past me, into Never-Never Land. Now and again, her eyelids would flutter. I believe these are what doctors call "absence seizures" or "petit mal seizures." Children tend to get these. Fortunately, I've suffered through enough therapy sessions while also absorbing a shitload of street rap, all of which allowed me to yank her down off that precipice. She struggled but still managed to absorb my efforts at restoring her stability and control. It was rough. I was right in her face, not mean or angry, just straightforward serious. And I may have raised my voice. It seemed necessary. That's how some counselors got through to me.

My only medicine was reality: "That was then. This is now."

Think about taking Shakespeare's "what's past is prologue" (the idea that history contextualizes the present) and turning this pedestrian adage on its head – saying bullshit to that. In fact, to successfully control deep-seated trauma, one must effectively believe AS GOSPEL the exact opposite:

"What's past is fucking gone." To hell with prologue. Dust in the wind.

Good counselors make it clear: It's all about defining the hard facts that exist RIGHT NOW, as opposed to fearing what no longer exists. Let that scoundrel called FEAR "out the closet." High-Noon the motherfucker. Charlatans in the biz love their shortcuts... they employ and embrace chemicals to create Band-Aids of amnesia – very Madison Avenue, very American.

Mother's little helper.

Donna held her as I rambled on...

Finally, Christina reached for my hand, now smiling as if the clamps were removed from around her temples. That's when I knew Christina had regained control of her reality. She was out of her cage. It was about 1:00am. She said she could drive home. I agreed but still asked Donna to ride with her, make sure she turned in safe. Stefanelli gladly obliged.

I wasn't expecting to divert this chronicle of my life into a situation that was unfolding in real time, but this unexpected encounter with a mix master comrade – a woman who washed ashore just like the S.S. Morro Castle back in '34 – cannot go unheeded nor undocumented. Some occurrences cry out to be catalogued as worthy, revealed as truth.

Let's be honest: this town, right now, is good for nothing. That's obvious. As for me, I'm next in line to be branded "good for nothing."

But before that eventuality takes place, this current shipwreck might be an opportunity to truly serve a holy sister in distress – even if it's only pointing her in the right direction. Just this morning, Christina asked me if there were any responsibilities attached to being the King of Asbury Park. I said no, not really.

Clearly I was wrong. "Uneasy lies the head that wears a crown."

Enlightenment hovers on the horizon. Something meaningful under my bullshit watch as some bullshit King. So please forgive the detour.

\#

40

Angel or Demon?

The night air pumped much-needed life back into Christina, and she wanted to drive Donna home first, wherever home was, but Donna insisted that she get Christina tucked in safely. "I know you don't need a babysitter, but that's what Fish made me promise," Donna lamented, "and who the hell feels like listening to him bitch and moan?" They laughed as they pulled up to the Sea Breeze—dark except for the dim light bouncing off the wood-carved sign. Christina probed, "What's his real name? Do you know?" Donna popped open her door, "Beats me. It's like this big fucking secret, as if anyone gives a shit."

They chatted over the car roof. Christina asked, "Are you okay? Safe to be alone tonight?" Donna lit a cigarette, "Oh, you mean Quentin? Yeah, don't worry. I'll crash at my Aunt's. She's not far." A train approached the not-too-distant station. "You want me to walk you in?" Donna asked half-heartedly.

Christina was already moving toward the front porch, "Nah, I'm cool." Donna gave a slight wave as she dusted off into the night. Christina called after her, "Hey Donna… thanks for helping me out." By now, Donna was a shadow moving by the church, "Hey, I owed you one." Christina tossed out a final offering, "Sorry I was so fucked up." Donna answered from the darkness, "No more fucked up than the rest of us."

A few blocks away and on schedule, the last train of the day—the 1:30am North Jersey Coast—screeched to a grinding halt.

The first thing Christina did upon entering the shelter of Room 204 was flick on her favorite white noise—and the old radio didn't disappoint (Thanks, Charlie!). She had no idea the song playing was 1941's "I Hear a Rhapsody," an ancient romantic lullaby that suited the Sea Breeze, especially with the tuner's amber light framing the ensuant time tunnel that transported the old place to happier times.

Christina glanced out from her large picture window, wondering if she should take one or two Ambien—and jeepers creepers, who was down there smoking but Father Marlboro. She figured that the good padre either had radar or was smoking four packs a day. Because a second later, a factory-sized smoke plume left his mouth, and then, almost robotically, his eyes locked on her like a tractor beam. She then realized in the ruddiness of the streetlamp that this guy resembled the priest from *The Exorcist*.

"Poor bastard," she thought, "a damn peeping pope." They stared at each other for a weirdly long and strained moment. A wicked thought quickly emerged, dark folly really, one of those "not for public consumption," except now, for some reason, it was gaining momentum: At some point she had to undress, so why not here? Why not now? Let's give this holy man something to remember while he's waxing his carrot. Her eyes never left his, and a few seconds later, she was naked. Her stare could have melted steel.

She made the sign of the cross and turned away, thinking, "What the fuck was that? Am I an angel or demon?" But in the bathroom, at the mirror, she smiled as the right answer floated by, "To Father Marlboro, right now, I'm nothing but tits and ass." She laughed when she declared out loud, "And a grateful church says THANK YOU."

She took two Ambien from her baggie filled with prescribed goodies—leftovers from her days before Doc Genovese. In fact, she's kept Big Pharma by her side all these months, a security blanket, just in case. Actually, these two pills were her first foray back into the world of "better living through chemistry." She flicked off the light and climbed into bed, her eyes fixed on the tuner's faint amber light. Just before Louise Massey's "My Adobe Hacienda" faded into another 40s classic, Christina thought, "How lovely a song." Room 204 agreed as it kept diligent watch over Christina, who slowly, gently, let go. Innocent sleep.

> ♫*In my adobe hacienda*
> *There's a touch of Mexico*
> *Cactus lovelier than orchids*
> *Blooming in the patio*
> *Soft desert stars and the strum of guitars*
> *Makes every evening seem so sweet*
> *In my adobe hacienda*
> *Life and love are more complete*

❖ ❖ ❖

Millie was dressed and ready by 7:30am.

By 9:30am, Millie figured Christina must have forgotten. Or "blew her off," as the kids enjoy saying. So, like most mornings, she made some toast and tea and watched life outside her kitchen window. There he was, young Father McBride. "Another cigarette," she thought, "How is this guy still alive? And why is he staring upstairs?"

A screaming, loud siren from a passing hook and ladder wrestled Christina from her Ambien sleep. The radio station was back to a news drone, which she flicked off on her way to the toilet. The small clock pointed at 11:33am. She sat on the commode and peed, realizing the sedative knocked her for a loop. "Oh fuck, Millie. Damn it. Shit."

By noon, sitting in Millie's kitchen, Christina had apologized at least three times. But now she was lost in a stream of Earl Grey landing in her floral cup. Whitefish's words from last night hit sporadically, machine-gun blasts of good and bad tidings. They resonated akin to Genovese's words at Peace House—powerful, but in a way that was even more authentic. It was like being back in the shit, and he was pulling her out by the arms, out of the quicksand, out of her gruesome nightmare. The beauty part? It was the first time Christina could differentiate reality from hallucination right in the goddamn moment. The visual recognition was a divine epiphany. She could still hear Whitefish's insistence: "What's past is prologue—bullshit! What's past is fucking gone!" The tea settled in her cup, the surface moving like rippled glass.

Christina watched Millie cut two slices of white bread from a solid loaf, dropping them into her prehistoric toaster. She relished her newfound strength. She wanted desperately to cling to that fragile knowledge of what was real and what was delusional. Did Whitefish say, "High-Noon the motherfucker?" Christina thought she knew what that meant, but she'd have to confirm. She smiled, thinking, "He could be one cryptic SOB."

"Christina? (long pause) Christina?"

Millie was holding butter and jam, "Are you okay?"

Christina snapped to, "Sorry, I'm a million miles away... and Millie, I'm so sorry for flaking out."

Millie sat down, "Stop apologizing, young lady. As you say, we will go to your Johnny Be Goode diner tomorrow." They raised their tea cups. Deal.

❖ ❖ ❖

First she read the sandwich board's announcement:

Sloppy Joes | Brats + Kraut

Then she spotted Whitefish hosing down an outside wall of the Club Southside, water cascading over 'SCUSE ME WHILE I KISS THE SKY. His hockey jersey was white with red and blue trim—a large number seven on his back with the name GILBERT.

"Hey, Gilbert," Christina called out.

He smiled, "It's French Canadian, pronounced 'Zhil-Bear.'"

She moved next to him, "I don't follow football."

He play-acted his exasperation, "IT'S HOCKEY!"

She acknowledged the front of his jersey, "Oh, yeah, the Rangers. I went once. They lost." He stopped spraying from his trigger mechanism, "You look like you're doin' okay."

❖ ❖ ❖

In the galley, Lou plated four lunches, singing an old Italian folk song, "Sicilia bedda, Sicilia mia, Ti pensu sempri cu nostalgia..." A chicken fillet flamed on the char-grill as Whitefish prepped his daily lunch. He scooped brown rice on his arugula and tomato salad, and then asked Christina, "You sure you're not hungry?"

With prayer hands, she said no, thank you, "Just had some breakfast."

Whitefish's finishing touches were a well-rehearsed ballet: ground salt and pepper, along with a perfect dollop of Roquefort, spin the plate. "My meals," Whitefish confessed, "are habitual, as you may have surmised." Christina wondered, "In what way?" Whitefish flipped the chix, "Your good buddy is one sad ritualistic bastard."

Flames shot up as he pressed on the fillet with his spatula, "Two of my three meals you've already consumed and hopefully enjoyed." She confirmed, "Very much so," and then she acknowledged the trilogy, "and here lies your third." Whitefish pressed on the chicken again, watching the flames dance as he ran through his culinary conventions: He's been eating the same three meals "since Nixon was squatting in the White House," and he enjoys every meal "at exactly the same time," and finally, he will not eat a meal prepared by anyone else, "with Lou being the lone exception." In one fluid motion, the spatula slid under the char-grilled cutlet and delivered it atop his masterpiece—the finale of his Swan Lake.

Bowled over, Christina stopped time: "Wait a second. Not once in twenty years did you ever eat anything different?"

He admired his plate, "Nope. Except for five or six of Lou's extravaganzas." She waved him off, "No way, you're full of shit." He picked up his lunch and moved past her, "Hand to God and pinky swear. Arnold Palmer?" He disappeared through the swinging doors—and then from beyond the doors, he shouted, "See? We're both looney tunes." She agreed. Lou was still singing as she headed out to the bar, "That's nice, Lou... 'Beautiful Sicily, my Sicily,' right?" He smiled, "Tu parli Italiano?" She gestured, "Poco ma."

Club Southside was about half full. Not bad for a lunch hour crowd. Christina recognized some of Fellini's ensemble cast, although there were a few new additions from Central Casting. Donna barreled into the kitchen, "Lou, where are my brats?" Besides Whitefish enjoying his lunch and Christina sipping her Arnold Palmer, only Lil Abner sat at the bar, writing with a golf pencil in a tiny spiral notebook. "Fish," he waved his notes, "I got the line-up for tonight. Eight definites and one maybe." Whitefish asked, "Who's the maybe? Johnny Pots, I assume?" Abner snapped sarcastically, "Of course. He has a hard time deciding whether or not to breathe."

Christina asked, "What are you guys talking about?" Abner looked at Whitefish, wondering if the newbie was truth-worthy. Whitefish smirked at him, "Tell her."

Abner was suddenly skittish when addressing Christina, "We're doing a stand-up thing, a sort of competition if you will." Whitefish interjected, "It's not a 'sort of' competition, it's a fucking competition. I'm offering prizes for crissakes." Abner continued tapping his list, "These eight or nine people will try to top each other, what have you, with their real-life Springsteen stories, some of which sound whaddayacall iffy at best."

Whitefish added a period, "And then the audience votes. It should be a real hit... an homage to our native son, although Brucie Boy hasn't been his 'man of the people' invention since he moved into that antebellum palace up in Rumson." Whitefish then charged Abner with (1) getting their phone tree going, (2) putting a notice on the sandwich board, and then (3) "Make sure the contestants know they have to bring three to four people each. This ain't the March of Dimes." Like a good soldier, Lil Abner straightened his red chapeau, tapped his notebook on the bar, and was off. "Nice chatting with you, Christina."

Whitefish waited a moment for Abner to be out of earshot, "If you want to see a real freak show, stop by tonight. Yours truly'll be MC'ing, and these folks, him included, all kneel at that Springsteen altar. I take pleasure in bursting their bubble. It's like shooting carp in a barrel."

Christina laughed, "Try and keep me away." She was curious, "How do you really feel about him?" Whitefish stood, "Who? Bruce? Why? You sensing some love behind the curtain?" She smiled.

Then, as he walked his empty plate inside, "Wait here a sec, I wanna show you something."

&

41
Solidarity.

MY OLD MAN was my hero.

As you know, first and foremost, Frank Delgado was a muckraking newshound. The man of Portuguese descent who hailed from Weequahic (the predominantly Jewish section of Newark) was a rough and tumble reporter, a devoted journalist honored to write in the shadows of giants like Izzy Stone and Pete Hamill. He also loved the great Jersey sportswriter, Jerry Izenberg, even though Jerry worked for the "competition" (as Pop never referred to the "Star-Ledger" by name). He thought Izenberg was a brilliant Everyman – a poetic sportswriter who still appealed to the boorish fanatic; hit 'em hard with direct and robust prose, not unlike Jack London banging out gritty tales for a changing America.

At night, I always looked forward to the old man reading aloud from Jerry's daily column. That's how I became infatuated with sports, and I loved Jerry's style – short, choppy sentences that sounded lyrical when Frank Delgado read them to me, his son, my bedtime stories.

For the sake of posterity, I've kept many of Izenberg's columns in a large accordion folder that gets thicker with time. Here's a taste of Jerry's no-bullshit poetry:

"Muhammad Ali and Joe Frazier did not fight for the WBC heavyweight title last night. They did not fight for the heavyweight championship of the planet. They could have fought in a telephone booth on a melting ice flow. They were fighting for the championship of each other and for me that still isn't settled."

That's the kind of fertile education I was expected to embrace, served daily by Mr. and Mrs. Frank Delgado. And what a kick it was to see Pop's byline in the evening paper.

Quintessential Delgado was the investigative series he authored back in '64, stories that covered an ongoing racial uprising at the Lafayette Gardens – a public housing project in Jersey City. The old man wanted to

269

use the term "rebellion" instead of "riot" to describe this citizen's revolt. But the editors, as they were apt to do, won the political battle. He used "riot" (under protest).

I love this series for a number of reasons, but mostly because the entire working press – along with Lyndon Johnson and New Jersey Governor Richard Wagner – were tongue-licking the mayor and his goon-squad cops for their sadistic and violent response to the community. Instead, my old man focused on the people of Lafayette Gardens, the victims... and then Delgado had the audacity to ask the all-important question:

"WHY did this happen?"

So often journalists forget or conveniently overlook the WHY (the real WHY – that sacred place where the truth hides).

Here's a short segment from the first installment in the series. The clipping is dated August 4, 1964:

> In the course of our investigation, this reporter has interviewed dozens of citizens, the clergy, as well as various city officials who spoke on the condition of anonymity. The picture they paint is ugly, but one that needs to see the light of day. In fact, these tell-tale interviews, coupled with recently obtained records by the Newark Evening News, depict the public housing communities of Jersey City as being managed and controlled by ineffectual bureaucrats and agencies, oftentimes fueled by their adversarial bosses who exhibit no regard for the general welfare of the tenants, most of them Negroes. Critics also point to widespread corruption within these same agencies. City Councilman Richard Conti, who did not request anonymity for this report, is a strong but rare government voice in support of the city's tenants. He believes that "Local slumlords also shoulder a hefty amount of responsibility for this dire situation."
>
> The Negro citizens of Lafayette Gardens have experienced years of overt and covert abuse stemming from racially motivated and illegal housing exclusions all across New Jersey's second largest city. A growing

percentage of the abuse has been documented by this paper and other sources. Conti added, "This exclusion mirrors the rigorous segregation practices underway throughout the [Jersey City] public school system." One city official called this parallel pattern of segregation "despicable."

`Finally, the city cops.` Our extensive investigation does not simply chronicle random prejudicial anecdotes about police neglect or the so-called isolated abusive and violent actions by law enforcement, but rather these powerful first-hand interviews establish an ongoing narrative that can only be defined as systemic institutional racism and violence throughout the Jersey City Police Department. This harsh reality frequently manifests itself in what the American Civil Liberties Union (ACLU) calls `"police brutality."` Our ongoing and in-depth probe reveals a blatant and willful disregard for constitutional rights including the malicious and violent treatment of the Negro population by both beat cops and their superiors.

It is no small wonder that the citizens of Lafayette Gardens decided to say, "No, that's enough." If history teaches us anything, it's that `power concedes nothing without a fight.`

The paper ran my old man's series in its entirety – but only in the Editorial Section; they needed cover for reporting the truth. This series was Ma's all-time favorite. She was proud of her straight shooter from the hard-boiled streets of Newark.

Throughout his career, he made great friends with his fellow scribes. He fancied press gatherings of any kind – conferences, conventions, and, of course, trading war stories at some local watering hole after the paper went to press. He loved being around reporters, be they good, bad, or ugly. Likewise, he reveled in the camaraderie, the friendships, and above all, the solidarity amongst journalists.

Funny enough, his favorite newspaper scribe, and a great friend in the biz, worked for the "San Francisco Chronicle." His name: Stanton

Delaplane. It seems like a stretch, right? Considering Frank Delgado was a mainstay in the northeast corridor. The Bay Area's legendary journalist, Herb Caen, dubbed Delaplane: "The last of the old irreplaceables." What a tribute.

And if Caen knew my old man, dollars to doughnuts, he would've said the same of one Frank Delgado.

Ma knew all about Stanton: He was at the Chronicle for half a century, won a Pulitzer in '42, spending most of his career as a "collaborative" travel writer – meaning Stanton infused himself with the cultures and people he visited and wrote about. And that's what my old man loved: Stanton was entrenched "in the moment." His column was called "Postcards," and no matter where he was in the world, he'd find a bar and write these enchanting articles over a martini, with his trademark cigarette always nearby.

Frank Delgado never experienced Hunter Thompson, but if he had, he'd declare Stanton Delaplane as an early prototype. His style was terse and uniquely opinionated. His story became your story. My old man engaged a copyboy at the Chronicle to mail him clippings of Stanton's column. I still have them. Delaplane showed up for Frank's funeral. Talk about mutual respect. Friendship.

And that's why I've detoured here again, right on the heels of my previous detour – the one that cradled a prone and vulnerable Christina MacKenzie, just like I've been prone and vulnerable (and exposed). Because the most important thing Frank Delgado left me was his unequivocal belief in friendships, especially those built on what he called "the solidarity of purpose." Pop had one religion: what many refer to as "the Fourth Estate" – or the People's check on the habitually corrupt three branches of government. Hanging over his desk (and now over mine) were two framed quotes, words to keep him honest in case he ever veered off the rails. The first from Thomas Jefferson (enlightened slave owner and world-famous rapist):

`"Were it left to me to decide whether we should have a government without newspapers, or newspapers without a government, I should not hesitate a moment to prefer the latter."`

The second is my favorite commandment from Chicago journalist Finley Peter Dunne (who used to love skewering Teddy Roosevelt like a stuck pig):

```
Job of the Journalist:
"Afflict the comfortable and comfort the afflicted"
```

You see, I'm not him (by any stretch), but he left me his beliefs, his foundations, his legacy. He once told me, "Friendships are like ice cream... they come in 31 flavors." Here, I paraphrase: Cherish the friendships you make in life. Work at them. Respect them. And if you're lucky, like I've been lucky, you'll have a few elite friendships built on "the solidarity of purpose." For him, it was all about unfettered journalism: "afflict the comfortable, comfort the afflicted." Enter into my life Christina MacKenzie – fellow wounded warrior.

Her woe, her damage? Mental. A classic mind-fuck.

My affliction, my loss? Physical. Explicit mutilation. (With a side order of mind-fuck.)

I can tell you this without reservation, even though the friendship is only days old: our solidarity is sacrosanct. I will treat our connection as holy territory. My expectation is that she will reciprocate in kind. I trust her. Implicitly. We will not be typical Veterans of the United States Armed Forces – i.e., two Vets who meet on the street with some woof-woof pom-pom bravado, you know, two Marines with that "Semper Fi" nonsense.

Nope, not us, no cult robotics here. Rather, two mortals thrown together in one small corner of the universe, two sentient beings facing the grim, meat-hook reality of their existence – two kids turned into state-sanctioned killers trained and brainwashed to do their master's bidding. We were sent to Hades and back and then expected to be joyful and proud – "C'mon, kids, wave a flag, bask in your stadium flyover" – and then fade back into society as if nothing happened.

```
Hell, gobble up some apple pie with that pretty girl next
door. What's her name? Betty Boop? C'mon, chest out, head
up... Remember! God was on your side.
```

It's truly amazing what these bastards have accomplished – over centuries, the wholesale indoctrination of untold millions. It's major league conditioning on an epic scale. "War is peace. Freedom is slavery. Ignorance is strength." With some masterful abracadabra, the warmongers pulled off the greatest parlor trick since the Virgin Birth.

THEY MADE THE UNTHINKABLE NORMAL.

Right now, I'd give anything to have Frank Delgado write the story. He'd probably win his much-deserved Pulitzer. The title?

Welcome to the American Berserk.

#

42

Alabaster Caddy.

Framed by a narrow doorway, Christina stood in silence, absorbing what Whitefish wanted to show her. The large subterranean space was indeed an odd sight to behold: an unsullied convertible Cadillac centering an immaculate brick-faced room, complete with museum-like lighting glistening off the car. Christina was experiencing the same bewildered feelings felt by those few who had visited before. Whitefish beeped the horn, "Don't be shy." She entered slowly, her smile dubious at best. She exchanged glances between the car, Whitefish, and every element in this—*what would you call it?* Cellar? Basement? Crypt? He broke the silence, "Not a bad showroom, huh?" She gently touched the car, making sure it was real. "All I can say is wow, you're full of surprises."

Whitefish began his tour, announcing, "The 1985 Cadillac Eldorado... this pristine original paint was dubbed 'alabaster' by the fine folks at General Motors." He knew how these initial visits played out: invitees (and there were not many) would scan and move about the room, looking past the artwork to probe the windowless walls for a possible way in, a way out, maybe a trap door, a false floor, how about a Jimmy-rigged ceiling? There were no clues. This damn catacomb appeared hermetically sealed. Whitefish suggested, "Check out the red leather." She wagged her finger, playfully warning, "Don't divert my attention, Mr. Clever Fish."

C-Mac tapped on the walls while circling the Caddy, "You know, it's not every day I venture down into basements with older men, albeit part-brother, only to find... what's the word?" Whitefish filled in the blank, "Entombed?" She pointed at him, "That'll work... only to find a beautiful entombed Cadillac, surrounded by brick walls with no apparent way in or out. You must admit this is fucking weird." He enjoyed these reactions: "No weirder than a lot of things." She stopped and gazed across the car at Whitefish, "You're a wizard, right? A sorcerer? The reincarnation of Harry Houdini." Whitefish smiled, "A real conundrum, eh?"

He reached in the car and popped the hood, "A wizard? Nah, just a God-fearing man. Have I ever told anyone my secret? Nope. Although, Ms. MacKenzie, you're currently the only person on the short list that might stand a chance of finding out." She smiled, "You're a tease." "Why thank you."

Whitefish's full tour continued with the engine. He gave C-Mac a complete walk-around, a literal dissertation on this elegant convertible—a product breakdown that would have brought the most hardened car salesman to tears. He pointed out the classic old straw-colored licensed plates and the fact that he continued to register the vehicle with the State of New Jersey, emphasizing "somewhat illegally" as he tapped on the inspection sticker, "Up to date." He also said that the insurance was current, "just in case."

Christina burst out laughing, "In case of what?!" He opened the passenger door and ushered her inside, "You'll never put your ass on more luxurious seats." As she slipped in, Christina's smile was still dubious. He shut the door, "Ricardo Montalban and his 'soft Corinthian leather' have nothing on this baby." He plopped down behind the wheel and fired up the powerful V8 engine. "Throaty, huh?"

Christina looked around, "Isn't it dangerous to run a car inside? Like the exhaust?"

Whitefish pointed out the large tube attached to the tailpipe that wound its way through a brick wall. He confirmed, "How'd you miss this? Straight to the ozone layer." Digging through a box of tapes, he asked, "You like The Beatles?"

She replied with faux ignorance, "Who?" He enjoyed her subtle dig, flipped in the cassette, and turned the volume up to somewhere around booming. It sounded like they were on an earsplitting runway at JFK just as the guitars ramped up. Whitefish yelled, "You ready?" C-Mac yelled back, "For what?" He nudged her to join in as the animated dude became the fifth Beatle—she tried, slowly at first, but then the lyrics came roaring back; she was finally in sync as Whitefish played every instrument on their dreadful flight from Miami Beach back to the U.S.S.R.

B.O.A.C.

The tune ended and they broke into laughter, offering themselves a round of applause. He popped out the tape and cut the engine. She asked, "What about gas?" But then answered herself, "You don't need much, you just bring it in." He added, "I change the oil every three months."

They sat quietly for at least a minute. It wasn't awkward, just peaceful. As if they were parked on the edge of a mountain lake. Whitefish broke the calm, "Sometimes I sit here and I swear I can see the road ahead."

She turned to him, "Okay, where we going?"

He dropped his hand over the wheel, "Anywhere you like. The other day, I listened to Johnny Cash while toolin' the Blue Ridge Parkway, right along the spine from Virginia to Tennessee, scatter my ashes right there... So? What do you see out there?"

She waited for a vision. "Same like you, mountains," she imagined, "We're heading west through Oregon. Columbia River Gorge. Steep canyons. Waterfalls. And we're taking a bunch of photos."

Again, they sat in silence. Christina's gaze far beyond the brick and mortar. Beyond those traditional ties that bind. And as far as Whitefish was concerned, she could exist in this moment, this quiet place for as long as she wanted. Even if that was forever.

He reached under the seat and pulled out Hendrix's double vinyl album, *Electric Ladyland,* followed by a baggie of weed and his Big Bambu rolling papers.

Christina smiled, "Now we're talking. Can I look through your tapes?"

He handed over the shoebox, "Go for it." Like Cheech and/or Chong, he cleaned away the seeds on Jimi's masterpiece and then rolled a flawless, thin joint ready for ignition. As she decided on music, he handed over the joint for their maiden voyage. The Caddy's lighter popped out. She inhaled a long drag off the coils—and they had liftoff.

"Whaddayasay?" She handed him the cassette, *Hotel California,* followed by the joint.

Whitefish fancied the choice, "Well done... legitimate masterpiece." He took a prodigious drag as he flip-flopped tapes in the deck. Then, with a tinge of sarcasm, "Hey, we both spent some quality time in our own special Hotel California." They shared a casual high-five as the track started—those familiar arpeggios, Don Felder's 12-string pumping through a Leslie, giving it that ethereal swirl. Christina blurted out, "Let's go, boss!" He laughed and again fired up the V8. She pointed straight ahead as the lyrics kicked in, half singing out loud.

♫*On a dark desert highway...*

"Hey Kingfish!"

"Yes, my lady."

"Step on it, we're losing daylight! Gotta be in Gallup by sundown!" They were both digging the tune, enjoying the drive. One might envisage wild and absurdist thoughts bouncing off the walls of their imagination.

With the music blaring, Whitefish let out a "Yee-haw!" and then pedal-roared the V8—the front seat travelers singing like they were onstage at The Garden; only now resembling two screwballs escaping from an asylum, you know, one of those super lockdown sanitariums for the seriously deranged, the Caddy fishtailing down suburban streets with these two PTSD whack-jobs firing their six-guns at the local paperboy, one shot blows off his kneecap, oops, there goes a shoulder. From her kitchen, an innocent housewife—a nosy lookie-loo—calls the cops, who then frantically notify their local FBI office:

"THE **HOUSEWIFE** IDENTIFIED THE BACKSEAT PASSENGERS AS FORMER PRESIDENT **DICK NIXON** ALONG WITH HIS BOMBASTIC SIDEKICK, **MISS MARTHA MITCHELL.** THEY'RE BOTH **TOPLESS,** WEARING RAY-BANS, AND PROBABLY HANDCUFFED. WE BELIEVE THEY'VE BEEN KIDNAPPED BY **DRUG-ADDLED MANIACS!** FOR GOD'S SAKE, **SAVE THE REPUBLIC!**"

The Caddy careens through a picket fence, tramples a rose garden, and then, with no regard for human life or grilled Americana, the demented driver plows through a backyard barbecue, leaving burgers-franks-and-broken-limbs in their wake. Finally, the Caddy blasts back into traffic, the front seat crackerjacks howling with laughter, guzzling from a bottle of gin—always a big help when washing down a handful of bennies.

You can check out any time you like, but you can never leave.

A few minutes later, the Insanity Express reached the station; the album played low, the joint now a roach. "There was only one good thing about the Army," Christina declared. Whitefish surmised, "The dope, right?" She acknowledged with a subtle thumbs-up, "And this, by the way, is very nice." Whitefish said, nonchalantly, "I've got a guy."

Listening to "The Last Resort," the album's final nihilistic gem, Christina closed her eyes, perfectly relaxed as Whitefish sang along softly...

> ♫ *You call someplace paradise*
> *Kiss it goodbye*

As the song ended and the room tone returned, Christina opened her eyes with a sudden and personal revelation, "You know why I drove three thousand miles to Asbury Park?" He just listened. "This might sound ridiculous, fucking crazy, but years ago I lost my red bucket and shovel. On the beach, right in front of your place. I mean, I didn't know it was your place at the time, I was a kid. But I came back hoping to find it. I thought maybe it might be under the Boardwalk or something. That's insane, right?"

Fashioning a ponytail, Whitefish pulled back his hair, "A bucket and a shovel?"

Christina elaborated, "Yeah, you know, a plastic pail with a handle and a small shovel. I was gonna make this great sandcastle. I got distracted and whoosh, it was gone." She buried her face in her hands and just sat there. Whitefish could tell she was on the verge of sobbing.

He tried, "Did you look for it?"

From inside her hands, "You mean recently?"

He shrugged, "Hell, you came all this way."

She looked up at him in disbelief, her eyes red with tears, "Are you being a wise guy?"

He knew this was dangerous ground, "Hey, you're the one that drove three thousand miles in search of a plastic pail from what? 1978? I figure you oughta at least look for it. I'll help."

She was hurt, "Are you fucking with me?"

"C'mon," he shot back, "Give me more credit than that. Why would I fuck with you? Christ, you wanna relive some childhood bullshit? Fine. I'll go with you. I'm a fucking professional at reliving everything I lost. And I would never fuck with you. Don't insult me."

They just sat there staring out the windshield. Christina smiled wryly, "If it helps, the pail was the exact same red as your bucket seats."

CUT TO:

The beachfront that borders Club Southside. Just beyond the Boardwalk. In the late afternoon of time. Christina walked Whitefish through the faraway moment when her bucket and shovel vanished "into thin air." She spoke about her panicked reaction. Jack & Darlene's empathetic response. Then they combed under the Boardwalk, between the pylons and posts. They even ventured out by the old Power Plant. They found a lot of useless crap but, of course, they didn't find hide nor hair of the red bucket. Or shovel. Lost almost twenty years before.

At the water's edge, dusk gathered around these two lone figures silently facing the great divide, the "pond," as some called it, with rhythmic white crests rolling in on cue. In a strange way, Christina felt some closure on this wacko and haunting episode. She previously shared it with Jaime, of course, and that was important. But sharing it with Whitefish was important in another way. It was like she gave Asbury Park one last chance to come clean, and he, more than anyone, seemed to represent this place. He was after all the King of Asbury Park. Who better to head this investigation—this cold case?

She was now convinced that the seaside town of her youth was innocent of all charges. The guilty party, this phantom thief, simply got away. Not unlike Jack the Ripper.

As they stood there facing Spain, facing what they shared in common, Whitefish buddy-draped his arm over Christina. After a long moment, she rested her head on his shoulder.

He wasn't leaving this moment any time soon, but gently declared, "I have to get ready for the Bruce thing."

Neither was she, "Should be fun."

Dusk lingered and that was a good thing.

43
Close Encounters
of the Third Kind.

WHAT CHRONICLE OF MY LIFE would be complete without a short mention of New Jersey's native son, Bruce Frederick Joseph Springsteen? For some time now, Lil Abner and I had been toying with the idea of a Springsteen night – an homage of sorts... Club Southside style. And tonight was that night.

Side note: For complete transparency, Asbury Park claims Springsteen as its native son, but his formative years were actually spent in Freehold, fifteen miles west.

We packed the joint – and my secret to generating great turnouts is to pull the trigger last minute. I like to call them "pop-up nights." Remember the old Carnies who would roll into town completely unannounced? They'd unfurl their wagons and pop up their tents for a rousing good time... and then skedaddle out of town.

That's us, except for the skedaddle part.

Abner did a nice job as talent coordinator, and Lou put together a terrific buffet: Mexican, of course – because nothing says Springsteen more than carnitas, arroz con pollo, chili con carne, guacamole, three types of salsa, and then churros for dessert. Young Christina was in attendance and had a wacko great time, the likes of which I doubt she'd ever experienced.

We showcased eight contestants vying for three prizes, in descending order: a two-night, three-day all-expenses-paid weekend at Trump Plaza in A-C; a six-bottle collection of high-end booze that included a full set of the Rolling Stones' tongue-and-lips shot glasses; and last but never least, we had three complimentary readings by Madam Marie – Asbury Park royalty herself. La Grande Dame.

Here's how this head-to-head battle worked:

The eight competing storytellers each revealed their alleged personal encounters with the man some call "The Boss." The audience then voted for the top three – and we made it clear: "authenticity" should weigh heavily in your decision.

Of course, I was the emcee and delivered what I thought was a brief but fitting monologue to an audience expecting an unabashed hagiography. I was simply stirring the pot (add devilish smile).

These are my notes and rough script for posterity.

ME:

(offer thanks to Abner, Lou, Tombstone, and Donna for their hard work; round of applause)

Okay, folks, welcome to the "First Annual Springsteen Schmooze Fest." And tonight, Miss Rosalita's gonna jump just a little bit higher. So grab on to your britches, we're about to enjoy some zany homespun tales regarding one man - the celebrated Columbia recording artist who just happens to hail from these here parts: Mr. Bruce Springsteen.

(take a beat for cheers and that B-R-U-C-E shit)

Now, we've invited eight outstanding contestants who all "claim" to have had a "Close Encounter of the Third Kind" with The Boss himself - and that's contact, baby. We'll evaluate their stories and then toss out the ones we believe to be fishy and/or blatant lies. There's a possibility that they're all full of shit... We'll also have a Q&A session, so feel free to ask questions, grill 'em good - see if their stories hold up under the bright lights... and then you'll vote for what you believe are the three best and bona fide encounters... and then our lucky winners - all chosen by you - will take home some great prizes. Abner, tell our studio audience what the participants can win...

LIL ABNER: (lists the prizes, 3-2-1)

ME:

Now, there's no doubt in my mind that many Jerseyites have experienced their own close encounters with our roaming troubadour... and I suspect that the closer you get to Monmouth County, the more frequent the sightings, the more outlandish the stories.

(take a beat)

Personally, I've never encountered the man except through his extensive "oeuvre" - and for you philistines in the crowd, that's French for "body of work."

(go back in history)

The story begins with famed record producer, John Hammond - who discovered giants like Billie Holiday, Aretha Franklin, and good ol' Bobby Zimmerman. His connection to us tonight? Well, Mr. Hammond also discovered Bruce Frederick Joseph Springsteen... and believe it or not, I consider his first album - "Greetings from Asbury Park" - to be his very best: The music and storytelling were exceptionally raw, beautifully stark and opulent all at the same time.

(read as poetry)

"Well I stood stone-like at midnight
Suspended in my masquerade
And I combed my hair 'til it was just right
And commanded the night brigade"

It defined who we were and how we existed in time. "I swear I lost everything I ever loved or feared, I was the cosmic kid in full costume dress." C'mon, that's killer... And then his second release, "The Wild, The Innocent, and the E Street Shuffle," was kinda-maybe similar, but a little over-produced for my taste. And let's all try to remember without those rose-colored glasses: these two albums sort of went nowhere.

(turn quick, make this big)

BUT THEN, exactly 20 years ago, there was what novelists and screenwriters call "the inciting incident," only this one was a career rocket ship to Mars. Here's what went down: Bruce played a gig at the Harvard Square Theater in Cambridge, Mass, opening for Ms. Bonnie Raitt - and who's sitting in the audience on that fateful night? None other than the very influential music critic, Mr. Jon Landau. And judging by Jon's hyperbolic and preposterous review - and let me tell you, this dude didn't just have an epiphany, no-no-no... it was like a lightning bolt upside the head, carrying the biggest payload of journalistic claptrap ever written.

(let that sit, move to Abner)

Lil Abner, tell the folks what he said -

LIL ABNER: (opens & reads from "THE REAL PAPER")

"On a night when I needed to feel young, he made me feel like I was hearing music for the very first time. I saw rock and roll's future and its name is Bruce Springsteen."

ME:

Public announcement: If anyone here feels the need to hurl, the bathrooms are thataway. Alright, I'm sure it's obvious by now that I've come here tonight not to praise Bruce, but to knock him around a little bit. But that's just me. I mean, c'mon folks, SOMEONE in the great state of New Jersey has to offer a countervailing force to the frenzied exaltation that surrounds our famous song and dance man.

(there will be boos, keep going)

I am that agent provocateur. C'mon, you got fanatics worshipping the man like he's Jesus of Nazareth, singing with that rockabilly Eddie Cochran vibe -

(sing it)

"Working on the highway, laying down the blacktop
Working on the highway, all day long I don't stop"

Ladies and gentlemen, I ask you: What the hell does Bruce know about laying down some blacktop? As much as I do - nothing.

(absorb the major vitriol, then pick the audience mole)

See, she knows exactly what I'm talking about, am I right?

(exchange high five)

Wait a second, hold on, I'm confused - are you all booing or yelling Bruce? It's very hard to tell.

(smile, keep it light, make them love to hate you)

Listen up. Listen up... Am I being unfair? A little harsh? Maybe, I'll give you that... but one day when you feel like finding out there's no Santa Claus, drive out to the country with yours truly - I'll show you where "Bad Scooter" buried that blue collar.

(beat)

Because when you actually look at the facts, the latter-day Mr. Springsteen resembles William Randolph Hearst more than Chuck Berry.

(acknowledge the anger & contempt, back off a bit)

Alright, calm down, let's just hope I've given you something to think about - or maybe at this juncture you just wanna tell me to go fuck myself.

(should get a rowdy chorus of "Go Fuck Yourself")

Okay, who am I to denigrate the American Dream? Just another feudal serf out here in the darkness...............

(turn on a dime, big surprise)

"ON THE EDGE OF TOWN! ! ! "

(cheering ensues)

Alright, judging by your reaction, you've come to the right place - because that's the kind of Springsteen adoration you're about to experience and embrace. On with the show.

(beat)

Our first storyteller and Springsteen devotee hails from Sea Girt. Ladies and gentlemen, please welcome...

#

CHRISTINA and the WHITEFISH

44

Red Bucket.

Years later, when self-publishing became the rage, Whitefish coughed up some hard-earned cash and self-published his "chronicle" (really a memoir). The 224-page book did fairly well, especially after a very nice review in the *Asbury Park Press*. Amazon sold the paperback as well as the Kindle version, and he managed to place the book in the few concrete bookstores that still existed throughout the Tri-State area. He even managed to do a few book signings and talks—those being the days when he actually began leaving Asbury Park on short outings. In one of those Manhattan bookstores, The Strand, an independent filmmaker by the name of Standish Adams picked up a copy and was enamored with Whitefish's bizarre story—as well as making the dramatic film adaptation.

File this saga under: "A Funny Thing Happened on the Way to the Forum."

Standish (a trust fund baby) purchased the film rights from Whitefish for a flat ten grand. Then, during a booze-fueled month in Asbury Park, he wrote the screenplay adaptation holed up at the Berkeley Carteret Hotel. He was arrested but quickly released after paying the hotel $1,750.00 for damages to his room. Also, as a favor to one of the hotel's managing partners for not pressing charges, Standish agreed to shoot and edit his daughter's bat mitzvah.

The filmmaker put up some family cash and also sought financing from foreign distributors. When he garnered about fifty percent of a two million dollar budget, Standish began production in and around Asbury Park. That was the spring of 2005. He insisted on utilizing a completely unknown cast of theatrical actors from New York and Philadelphia, except for one cameo—Roseanne Barr would play Madam Marie.

Unfortunately, the film was never completed. The money dried up after ten days of principal photography. Bottom line: Standish proved to be an incompetent fool—good at making deals, bad at making movies.

Standish also subscribed to the Kubrick method of filmmaking: multiple takes until the actors and crew were throwing up from exhaustion. He did attempt to secure a commitment from Springsteen's people for a simple cameo—one shot: the Boss walking down the Boardwalk. But before Springsteen's people hung up on Standish, Bruce was heard yelling in the background, "That Whitefish jackass is delusional AND an asshole. Hang up the fucking phone!"

The good news is this: We were able to obtain pages from Standish's screenplay that covered the night Whitefish held the Springsteen competition. Sources have confirmed that this was one of the scenes actually filmed before production on *The King of Asbury Park* shut down. For good. Here's an excerpt:

```
                                            CUT BACK TO:

INT. CLUB SOUTHSIDE/STAGE - NIGHT

The evening has progressed - the packed house
antsy as Whitefish prances about, doing his best
over-the-top Pacino.

FAST CUTS as time keeps jumping ahead—

                    WHITEFISH
        If you ever feel like finding out there's no
        Santa Claus, drive up to Colts Neck or Rumson
        and check out Bruce's extravagant and genteel
        properties.
                (next)
        Actually, when you look at the facts, this
        dude's more like William Randolph Hearst than
        Chuck Berry.
                (next)
        AGENT PROVOCATEUR! That's me, baby. Hopefully
        I've given you some shit to think about -
        or maybe you just wanna tell me to go fuck
        myself!

ECU of mouths shouting:

                    FACES
        GO FUCK YOURSELF!!! ASSHOLE!!! DOUCHEBAG!!!
        GIMP!!!
```

JUMP AHEAD

EXT. BOARDWALK/CLUB SOUTHSIDE - NIGHT

> WHITEFISH (O.S.)
> Ladies and Gentlemen, please welcome to the
> stage, Vinnie Cusumano!

Applause.

INT. CLUB SOUTHSIDE/STAGE - NIGHT (CONTINUOUS)

In his grease monkey greens, Texaco Vinnie stands
under a harsh spotlight. He's all attitude a la
Vinnie Barbarino.

> VINNIE
> Lemme tell ya about the time I ran into Bruce
> outside the Route 35 Shop-Rite.

> HECKLER
> WIFE SEND YOU FOR TAMPONS?!

Laughs, ohhs and ahhs…

> VINNIE
> I was actually pickin' up gin and
> prophylactics for your mother.

Laughter now directed at heckler.

> VINNIE
> (collects himself, continues)
> Alright, okay, here we go... I'm sittin'
> in my car, believe it or not, listenin' to
> "Thunder Road" - and of course I can't exit
> the car until the song wraps up.

> HECKLER
> BORING!

> VINNIE
> (fires back at Heckler)
> Why don't you get prostrate cancer and fall
> on the floor?

                WHITEFISH
            (to Heckler)
Hey Beans, shut the fuck up.

                VINNIE
            (steadies himself, continues)
Thanks, Fish... so I'm right at the
whaddayacall climax of the song...
            (sings)
"It's a town full of losers, I'm pullin' out
of here to winnnnn"-
            (asks audience)
And who pulls into the spot next to me?

                AUDIENCE
BRUCE!!!

                VINNIE
Bingo. '65 convertible "GOAT" in what Pontiac
dubbed their Montero Red. Headers wide open,
kick-ass Cragars, the whole nine yards.
            (long pause, dramatic)
After a sec, Bruce gets out, looks over at me
kind of concerned - and being the gentleman
that he is, says, "Excuse me, did I park too
close?" And I say, "No, man, you're fine. No
problem." And then just as he turns to leave,
he winks and says, "By the way, good taste in
music."

JUMP AHEAD

STAGE - SHORT TIME LATER

A new contestant - Cis, a rough and hearty woman
maybe forty.

                CIS
So, I get a call, an emergency gig down the
Stone Pony. And what most people don't
understand is that a career in plumbing is
just like surgery, you gotta be twenty-four
seven. No pun intended, but I take this shit
seriously...

          (laughter)
So Butch **says** one of the stalls in the men's
room has reached the danger zone. And this
dude was not exaggerating – there's shit
everywhere, including his plunger and three
empty bottles of Drano. So, of course,
I gotta snake the fucker—
          (asks audience)
And who walks in to take a leak?

                    AUDIENCE
BRUCE!!!

❖ ❖ ❖

On the real-life night of the "First Annual Springsteen Schmooze Fest," Christina laughed her ass off. She told Whitefish she couldn't remember the last time she laughed so hard. And per management's decree, bar service was halted during the show, so Donna grabbed a seat next to Christina, both ladies hanging on to each other, they were laughing so hard.

The scripted "mole" or "plant" in the crowd (who high-five's the Agent Provocateur) was Christina. Whitefish later remarked, "She underplayed her role beautifully."

Around midnight, once everyone scampered home to their boxes, Christina, Abner, and Whitefish shared a joint on a bench near the empty Carousel House. It was nice, Christina thought—minutes went by and nobody felt compelled to say anything. The ocean articulated everything that needed to be said—finally, the mighty Atlantic must have inspired Abner's arbitrary libretto, "You know, when those bastards ripped out the horses," he mused and gestured to the Carousel House, "It felt like they ripped the heart outta this town." Whitefish added, "Four years ago." Christina wondered, "Where did the horses go?" Abner toked, "Myrtle Beach, South Carolina. Those beauties spun around in there for more than fifty years. The kids loved it." Whitefish concurred, "We all did."

There was another long discourse by the nearby and verbose Atlantic. This time it inspired Christina's libretto, "Tell me, Mr. Fish, how do you really feel about Springsteen? That was an act tonight, right? The old fly in the ointment. Clearly, you know your shit, but I don't know, it still kinda felt like a tribute. Hate doesn't usually traffic alongside the embrace of knowledge."

Abner was blown away, "Whoa, that's heavy. Jesus." Whitefish smiled and nudged Christina, "Ah, you may have unmasked the Whitefish." He took a quick hit on the doob, "I do in fact hold a few positives about our famous rock n' roll legend... and I will offer you this: a few years back, he had another release that caught my attention—" She cut him off at the pass, "Nebraska... like our nightmares, stark and haunting." Abner took the joint, "Wow, this chick is smart AND poetic. Are you single?"

They all laughed.

That night, when Christina returned "home" to the Sea Breeze, there was a Shop-Rite supermarket bag sitting outside her door. She picked it up and gingerly looked inside. First she smiled and then broke out crying. Real-time water works.

She pulled out the gift: a red plastic bucket and a white shovel.

&

45

Parting Shot: Bruce.

Lest we continue without revealing who, in fact, won the "First Annual Springsteen Schmooze Fest," here is the abbreviated story. Standish Adams' screenplay called for this sequence to be included alongside his closing credits. You may recall that Johnny Pots was a "maybe" for the competition, but in the end he decided to show up—and good thing he did because he won first place, claiming the all-expenses-paid weekend in Atlantic City. He later told Whitefish that the weekend may have saved his moribund marriage, "a union that was basically dead on arrival."

Johnny Pots was the head butcher at the Ortley Beach A&P for more than thirty years. This one-armed butcher was a legend in Jersey meat-cutting circles, a renowned wiz with his magic cleaver. Johnny was also a union man—the UFCW shop steward at his beloved store: The Great Atlantic & Pacific Tea Company.

For dramatic impact on this historic evening, Johnny arrived in costume: a long white smock-apron splattered with blood, cleaver in his right hand. Many of the contestants cried foul, thinking he won simply because of this absurd stunt. But let it be known, here and now, that the audience overwhelmingly embraced "Johnny the Butcher." He was the clear-cut winner (pun intended).

In fact, Christina needed to help Donna back on her feet after she collapsed to the floor in laughter.

UP FROM BLACK

EXT. BOARDWALK/CLUB SOUTHSIDE – NIGHT
(ROLL CREDITS)

A few folks stroll the deserted Boardwalk. Under a nearby streetlamp, the familiar little girl rides her bicycle in freewheeling circles.

>   WHITEFISH (O.S.)
>   Alright folks, please welcome our last
>   contestant to the stage - and apparently he
>   came here straight from work. Ladies and
>   gentlemen, Mr. Johnny Pots!

Applause.

INT. CLUB SOUTHSIDE/STAGE - NIGHT (CONTINUOUS)

Johnny Pots (early 50s with a hefty salt & pepper
beard) wears his bloody butcher apron over his
industrial garb. He speaks with a pronounced
Jersey accent.

>   JOHNNY
>   Hello there, folks... I may be a supermarket
>   butcher, but I am *Bruce Springsteen's*
>   *supermarket butcher.*

>   CONTESTANT #1
>   THIS IS BULLSHIT! I CRY FOUL!

>   HECKLER
>   FAKE BLOOD! BUTCHERS DON'T SLAUGHTER ANIMALS!

>   CONTESTANT #2
>   NO ONE SAID ANYTHING ABOUT WEARING COSTUMES!

>   WHITEFISH
>   (to Contestant #2)
>   Hey Wimpy, who said you couldn't add ward-
>   robe? Quit your yammerin'.

>   LIL ABNER
>   (yells his Wimpy impression right in
>   contestant #2's face)
>   "I'LL GLADLY PAY YOU TUESDAY FOR A HAMBURGER
>   TODAY!" Shut the fuck up... Alright, JOHNNY,
>   the stage is yours.

Crowd laughs and cheers.

>   JOHNNY
>   In the old days, before he got famous, Bruce
>   came in all the time - loved his rib-eyes,
>   which are always a nice balance of muscle and

fat. The man knows how to feed those E Street boys.

(moves offstage, engages audience)

So flash forward, it's late summer 1979, and the shop phone rings. Guess who?

AUDIENCE

BRUCE!!!

JOHNNY

Bingo... and he says, could I put together a dozen rib-eyes for the grill, deliver 'em up to Holmdel? I tell him, "No problem, Boss. You got it." But then he says, "Listen, Johnny, I don't trust just anyone coming out here. Would you mind doing it personally?"

(awestruck)

Would I mind doin' it personally? I'm fuckin' flabbergasted, so he gives me the directions. "I'll be there A-SAP."

(paints a detailed picture)

I get right to work, package up the best rib-eyes we got - a Baker's Dozen because hey, it's Bruce, you gotta throw him a little sumpin' sumpin', right? So I head out to what he calls the "Telegraph Hill Studios," which is actually a barn on his Holmdel property. Beautiful spread. And luckily, when I got there, the band's on a break. Bruce jumps up, greets me like a long-lost brother, and then introduces me to the band - Little Stevie, Max, Roy-Danny-Garry, and then holy shit, the Big Man, Mr. Clarence Clemons. They're all there working on "The River" album, which, at the time, not too many people know this, was entitled "The Ties That Bind."

(drives his cleaver into the table where Donna and Christina are seated)

NOW SONOVABITCH! if he doesn't offer me a beer and says, "Johnny, relax, hang out, we're gonna try to pull together this new song, it's called 'Two Hearts.'"

(to audience, sing-songs)

You know the tune, "Two hearts are better than one, two hearts girl get the job done."

(plops down in a chair, emotional)

Lemme tell ya, being that close to when they kicked it all into high gear was like being at the Big Bang when God himself said, "Fuck it, let 'er rip." Bruce on that geeked-out Telecaster, something he calls "The Mutt." Ya got Danny on organ – shit... this was Christ on a stick.

(long pause, a pin dropped)

There I was, Johnny Pots, suckin' down a Mich not ten feet from rock 'n roll history.

(pulls out a photograph, holds it up to the audience)

Just before I headed back, we took this picture of me and the boys right next to the A&P van.

(long pause, looks at photo)

Lord have mercy.

♫

THE KING OF ASBURY PARK

Screenplay by Standish Adams

Based on the Memoir
of the same name

by

"The Whitefish"

Part Three

"There are no uncontaminated angels."

Philip Roth

ANGELS

CHRISTINA and the WHITEFISH

46

Millie, Shanice, and Mr. Cool Pants.

The next morning, as promised, Christina was up bright and early to take Millie to breakfast at the diner. In fact, she was waiting for her in the Sea Breeze's parlor when Millie emerged, almost surprised that her young guest had actually followed through. "Good morning," Christina chirped, closing the large coffee table book entitled *Antique Radios*. Her mood was playful, "I'm starving. Wanna hit the road?"

As they stepped outside, both women immediately felt Mother Nature's handiwork—one of those late summer New Jersey days that suddenly hinted at fall; crisp air that strangled the goddamn humidity into submission, along with a cobalt blue postcard sky—even a few leaves from a nearby elm were rocking themselves earthbound. There were no words as they stood on the porch, just acknowledgment of sharing this moment, drawing gentle breaths, instinctually knowing that change was in the air.

On the ride over to the Johnny Be Goode, Millie confessed that it's been years since she went out for breakfast. Or any meal for that matter. Her husband never liked restaurants. Luckily for Millie, her younger sister Greta enjoyed dining out, and they had a standing date every Wednesday. But Greta passed two years back, and Millie said she dearly missed their weekly luncheons, especially at the venerable Grenville in Bay Head. Christina revved the engine at a red light. "This is all very exciting," Millie stressed, as if the morning ride was a great escape.

Millie thought the Johnny Be Goode Diner was just extraordinary. "My husband and I used to listen to the rock and roll," she recalled, casually perusing the festive interior from their window booth. "We'd light candles and sip port wine," Millie remembered, "listening to singers like Brenda Lee and The Platters on one of his big cabinet radios." From their corner booth, Christina followed Millie's gaze outside, but judging by the light in her faraway eyes, Christina wasn't privy to her keepsake. "Did I tell you how much Charlie loved radios?"

Christina smiled, "Yes, you did. I love the one in my room. It's a gem." Millie looked at the giant menu, "Room 204. The best."

During breakfast, they shared stories about the Asbury Park that now only exists in antiquity. Christina submitted, "Like old photographs." Millie mused, "I agree, only mine are much more faded than yours."

Christina touched her hand, "Not true. Yours are beautiful." And then, as if Scotty beamed them down from the Enterprise, our three shining Texaco stars hovered over the booth.

Vinnie was working the remnants of his breakfast with a toothpick, "Hey Christina, what's shakin'?"

"Not much, Vinnie," Christina hesitated, realizing she was now forced to introduce the trio: "Millie, this is Vinnie-Danny-and-Joey, Asbury Park's finest mechanics."

Millie smiled, "In my day they were called 'grease monkeys.'" She sipped her coffee as Christina swallowed her smile.

Danny wondered, "Is this your mother, Christina?"

Christina clinked coffee mugs with Millie, "Dear friends."

Vinnie sniffed with faux confidence, "Christina, I know we're on display here in public, but I was wondering if you might like to join me for dinner and drinks? Of course, my treat. Maybe tonight? I am available."

Christina shared a knowing glance with Millie, "You know, Vinnie, as great as that sounds, and it does, I'll have to say no, but thank you."

Joey laughed way too loud, "N-n-nice try, B-B-B-B-Bozo." Then, with faux arrogance, Vinnie gathered himself, absorbed the nuanced kick in the nuts, and sauntered away, "Hey, no problem." Danny smiled and flashed Christina the thumbs-up, as did Joey upon their exit.

After a long moment, Christina asked Millie, "So, how are your pigs in a blanket?" A few pregnant seconds later, they broke out laughing.

That afternoon, Christina called Ricky, her manager at Starbucks, and apologized for still being away; yeah, it's been longer than expected, but all was cool and she was no doubt still coming back, just attending to family matters. Ricky was a decent guy and considered her a valued team member, "No worries. Your job's here when you land." She also called Julian about his car; don't worry, it's running well, still in one piece, "I should be heading back soon, maybe ten days." Julian was so cool, easily one of her favorite people.

He seemed only concerned about her.

When she hung up the receiver in the beat-up phone booth on the corner of Ocean and 2nd Ave, she glanced across the street at the venerable music club, The Stone Pony. She chuckled as she remembered Cis' ridiculous Springsteen toilet story from the night before.

Christina grabbed a coffee at the Boardwalk HoJo's and found an empty bench facing the water. She figured if she ever jotted down the positives about current-day Asbury Park, finding empty benches would be top of list. She sipped her spineless coffee delivered from the 1950s and realized how much she missed her Starbucks rocket fuel. On the horizon, an oil tanker headed south. She smirked, mostly at herself, since she was recently in the employ of the American government, helping secure its oil supply that somehow found its way underneath the sands of Iraq. She asked herself a recurring question, "What the fuck were you thinking?" The move so pathetic, so out of character, almost laughable—except when she factored in the very real and scary contemplation of offing herself.

Was self-destruction still a possibility? She let the question and possible answers dissipate away. Although watching the treasured oil travel south, offing oneself may have dropped a bit on her list of things to do. She counted that as a win, sipped her crappy coffee and closed her eyes, thinking about Jack & Darlene, as she so often does. Her thoughts weirdly morphed into Jaime. "How much does she hate me right now? How much did I hurt her? She didn't deserve any of this."

"Hi, Christina."

Who was that? It sounded real. Christina opened her eyes—and against that striking blue sky, she was staring into the beautiful little face of that beautiful little girl, smiling, straddling her familiar Schwinn. "Were you asleep?" she asked.

What a sweet kid, "No, just daydreaming."

"About what?"

"A friend."

"Was it a boy or a girl?"

"A girl. Her name is Jaime."

"That's a pretty name."

"So is Shanice."

"That's what they tell me."

Christina laughed. "When do you go back to school?"

"My mom says soon. Do you go to school?"

"I used to. You think I should go back?"

"My mom says school's the best thing in the world except for love."

"Your mom is very smart."

"I know." Shanice hopped back on her seat and pedaled away. "Bye Christina."

"Bye, Shanice."

Christina watched the girl ride toward the not-too-distant necropolis, you know it... Convention Hall. Shanice stood up pedaling as she veered through the large doors and inside the massive boneyard, suddenly gone from this promenade, just like the straw hats and petticoats that disappeared decades before.

For some reason, C-Mac wiped tears from her eyes.

❖❖❖

Walking up the stairs and then knocking on his upstairs door, she heard Italian music. When Whitefish opened the door, it was like Mario Lanza burst into the hallway. "Ciao bella... Arrivederci Roma!" She laughed, "Sorry to just drop by." He threw the door wide open, "I'm making dinner, you want in?"

As he chopped and diced and moved about the small kitchen, she was browsing his books in the contiguous parlor. "Is this good?" she called out, "'World Without End, Amen?'" He tossed a pile of fresh slivered garlic into sizzling olive oil, "If it's Breslin, it's always worth a read." Christina recited from the book, *You would never know you were in New York City if you stand on the beach in the late afternoon at Rockaway.*

With his old-school can opener, Whitefish released 28 ounces of Progresso crushed tomatoes, "First line of the prologue, classic Breslin." Christina was impressed, "Good recall." He poured the tomatoes into a larger pot, "It's like a parlor trick. I have most of the first lines memorized or at least close to it. Try me."

Suspicious, she scanned the shelf, grabbed a book, and flipped to the first page, "Keep your eyes over there, don't cheat. Okay, here we go: *I am blind. But I am not deaf. Because of the incompleteness of my misfortune—*" He cut her off, "Gore Vidal's 'Creation.'" She smiled, "Oh, man, you got lucky!"

"G'head, hit me again."

She grabbed another, and this time turned her back to hide the book, "Okay, Mr. Cool Pants, here we go: *Elihu B. Washburne opened his gold watch.*" Whitefish casually jumped in, "Piece of cake, once again, Gore Vidal, this time from 'Lincoln.'" Then, with refinement and grace, Whitefish added, "Mr. Vidal continues, *The spidery hands showed five minutes to six.*"

She was impressed, "Damn."

He suggested she get off that shelf. She did, crossing to another bookcase, determined to stump his annoying confidence. "Alright, third time's a charm for beating your sorry ass, let's see, okay, okay... ready?" Whitefish calmly stirred his gravy, "Born ready." Christina was confident, "We'll see... *Later than usual one summer morning in 1984—*" He immediately took over, *"Zoyd Wheeler drifted awake in sunlight through a creeping fig that hung in the window...* blah-blah-blah. Thomas Pynchon, 'Vineland.'"

Christina was absolutely stupefied, "Jesus, you have a photographic memory." He shrugged, "I don't know about that... shit just sticks."

❖ ❖ ❖

Christina loved the cozy dinner—the only difference from her first sit-down at Chez Whitefish was that the chef swapped Penne Rigate no. 41 for Thin Spaghetti no. 11. As *Cavalleria rusticana* reached its finale, their plates were empty and the bottle of Percarlo Sangiovese was bone dry. That's when Whitefish opened a nearby drawer and retrieved Christina's *Outdoor* magazine. He tossed it on the table.

"Let's talk about Mr. McCandless."

47

A Failed Seeker.

And talk they did. "Of course we all see what we want to see" was Whitefish's underlying supposition throughout their impromptu analysis of Chris McCandless: the dichotomy of his existence—or more accurately, the yin and yang of his death sentence. Whitefish had clearly given great thought to the overriding conundrum of the story—a story he knew was rattling around inside Christina's terrordome. As Whitefish spoke, C-Mac was immediately reminded of her father. Indeed, the more the self-proclaimed King of Asbury Park spoke, the more he took on the persona of a teacher, a legit professor, offering up questions and ideas to be considered, realities to be explored.

Whitefish viewed this McCandless character like a Buffalo nickel, with two sides: heads, an indigenous male; tails, an American bison. Both are real. Both are to be considered.

As he held court pacing the kitchen, Christina quickly realized that she was right: Mr. Cool Pants belonged in some ivy-covered edifice off Nassau Street in Princeton or at least a visiting adjunct at Rutgers.

No doubt a multifarious story, eh? Was Mr. McCandless an intelligent ideologue who earnestly believed that life for him could be best lived alone, in nature? Was this twentysomething in fact searching for that elusive holy grail? You know, the heavy shit—answers to life, death, existence. Why is there air? Or maybe, maybe, the boy was simply on the run? Sprinting from his own central demons? Let's face it, demons that ultimately destroyed him.

Regardless, Krakauer, our journalist, eventually positions his subject as a mythic figure longing to embrace the meaning of life. Mr. Krakauer—when framing this heretic, this outlier—presents a narrative of a brave young man. Stimulating. Quixotic. But then this guy just ups and vanishes, goes AWOL from what he perceives to be the dead-end and predetermined trappings of his own life, right? He craves communion with the birds and the bees. I get it... I think all of us at one time or another contemplate that kind of disappearing act. Poof. Gone. See ya down the road. But damn, if the kid doesn't come off endearing. And so Krakauer had his folk hero. Was Mr. Chris naïve? Of course he was, beyond a shadow of a doubt naïve. Why? Because he's steeped in his own abject stupidity. The boy ends up killing himself. But here's the rub: Mr. Chris is a character who's both appealing and baffling all at once. Philosophers throughout the ages, like Carl Jung, have scribbled about "the duality of human nature." Mr. Krakauer presents us with this trope.

Christina hung on every word as she drained her glass dry.

Whitefish took a quick off-ramp, grabbed an already opened second bottle, tossed the cork and poured them each another hit. "You'll love this... '92 Silver Oak cab... classic Sonoma beauty... ruby hue, red fruit but still bold, long finish. My guy has this once, maybe twice a year." Suddenly, he was back on the highway—

Okay, let's flip this Buffalo nickel over, let's look at Mr. Chris from another possible POV. Did mental illness drive McCandless over the delusional edge? Could be... he takes on another name, one that sounds like a cartoon character.

"Alexander Supertramp," C-Mac inserted, sipping the cab.

Bingo. "Alexander Supertramp." Was he trying to create a completely different persona? Some kind of dime store deity? I'll bet you dollars to doughnuts, if you let a competent shrink study those journals he left behind, schizophrenia will scream off those pages with a goddamn bullhorn. Break it down: one, he operates under faulty perceptions— that's clear... two, he embraces ridiculous and reckless actions, it's like stupidity 101... three, he clearly withdraws from reality as well as his own personal relationships, people that care for him—that's tragic... and then finally, all of it descends into fantasy and delusion. I mean that's textbook schizo. I think if you glanced at the back of Mr. Chris' baseball card, that description would be his biographical takeaway.

Christina remained laser-focused. Her immediate reaction was to challenge and argue against Whitefish's take on Chris. But this angle had never even occurred to her. He was damn convincing, his analysis like a runaway freight train.

A pit stop as he poured himself another inch of the California cab. He held his glass up to the light, "A real motherfucker, right?" They clinked glasses, she concurred, "A righteous motherfucker." He laughed, "You punched that up. Love it." He dove back in—

Now, is it possible the kid was suffering from an undiagnosed psychosis? Absolutely. In fact, that would be my unprofessional shot in the dark. But you may be thinking otherwise—hence this conversation: Was McCandless simply a very unique rebel? Albeit, it seems, a rebel without any cause whatsoever. But for the moment, let's accept him at face value—because having alternative worldviews or deciding to live your life in a way that others regard as odd, well, that doesn't necessarily pigeonhole you for mental illness. Take one good look at me!

She smiled. A brief respite.

So, parting thoughts: Was Christopher McCandless a trailblazer at the vanguard of his own narrative? Was he eccentric? Ethereal? Heroically living on the edge? If indeed he really was all those things, I can see why you might be enamored with this cat. But to others, and I count myself included, the dude was sadly disturbed. Certifiable with a kind of peaceful rabidity, if that makes any sense. In the end, Christina, I think the only honest conclusion we can come to is that we may never know. We are stuck to decide for ourselves. The poor kid is gone.

Whitefish picked up the magazine as Exhibit A.

But I said all of that to tell you this: By looking the other way and accepting Mr. Chris as the aforementioned "folk hero," are we then memorializing suicide? Are we accepting, as operational, the thesis of a failed seeker?

She raised her glass, "Geez, you should teach a course." With a devilish smile, Whitefish knocked back the wine in his glass, "I do every day. Haven't you noticed?"

A long moment passed as they comfortably shared the silence, then Whitefish broke ranks with a thought, "Failed seeker, hmmm... I want you to hear one more thing." He moved to his books, one book in particular, and pulled it from its parking spot. Christina waited, wondering what was next as he flipped through *Fear and Loathing in Las Vegas*. Finally, Whitefish announced, "Here it is. Hunter Thompson writing about what he called 'the fatal flaw in Tim Leary's trip.' You're familiar with Leary, right?" She nodded with shaky confidence, "Drugs, LSD, hallucinations?" Whitefish held up the book, "You got it." He mumbled, searching for a good starting point—*"Wired into a survival trip... Crashed around America selling consciousness...* yeah, yeah, yeah—ah, here we go." He looked to Christina, "I offer this as an accidental glimpse into Mr. McCandless."

Whitefish read the passage as if the words were pulsing through his veins:

> All those pathetically eager acid freaks who thought they could buy Peace and Understanding for three bucks a hit. But their loss and failure is ours too. What Leary took down with him was the central illusion of a whole life-style that he helped create... a generation of permanent cripples, failed seekers, who never understood the essential old-mystic fallacy of the Acid Culture: the desperate assumption that somebody... or at least some force—is tending the light at the end of the tunnel.

He shut the book, "That's why you gotta burn that magazine right away. You ain't him... and he ain't you. In my not-so-humble opinion, McCandless has nothing to teach you, trust me, nothing to guide you anywhere. If you agree with me, burn that magazine."

He tossed Thompson on his desk and moved back to the table. "Kiddo, you and me, we share the same bullshit, the same pain. I bet every day you imagine that plane slamming into some Alaskan rock face, right? You imagine what they went through: Did they suffer? Did they linger? Did they know they were dying? We share this because those are the exact same thoughts I have about my old man. I play that movie over and over in my head. Shot in the chest, in the gut. Bleeds out on the floor in some fucking Grand Union. Did he suffer? Did he know he was dying?" Whitefish struggles, "That was my Daddy."

There were tears in both of their eyes. He took a prodigious pull from the '92 Silver Oak, straight from the bottle, then handed it back to C-Mac with a skyward gesture, "Blood of Christ, the rest is yours." He reclaimed his seat at the table. Christina added, "And then we both knocked on

Uncle Sam's door." Whitefish picked a crumb off his plate, "Gasoline on the proverbial fire."

Straight from the bottle, she matched his prodigious pull, "So fucking good... by the way, thanks for the red bucket. Best Christmas present ever."

"My pleasure. Wanna burn that goddamn magazine?"

&

CHRISTINA and the
WHITEFISH

48

Fred & Ginger (Part Deux).

They walked down the creaky stairs to Club Southside's subterranean Disney World. For a moment, Christina couldn't figure out if she was standing in the midst of genius or madness. Or both. For magazine burning, Whitefish suggested the floor of what he called "my art-making room."

At first, she wasn't sure where to focus—there were white mannequins without arms or heads; there were pastel-colored papier-mâché busts and masks of nondescript humans; there were urban-rusted car grills, quarter panels, and a few tires leaning against the walls; there was a tattered silk parachute that hovered above, one that imitated a circus big top; and an old Raleigh road bike (with ram handlebars) hung from the rafters.

But suddenly where to focus became obvious: the large collection of painted trash cans, expertly crafted as Progresso tomato cans. They were piled and stacked everywhere in this cavernous basement. And there was paint. Cans and excess splatter bejeweled the place.

She smiled, thinking, "Warhol had The Factory, Whitefish has this."

"You painted all of these?" she asked, blown away. He sat down on his mushroom-like toadstool, "Somehow it's strangely satisfying." She followed up, "And the papier-mâché? Doesn't that take a lot of work?" He offered details, "I started with the no-cook paste formula, but then shifted to a resin paste recipe. Gives your project a nice hard finish. Much more durable."

He gestured far and wide, "Pick a spot where you want to burn the magazine." She had an idea, "Can we burn it in one of your tomato cans?" He smiled, "An exceptional idea. Whichever one you want." She spotted the turntable and vinyl, "Who's on the record player?" He mimed a conga drum, "Mr. Desi Arnaz, 'Babalú.' It's my inspiration when I start painting a new can."

Christina grabbed the Progresso trash can she fancied, "'I Love Lucy' was my favorite show. Can we listen while we burn?"

"Abso-fucking-lutely. Here." He tossed her a book of matches. She pulled the can center stage. Whitefish pushed open a window, then flicked on his amp, "You ready?" She pointed to him in the affirmative. He picked up the turntable's stylus, and at thirty-three and a third, the eagle landed— the drums and percussion of "Babalú" began thumping as Whitefish moved to the beat. "Fire that fucker up when Desi first hits 'Babalú,' about fifteen more seconds." Christina stuck the magazine under her arm and lit the match. He anticipated the timing he knew so well and then pointed. She lit the corner right on cue.

Desi wailed, "Babalú... ¡Ba-ba-lú! ¡Babalú, aye!"

A decent flame emerged, and she dropped Mr. Chris into the can, followed by the book of matches as she gently grooved to the beat. He walked past the can and suddenly squirted in some Ronsonol Lighter Fluid—whoosh! Together, they danced around the flaming and smoking can, enjoying the weirdness of it all.

She offered her hand as they moved in locked unison, the Fred & Ginger they both craved.

&

49
Suicide is Painless.

IT TOOK A WHILE, but in the minutes before dawn, we drained the bottle.

Me, Christina,
and our good friend Jack D.

Considering how much we drank, I was remarkably lucid. Although, I wasn't sure if I could actually get up and walk. Christina also seemed none the worse for wear, but she's a helluva lot younger. She still has staying power, as they say.

Like me, C-Mac – this new addition to my life – also danced with the God of Suicide. Or maybe it's the Devil of Hara-kiri. Nevertheless, who could blame her? Or me, for that matter.

The bastards who wage war create...

INFERNOS that engulf
FURNACES that scar
HELLHOLES that devour

Ending your life seems much less painful (and quicker) than absorbing the constant body blows.

At this moment, I'm not convinced that Christina is truly suicidal. Months ago, felo-de-se might have been a reality, back when the VA hacks had their claws buried inside her psyche. But thankfully, she met those "dissident" docs and Vets that yanked her from the VA quicksand. They also knocked that drug monkey off her back. And then coming here, as fucked up as this place is, Asbury Park – or at least the place she remembers – is offering another healing hand. To me, her smile feels genuine. Her heart appears open. Is she out of the woods? Who the hell knows? Based on my personal history, probably not... because it's never really over. You face continuous speed bumps, not to mention those wicked left-hand turns down shock corridors.

But it gets better. Sometimes. I've personally known two GIs that were sure they left all this shit behind. "Free at last, free at last...." Turns out they weren't. Both men – good, repentant, and smart guys – fell into latent and dormant depressions. They both hung themselves.

Thank you for your service. Now cut 'em down.

Christina was carrying around this "Outdoor" magazine that lionized the life and strange death of a decent young man named Chris McCandless – a guy I surmised was extremely naive, probably depressed, and almost definitely schizophrenic. The Hat Trick. But in the end, many folks (Christina included) positioned the kid as an American folk hero. She absorbed his intriguing narrative – it spoke to her. And I get the intrigue, the rebellion of it all. But in my not-so-humble opinion, she mistakenly conflated her plight with McCandless' foolish and/or deadly escape (slow-motion suicide).

Ultimately, her take on this story was a misguided read of history. But give her credit: Once presented with alternative views, she was smart enough – and tough enough – to see through the embroidery. She then agreed to ceremoniously burn the magazine upon my recommendation. My guess? She suspected these alternatives all along. Our chat simply offered a clear passageway out.

We had dinner. We had wine. Great wine. And then we dissected McCandless' story every which way but loose. Truth be told, I did most of the talking. I brought Tim Leary and Hunter Thompson into the mix, so that's always fun, and then we burned the magazine in one of my Progresso cans. Afterward, we needed a denouement of sorts, so we hung out in the bar for a short while. Of course I had to break up a verbal tete-a-tete between Bagel and Texas-T that was probably ten seconds away from someone throwing a punch. And then, with a bottle of Jack D in hand, we ventured up to the roof, where I have two Adirondack chairs for just such occasions.

I find this unorthodox relationship between Christina and myself to be a wonderful thing. It's an absolute learning experience for me because even over the chasm of our ages, it's apparent that C-Mac and I can damn near talk about anything. She actually seemed interested when I spoke about the history of the Adirondack chair and its birthplace in upstate New York. Talk about useless and pointless knowledge. She told me about her dog growing up – a Yorkie named Albert. But then she dramatically catapulted, confiding in me about her long-standing love affair with Jaime, including the expected trials and tribulations of keeping their relationship veiled during high school, not to mention a covert action around a town like Belvidere – puritanical bullshit a la Ocean Grove.

It's obvious how much she misses Jaime and how she yearns to be free from these demons so they can try again. Clearly, she doesn't blame Jaime for leaving. "Plain and simple," she confessed to me, "I was a toxic asshole. I'm surprised she stayed as long as she did."

I'm not. In fact, I told her how much I envied what she had with Jaime and what she could still have with this young lady.

In all my life, I told her, I've never once loved a woman. Or had one love me back. Sure, I got a hand job from Grace Nowicki in tenth grade, and then one night after a Knicks game, in my car, I banged a professional just outside the Lincoln Tunnel. Such sweet memories of losing one's virginity. Of course, in 'Nam, I rendezvoused with a few ladies in country. Truth be told, I asked one young lady for her hand in marriage – what they call "war brides." Her name was "Mary," although I have a sneaky feeling that was her stage name. But alas, my only takeaway from those various romances were two bouts with gonorrhea... and like they used to say, "VD is nothing to clap about."

At first, Christina teared-up when I spoke of my tragic void to find passion and love in all the wrong places – but then her tears turned to gallows laughter as I detailed my slaphappy "love life" with Grace and Mary, as well as the patron saint of venereal disease.

Earlier in this chronicle, I discussed the importance of inciting incidents. We looked closely at Mr. Springsteen's – that rocket ship to Mars review penned by Jon Landau. Well, last night there was another "inciting incident" that occurred up on the roof, and this one involved Christina. About halfway through our slow-drinking marathon, she began sketching out the sky for me like she was describing her old neighborhood. It felt like I was back on a field trip to the Hayden Planetarium. She sat up and pointed with a buoyancy I had yet to see from this young woman, "That's Saturn right there, the brightest one in that dim constellation called

Capricornus, see it?" I did. "You know, it's amazing... Saturn spins so fast on its axis that it literally flattens out into what scientists call 'an oblate spheroid.'" For some reason, we both cracked up, with me wondering if those were even real words. "Absolutely," she continued, "When you see a photo of Saturn, it's like someone squished it a little. The speed causes the equator to bulge out. Holy shit, right?"

Next thing I know, she's off and running about other stars – Vega and Sirius – and then starts filling me in on Carl Sagan, her "favorite writer of all time."

She talked about Sagan's idea that "science was like a candle in the dark" and how it's not only compatible with spirituality but that science can actually be a profound source of spirituality. It was beautiful. And no doubt poetic. And then we drank some more... and I watched her watch the stars. I thought about the moment I first saw her, right on my boardwalk, standing there in those red sneakers, that moment locked in a sunrise – and maybe it was the booze, or maybe it was something else, but my thought-question was epic if nothing else:

Holy Christ, was this chick delivered from the stars?

And then McCartney and Lennon were singing in my fucking head:

"Well she was just seventeen, and you know what I mean, and the way she looked was way beyond compare, so how could I dance with another, oh! When I saw her standing there."

Well, she wasn't seventeen and she wasn't standing there, but you get what I mean.

The last few days of my life added up to this moment – a moment that will unfortunately come and go, like us, like the planet, like the whole damn shebang. But it was a moment nonetheless. And it was my moment. Fleeting. Intimate. And absolutely delusional.

BUT...

Christina will never know because I'm not planning on saying or breathing a goddamn word to her. But on this night, on the roof of my venerable old Club Southside, sitting in Adirondack chairs from upstate New York, I began to experience the mystery I so often wondered about. There

I was on my cloistered and lonely one-way street, suddenly knowing what it felt like to actually love someone, to love a woman other than your Ma.

Now, I suppose you can't truly fall in love with someone unless that individual returns the favor with equal vim and vigor. But at least I have my puzzle piece, my fifty percent. And dig it, I questioned myself thoroughly: Was I indeed fucking delusional? (Like McCandless?) Or was I simply enamored with the idea of our connection, of falling in love? But remember this: When you've been through what I've been through, when you've built a sturdy and dependable bullshit detector like I possess – one that you can even point back at yourself – there's a good chance you can trust your feelings as being authentic. Because this feels as real as the salty ocean breeze on my face. I've never felt anything like it... don't want it to end... and I'll take this secret to the grave. (Unless this pile of tripe gets published – and then I might simply omit this chapter.)

Ah, this woman. So much younger than me and in many ways so much brighter, like her star Sirius, "the brightest!" Christina has unknowingly bestowed upon this wretch a remarkable gift. It might be unrequited love (of course it's unrequited!), but at least now I have something to embrace.

I watched her take a pull from that bottle of Jack Daniel's... and now, in the damp recesses of my tangled brain, it continues to play like an overproduced TV commercial... but in my thirty-second spot we had a real wind machine called the Atlantic that gently eddied her long and flowing black locks. We had real moonlight that some Hollywood schlub couldn't duplicate in a million years; she was a vision of beauty, an American beauty. Like me, ripped apart and then pieced back together with spit and glue. Sure, Christina's pretty. Actually strike that – she's magnificently pretty, whether she's an inch away or a hundred yards down the road. And of course that reality helps the magnetic forces. As I've said numerous times: I'm a plain, straight male, so give me a fucking break. Every time I see her, the attraction, like a magnet, grabs me by the throat (can't grab anything else).

So, without wanting to sound maudlin or mawkish, her beauty alone is not what generates these unexpected feelings. It's the way we click. It's the HOW & WHAT we share. We've had perfect integrity from the get-go. It was unspoken but oh-so-obvious.

As you've probably figured out by now, I'm not exactly the kind of guy that gives a shit about what others think, or what they know, or even accomplish for that matter. I'm all about me. I'm a constructive and benevolent self-serving bastard. Scribble that on my urn.

But with Christina – the woman I'll never have, the woman I can't have, the woman who might as well be a sweater model in a Sears Catalog – I suddenly care about what she thinks... and not just what she thinks about me, that's cheap grace, but what she thinks about everything. Like the stars.

I'll settle on being her knight-errant – a medieval horseman in constant search of chivalrous adventures. I want to see her move on. I want to see her drive away from this dying ember of a place, ready to re-enter the land of the living, hand-in-hand with Jaime.

I want her to remember Jack & Darlene with a smile on her face... and then, I want her to forget... disremember... fail to recall... erase from her mind... this evil Uncle Sam... and what he tried to do to her –

but failed.

#

50

Tadasana (Part Deux).

Christina slept with the windows open. Silence was never an option. She needed the faint incidental sounds that would permeate the room like a soft blanket. The low-volume radio was also a must; preferably music, but news talk would suffice in a pinch. Pretty much anything but a religious channel. She turned over in bed and hugged the cool sheets close. Twenty-four hours had passed since she successfully slogged down off the roof of the Club Southside. She hugged a few more inches of bedsheet, feeling relieved that her hangover seemed to have left the premises. The pounding headache was gone. She tunneled deeper into the bed. It felt so good to feel good again.

She noticed what appeared to be the first hints of daybreak. The hands on the small clock hit 5:37, must be AM. The familiar and muffled sound of a commuter train joined her early morning soundtrack—and then a distant siren. The almost unintelligible voice on the radio reported that "The 29th Annual Jerry Lewis Labor Day Muscular Dystrophy Telethon raised a whopping $47 million dollars." She smiled, remembering how much she loved watching the telethon with Jack and how excited they'd get when Ed McMahon hinted that the tote board was about to change. Jerry: "Timpani... hit it!" Another cool million. Father and daughter would jump up cheering with the Vegas crowd.

Wrapped in a sheet, Christina slipped out of bed and moved to the windows. Thank Jehovah that her buddy, Father Marlboro, the Pope's errand boy, wasn't glued to his cancer bong because the church, with its reddish-brown stone, was bathed in perfect light. *The Exorcist* priest would have certainly ruined the moment—with the trees rustling and the bronze cross sitting against a changing sky. It was art, really.

C-Mac had a thought, a really good one, about the Whitefish. But damn, wouldn't you know it, the good padre wandered across the courtyard to his customary spot and, presumably, fired up his first of the day. He looked disheveled and lonely, a sad sack even though he was showered in this heavenly light. Wow. The scene reminded her of a Pissarro painting she and Jaime loved at The Met.

And for some reason, on this early September morning, Christina felt sorry for her chain-smoking nemesis, this agent of the Roman Church, the Catholicism the MacKenzies rebelled against so long ago. He stood there looking like a man against the world, maybe against himself, looking younger than she first thought. Did he want out of this medieval bullshit? Maybe his demons were closing in, forcing the young priest to look more like a chimney sweep than a vibrant spirit living free of his priggish leg irons.

Then, for some bizarre fucking reason, she summoned a distant thought, "When two of you gather in my name, I am there with you" or some such—Oh shit, Father Marlboro glanced in her direction, and once again their eyes locked—only this time his innocent face longed for something more than just a cheap thrill. More than perfect tits and ass. She felt it, so Christina smiled, and shyly waved. He smiled and waved back. "What a sweet smile," she thought. Her second wave shape-shifted to a peace sign; he nodded his acknowledgment and returned the same—and then took a deep drag. They both turned back to their lives.

Christina threw on her yoga pants and a top, tied back a ponytail, grabbed a large package of developed photos and headed out. The day before, she had picked up her Asbury Park memory pics at the local Fotomat. Millie said she was interested in seeing her "photo essay." C-Mac laughed, "I don't know about that. Just snapshots from throwaway cameras." She dropped the photos on Millie's desk.

She had to run to catch up to Whitefish on his daily routine. He was already off the Boardwalk and passing Deal Lake when she jogged up. "I have an idea," she boasted.

"Hey kiddo," he was happy to see her. Just then, a car passed from behind with the horn blaring as the driver yelled out, "Hey Whitefish!" Then flipping him the bird, "Go fuck yourself, you dipshit!" The young passengers shared a big laugh as they roared off. Whitefish was like the Teflon man as he saluted, "Good morning, boys!" His attention quickly turned back to Christina, "Just a few of my loyal fans. So what's up?" She was stretching as they walked, "I'll show you when we get to the turnaround point." Christina punched him in the arm. Surprisingly hard. He smiled. Jesus that felt good.

❖ ❖ ❖

On this particular morning, had you been standing on the corner of Ocean Place and Spier Avenue in Allenhurst, right under that rusty street sign engulfed by exclusive beachfront homes, and you gazed out over the beating Atlantic, you would have glimpsed two silhouetted figures near the water's edge. That's where Christina decided to give Whitefish his first yoga lesson. She wasn't sure how he'd react to the idea—being told what to do, breaking out of his regular regime. But she trusted him, and to her joy and surprise, he was remarkably compliant. One might even say, "into it." She explained how she wanted to guide him through some moves and then meditate for fifteen minutes.

She wanted to make sure, "Are you cool with this?"

"Absolutely, my Yogi Berra."

With bare feet, they sat on the hard sand as Christina began with an easy pose, something she called, "Sukhasana... this will help relieve stress... follow me, palms up, legs crossed like this. It's also called the Lotus position." It sounded good to Whitefish, except as he struggled into position, he moaned, "You might have to put me in traction at some point." They sat facing the ocean as she transitioned into Cat-Cow. "This will wake up your spine and also ease any back pain." Accepting his assignment, he followed her exactly, "I'm all for that." Next they stood up for Tree pose, "This will help greatly with your balance." He was having a tougher time pulling this one off, groaning as he fought gravity, but she lent a helping hand—that's all he needed. "Don't let go," he warned, "or you'll have to call an ambulance." She was trying not to laugh. "Alright, let's get back down for Child's pose, or what's called Balasana. You'll like this. It's very healing." At first, the stretch was tough, but then he melted into the pose.

Christina popped to her feet, helping him up as he labored, "After this, it's back to the old folk's home, right?" She waved him off, "Are you kidding? You're doing just fine. Only one more position, my favorite before we meditate. It's called Mountain pose or Tadasana." Whitefish was a good student—very attentive as C-Mac illustrated, "Tadasana looks simple, but inside your muscles are really working hard. So... stand perfectly still with your chest wide open, hands at your side, like this." As he glanced for instructional purposes, he suddenly realized he wasn't glancing for instructional purposes. He was trying desperately to hide his guilt, you know, that *"Playboy* back under the bed" look. In the nanosecond that all of this transpired, he chanted to himself: "Yoga. Yoga. Yoga. You stupid idiot." She wondered, "You okay?" He was back, "Yes, chest wide open. Hands by my side."

The lesson continued, "Perfect, now grasp the sand with your yoga toes, see? Root down through your feet. Concentrate. Do you feel the sensations in your legs and back?" He did and nodded as he focused. She emphasized, "Don't clench your teeth. Root yourself... but then let everything go, don't pressurize your body. She gently guided her hands over his body as she explained, "Make sure to elongate your spine from your pelvis, here, right up through the top of your head."

Five minutes later, eyes closed, they meditated—Christina in the Lotus pose, Whitefish seated with his legs stretched out. She added some peaceful guidance along the way. After a few minutes of uncomfortable nothingness, he suddenly felt like he was floating.

Christina offered a soft landing, "Hands to your heart. Like this... Namaste." Under his breath, he repeated, "Namaste."

They walked back to the Boardwalk in a pleasant haze. Whitefish expected to make them his regularly scheduled oatmeal, but instead Christina offered to drive them to the diner for breakfast. Her treat. Whitefish slowed to a complete stop somewhere between the 1st Avenue Pavilion and the Carousel—as if the world suddenly stood still. She could sense an internal battle raging on the good ship Whitefish. For him, this decision felt like Grant at Vicksburg. A diner breakfast was wanton heresy.

He was locked on her gaze, which offered nothing more than a patient and gentle smile. And then, after a few weird seconds, she added a subtle little Irish jig that said, "C'mon, it'll be fun." Struggling to get past the lump in his throat, he finally uttered just above a whisper, "Sure. Let's go." Had anyone ever been allowed to witness Whitefish so vulnerable?

So with the windows down, the Pulsar tooled along Route 35—Van Halen's "Panama" blaring on the cheesy tape deck:

♫ *Hot shoe, burning down the avenue*

Clearly, C-Mac and the Fish enjoyed the jaunt, their hair coasting on a wave. She downshifted seamlessly as they galloped in hot, parking underneath the neon-gyrating sign: Johnny Be Goode. Whitefish was duly impressed, "Man, you can really drive this thing." She yanked up the parking brake and killed the engine, then, like a robot, "I-am-one-with-machine."

When they walked in, a number of heads turned toward Whitefish as if they were witnessing the rarest of white elk sightings. They slid into an open booth. "Seems like they know you," Christina said with tongue in cheek. Whitefish studied the song selection on the push-button jukebox, "Yeah, it's been a while." C-Mac's familiar waitress, Doris, sauntered up with menus and tossed them down, "Lordy, Lordy, look what the cat dragged in." She was quick to add, "Sorry, not you, sweetie."

Whitefish picked up a menu, "You haven't changed a bit, Doris." Followed by the most exaggerated eye roll of all time.

She continued to size him up, "I didn't think you ever left that dive of yours." Doris nudged Christina, "How the hell did you extract him?" C-Mac smiled, "I just asked nicely." Doris smirked, "Yeah, I bet you did." Then to Whitefish, "Okay, Charlie Tuna, whaddaya have?"

Whitefish closed his menu and then announced to the diner with no reserve:

> "LADIES AND GENTLEMEN,
> LET'S HAVE A BIG CAESARS PALACE WELCOME
> FOR MISS JOAN RIVERS!"

Then he calmly ordered, "Oatmeal, brown sugar, and a cup of your shitty coffee." Doris jotted on her little pad, "How 'bout you, Baby Cakes?" C-Mac laughed out loud, "Baby Cakes. I like that. I'll have the same."

As Doris moved away, Whitefish winked at Christina and then summoned back their waitress, "Excuse me, Miss Rivers..." Doris swung around, "Yessir, Tuna Melt." Deadpan, he advised, "Listen, sweet cheeks, I'd suggest not giving up this amazing day job, comedy ain't your thing... but I'd like to change my order because this is a big day and we're celebrating."

Doris grabbed her pad, "Go 'head, it's a free country."

Whitefish snickered, "Actually it's not, but two eggs over easy, crispy bacon, hash browns, and toss in an English muffin, dry and well-done. You can damn near burn the motherfucker." Christina offered her second peace sign of the day, "Make that two."

Doris grabbed the menus, "Geez, the Bobbsey Twins," then grinned a solid "drop-dead" at Whitefish and just walked away.

Whitefish pulled some coins from his pocket, "See, they either love me or hate me... and Doris hates me ever since we did high school together. The Neptune Scarlet Fliers." He popped a quarter in the jukebox, "Pick one, then I'll pick one." Christina flipped through the tunes and plugged in D-5.

Whitefish liked her choice, "Van Halen to Van Morrison, nice symmetry."

On their way back, Mario Andretti was forced to stop at a construction backup, right in front of the old gothic Asbury Park Armory on Lake Ave. The sign read, "Home to VFW Post #1333." There were two large flags flying out front—the American and the black POW-MIA; they snapped briskly in the ocean draft.

These two ex-GIs weren't talking about war, nor were they even thinking about it, but the flags and patriotic lawn drivel opened the door.

In the screenplay for his aborted film, Standish Adams included this scene based on Whitefish's very short account of the interaction. We don't believe the scene was filmed before production was unceremoniously shut down.

EXT. ASBURY PARK ARMORY - DAY

Old Glory and the POW/MIA flags crack in the breeze as the Pulsar sits in a traffic jam - heavy construction. A jackhammer thrashes nearby.

EXT. ASBURY PARK ARMORY / INSIDE THE PULSAR - DAY (CONTINUOUS)

A toothpick hangs from Whitefish's lips. The Armory's lawn offers patriotic placards. Christina points to a red-white-and-blue sign with a large peace symbol; she reads the headline—

> CHRISTINA
> "Footprint of the American Chicken."

> WHITEFISH
> That was big during Vietnam. John Birch
> Society.

> CHRISTINA
> (reads another)
> "America - Love It or Leave It." That one I
> know.

> WHITEFISH
> (taking in the symbols)
> General public has no grasp of history...
> indoctrination instead of education...
> and whaddaya get? Bumper sticker mentalities.
> A true formula for disaster.

> CHRISTINA
> We were pretty fucking gullible, huh?

Traffic starts to move. Christina shifts into gear.

> WHITEFISH
> But there's good news...
> (a la Roger Daltrey)
> *"We won't get fooled again."*

> CHRISTINA
> Unfortunately others will.

> WHITEFISH
> (as it sinks in)
> Yep.

❖❖❖

Christina pulled up behind Club Southside. She told Whitefish she'd be leaving in the next day or so. A trip north to Belvidere to see Jaime and then the trek back to Los Angeles, hopefully with Jaime. "Maybe it's a pipe dream," she admitted. He offered hope, "Then again, maybe not. Leave the baggage down here."

Whitefish told C-Mac that he wanted to "throw her a little bon voyage party." He also had a parting gift, "You know, like on 'The Price is Right,' *thanks for playing!"*

She was touched, "When's the party?"

As he climbed out of the Pulsar, "How's tonight? Seven-ish?"

She smiled, "Sure, that's so nice." He shut the door and limped his usual limp toward the club. She watched him in his faded jeans and long white hair, a cool trademark, she thought, that fell easy on his pink-flowered shirt that screamed Maui—the colors almost day-glow, jumping off the Boardwalk's grunge canvas, a palette populated by what only could be called "Desolation Brown."

She pulled away down Ocean Ave.

&

51
Tectonics.

FOR MOST OF US, it seems, there are any number of instances during our time on this rock when some event or a fellow space traveler might force a tectonic shift in who we are, where we're going, how we view the world, even how we might live out our lives. These dramatic moments usually fall into two simple categories: good shit or bad shit – and if we're truthful, they will by definition never be indifferent.

You've spent some time with me, so you know I've had my share of tectonic shifts. I count two events that clearly fall on my bad shit list: the old man getting plugged during a random hold-up and, of course, the day I stepped off that Boeing 707 transport at Tan Son Nhut Air Base in Saigon – new meat for the American Empire.

But following these two major FUCK YOUs, courtesy of the home office, my experiences in life turned a decisive corner. I count five angels on my good shit list, so in that regard I consider myself fortunate. First, there's Ma – my "Madonna," who embodied unconditional love; no explanation necessary. Secondly, there's Lou and Lorraine – two absolute archangels who selflessly afforded me the opportunity to become a fiercely independent business owner, and therefore a fiercely independent human being. Thirdly, there was sweet Lorelei Antuofermo, my partner in the gaming business; over the years we made good money together, never fought about a thing (except who was better, Mantle or Mays) – and I learned volumes about commerce and life in general from this wonderful and tough old broad.

And now there's Christina MacKenzie, number five; a tough young broad who blindsided me on my own boardwalk – another archangel, this one locked in a sunbeam, resembling one Dorothy Gale, an itinerant day tripper searching for her way back to Kansas.

Maybe I'll see her again... and maybe I won't. But in case it's the latter, I want to scramble up a going-away party as well as a parting gift that might ensure me a place in her heart. After all, you know about the gift she's bestowed upon me, one that's engendered my latest tectonic shift.

She gave it unselfishly (not to mention unknowingly).

That's the beauty part.

My clock says 11:11am. Time to get crackin' on this going-away shindig. I also have to call Joe Fats about his connections at Regal Construction (I know that sounds like a "note to self," but in actuality it's a story point – so hang in there, baby).

More on both of these after midnight.

Oh, and it's #24 – Willie Mays. The "Say Hey Kid."

#

52

The Favor.

Without the help of his loyal following, the King could never pull off these last-minute soirees—his track record chock-full of well-attended and memorable gatherings. He had it down pat: engage the necessary triggers and phone trees, and voilà, Instant Karma's gonna get you.

For Christina's going-away, he wanted the menu to be special. Invitees would have a choice of three entrées: petite filet mignon, shrimp scampi over linguine, or one of Lou's favorites, chicken cordon bleu. At 11:20am, Whitefish called his liquor guy, who was actually a woman, and personally picked out the red and white vino—a 1990 Valdicava Sangiovese from Tuscany and a '91 Sauvignon Blanc from Napa's Sebastiani Winery, "Both award-winning... and as you may or may not know," Whitefish told his distributor, "1990 was a historic vintage for Tuscan Sangiovese. I'm happy to see it in your inventory. I need it all by five."

Also, in Christina's honor, this Club Southside evening was on the house for all invited. Whitefish was picking up the entire tab, although if some of the less couth in attendance wanted beer, a shot, or a mixed drink, "It's a cash bar," he told Tombstone, "Fuck 'em."

The last-minute live music would be tough. Two Jacks and a Jill, usually a phone call and a cheeseburger away, had a three-night gig in King of Prussia, PA, so they were out. Johnny Maestro and his Fucking Brooklyn Bridge were booked for some robber baron's bar mitzvah up in Tenafly. And then his last choice—the Cranky Tampons, an all-girl band from South Philly—was available, but he vowed two years ago never to hire them again. He hated their name, their logo, and it seemed everyone hated their music. "Why do I still even have their goddamn number?" he asked Abner rhetorically. His friend in the red fedora straw-sucked down the remnants of a Diet Coke and then looked Whitefish square in the eye. As the pregnant pause passed, Abner asked the proprietor a query with all the gravity and hushed drama you might expect in a much different scenario: one where a five-star general asks the Commander in

Chief if it's time to launch that 25-megaton nuclear warhead into Beijing: "So, do you call in... drumroll... *the favor?*"

❖ ❖ ❖

"What a turnout!" Whitefish exclaimed to anyone within earshot. Although, what else did he expect? mumbled Madam Marie. "Free grub and wine. This ain't magic."

Christina was taken aback when she walked in, shocked really at the bizarre number of Asbury Park denizens in attendance, not to mention Whitefish's generosity of food and drink. She never saw him dressed as he was on this evening—the faded jeans and dark blue Hawaiian shirt were familiar, of course, but the gray sport jacket was a nice addition, as was the white straw fedora with a fancy blue feather. The jukebox played at a background level that made conversation easy. And Whitefish had his full complement of staff: three waitresses, including Donna, all of them now circulating with hors d'oeuvres (miniature egg rolls and pigs in a blanket), two busboys roaming and cleaning, Lou had ample help in the galley, and Tombstone split his time between pouring the vino and mixing the occasional drink.

The joint had a pleasant and friendly buzz.

Millie walked in a few minutes after Christina. Clearly, the Fish had considered every detail. Christina hugged her favorite innkeeper, who whispered, "Luckily I only had to keep the secret a few hours." Millie giggled—and at that moment Christina had a strange realization: Millie reminded her of Darlene, had her mother been allowed to grow old.

Individuals Christina barely knew, like Bagel, Joe Fats, and Madam Marie, as well as the rest of the King's gang, wished her well. People she never even laid eyes on did the exact same. For one crystalline moment, in these four walls, Asbury Park was alive again.

People gathered randomly at the various tables and booths, except for one table that was reserved for the guest of honor, along with Whitefish, Millie, Lil Abner, and Donna. The owner cut Donna's shift short and invited her to join, which she did, gladly.

As the spectacular dinner wound down, Joe Fats caught Whitefish's eye and strenuously nodded in the affirmative. Whitefish casually excused himself and moved to the small stage with his red wine, grabbed the mic stand, and tapped the hot mic, "Is this thing on?" A few laughs as the room fell silent. Unbeknownst to the guests, a man carrying something mysterious moved through the dark shadows behind the stage. Whitefish addressed the crowd.

"Thank you all for attending our celebration on short notice. I thought it was important to give my new and dear friend, Christina, a proper Asbury Park-Jersey Shore send-off." A friendly applause with some whistling ensued. "Most of you don't know Christina," he continued, "But you do know me, so this pedigree of a friendship and evening falls under the old adage, 'Any friend of my brother is a friend of mine.'" He raised his glass, "A toast to the future travels and endeavors of Ms. Christina MacKenzie. Here-here!" The room obliged with gusto. Christina smiled shyly, half stood and waved. She felt embraced, and that was nice, but as she glanced around the room, it also felt kind of strange—the attendees continued their long applause, but she really didn't know anybody, and they didn't know her. In many ways, this surreal snapshot of jubilance, this outpouring of love, felt weirdly artificial.

Was Fellini stationed in the dark, triggering his Arriflex loaded with Ferrania P30? Probably not, so she ignored her doubts because it was important to Whitefish and Whitefish was important to her. "Any friend of my brother is a friend of mine."

The King quieted the room and continued, "My unlikely bond with C-Mac, that's her nickname by the way, is actually threefold: First and foremost, our union is rooted in two failed wars. Christina bravely served in the blowing sands of Iraq... my stint, as you all know, tap-danced through the jungles of Southeast Asia. Our bond is also deeply rooted in the fact that we're both only children who tragically lost parents at an early age... but now, on a much happier note, thank god, we both share fond childhood memories of the holy Jersey Shore... historic Asbury Park in particular." Whitefish encouraged warm applause.

"Now, would this be a typical Club Southside moment without some bravado from atop my trusty soapbox?" More laughter and numerous hoots of "NO." He chuckled, "Indeed... but tonight, in deference to Christina and also not wanting to upstage our special guest, I shall wire my mouth shut for just this once." The room breaks into spontaneous and uproarious applause and cheers.

Whitefish grinned from ear to ear, blowing kisses across the club.

Christina enjoyed the shenanigans, feeling a little less weird. Whitefish waited for the room to settle, "Alright, alright, it's in the air. I can feel the love. Okay... I'd like to introduce our special musical guest. Now, I tried to book Two Jacks and a Jill, Johnny Maestro and his friggin' Brooklyn Bridge, the Cranky Tampons, and, believe it or not, Southside Johnny and the Asbury Jukes. Oddly enough, everyone was booked. But luckily, an old friend was available and agreed to play a couple of tunes in honor of my fellow Boonie Rat buddy, Private Christina MacKenzie. Ladies and gentlemen, please call to the stage, Columbia recording artist, the Boss—

MR. BRUCE SPRINGSTEEN!"

As a lone figure emerged from the shadows carrying an acoustic guitar, the joint erupted. Stunned, really. It was indeed Bruce Springsteen, dressed in all black and wearing a classic harmonica neck rig. When Christina realized this was real, she stood with rubber legs and joined the already vertical crowd, gasping, "Oh my God."

Bruce waved and grabbed a stool as Lil Abner delivered a double mic setup for voice and guitar. The cheering waned as everyone sat with anticipation. Whitefish plopped next to Christina, who was shaking her head in disbelief, then gave him an embrace for the ages.

"Thank you, folks," Springsteen modestly offered, "My friend and proprietor of this venerable establishment, Mr. Whitefish, apparently the undisputed King of Asbury Park, invited me to sing a couple songs for a United States Veteran who experienced the hell of war but luckily came back home... to New Jersey. Ms. Christina, welcome."

Shyly, Christina waved as the house offered another round of warm applause. Springsteen played a few notes and strummed his Takamine acoustic to make sure things sounded just right. They did. "This first song is called 'No Surrender.'" Brief applause as the house lights dimmed.

C-Mac decided that somewhere along the line she had died and this was heaven.

53
Juxtaposition.

EVER HAVE ONE OF THOSE MOMENTS when a tune gets stuck in your head? Over and over like a broken record? Of course, we all do. Well, tonight, as I sit here writing my notes and thoughts post-Christina's going-away gathering, I'm stuck on that Four Seasons song "Oh, What a Night" – their big hit that's actually entitled "December, 1963 (Oh, What a Night)."

Side note: One evening back in '84 or '85, The Four Seasons (Frankie Valli, Bob Gaudio, Nick Massi, and Tommy DeVito) rolled in for a quick drink. They ended up hanging at the bar for probably two hours. Never met these guys before, but damn, the stories they told about launching that band from the streets of Newark. Unbelievable.

And I never knew they were first called "The Four Lovers," later rebranding themselves "The Four Seasons" - funny enough, named after a bowling alley lounge in Union, N.J. (some joint where they bombed an audition and hit rock bottom, ballsy move).

I still have this weird double album concocted back in '63 by some Crackerjack record company called Vee-Jay... the recording billed as "The Beatles vs. The Four Seasons." The marketing savages were trying to capitalize on teenyboppers tussling about which band was better. The cover was set up like a prizefight – "The International Battle of the Century" and "You Be The Judge & Jury."

My vote? Let me put it this way: Buried somewhere, I have a decent photo Abner took that night of me with Frankie and the boys. Right now, I have no idea where it is. But if I had a similar photograph of me along with John, Paul, George, and Ringo, well, that piece of history would be blown up, framed, and hung prominently down in the Club.

Does that answer the question?

So, yes, what a night. I wanted things to be special for Christina, especially at this fragile moment in her young life, an evening to remember. I believe we accomplished that objective. I'm almost certain that she arrived in Asbury Park desperate for answers, muddled in depression, and probably on the edge of despondency. One wrong push, who knows? But over these last few days I've sensed a brilliant inner light, one that will take a great deal to extinguish.

Ultimately, she's a fighter. Float like a butterfly...

A note on the following thoughts:

Some of these anecdotes are specific and distinct memories that Christina shared with me; others I've extrapolated and/ or deduced by reading between the lines; and the rest are what I like to call "connective tissue" - those communal moments that pretty much belong to all the families, large and small, that rotate through the hundred or so miles known as the Jersey Shore.

She landed here in a Datsun eggbeater seeking the innocence she recalled with great affection, the innocence this place once offered in spades. Jack, Darlene, and the little girl they called Tina would joyfully check in at the Sea Breeze – that blue tribute to Victorian panache. They'd walk these sanctified planks where familiar sounds and unmistakable aromas invaded their sense memory forever – massive piles of sausage and peppers sizzling on a greasy grill, giant tomato pies sliced by hairy and garrulous Italians, lunatics wielding rotary blades traveling through pizza crust at the speed of light. And then, oh my Lord, at every turn, the incessant and perpetual clicking of spinning game wheels that spewed subversive and intoxicating messages: "Hey, kid, wanna do what's never been done? Wanna win what's never been won?"

Every day, the MacKenzies would seek out the colossal saltwater pool and swim in its magic buoyancy. They'd rent beach umbrellas and become simpatico with the hot, gravely sand and rugged Atlantic. Even when that occasional strand of seaweed wrapped itself around their ankles, no problem, just a mermaid saying hello. The MacKenzies didn't even mind the various pink shades of sunburn that covered their white North Jersey bodies. Hell, it was a badge of honor. (Although nowadays, you can buy sunblock with an SPF factor that'll stop a bullet.)

The MacKenzies would scream bloody murder on those big-time amusement rides and then yuk it up in the god-awful fun house. They'd revel in bumper cars, which Christina found to be the great equalizer between parent and child. She'd wallop Jack from behind; he'd slump over the wheel, feigning a blackout, only to wake up with a fevered vengeance!

The nights would begin with a relaxed dinner – sometimes Italian, but most of the time seafood, and usually with a great view of the deep blue sea. Christina always picked their lobsters from a giant tank; she'd even give them names... but alas, that tradition ended abruptly one evening when she finally put two and two together and realized she was singing the executioner's song. Once the crying stopped, her entree on that fateful night (and many nights to follow) was salad.

After dinner, they'd return to the Boardwalk, except now under pulsating and glistening lights, their stomachs full but somehow able to enjoy one more treat: "CUSTARD ON A CONE!"

What the hell – it was summer, it was vacation, and it was the Jersey Shore.

And that's what Christina came here to find, that innocence lurking in the histories of her life. Sometimes we all need a lifeboat... and last night we all tried to Titanic her home. The townspeople were summoned and came out in force. Club Southside did what Club Southside always does – food, drink, and revelry. And then I called in "the favor" – that's what Lil Abner calls my long-standing ace in the hole with Mr. Springsteen. This voucher goes way back to the early seventies, the substance of which will remain between myself and the guitar player from Freehold.

So now, in 1994, we're even. I was just waiting for that no-doubt-about-it perfect moment.

And Christina was it.

And Bruce was Bruce – playing like Club Southside was the last venue on Earth.

Side note #2: Springsteen played two songs on his acoustic... the defiant anthem "No Surrender" that he performed with appropriate swagger... and then his seminal "Thunder Road." What a choice and such a complex narrative: The melody

337

hints at a new day breaking, but then the story turns on a dime and speaks with absolute dread about a **very** uncertain future... all of it followed by another sudden turn as Bruce ties up all the loose ends and his fable rides off drenched in hope: "It's a town full of losers, I'm pulling out of here to win."

All of it drawing parallels to Christina's precarious journey.

When he finished and the joint was on its feet cheering, I subtly pointed to Christina. He approached with the guitar slung over his shoulder, kissed her on the cheek, gave her a hug, and then disappeared into the night.

Who the hell can tell that story?

On this cool September night, nineteen hundred and ninety-four, it's ironic that a soul may have been saved in a place that died years ago. Give her credit. She knew we were all but dead, yet she still came searching for hope – even a shred of hope – amidst the burning rubble.

A real juxtaposition, eh?

Tomorrow, when we say arrivederci, I'll have Christina's going-away present wrapped up with a big red bow. But first I need to get some shut-eye. Got to be up by five.

# #

54

Garden State Parkway.

After her soirée, Christina drove Millie back to the Sea Breeze, although the recent guest of honor wasn't ready to turn in for the night. Her brain chugged in overdrive. She waited for Millie to disappear safely inside before disappearing herself, taillights into the night.

With her windows down, she headed toward the Parkway, the great artery that bordered the notorious coast, the famous toll road that carried New Jerseyans and accidental tourists north and south through pine barrens, marshes, and swampland—Mother Nature's buffer between civilization and the Jersey Shore.

Sans her trusty Trip-Tik, she wound her way through Neptune and Wall, confident that if she just headed west, she'd soon somersault right into the pride of New Jersey. And, of course, she did, happily alerted by a familiar green entrance sign with its amber Parkway logo: "Toll Road, Parkway Entrance, South, No Pedestrians – Bicycles." Christina easily navigated the circular on-ramp and was soon headed south on the dark, empty highway toward Toms River, Barnegat, and who the hell knows. She followed a half moon rising in the clear eastern sky.

She wanted desperately to hear Springsteen songs, especially ones that would fit the mood like "Drive All Night," "State Trooper," "Wreck on the Highway"—wait, no, nix that one, how 'bout, "Open All Night?" Yes, perfect, except there were no Bruce tapes in her box. Idiot. How do you drive to Jersey without the E Street Band? But then she smiled, thinking, "Who the hell cares? The man was just singing FOR ME. Ten feet away! In the flesh! He hugged me, for god's sake. Bruce Springsteen. Hugged me. At my cockamamie going-away party. Going away where? Where the fuck am I going? Do I dare show up in Belvidere? THEN WHAT? Do I have a plan? NO. Can I formulate one in time? PERHAPS. Will it be stupid? PROBABLY. Will Jaime kick me to the curb?" MAYBE. And on that note, Christina flicked in a Bruce substitute, although Mick and Keith proved to be star-studded substitutes with Richards' trademark riff launching "Start Me Up."

And damn, way out in the distance, to the east, she had company—giant radio relay towers, red lights flashing, watching, guarding, stoically guiding her south.

❖ ❖ ❖

Christina decided to abandon the Parkway at the confluence of Exit 10 and 1:15am. She needed gas and knew the ocean was close, at a place called Stone Harbor. After grabbing a 7UP at the Gulf Station, she parked and wandered down a short wooded path toward the ocean. She could hear the waves. And then the path revealed a magnificently large beach.

It was dark, but the moonlight helped details to emerge, especially the breaking white caps. She spotted a lifeguard's stand and climbed up to the large bench seat—a position that made her feel like the last human on Earth, until a distant siren reminded her that she wasn't. A dog barked. Followed by unintelligible voices that came and went, probably from those nearby oceanfront McMansions. But then solitude came back, just Christina and the waves.

She noticed that the surf sounded loud. Was that a thing? Could the crashing surf be louder at night? Maybe Whitefish knows. She curled up cozy, deciding to rest for a little while, watch the dark ocean, and then head back up Parkway North.

At first, it sounded like a massive sea creature lurching from the tide, squealing and wailing like a harpooned behemoth. But this was no giant sea creature, no sirree! This was mouth-gaping, stone-cold freakish— like watching the Empire State Building suddenly topple onto midtown Manhattan.

Christina watched in horror as a colossal and monstrous cruise ship approached the shoreline, thundering in at god knows how many knots, its horn howling at earth-shattering decibels, its bow and hull grinding through rock and sand, screeching to a terrifying and shuddering halt just before this modern marvel of navigation plummeted over sideways, shaking the once quiet beach like a South American earthquake. The lifeguard's stand rocked violently, collapsing to the beach, but somehow Christina was left standing, unscathed—and now she heard passengers screaming; she could see them leaping to their deaths. Did a fiendish captain gain control of this vessel and ground it ashore like a bullet train? Was this the next scheduled cruise ship disaster for Asbury Park—but this fiend miscalculated and landed in Stone Harbor? She watched blood flow from the enormous dead ship, flooding like a teeming Tigris River. Broken survivors crawling through the killing fields of suitcases and still-moving body parts. Christina wanted to help, but how? She was frozen, petrified, wanting to grab her car keys, to get the fuck out of there, but she couldn't move, paralyzed!

When she opened her eyes, it was still dark.

Serenely quiet except for the surf.

She remained curled up, heart thumping, but was still able to thank Jesus—or maybe she should thank Poseidon—for segregating that cataclysm in her warped dreamworld and not actually dropping it on the good folks of Stone Harbor.

"Fucking PTSD," she groaned-sighed-and-swallowed as she climbed down off the lifeguard's stand.

❖❖❖

Ten minutes later, she was heading north on the Parkway. It was just after 3:30am as a State Trooper flew past her, siren and klieg lights on full tilt. She munched on a leftover stale doughnut and flicked on the radio—WMMR-FM out of Philly. She was in luck. "This next tune is for all you lonely hearts out there in the Delaware Valley," the soothing voice teased, "Lying awake or driving through some backwater town... Here's Bruce with 'Drive All Night.'"

Lucky indeed. Christina turned up the volume, and like magic, Jaime was sitting right next to her, eyes closed, with love and whispers in the cool night air.

❖❖❖

Whitefish had a hard time sleeping. His 5:00am meeting was simmering on the brain.

Clock radio, 3:47am. "Fuck it," he said out loud, "I'll sleep when I'm dead." He climbed out of bed and moved slowly to the shower. The steaming hot water washed away any early morning haze. He felt invigorated. Ready for action. Again, out loud, "Let's get this show on the road."

Wrapped in a towel, Whitefish hit the grinder on his Guatemalan roast. The coffee smelled good.

❖❖❖

By the time the song ended (Bruce's eight-minute true blue love note), Christina wiped the tears from her eyes and passed the Cape May Toll Plaza thirty-five cents lighter—but with her mind made up:

Tomorrow was Belvidere. Tomorrow was Jaime.

She figured, "What's the worst that could happen? They'd talk. Maybe agree to talk again. Maybe. Maybe. Maybe." But then she realized that could all be very naïve. Maybe super naïve. Jaime probably wants nothing to do with good ol' C-Mac and she'll end it right there.

Christina played ping-pong with these thoughts until she parked at the Sea Breeze around 5:00am. Fortunately, the mental torture fizzled as she climbed into bed; the radio, as always, played softly.

Tomorrow was Belvidere. Tomorrow was Jaime.

❖❖❖

Whitefish made himself a second cup of coffee and was outside sipping his perfect brew at exactly 5:00am—waiting for those boys from Regal Construction.

♫

55

Resurrection.

Regal Construction was owned by Joe Fats and his three brothers, triplets: Wyatt, Virgil, and Morgan (Mom & Pop had a unique sense of humor). Joe founded the company back in '72 and then brought in his three brothers—"the Earps"—as they were caustically dubbed by shore locals. They were good contractors and became one of the most successful construction firms in a three-county radius. But the 1980s proved difficult. Jobs dwindled with the bad housing market, forcing Joe to take on other things to make ends meet. Plus, he learned to hate construction, so he let the brothers pull salaries until things turned around. It was not surprising that at 5:00am Joe Fats was nowhere to be seen.

"Okay, boys, let's roll away the stone."

Wyatt wondered, "What stone you talkin' about, Fish?"

Whitefish laughed, sipping his coffee, "It's a joke, you know, a saying, when Jesus told them to roll away the stone?" The Earps had no idea what he was talking about. Incredulous, Whitefish pressed on, "Out walks Lazarus, who's been dead for like a week." Blank stares. "C'mon, guys, everyone knows this shit... when Jesus raised the poor bastard from the dead, proving once and for all that he really was THE SON OF GOD!" The Earps were still stone-cold lost. Dumbfounded. Whitefish groaned, "You're telling me that the name 'Lazarus' doesn't even ring a bell?" They shrugged. Desperate, he addressed the three other workers over by a dump truck, "HEY, YO... YOU GUYS EVER HEAR OF LAZARUS?! ROLL AWAY THE STONE?! THE GOSPEL ACCORDING TO JOHN?! DIDN'T ANYONE GO TO SUNDAY SCHOOL?! Jesus Christ."

Exasperated and laughing, Whitefish waved his hands and it was down to business, "Holy shit, forget it, let's start this thing... and remember, you gotta be exact. Surgically open the wall right here, right where we went in last time. Wyatt, remember? You see right here? I marked the parameters." Wyatt scratched his stomach, "Yeah, right, okay." Whitefish continued, "And then once you're in, you'll remove eight ceiling panels... and that's easy as hell because the floor there was never replaced. Got it?" Wyatt nodded as Whitefish finished his coffee, "Once clear, we'll lower in the makeshift ramp and extract the vehicle. Then you'll cart in all the new materials, build back up the ceiling and wall, and bingo, we're good as new. Easy as pie if you don't fuck it up. I'll be guiding you every step of the way. Really, Lazarus... doesn't ring a bell?"

With the speech over and his directions delivered, the three brothers and their dutiful workers moved into action. Bright work lights flashed on. This was basically the same team that first opened up the tomb a few years back. They were simply reversing the process: remove an entire section of the club's only cinder block wall, open up the ceiling, lay in a ramp, drive the car out, restore the wall and match the paint, "which might be the toughest part of all," Whitefish predicted.

As the workman finished carving out the side wall and the debris was being piled into a dump truck, Wyatt asked Whitefish, "Gonna enjoy the Caddy?" Whitefish was nonchalant, "Nah, donating to the church. Let 'em raffle it off, make a few bucks." Wyatt was impressed, "That's very generous. You a religious man?" Whitefish walked toward the hole, "Why do you ask?" Wyatt followed, "You know, you're donating the car and you knew all about this Lazarus guy. I mean, did Jesus really raise some guy from the dead?" Wyatt couldn't see the devilish smile on Whitefish's face, "It's in the Bible, so what do you think?" Whitefish let the workers know, "Yo, when you're done, make sure this is cleaned up, spic and span. Like it never happened. No half-ass shit or you'll be back here in a nanosecond."

As Virgil and Morgan began prepping the ramp, lowering long planks through the hole, Whitefish headed inside, "I'll be downstairs, just give me the word. And Virgil, make goddamn sure that ramp is rock-solid."

When he walked around to the front entrance of the club, he noticed another brilliant sunrise just about to happen. He also acknowledged that over the last four or five sunrises, his life had changed in abundant ways, all for the good. He laughed to himself, wondering if he wasn't his own expression of Lazarus.

❖ ❖ ❖

344

In the basement, Whitefish sat behind the wheel as Virgil and Morgan reinforced the ramp. A million thoughts ran through his mind: first and foremost, Lorelei, and how this Cadillac embodied her spirit—iconic, unexpected, classic; he thought about the hours he spent in this basement, behind the wheel, high as a kite, visiting various locales from here to Timbuktu; he also thought about what a fucking whack job he had devolved into, interring this sweet ride in a self-prescribed mausoleum, "Shoulda been out there driving for real," he mumbled.

Confident with the ramp, Morgan yelled, "Hey Fish, we're looking good. Steady as she goes!" With Virgil guiding from above and Morgan below, Whitefish fired up the V8, shifted into drive, and then slowly navigated the ramp, climbing toward the light of a new day.

❖ ❖ ❖

For some reason, Asbury Park never looked so good.

And thank god for those boys from Detroit: The Caddy responded well as Whitefish cruised down Asbury Ave, past Library Square Park, finally accelerating hard through Emory-Bond-and-Main Streets. He hadn't driven this car, or any car for that matter, in a few years. He felt alive as the fiery sunrise spread wide over the empty streets. Hell, he laughed out loud, thinking there were people in this seaside hamlet that would shit themselves brown if they spotted him roaring down Memorial Drive in Lorelei's unsullied Eldorado—top down with Van Morrison swoonin' brassy on the stereo. "Tupelo Honey."

> ♫ *You can't stop us on the road to freedom*
> *You can't keep us 'cause our eyes can see*

When he swung into the Route 35 Texaco, bells rang as he pulled straight into an open bay. Vinnie, Danny, and Joey emerged awestruck, as if this vision arrived from another dimension. Whitefish cut the engine and boomed, "GOOD MORNING, ASBURY PARK!" Joey was the first to speak, "Wha-wha-what the, what the fuh-fuck?!" Whitefish stepped out, "C'mon, fellas, ain'tcha ever seen a ghost before?"

He quickly explained what he wanted and left no wiggle room for debate. He limped around the Caddy as his laundry list unfolded, "Check out and inspect every motherfucking thing on this vehicle... I want new tires, new brakes, new shocks or struts, or whatever the fuck this thing takes.

Change all the fluids, flush out the fuel injectors. And no fuckin' around, this is a throttle-body Olds V8. Treat it with respect." He stopped for effect. "Remember, I'm not one of your Bermuda short-wearin' assholes down for the summer. Make believe it's your mother's car—perfectly safe and street legal. I don't care what it costs, but I will expect a healthy discount. And when you're done, buff it up nice and spiffy... and make sure you throw in a full tank of gas. Hi-test." For a very long moment, the three Texaco stars resembled the pack of apes in Kubrick's *2001: A Space Odyssey*—scratching their balls and staring at the black monolith.

Whitefish ambled toward the busy thoroughfare, "I need it by noon. So get started, chop-chop. I'm going for breakfast."

56

Sanctuary.

Christina woke up on her own around noon. She didn't remember dreaming about anything, and that was just fine, especially after her raucous cruise ship extravaganza. The rhythmic ceiling fan was mesmerizing as she mused why she adored this room so much. Sure, on the surface she understood the allure—her family's history here, the charm, the quaintness, Millie's tea and cookies, her favorite radio of all time, the absolutely serene view, even Father Marlboro across the way, their peace pact firmly in place. But there was more to this room. Something bigger. Something deeper.

The answer became manifest as she rolled over and glimpsed the rustling trees outside: it was her sanctuary, her place of refuge, what the ancient Hawaiians called Pu'uhonua. Curled up naked in her perfect sheets on this perfect bed, she replayed her recent past like a Kodak slide show, her strange quest for sanctuary snapped in vivid Ektachrome. And pow— when she laid out the past few years side-by-side, damn if her journey's trajectory didn't ping-pong the planet. Belvidere to Vegas. Fort Jackson to Kanagawa Prefecture, beautiful Japan. Germany to the Arabian Desert. The Highway of Death to Wilshire Boulevard. Santa Monica to Asbury Park, via her ever-so-helpful Trip-Tik.

She also wondered if Cletus ever got any.

And along the way, amidst the madness, she lost Jaime. The last vestige of her heart.

But here she was in the safe confines of Room 204, Sea Breeze Hotel, Asbury Park, New Jersey. The ceiling fan more metrical now than ever before. And then happily, ecstatically, she realized the Ektachrome slides that just sped through her mind like a frenetic peep show were all in the rearview mirror. Relics. What's past is prologue—"NO," she remembered Whitefish's echo, *What's past is fucking gone! To hell with prologue!*

Was there hope?

Christina sat up in bed, smiling; she might see Jaime today. The commuter train pulled into the nearby station—the clarion screech now so familiar. She liked familiar. She also felt strange in a really good way. Lighter? Wispier? "Is this what freedom feels like?"

She took a very long shower, another one of those "empty the hot water heater" showers. She envisioned the forest high atop Mt. Charleston in Nevada, that place she'd hike with Jaime to escape Vegas at 117°, wildflowers leading to Cathedral Rock.

In her mind, she whispered her Sanskrit mantra, "Aham Brahmasmi" or "I am the Universe," the water curving down her body, a makeshift womb.

Christina packed what little she had and headed out, stopping briefly before she pulled the door shut. To look back inside her unexpected sanctuary. She wanted to remember: the bed, the chair, the ottoman, the windows, and, of course, Marconi's invention: Charlie's perfectly refurbished RCA Victor.

Thanks, Charlie.

She knew she'd never visit Room 204 again.

She headed down the creaky stairs and heard familiar voices in the lobby. A playful conversation. Millie and the Whitefish?

57

Freedom with 170 Horsepower.

Millie and the Whitefish sat in the parlor sipping tea. Whitefish was enjoying a butter cookie as Christina turned the corner. "My goodness," Millie quipped, "The joint is jumpin' today." She stood and moved toward the kitchen, "The tea is made, let me get you some."

Christina dropped her bag and sat on the sofa, "Thank you, Millie. That's sweet."

Whitefish asked, "Checking out?"

She swiped a cookie, "I am. I was just heading your way."

He sipped his tea, "Beat you to it."

There was a long silence, unusual for these two, but this was getaway day, and they both knew it, and felt it, and for the most part, endings are always hard. Christina broke the silence, "Did that really happen last night?"

He raised his cup as a salute, "From what I can tell, most likely." He took a sip, "Earl Grey."

She grilled him, "C'mon, how did you pull that off?"

His turn to swipe a cookie, "These are amazing and I just ate a monster breakfast. Went back to the diner, had a few laughs with Doris. Oh, yeah, the Springsteen thing."

She laughed at his minimalist attitude, "Yeah! The Springsteen thing."

Whitefish waved her off like it was no big deal, "He owed me a favor. I finally called it in. We're all square, me and The Boss."

She sat back, "It's good to be King."

He was ready to fire back with a pithy jibe but decided to moan his love for the cookie.

Millie returned with another pot of tea. "Here we go, Christina. Enjoy." It was quiet as Christina poured her tea. The tick-tick-tick of the wall clock seemed to grow louder. Millie asked, "So, where you off to next, Christina?"

She blew on her piping hot tea, "Belvidere. Up north. Near the Delaware Water Gap. Maybe an hour and a half, depending on traffic."

Remembering a task, Whitefish reached into his bulging shirt pocket and revealed a small Minolta camera, "Hey, Millie, mind taking a few shots of me and Christina?" He handed her the camera, "Then I wanna take a shot of you two. Just press that button." Millie knew her way around a camera, and the parlor light was perfect, so when Whitefish picked up his photos a week later, there were three or four really good shots— three with great smiles and one where Christina surprised him, turned and kissed him on the cheek. His wide-eyed look of surprise was silly as hell. Millie captured the moment like a pro.

❖ ❖ ❖

Outside, Whitefish and C-Mac moved off the porch and across the lawn toward the Datsun. She carried her small suitcase and finally asked, "So what's this going-away present you were so cagey about? I want one of those Progresso cans!"

It was time, "Here," and when she turned, he tossed her a key ring with four keys. She caught them with her free hand. She was confused, "What's this?" He pointed across the street. To the sparkling alabaster Eldorado, convertible top down. If this vision had a soundtrack, it would be a quick but ridiculously divine chorus of angels.

Christina was truly flummoxed, exchanging glances between the car, the keys, and then the Whitefish. She finally managed, "What are you doing? Wait, how did you get it..." Her words trailed off.

"Follow my thinking," he suggested, "This car meant a lot to my old partner in crime, Lorelei Antuofermo. She gifted it to me from the grave... and I, being the head case that I am, buried this work of art in the goddamn basement." C-Mac, still holding her small suitcase, listened intently, trying to absorb the moment as Whitefish paced a bit. "But then, like second nature, you jumped in the car for one of my idiotic psycho rides 'cause you actually got it!"

She nodded, "I did... I do." She held up the keys, "The keys are gold."

"Nice, right? Factory issued." He held her gently by the shoulders, "We headed west through Oregon, remember?" She nodded, smiling. Whitefish kept painting, "Steep canyons. Waterfalls. You were taking photos, right? Clear as day. Columbia River Gorge. We sat there, you and me, fuck 'em if they can't see it, we did." She nodded yes. "You just got it!" Then he motioned to the Caddy with sustained gusto, "And that's when it hit me: This car represents freedom. High time I set it free. No more solitary confinement."

Thoughts rifled through her brain. Did this pied piper, this alchemist or Mad Hatter, did he regard the car's escape as her escape? Her release? By extension, his release, too? Was that it? Before she could answer—

He closed her hand around the gold keys and held on, "That's why it's yours, kiddo. You've been to hell and back and you're still standing. You beat the odds... more importantly, *you beat the bastards.* But you gotta stay one step ahead. Forever. The torment will be un-fucking-relenting. That's our reality, *our beast of burden...* and I guarantee that your doc in L.A. will say the same thing."

She confirmed, "He did."

Whitefish lowered his voice to a whisper, "Freedom for us ain't easy, but it's our Kryptonite to their plague." He lightened up, "That's why you need one hundred and seventy horsepower." She looked comically confused as he followed up, no longer whispering, "You gotta break free from its gravitational pull." Then he upped the ante, almost demanding, "Christina, this car will take you anywhere. There's nothing holding you back... *like it held me back.* We both know I exist in some open-air prison. Granted, no doubt, by choice. I get that. Back then, I looked at my pathetic situation and figured out how to exist in my own hell. The trick? I made it look like heaven. I became the King of a dying nightmare... and the characters in my nightmare don't really know it's a nightmare. For them, it's just something to do. For me, it's the necessary illusion, whatever gets you through the night... thank you, John Lennon. But for you? This car's a launching pad the fuck out of here."

Somehow, Whitefish recognized the look in her eyes, that look when two souls touch. He sensed this was intimidating for them both, so he eased up. "Go ahead, drive out of here in style. Like you, this car still has life. Damn thing's only clocked seven thousand miles."

Christina dropped her bag and then turned the tables, holding his hands, "Let's assume for one second that I go along with this... that I accept your beautifully outrageous gift, which is crazy, but let's say that I do... *what the hell am I gonna do with Julian's Datsun?*"

He smiled a big shit-eating grin, "You don't think I thought about that? C'mon." Whitefish reached into his back pocket for an envelope. "Wholesale book value on the Pulsar is about twelve hundred," he plopped the envelope in her hand, "Here's two grand. I have a buyer. Julian will be thrilled with this windfall."

C-Mac knew Mr. Smarty Pants was probably right, but she was still apprehensive. The keys were anxiously jangling in her hand. Whitefish sensed her trepidation, so he put his arm around her as he dramatically referenced the Caddy, taking on the playful persona of an insufferable car salesman, "Listen, lady, I put a few bucks into prepping this sled: brand new steel-belted radials, new brakes-new shocks, flushed out the fuel system, changed all the fluids, aligned and balanced every nut and bolt. This here tank purrs like she just rolled off the assembly line. Imagine driving up to Jaime's in this fine General Motors product? Talk about your icebreaker. And it's a fucking convertible!"

She broke out laughing and gave him a loveable push, "You're such an asshole. This is so—oh, wait," she thought of an obstacle, "What about that thing, you know, for owning the car?" He was cool as a cuke, "You're referring to the title, which is in the glove box, along with the registration and insurance. Keep it in a safe place... and when you get back to LA, simply change the paperwork over to you. And then send me the title for the Pulsar."

There was a long, pregnant silence as a commuter train pulled into the Asbury station. A motorcycle cruised by. That's when Whitefish grabbed her bag and moseyed toward the Cadillac, wanting to push the moment forward. "C'mon, check out your new ride... and I need the—"

"Hey," she interrupted, digging out the Pulsar keys from her pocket, "Here." She tossed them his way. "Good catch, Mr. Fisherino, but I got the better of this deal."

He stopped and smiled, "Trust me, you didn't." His response hung in midair. He kept walking, "C'mon, Dorothy, your chariot awaits."

As they crossed the street, Christina thought hard about his response, "Trust me, you didn't." She knew him well enough to know that Whitefish doesn't just randomly say things.

He asked, "Can you pop the trunk?" Realizing she had the keys, she unlocked the trunk, "Oh, sure, sorry." He tossed her bag in, pointing out, "Real spare. None of that donut shit." He closed the trunk, "So, first stop Belvidere and Miss Jaime. I have good feelings." A city bus roared by as he opened the driver's door.

Christina said, "I'm gonna miss you, that's for sure."

"What?"

She waited for the bus to clear. "I'm gonna miss you, that's for sure."

Rarely, if ever, was the King of Asbury Park at a loss for words, even for just a few seconds. Although here he was in the light of day, under a crooked elm, gut-punched in the shadows of an old stone church, desperately grasping the car's door as his rubbery legs fought for strength. But like any great boxer, he recovered quickly, hoping his adversary—in this case, his damaged yet beautifully perfect comrade—didn't notice his sorrow over her imminent departure. He counterpunched, "C'mon, Private MacKenzie, screw your helmet on tight. No room for schmaltz. Look at us: two ships lucky enough to have passed in the night—and with the history of shipwrecks in Asbury Park, count us lucky."

She smiled sweetly and shook the gold keys as if ringing a bell, "I have one other question for you, Mr. Fish, and I'm not leaving or taking this gorgeous car if I don't get an honest-to-god, no-bullshit answer. That's a promise *and* a threat."

Whitefish smiled and crossed his arms, "Oh, is that so? Alright, hit me."

Christina knew this was a big ask, "Tell me your real name."

He knew this day would come. He had successfully hidden it from a throng of inquiring minds that he really didn't care about. But in his heart of hearts, he wanted so much for her to know his name. And he wanted this escaping angel to be the only one. "So I guess you won't buy the fact that they named me Whitefish at birth, huh?"

She leaned against the car, "If you tell me it's the honest-to-god truth, I'll accept it." She offered a playful curtsy, "How can I not trust my King?"

He glanced up through the branches of the old elm, "You remember I told you a bunch of stuff about my old man?" She nodded, "Of course I do... 'a classic muckraker, a force to be reckoned with.' *Newark Evening News byline: Frank Delgado.*" He loved her 1940s delivery and then motioned in the air to an imaginary signature, "Well, Christina MacKenzie, just add junior."

She didn't have to say anything. Her body language confirmed how much she loved that he was named after "the old man." And in the ensuing silence, she quickly understood why he barricaded himself behind WHITEFISH: He didn't want to go through life hearing his slain father's name over and over and over again. But she was going to say his name once, right now, knowing he'd allow her the privilege. "One more thing, *Frank Delgado, Junior*—'thank you' is ridiculously inadequate, but thank you for caring enough to show me the light. You are, without a doubt, no matter what they say, a benevolent king."

They smiled... and she hugged him tight. When it was over, he gently brushed some hair from her eyes. She tenderly held his face before turning to leave.

Christina sat behind the wheel and sighed, knowing she was embarking on the unknown. But hell, she thought, I'm getting better at this. The red leather seats felt soft and perfect as Frank closed the door. He put his sunglasses on, "Yo, C-Mac, break a leg up there."

She fired up the V8 but wasn't used to the power and the roar. "I'm sure as hell gonna try."

Frank snapped his fingers and pointed at the dash, "Oh yeah, there's a mixtape in the deck. A little road music." There was nothing left to say.

He turned toward the Datsun, which by 1994 was considered a Nissan. He nonchalantly slipped into the eggbeater and started up his new car. And then without rehearsal—

He made a U-turn heading east, while she made a U-turn heading west.

Movie-ending glances were not exchanged as they passed.

It was just like Frank said, "two ships."

&

58

Happy Motoring!

As she pulled out of her U-turn on Asbury Ave, Christina drove a few yards and then immediately pulled over next to the Sea Breeze. She needed a moment. This strangely beautiful yet infinitely weird farewell was tantamount to getting shot out of a cannon. Even the Army had orientation week. It all happened so fast—and maybe that was a good thing. Baptism by fire. But midway through that life-altering U-turn, thoughts were sprinting through her brain, starting with "What the fuck just happened?" and ending with "Would Julian care about his car?" She also had to get a handle on this giant Cadillac, feeling like Lily Tomlin's "Edith Ann" perched up in that giant rocker. And the dashboard was daunting, filled with strange buttons and knobs.

But parked next to the Sea Breeze, her fleeting sanctuary, Christina realized that this sudden wave of angst wasn't about the car, or Julian, or Whitefish, or anything else on her mental list of diversions. Whatta-you-know? It was all about her: *What was she going to do with the rest of her life?* Okay, first things first: Up periscope on Belvidere, of course on Jaime, and then what to do with the old house and all that money? The time to confront reality had arrived.

Daunting? Yes. Necessary? Also yes, "Especially if I want to move on, survive."

She turned the engine off and closed her eyes. Jen, her yoga teacher, was very clear about this: "You can meditate anywhere, any time. Wherever you are becomes your sacred space." Christina could hear Jen's sweet voice: "Pay attention to your breath... breathe naturally... take a deep breath... exhale through your mouth... again... once more... now scan your body. Notice any physical sensations? Imagine yourself somewhere special, peaceful... a forest, a beach, maybe on a desert mesa." Christina floated by all three with her anxiety slowly melting. At least for now, and that was enough.

After five minutes, she opened her eyes with an exhale, "Okay, let's deal with this car. Lights, check... radio – shifter – parking brake – blinkers – A/C... got it." She adjusted the mirrors and the electronic seat... ahh, no more Edith Ann. A quick rummage through the glove box revealed, as Frank promised, registration, insurance, and title. There was also the original owner's manual. Perfect! She'd be able to get the top back up. Plus a New Jersey state road map courtesy of Exxon: *Happy Motoring!* She smiled and tossed the map on the seat. Frank thought of everything. Then it hit her, finally picking up the paperwork. His name was on all the official shit. "That's how he intended to tell me!" She laughed out loud, "You sonovabitch!" She happily closed the glove box.

She started the car. Indeed, this was no Datsun. What did Frank say? "One hundred and seventy horsepower?" Is that a lot? Then she realized she didn't even see him pull away. Christina looked left as if he might still be there. Of course he wasn't. Instead, Father Marlboro was standing across the street—in his familiar spot, puffing away. They exchanged smiles. Light traffic passed east and west.

"Nice car, Christina."

The tiny voice came from the passenger side. It was Shanice straddling her bike on the sidewalk. "Is it yours?"

Christina thought for a second, "Thanks, Shanice... yes, it's mine."

Shanice asked, "Did you buy that car?"

Christina smiled, "No, it was a gift."

The little girl peddled away, "You know I don't believe in Santa Claus anymore. Bye Christina!" "Bye Shanice." The church bell rang once. Dashboard clock read 1:29pm.

She dropped the Caddy into DRIVE.

Before she left town, Christina picked up two Snapples and a bag of pretzels for the trip, which she mapped to Trenton. From there she knew her way up the river. To Belvidere.

To Jaime.

❖ ❖ ❖

Crossing the flat farmland of Central Jersey was like traversing a fruit salad. If she had a home with a kitchen, Christina would have stopped for blueberries, raspberries, apples, peaches, and cherries, not to mention a bushel full of vegetables. It would be an homage to Darlene, who loved farm stands almost as much as old churches.

This reverence for produce sparked Christina to recall one of Whitefish's, err, Frank's recent tête-à-têtes with a soused bar patron who hailed from Long Island, which Frank later called "the asshole of the planet." It started with this obnoxious character cackling and guffawing about Jersey being called the Garden State. Frank moseyed over, "Hey, pal, you know what I tell people who mock the Garden State?" The guy slapped the bar, "How the hell should I know? Why don't you tell me, barkeep." Frank towel-dried his hands, "I tell 'em two things: Don't be ignorant, educate yourself." And then slurring his words, the guy muttered, "And what's the second thing, professor?" Frank smiled, "That's what I'm about to tell you—" Frank grabbed the guy's Islander hat and frisbeed it across the room. "Go fuck yourself."

Christina remembered busting out laughing as the guy stood with rage, holding up his fists like John L. Sullivan. Regrettably, the dude just toppled over, face-planting first into the bar and then the floor. Nothing broke his fall. Tombstone had to mop up the mess. She missed Frank already. Club Southside, what a hoot. Wait, the mixtape! Perfect. She flicked it in and turned up the volume.

High above the planet, not satellite high but high enough, a soaring hawk spied an alabaster and red convertible dissecting September-green farmland; a woman's wavy black mane floating free just like the hawk a way up yonder. Now this eavesdropping bird of prey didn't recognize the tune playing in the car, but Christina did—from the very first drum hit and piano sting, she sang a raucous duet with Mr. Warren Zevon, a performance loud enough to turn the heads of every strapping farm boy in a three-mile radius, and damn if she didn't know all the lyrics about some hungry werewolf beatin' the streets of Ye Olde London, looking for a big dish of beef chow mein. *Ah-hoo.*

❖ ❖ ❖

With the Delaware to her left, she tracked the river north. When she approached historic Washington's Crossing, Jack's silly joke popped into her head, "Hey Tina, why did Washington cross the Delaware?" She'd play along, "Why, Dad?" And then together they'd spout the punchline,

"Because he had a girl in Jersey!" Jack would laugh every time. So would Tina, although she hated to encourage his corny jokes. And then she realized, "What a great mixtape, good ol' Whitefish." Eclectic to say the least: Zevon, Lou Reed, Zeppelin, Leonard Cohen, Patti Smith, Sinéad O'Connor, the Ramones, and then Side A ended with Ice Cube's "It Was a Good Day." How great and arbitrary, she thought. Weird he would even know this stuff, even weirder he was listening to Ice Cube.

Route 29 ended in Frenchtown, and from this dot on a map, it was back roads into Belvidere, the pastoral America that Christina knew well, passing the places she'd hide with Jaime, away from those nosey and judgmental eyes. Savages who might finance billboards to destroy their love: HEATHENS. DEVIANTS. PERVERTS. GODLESS PAGAN INFIDELS!

The Caddy crossed the southern border of Belvidere on a tree-lined country road. Christina knew she had to see her Uncle Charlie about the financials and about the house. She'd been woefully out of touch with her Dad's brother, so rudely AWOL, but he was a forgiving and sweet man. She wondered if she had taken advantage of his good nature. Side B ended with a song she'd never heard before, but damn if she wasn't hooked on this folk singer's sweet voice, a tenor singing about serious shit with this recurring and haunting line: "But I ain't a-marching anymore."

She knew it was no accident that Frank placed the song last.

❖ ❖ ❖

Jaime Nguyen's house on 4th Street was only a few blocks away. Christina pulled the Caddy to the curb, shut off the engine and simply sat there behind her shades—sunglasses she didn't need as the Sun dropped lower in the sky. She'd left this place more than five years ago. On the run from the reality of catastrophic death. Little did she know that her blood-and-thunder exit was only the beginning. The inaugurating event. But not the fucking apocalypse she was about to endure in Western Asia.

Lo and behold, she was back, returning to Belvidere on this sunny day in September of 1994, a day that witnessed her rather unique re-entry: In a glitzy '85 Cadillac Eldorado, first gifted to a woman named Lorelei Antuofermo by her gangster husband, a cog in the Boiardo Crime Family. She then bequeathed the alabaster convertible to a guy named Whitefish, aka Frank Delgado, Jr., who subsequently entombed the vehicle in his basement for reasons only the jungles of Southeast Asia know for sure. A few short years later, the Whitefish, a Jersey Shore tavern owner, was so moved by one, Christina MacKenzie, that he magically exhumed the beast from its subterranean hideout and then bestowed it to her as a parting gift from Asbury Park. Just a few hours ago. She even has the title. Christina thought, "You can't make this shit up."

Her first order of business could be the toughest or possibly the easiest. It could be ridiculous and delusional or simply "in the bag," a fait accompli. Grave doubts swirled.

Christina had to convince Jaime Nguyen (the most beautiful & hip & sweet & cool & sensuous woman in the entire world) to give her another chance. She closed her eyes; a stream of consciousness flowed:

> **"**Let's try again. Run with me to California. We can be ourselves there! No hiding from BILLBOARDS. And please James, forget the monster I became, the pill-poppin' pincushion psycho bitch. I fucked up so bad. But I heard what you said and did what you wrote. I wouldn't be here if I didn't. I read your letter every day. It's my saving grace. So many times I wanted to call you and tell you how brave you were to write that letter and how I wouldn't have survived without you and how I loved you more than ever. I see the letter clear as day, like paragraph four, the one that starts—
>
> > *But then the monsters from hell arrived and somehow, some way, behind my back, they stole your soul. Wrapped in flags and fucking experts at brainwashing, the lies that we're all forced to swallow*
>
> Sick, right? I have some of it memorized, like from the same paragraph—
>
> > *They steal brains DAILY! and then the bodies & souls follow. And there's no doubt in my mind that if Jack & Darlene were around none of this would've ever happened!*

Can you remember the original me? *Remember us?* We can still be what we always wanted. Trust me.**"**

Sitting there, she kept listening to herself on internal rewind until it sounded like gibberish. She realized, "Oh Christ, I only have two things going for me: California and the Cadillac." She took off her sunglasses and scoffed at the sky, remembering the words, "Imagine rolling up to Jaime's in this fine General Motors product? Talk about your icebreaker. And it's a fucking convertible!" She laughed, "Delgado, you motherfucker."

❖ ❖ ❖

Christina walked up the familiar long stone stairway that led to the Nguyen home. Potted begonias lined the entire flight up. So pretty. She took a deep breath—and just as she reached for the doorbell, the front door opened. Mrs. Nguyen was in a joyful shock.

Her Vietnamese accent so etched in her spirit, "Christina!" They hugged. C-Mac had forgotten that Jaime's mom was so petite. "Jaime's not here, she's at work." It felt so odd that Christina didn't know the answer to her own question, "Where does she work?" Mrs. Nguyen seemed surprised that Christina didn't know, "Oh, at the flower shop on Front Street. Anna's Secret Garden." Mrs. Nguyen offered for Christina to stay, "Wait with me. I'll make dinner. Lang will be here soon." Christina thanked her but said she'd go meet Jaime down on Front Street. They hugged again, and as Christina started down the stairway, Mrs. Nguyen called to her, "Christina... I know about you and Lang. It's okay. We understand."

Christina was frozen. She had no idea what to say. She forced a smile and simply said, "Thank you." And then, after another few steps, Mrs. Nguyen called out, "Nice car!" Christina waved back.

As she took off for Front Street, Christina was bemused on three fronts: First, Jaime's working in a flower shop? Jaime a florist? That's too weird. Secondly, she hadn't heard Jaime's Vietnamese name in such a long time, and for good reason: Jaime hated "Lang"—it meant sweet potato. And finally, Mrs. Nguyen knows about us... and "It's okay... we understand?!" It all seemed so strange and so foreign as she passed their old high school.

It felt like there were ghosts lurking everywhere.

She parked across the street from Anna's Secret Garden. Christina remembered this place as a vintage clothing store. One step at a time, she told herself. Jaime's tough, but this will still be a sudden shock, a thunderclap out of nowhere. Be yourself, be gentle, you've come so far, mostly for this moment. Don't get weird. Be cool. She closed her eyes for a one-minute meditation.

"Anywhere, any time."

When Christina walked inside, the shop's little bell jingled overhead. From behind a refrigerated flower case door, Jaime peered out to see who it—

Through a maze of daisies, tulips, chrysanthemums, balloons and greenery, their eyes met somewhere in the middle of this perfumed jungle. Jaime was holding a wrapped bouquet of roses. A sweet smile blossomed between the roses and the flower case door.

"Lord, she's beautiful" was Christina's only thought.

❧

CHRISTINA
and the
WHITEFISH

59

Crossroads.

On the third of October 2019, the Crossroads Diner in Belvidere, New Jersey, was lifted off its foundation and moved to Hudson, New York—a small town about thirty miles north of Woodstock, right on the river. For more than forty years, this landmark diner occupied a prominent corner on U.S. Route 46 and served two distinct sets of customers: the good folks of Belvidere as well as interstate truckers rolling between America's two coasts. Before the emergence of Ike's interstate highways, Crossroads was also a popular stop for Greyhound and Trailways buses. The diner was built by the Campora Dining Car Company of Kearny, New Jersey, and was one of those classic stainless steel throwbacks to another era. And just small enough to move.

Working through a steady drizzle on that October morning in 2019, the moving crew prepped the old diner to leave its foundation, where it was then elevated by hydraulic braces and set down on a giant tractor-trailer for its journey to upstate New York.

Jerseyites sure as hell love their diners, as evidenced by the pack of Crossroads devotees who showed up in the rain to say goodbye to their beloved old place, take photos and share memories with friends. Escorted out of town by two cop cars, the tractor-trailer rumbled away. The funereal crowd held their gaze down Route 46 as the diner receded into taillights and then was gone.

The canopy of umbrellas scattered in separate directions as the drizzle became a downpour.

❖❖❖

Twenty-five years prior to the Crossroads Diner being lifted off its foundation and commandeered north, the convertible Caddy was parked out front. It was twilight. Dinner time. Customers came and went; some lingered by their cars, their toothpick finesse an absolute art form. Beyond the foreground action, Christina and Jaime sat in a window booth, like they had so many times before. Funny enough, Edward

Hopper recognized the dark realism of this moment and decided to paint the scene here and now, even though he died in 1967. Nevertheless, he set himself up in the parking lot, envisioning a unique amalgamation of his best work: *Nighthawks, Room in New York,* and *Chop Suey.* It would be oil on canvas.

A waitress approached to take their order. Question was: Would Hopper include the frumpy young woman holding a pad? They ordered Cokes and French fries. Dinner was too formal and messy for this conversation. In fact, before driving to the Crossroads, they only hugged briefly outside the flower shop. Their reunion was not epic, measured at best. But then Jaime lost it, laughing hysterically when she laid eyes on the Eldorado.

"Oh my god."

Ti promised to get her up to speed. There was obviously so much to tell.

Hopper decided against the waitress. At least at this point. He had already sketched the window frame dead center on the canvas; he also included a piece of the Eldorado that sat beneath the window, as well as a wedge of the "Crossroads" sign that hung above. The boundaries were set.

Jaime explained Anna's Secret Garden. She liked Anna, the owner; the hours were flexible, the money not half bad, and she could finally put to use all the flower stuff she learned from her mother. Jaime figured it was a good holding pattern. She was also taking two classes at Warren Community—Jaime suggesting that Ti's recent exploits were surely more adventurous than apricot carnations and Creative Writing with Professor Numbnuts.

Hopper was concerned that his two young women were smiling and laughing, since that depiction would be odd for him. He needed a more somber tone, a characteristic more akin to his other work.

A second round of Cokes seemed to signal it was Christina's turn, and yes, it was more adventurous because, as she acknowledged, it had to be. The repeated punches in the face that Jaime's letter delivered, busting up the bathroom, losing all control, all sense of reality, crawling across cut glass, blood and vomit, praying to her father for salvation—all of it somehow, someway leading to the intercession and redeeming work of Doc Genovese, the Vets at Peace House like Eugene who got royally fucked during the Tet Offensive, and then there was the personal impact of Ron Kovic. How mesmerizing, debilitating, and revelatory it all became. It was an avalanche. And now at the Crossroads, where they used to talk shit about high school crap, Christina laid bare her ongoing face-to-face with pain.

And now Hopper had what he wanted: that sober and lugubrious moment between his two young women, their eyes locked in those precious seconds when not much else existed. Except them.

Luckily, the painter already had the cheerless moment sketched as Ti shifted the narrative to Julian's Datsun, the cross-country pilgrimage, the creepy Texas pervert, Mr. Hershey Bear, and finally Asbury Park, or as some called it: *Newark by the Sea.* Smiles returned to the diner window, as did the waitress dropping off a gigantic slice of lemon meringue pie, a treat these two silly hearts would often share, most of the time baked and flying high.

Clearly, Hopper didn't appreciate the idea of a lemon meringue mountain in the middle of his vision.

Christina ran her hands through her thick black hair. My God. Where do you start with the Whitefish? But she did. And then told the entire story, this wonderful, wacky magic carpet ride that ended with that convertible hunk of steel sitting outside. One hundred and seventy horsepower. Vroom.

And here they were. Caught up. What's next?

That's when Hopper's brush, loaded with dark green, stopped mid-stroke as he watched this rare flash of silence between these two connected beings. He couldn't read lips but wished otherwise as one woman (Jaime) seemed to ask a serious and emphatic question. It was only one word, but her body language filled in the question mark.

Fortunately for Hopper, the waitress walked by at that very instant and heard her customer blurt out the query. Later that evening, when Hopper went inside for his own slice of lemon meringue, he interrogated the frumpy and po-faced waitress ("She's perfect for my next painting, *Diner,*" he decided).

Her name was Deb... and Deb gave it right up:

"Oh yeah, the Oriental yelled, *'Springsteen?!'*"

By the time Christina convinced Jaime she wasn't hallucinating about the Bruce thing, Crossroads Diner was well under the cover of night. It had been three plus hours, probably time to leave. As they crossed to the register, Hopper stood from his easel and stretched, somewhat pleased with his new tableau vivant.

Just then, Hopper's two subjects left the diner. He noticed it was a subdued and melancholy walk to the car. They slid in without saying a word, backed up (he had to grab his easel or they would've crashed into the wet painting), and off they cruised into the night.

He decided to title the painting *Two Young Women*. It seemed to fit.

❖ ❖ ❖

Even though this was 1994, and Crossroads would go on to host many more hungry souls before its relocation north, this face-to-face *twinkle in time* between these "Two Young Women" would be remembered (by the angelic historians who keep track of shit like this) as probably the diner's most significant get-together.

&

60
Prelude to Act Three.

I **DIDN'T WANT** a long or drawn-out goodbye.

It wasn't Christina I was worried about. It was me. A quick exit stage left was a fail-safe mechanism – no opportunity to spill my guts or even hint at my feelings. I didn't think I would, but who the hell knows? It's like having a full tank of gas and then you pass a sign that reads "Last Gas for 100 Miles," and you still pull over and top off the tank. Pity the man who doubts what he's sure of.

I was also concerned about the Caddy. If we didn't do the fast switcheroo, Christina might have had second thoughts. Hell, the Datsun was barely worth a grand retail and was ready to fall apart. My hope is that the Eldorado will always represent freedom in the ongoing narrative of her life. Even if she kept it for just a few months – beautiful, that's the horse and buggy that took her away.

As the reader, you already know that this chronicle of my life is an ongoing and transparent work. The story itself (and my process) has been an open book (ha!). In my mind, the shooting star that was, or that is! Christina MacKenzie, wraps up Act Two. Soft landing.

And damn if she didn't inject an atomic dose of love and exhilaration.

Right now, sitting at the Underwood, I'm at two hundred typewritten pages. You've experienced a childhood defined by the loss of a giant, my father. A childhood held together with the grace of an angel, my mother. You were there when early adulthood was shattered by the betrayal of my own country. You were privy to one human's rebirth at the hands of three sacred souls: Lou and Lorraine Fontaine and Lorelei Antuofermo ("Hey, nuggy! Giants minus three and a half"). And through it all, one character – derelict and disintegrating – has stood tall, and that's Asbury Park.

So here's your heads-up:

Act Three will focus completely on the denizens and dwellers that make – or have made – this seaside metropolis prosper... or tumble full throttle into everlasting perdition. The Whitefish, like his old man, will bring to life the stories of our people: the heroes who acted in service to this place... and the villains responsible for its ongoing and slow-boiled demise. Suicide, truly.

The great transcendentalist, anarchist, and lifelong abolitionist, Henry David Thoreau, will philosophically live at the heart of Act Three. I might even work him into my stage act. Lil Abner can't wait. Here's Thoreau, from "On the Duty of Civil Disobedience" –

"The mass of men lead lives of quiet desperation. What is called resignation is confirmed desperation.

From the desperate city you go into the desperate country, and have to console yourself with the bravery of minks and muskrats.

A stereotyped but unconscious despair is concealed even under what are called the games and amusements of mankind."

Sounds right... so does "Giants minus three and a half." Do it.

# #

61

Second Chance.

In the car, presumably on the way back to the Nguyen's house, Jaime reached across the red leather seats and held Ti's hand. This gentle gesture became a playful dance and then a sensual reminder for both women. A few minutes later, they were parked on a dark street that bordered a deserted park between the Warren County Courthouse and a small country church.

Were they defying both church and state?

This moment could have been any high school night in 1987—their necessary hideaway in one of their family cars. It felt like forever since they were in each other's arms, their mouths immediately falling back in love. Suddenly, lights rolled up from behind. The Belvidere bluecoats with their Christmas lights flashing. Christina and Jaime started laughing into each other and then straightened up, as they did on so many Saturday nights when the cops showed up uninvited. At least this time, they didn't have to swallow a joint.

Officer Dibble sauntered up with his stupidly large flashlight, "Good evening, ladies. Everything alright?" Christina smiled, "We're fine. Haven't seen each other in a while. Just catching up." Belvidere's finest looked over the Caddy with prying eyes, "Helluva nice car." Jaime's inside voice grumbled something along the lines of "Fucking prick."

"Thanks," Christina gripped the steering wheel, "One hundred and seventy horsepower." The cop laughed, "Is that a fact?" Christina tapped the dash, "Bet I'd get a speeding ticket with this baby." The cop laughed again, "By the way, any chance you have a license, registration, insurance card?" Christina grabbed her purse and then reached over into the glove box, "Sure do, just gimme a second." Officer Dibble addressed the passenger, "How are you tonight, Miss?" Jaime smiled, "I'll take the Fifth." The cop liked that one, "Ah, Laurel and Hardy, huh?" Jaime quietly said, "Hey, Abbott!" The cop corrected her, "That's Abbott and Costello." Jaime smirked, "I know." Christina had everything together, "Here you go, Officer. License, registration, insurance, and my United States Army ID just in case."

The cop took the paperwork and shined his light, "Army, eh? I was Coast Guard." He became curious, "Who is Frank Peter Delgado, Junior?" Christina reached back in the glove box and handed the title to Amphibious Kojak, "He's a dear friend, gifted me this amazing vehicle just this morning. That's the title. I have to transfer the other stuff." The cop tilted his hat back with the flashlight, "Must be a really good friend. Sit tight."

Deputy Fife sauntered back to his squad car.

Jaime whispered, "Like this idiot has nothing better to do." Christina sniffed playfully, "Do you smell bacon frying?" They both giggled. Jaime held her hand. Ti smiled, "Maybe we should get a room, as they say." Jaime liked that, "Even if they don't say... and the Army ID was a nice touch." Christina leaned back, "I thought so." Jaime glanced back toward the cop to make sure he wasn't on his way and kissed Ti's hand, "Frank Peter Delgado, Junior?" Christina reminded her, "The Whitefish. I'll explain later." Jaime spotted T.J. Hooker on his way back, "Here he comes. *Ixnay onyay ite-fish-whay.*"

They snorted like teenagers.

"We're good ladies," as he handed back the paperwork. "Probably not a great place to park such a nice car, if you know what I mean." Jaime piped up, "Oh, we do." Christina played nice as she put the paperwork away, "No problem, officer. We're out of here." "And Private MacKenzie," the cop waited for her to look, "Thank you for your service." She offered a casual, half-assed salute as he left. Christina closed the glove box, whispering to Jaime, "Didn't we go to high school with this guy?" Jaime couldn't care less, "Feels like old times." Christina agreed, "Yeah, it kinda does."

She fired up the throaty V8, looked in the rearview as Columbo made a U-turn—likely on his way to Dunkin'—and the duo pulled away. Free at last. They picked up some Chinese and checked into the Howard Johnson's over in neighboring Budd Lake. Together, they navigated the Owner's Manual and secured the convertible top.

They stayed up until damn near dawn.

❖ ❖ ❖

Minutes later, at 6:11am, Whitefish emerged from the Club Southside, stretching his creaky body, ready to kick off another day: fifty-five… forty-four… twenty-two. "Jesus Christ," he blurted out as he climbed back to his feet, thinking those twenty-two push-ups felt more like two hundred and twenty-two. "Work through it, work through it" he told himself as he shadowboxed:

Feeling good, feeling better…
like Cassius Clay,
ready to cartwheel out of Louisville.

The flurry of punches must've kicked in the endorphins or peptides or whatever the fuck: "Bring on Liston." He threw some fast jabs and then a right cross toward that faint glimmer of a new day, another beauty emerging over his beloved Atlantic—and there was no doubt about it: Frank Peter Delgado, Jr. will never stand on this rented boardwalk without seeing those red slippers, magnificent black locks, and that first smile when she turned around, all of it haloed by God's shining light.

When Whitefish reached Allenhurst, he didn't simply turn around as per usual. Nope. Not today. Not ever again. He carved a new path down the beach, toward the large driftwood log close to the water's edge. He took a deep breath and began his embryonic yoga practice—this being his maiden voyage on a newfangled addition to his routine. He remembered (almost) every move perfectly, right into the closing meditation, which he continued with eyes closed, recalling fragments of Christina's guidance, just enough to gently point him toward Eden. She told him, "Hands to your heart. Namaste."

The kitchen wall clock suggested it was 8:27am—later than normal when making his coffee. He would note the schedule change. The stove's blue gas flame whooshed on under his old teapot. The French press on standby next to his newly cherished Guatemalan roast, the beans that replaced A&P's "Eight O'Clock." He nodded, acknowledging his coffee evolution.

As the water heated, Whitefish hammered in a small nail right next to his framed recipe for gravy, then hung his new framed photograph of Christina surprising him with a kiss on the cheek. Great job, Millie.

One sugar, a splash of cream, and then the anticipated first sip, "If that ain't perfection, I don't know what is." He picked up the paper. Headline:

U.S. INVADES HAITI TO INSTALL DEMOCRACY.

A large guffaw was heard coming from the Whitefish's residence. It echoed straight down the eastern seaboard, making a sharp right through Delaware, across the Chesapeake, up the Potomac, past The Ellipse, and then right inside the White House, where this powerful guffaw kicked Bill Clinton right in his useless nutsack.

❖ ❖ ❖

It was now a mid-October afternoon in nineteen hundred and ninety-four. Northwestern New Jersey was a Technicolor Dreamcoat. And the "Lorelei >>> Whitefish >>> Christina >>> Express" was packed and pointed west toward Bob's Big Boy.

Hugs, kisses, and good wishes. They'd be leaving in the morning. Santa Monica or Bust.

Unbeknownst to anyone, that nosy, high-flying hawk was back—red-tailed and carnivorous, scientific name: *Buteo Jamaicensis.* Or maybe it was his brother, or sister, or possibly a long-lost cousin once removed. Doesn't matter. It's of no consequence. All that mattered was that this gorgeous and powerful hawk was on assignment: follow the alabaster Cadillac straight across America—and this time, unlike the recent trek across Jersey, the hawk was wired for sound. Communiqués back to HQ would be on a daily basis.

On the first day, as they backed out of the driveway, it was raining hard, so of course the top was secured, water dancing on the canvas in a rhythmic patter. Our travelers immediately spanned the Delaware and then chugged through the Pennsylvania countryside. Christina recapped all the financial gibberish for Jaime, most of which Jaime already knew. Uncle Charlie was the executor of the will, and Christina inherited everything, including the old house with no mortgage, which was now listed for sale. All the books and bric-a-brac that Christina wanted to save were safely resting in storage. Good ol' Uncle Charlie took on the rest. Estate and garage sales were planned. Besides clothing and a few books and photographs, the only other thing Christina took with her was her telescope.

Jaime drove a lot. She loved the Cadillac. Over the last month, their relationship grew closer and deeper than ever. Before Christina's hellscape of death and mayhem, their connection was wonderful and fun and oftentimes chancy in various and intriguing ways. But after life was blown to smithereens, here they were, dedicating themselves to piecing it all back together—by any means necessary—and to hell with all the king's horses and all the king's men not being able to put that anthropomorphic egg back together again. Christina and Jaime were different. They knew they were different. It was about shifting their field of vision: Nothing mattered now except what was in front of them. A new gospel must be embraced. *What's past is fucking gone! To hell with prologue!* "Who said that?" Jaime wondered.

Christina would never forget who said it and when: Frank Peter Delgado, Junior—his appeal to her on that night Iraq slammed into Asbury Park, seeking vengeance, thrashing her hard to the boardwalk planks.

She told Jaime about Whitefish's plea (a prayer, really) as they roared through Evansville Goddamn Indiana. That's where they were presented with their second speeding ticket. But then an hour later, they were giddy about shopping for a car phone once they arrived home: "How cool is it gonna be to take a phone with you everywhere?" In fact, in the daily dispatch, the hawk noted their healthy point of view: "They called Los Angeles home."

A week later, there was little doubt in the hawk's mind regarding the trajectory of their relationship, with the hawk reporting: "Their cross-country trip proffered the necessary solitude that maturity required. Healing is close, if not attained."

How fortunate it was to have this angel flight soaring high above Santa Monica, cataloging their every move, sending daily dispatches back to HQ. Okay, so the hawk ate an occasional field mouse. Who really cared? Nothing but the damn food chain. Besides, this industrious and kindhearted hawk was getting the entire story—and the powers that be were quite pleased. The boss even mentioned in passing, "A real workmanlike performance. Good job." This informal pat on the back occurred right after a specific communiqué that underscored the fact that Jaime was hellbent on moving them to Santa Cruz and helping to get Christina re-accepted at the University of California's astronomy and astrophysics program.

Even dreams need cheerleaders.

❖ ❖ ❖

The hawk stayed with Christina and Jaime for years. Hung out on the Left Coast, wrapping things up in Santa Monica before flying up to NorCal, where Christina's military service helped bridge the gap back into UC's undergrad program, where she flourished.

The hawk was there when Jaime opened "Flower McBlooms," her own quaint and funky flower shop on Pacific Ave, downtown Santa Cruz. The hawk still soaring around when they celebrated Jaime's fifth anniversary of a thriving enterprise.

Indeed, the hawk kept close tabs on Christina as she penned the dissertation for her Ph.D., even editing some of the more blustery sections—most notably her overplayed hagiography chapter on Carl Sagan.

On the morning of 11 September 2001, the hawk glided past their large upper story windows, where Christina and Jaime watched the surrealistic attacks on Lower Manhattan and the Pentagon. The hawk was struck by Christina's prescient, almost clairvoyant thoughts regarding a violent future: "Our lives will never be the same. Trust me. The bastards will seize this moment." Jaime squeezed her hand, offering a postscript, "At least you're no longer a part of that."

In 2003, Christina secured a position with the University of California's Lick Observatory on Mount Hamilton near San Jose. The hawk loved the days when Christina would leave her office on campus and head to the Diablo Mountains to visit one of her beloved telescopes, four thousand feet above sea level. 2003 was also the year of America's second bloody occupation of Iraq. This incursion considerably more murderous than the first. The death and destruction turned Jaime and Christina's combined stomachs; they sought refuge from these tellurian madmen— Jaime tending to the beauty of flora while Christina gazed into dazzling portals that revealed remarkable and faraway worlds. Alpha Ophiuchi (aka Rasalhague) never looked so glorious. She imagined her Belvidere backyard, Jack peering with her as the heavens came alive.

On clear days, Christina would eat her lunch on the upper slope of Mount Hamilton. She could see the entire Monterey Peninsula; even Mount Tamalpais and Yosemite were visible from various overlooks. It was all breathtaking. She took Jaime there many times, and often, they'd see a hawk circling and gliding above. For some reason, they decided it was always the same hawk; must be a local. They named him Ralph.

A year later, in 2004, the hawk (or Ralph) followed Christina and Jaime to San Francisco's City Hall, where the city was joyfully breaking California state law—issuing same-sex marriage licenses and conducting brief weddings. Civil rights flourished as the Golden City married more than four thousand couples in one month. Christina and Jaime were one of those couples. They both cried. As did Ralph, coasting his way back to Santa Cruz. A few months later, these marriages were ruled illegal and nullified by California's Supreme Court.

No matter, these two Jersey Girls unanimously overruled the lower court's decision.

❖ ❖ ❖

In May of 2011, the hawk received word that it was time to retire and that the 20th of the month would be his final day of service. Time for one last visit over Santa Cruz's Grant Park, where you'd find Christina and Jaime's quaint Spanish-style home—a small corner lot with lush gardens front and back. It was twilight as the hawk casually circled the property, only hours from a well-deserved retirement.

In the backyard, Christina leaned down over a little boy wearing jeans and a red flannel shirt. The boy, named Jack, was six years old and trying mightily to focus his telescope as Mom lent a helping hand. They were trying to find that faintest first starlight. Focus, focus…

Finally, they zeroed in on a bluish twinkle. Jack was filled with excitement, his gaze locked to the heavens. Christina shared his joy, "Eureka, kiddo. You got it!"

The screen door opened and closed as Jaime wandered over to Jack and Christina. She held Ti's hand in solidarity—the young family stargazing, protected on all sides by multicolored sweet flora, not unlike Camille Pissarro's painting, *In the Garden.*

It was almost time for supper. "Mama," Jack tugged on Jaime's arm, "Take a look!"

She did, "Wow, what star is that?"

"Mom says Vega, lemme look," as he snuck in for another peek.

Christina stuck her tongue out at Jaime, who smiled and rubbed Jack's back, "She would know."

A few minutes later, Christina asked Jack to please pack up the telescope and put it away. She was going inside to help with supper.

"Okay, Mom, one more look." Jack peered back out at Vega, "Wow, it's brighter," and then methodically broke down the telescope, carefully placing all the pieces back in the case along with the folded-up tripod. He snapped it shut and headed for the garage.

He passed their new Prius, their old Saab, and then ducked inside the garage through a side door. He flicked on the light and carefully maneuvered past the large convertible, sliding in the telescope on its proper shelf.

Jack flicked off the light and closed the door behind him.

"Jack, supper!"

By now the hawk was gone.

$$\Omega$$

CHRISTINA and the WHITEFISH

ACKNOWLEDGMENTS

This book began decades ago, as an original screenplay: first entitled "Asbury Park" and then "Whitefish." At one point, the script was optioned and the movie was semi-financed, then fully financed, and then suddenly the money left town. Numerous well-known actors were committed to the film—most notably Danny Aiello (such a sweet and talented man). Along with the production team and co-producer Hanif Shabazz, we began scouting locations in and around Asbury Park, walking the boardwalk and surrounding environs during the exact period of time that the novel takes place, when New Jersey's once famous seaside haven was a battered and deserted ghost town. Whitefish: "Even the parking meters are rusted shut."

Transforming a limited and hollow screenplay (nothing more than a structural blueprint for a motion picture) into a fully-developed and crowded novel was an invigorating and creative experience. In fact, writing the novel became a clarion reminder about the importance of literature, and therefore reading, in a world dangerously severing itself from a book-based society, be it paper or pixels; a society diving headfirst into what author and journalist Chris Hedges calls a "meaningless spectacle"—a culture hooked on podcasts, Insta-stuff, and TikkyTak, and yes, I'm guilty as charged. But these diversionary platforms are not replacements for reading the great thinkers and critics of our past... from Aristotle to Twain and then Mailer, and today... from Margaret Atwood to Percival Everett and Viet Thanh Nguyen. Indeed, American and international society has marched well beyond this icy and slippery slope. We're a global community dangerously mired in a cheap candy store of lies and infotainment—an avalanche of diversion that will destroy the capacity for complex thought and empathetic change. Clearly, this tragedy is on a speedway to perdition.

I'd like to thank the cadre of folks who have supported this book project from the beginning, starting with our Beta Readers, offering thoughtful and insightful feedback, including Ellie Whelan, Cliff Allman, Karen Briner, Katy Farzanrad, Justin Lebanowski, Gail Kelch, Jim Kelch, Ed Novick, David Rucker (whose hauntingly gorgeous photograph also graces the front cover), Cassidy Hart (who also designed the book's front cover as well as the interior), and the ever-supportive Rob Guillory, also responsible for the book's interior and back cover design. As always, a big thank you to proofreader Jennifer Grubba, who found my various and sundry hiccups. And-and-and to Kathy Kremins... my first de facto editor and the unflinching champion of this narrative—a creative force who continues to go the distance. Kathy's stunning poem, "Wild West," sings to us in the front matter of this book. And no acknowledgment would be complete without a loud "thank you" to my agent, Francine Taylor, whose research and deep dive into the dense publishing forest was exceptional.

And to the good folks at Alternative Book Press: the Publisher, Prasanna Chandrasekhar, and Senior Editor, Tracy Haught, for their faith and desire to bring "Christina and the Whitefish" to you... no small order. What's more, Tracy's editing and stewardship that delivered this book into the marketplace has been nothing short of sensational.

Finally, a heartfelt thanks to the COVID pandemic for giving me the time and solitude to write; most of the many hours sitting in a parked car, a Volkswagen, in Playa Vista, CA—laptop engaged, snacks nearby, shaded by a host of Australian willows.

— Stephen Vittoria, Los Angeles, Spring, 2025

About the Author

Stephen Vittoria is an award-winning filmmaker and author.

His last two feature documentaries – *Mumia: Long Distance Revolutionary* and *One Bright Shining Moment: The Forgotten Summer of George McGovern* have been embraced by moviegoers and audiences worldwide. Vittoria was also a producer on two feature documentaries by Academy Award winner Alex Gibney – *Gonzo: The Life & Work of Dr. Hunter S. Thompson* and *Magic Trip: Ken Kesey's Search for a Kool Place.*

Along with journalist Mumia Abu-Jamal, Vittoria co-authored the three-book nonfiction series *Murder Incorporated: Empire, Genocide, and Manifest Destiny* with forewords by Angela Davis, S. Brian Willson, and Chris Hedges.

Vittoria is the founder and creative director of two Southern California production companies: Street Legal Cinema and Deep Image.

Christina and the Whitefish is Vittoria's debut novel.

About the Publisher

Alternative Book Press was established in October of 2012 by Columbia and Cornell University graduates. We originally offered a powerful and straightforward mission: to identify and disseminate genuine, groundbreaking work that stands the test of time. In fact, our mission grows stronger with each passing year – publishing captivating books, both fiction and nonfiction, from intriguing voices that reflect various points of view. In addition, our pursuit of excellence champions new writers, diverse cultures, and important works of intellectual and literary merit.

Our bottom line? Share memorable writing with our readers – books that will sit proudly on their shelves for years to come.

www.ingramcontent.com/pod-product-compliance
Ingram Content Group UK Ltd.
Pitfield, Milton Keynes, MK11 3LW, UK
UKHW040926140725
6876UKWH00041B/508